See you at the TOXTETH

PETER CORRIS is known as the 'godfather' of Australian crime fiction through his Cliff Hardy detective stories. He published in many other areas, writing a history of boxing in Australia, spy novels, historical novels, a collection of short stories about golf, and co-authoring an autobiography of Professor Fred Hollows (see www.petercorris.net). In 1999, Peter Corris was awarded the Lifetime Achievement Award from the Crime Writers Association of Australia, and in 2009 the Ned Kelly Award for Best Fiction for *Deep Water*. He was married to writer Jean Bedford and lived in Sydney for most of his life.

Peter Corris's Cliff Hardy novels include *The Empty Beach, Master's Mates, The Coast Road, Saving Billie, The Undertow, Appeal Denied, The Big Score, Open File, Deep Water, Torn Apart, Follow the Money, Comeback, The Dunbar Case, Silent Kill, Gun Control* and *That Empty Feeling. Win, Lose or Draw*, published in 2017, was his forty-second and final Cliff Hardy book.

THE BEST OF
CLIFF HARDY AND
CORRIS ON CRIME

See you at the
TOXTETH

PETER CORRIS

Selected by
JEAN BEDFORD

First published in 2019

Allen & Unwin
83 Alexander Street
Crows Nest NSW 2065
Australia
Phone: (61 2) 8425 0100
Email: info@allenandunwin.com
Web: www.allenandunwin.com

A catalogue record for this book is available from the National Library of Australia

ISBN 978 1 76087 563 3

p. 221: Illustration by Michael Fitzjames
Set in 12/17 pt Adobe Caslon by Midland Typesetters, Australia
Printed and bound in Australia by Griffin Press

10 9 8 7 6 5 4 3 2 1

The paper in this book is FSC® certified. FSC® promotes environmentally responsible, socially beneficial and economically viable management of the world's forests.

CONTENTS

INTRODUCTION

Peter was a born storyteller. He didn't have to work at it the way many of us writers do, every word blood squeezed out of stone.

As he said several times in interviews, he never really plotted—it was as if he were watching a film unfold before him and he simply wrote it down. (He did make sketchy notes after each writing session to guide himself.) Frustrating to live with, if you're the blood-from-stone type.

He began writing as an historian. His MA thesis was about Aborigines and Europeans of western Victoria; his PhD thesis examined the Solomon Islands labour trade. Both were narrative histories—as he often said, it was the only sort of history he wanted, or felt able, to write.

He was a modest man. He wrote many books—42 Cliff Hardys, eight Ray Crawleys, eight Brownings (drawing on historical knowledge and interest), three Luke Dunlops and various other specifically historical novels, as well as several 'as-told-to' biographies, among others. His short stories were widely anthologised and collected—yet he was never boastful. Self-deprecatingly, he called himself an 'entertainer' and never quite understood, or gave credence to, the public and critical acclaim for the place he had carved out as a uniquely sharp, but also appreciative, chronicler of Australia, Sydney and our times. He spoke for a generation that had grown from hope and prosperity to cynicism and social deprivation, from a generous society to a mean and self-protective one. As he also said several times, he never wanted to give solace to religion or to right-wing politics, and he was scathing about both, as well as the exploitative rich, in his books. Hardy was a great conduit for Peter's own convictions.

His first Cliff Hardy novel, *The Dying Trade*, was rejected by several publishers who thought no one wanted to read contemporary Australian crime fiction. 'Why don't you write a thriller set in the Philippines?' one asked. Fortunately, he finally hooked up with Lindsay Brown at McGraw Hill and the book was published. (It has since been republished by Text Classics.)

He already had the second one, *White Meat*, written, and the rest is history.

After his family, writing was the love of Peter's life. He was never happier than when engaged on a book, and he was bored and depressed when there was nothing on the go. Fortunately, there usually was. He wrote for two short sessions a day, morning and afternoon, but was continuously preoccupied with the story—to the extent that I would sometimes ask, 'Are you okay?' when I saw him staring into space, suspecting a diabetic incident. 'Yes, love. Just thinking about what happens next.' Only other writers can understand this, perhaps? I often wonder about the non-writing partners of writers. Do they get it? Or do they feel shut out?

He also loved sport. He had been a promising amateur tennis player in his youth and in later life he took to golf. He liked watching the boxing, though his only painful attempt at it left him feeling it was not for him. I hate boxing and would sometimes ask what he saw in it. 'Great skills,' he said. 'And also they're braver than me. They don't cry when they're punched on the nose.'

His interest in boxing had a local flavour, too—he admired the way Indigenous boxers could make their mark and also some money (and keep it, if they were lucky), and this applied to Australian Rules football as well. He was an avid AFL follower—a lifetime Essendon supporter. In years when Essendon wasn't doing all that well, he would sometimes yell at the TV, 'More blackfellas! Recruit more blackfellas!'

What else did he love? Books, of course. Books, always. He always had at least one book on the go. Usually a novel and something non-fiction as well. His tastes were eclectic, much more than mine. He read a lot of literary fiction. He particularly liked biographies of people who 'had *done* something'. This category included other writers, adventurers, politicians, kings and knaves. He liked Stephen Hawking (for his atheism) but admitted he couldn't quite follow the argument. He loved Orwell and Somerset Maugham. He liked Hemingway and F. Scott Fitzgerald, even when I said he was a literary predator on Zelda and he agreed. (But who can argue about *The Great Gatsby*?) He admired James Ellroy, but thought he'd gone feral in his last few books.

He didn't read much fiction by women but he liked Ruth Rendell and the Morse series. He read Hilary Mantel, but hated the strange new narrative voice she'd introduced. He preferred C.J. Sansom's Shardlake series about Cromwell.

He was very selective about the crime fiction he read—Michael Robotham, Barry Maitland, Lee Child (until the later books, when he got bored by them), Michael Connelly, Elroy Leonard . . . I tried to get him interested in the Nordics, but with limited success.

The stories in this collection represent some of Peter's major interests.

'An ABC of Crime Writing', while tongue-in-cheek, shows his deep understanding of both crime fiction and the art of writing crime fiction, with his own prejudices and preferences clearly showing. He was disappointed that this couldn't find a publisher—too short, and he didn't want to rewrite. I think he envisaged a *de luxe* collectors' edition, lavishly illustrated with Michael Fitzjames's wonderful drawings. He would be extremely pleased that it now sees the light of day.

The selection here from his Godfather columns mainly concentrates on writing or reading-related themes. He wrote many more than these, on many other topics, for the *Newtown Review of Books* (https://newtownreviewofbooks.com.au) over nearly seven years.

In the last few years of his life, Peter's eyesight deteriorated further, he became deaf and his heart condition worsened, as did his arthritis. He became virtually house-bound, except for doctors' appointments and occasional—highly orchestrated—lunches with friends and the odd family event. His last book, *Win, Lose or Draw*, drew the final line under his writing career. He had typed it in 36-point font size and still found it difficult to see what he had written. He was unable to cope with the edits to this book and Angela Handley from Allen & Unwin and Jo Jarrah and I dealt with them, with constant reference to Peter.

He could no longer summon the concentration or energy required to write at any length, though he continued to provide interesting, amusing and knowledgeable weekly Godfather columns for the *Newtown Review of Books*, usually of 500 words or so, which he could just cope with. A column on golf remains unpublished.

Not having a book on the boil left a huge gap in Peter's life. Writing had been his main preoccupation for over 40 years and he missed it dreadfully. But as his physical debility increased, so did the range of activities he could perform or work up much interest in, and the gap writing had left seemed to shrink as health concerns grew.

In the last year of his life he did remain interested in politics and sport and always listened to the ABC's Radio National and watched the footy every week.

In his final few weeks Peter was in a lot of pain from arthritis, which they didn't think they could alleviate except with stronger painkillers. He was at the end of his tether by then—over-medicated, over-diagnosed, over-doctored. Cliched as it might sound, it was a blessed relief for him to die when he did. Not, perhaps, for those of us—family, friends and readers—he left behind.

But he also left behind a great legacy of pleasure and entertainment for a great many people through his books and he will long be remembered for that.

—Jean Bedford, 2019

THE BEST OF CLIFF HARDY, THE SHORT STORIES

What follows is a selection from the Cliff Hardy short stories, published in six separate volumes, from *Heroin Annie* in 1984 to *The Big Score* in 2007. These were good ideas that couldn't be incorporated into a full novel, or they were written for publication in magazines or other anthologies. On one occasion, they accompanied a novella, *Man in the Shadows* (1988). The stories demonstrate some of Peter's favourite themes—battlers, sport (especially boxing), his love of Sydney (corruption and all), his concern for and admiration of Indigenous people, as well as politics, local and national. Plus of course, crime.

Re-reading them, I'm struck by his graceful facility with the short story—his instinctive understanding of its shape and his unerring sense of when to finish, sometimes with the case unsolved, but always with some sort of resolution along the way. These stories are clever and humorous, sympathetic and cynical, and they do what all the best short stories do—they open small windows out to a larger world.

—JB

MAN'S BEST FRIEND

From *Heroin Annie* (1984)

I was walking along Vincent Street in Balmain, down near the soapworks, minding someone else's business, when a brick hit me, then another brick hit me, then another and I lost count; it felt as if a brick wall had moved out of line and wrapped itself around Cliff Hardy.

When I woke up Terry Kenneally was sitting beside my bed. My first thoughts were that my sheets had got very white and my windows very clean and that I'd finally got Terry to stay the night; and then I realised that I wasn't at home, I was in hospital. I've been in hospital before; the first thing to do is to check that you've still got all your bits and pieces and that they haven't mixed you up with the guy who had gangrene. I moved and wriggled and blinked; everything seemed to work.

'Don't move,' Terry said. 'They say you're not to move.'

'They say that to break your spirit,' I said. I grabbed at her brown left arm and the movement sent an arrow of pain through my head. I groaned.

'They're right, I won't move. How did you get here, love?'

Terry showed her nice white teeth. 'Someone found Dad's cheque in your pocket and phoned him. I came, he sends his regards.'

'I'm glad you came and not him, waking up to his face would be a shock. I wonder how your mum stood it.'

'Shut up.' She was holding my hand now, and it didn't hurt a bit.

'Did they find anything else? I mean my wallet . . .'

'All that,' she said. 'And your bloody gun; there's a policeman outside who wants to talk to you. I made them let me in first but I can't stay, I have to get back to work.' She leaned forward to kiss me and then pulled back.

'Possible fracture, they said.' She backed away and blew the kiss. 'Be back tonight, Cliff.'

She went out, the door stayed closed for ten seconds and then fourteen stone of plain-clothes copper walked in. His name was Detective Sergeant Moles and, although he didn't have much of a bedside manner, I told him all I could. I told him that I was a licensed private investigator, fidelity bonded and all, and that I was working for Pat Kenneally, who is a greyhound trainer. I didn't tell him that I was trying to find out who was doping Pat's dogs. I had a bit of trouble remembering what I'd been doing in Vincent Street, but it came: I'd been going to see the Frenchman. Moles nodded at that, he knew the Frenchman. Pierre Cressy knew all there was to know about racing greyhounds in New South Wales, he'd know who stood to win if Pat's dogs lost.

'Did you see the Frenchy?' Moles asked.

I had to think about it. 'No, I was on my way when the wall fell on me. What's your interest?' Moles scratched his ear and fidgeted, the way cops do when you ask them something. They figure ten of their questions to one of yours is about the right ratio. 'Bloke who found you saw your weapon, and called in. The boys who answered the call poked around a bit and asked a few questions. Seems people saw a man hanging around that spot before you came along.'

'What about the poking?'

'The wall didn't fall, Hardy, it was pushed. Someone tried to hurt you. Any ideas?'

I said, 'No,' and lay there with my possibly broken skull, thinking about it. Moles had talent, he read my mind.

'The Frenchy's okay,' he said. 'That all you've got to say?'

I said it was and he shrugged and left. I didn't tell him that I was in love with Pat's daughter or that I was afraid of greyhounds; I didn't think he'd be interested.

Doctors and nurses came and went and the time passed slowly. They told me I didn't have a fractured skull, just a lot of bruises and abrasions. I was grateful to them. Terry came back in the evening and we did some more hand-holding.

'Dad's worried about what happened,' she said. 'He's thinking of calling in the police.'

'He can forget about half his income if he does,' I said. 'You know what the greyhound people are like, Terry, any whisper of trouble at Pat's place and they'll pull their dogs out. Most of 'em anyway.'

'I know, but if someone's trying to kill you . . .'

I squeezed the upper part of her arm where she has a long, hard muscle under the smooth skin. 'I'll be careful,' I said. 'I'm used to it. Tell Pat to give me a few more days.'

'All right.' She kissed me the way you kiss invalids, as if they're made of feathers. Terry is tall and brown, as befits a professional tennis player. She has a terrific serve and aced me three times the day we met. She was overseas a lot reaching the finals of tournaments; we packed a lot into the time she was in Sydney, but I came a distant third in her life after her father and tennis.

They let me leave the hospital the next morning and I went home and read books and drank a bit and slept. Pat phoned, and I convinced him that I was fit to go on with the enquiry; Terry phoned, and I convinced her that I was fit to see her the following night. In the morning I took off some of the bandages and admired the deep blue bruises on my arms and chest. I'd been keen enough on the job in the first place on account of Terry, and now it had got very, very personal.

It was hot when I got to Vincent Street and a sweet, sickly coconut smell was coming up from the water, as if the bay were full of copra. I parked and walked up to the Frenchman's place; the crumpled wall had been tidied back on to the empty lot behind it, and soon the grass and weeds would be creeping up to the bricks and covering them like a winding sheet.

The Frenchman's house is a tumbledown weatherboard on rotting stumps; developers and trendies eye it greedily, but Cressy has some kind of protected lease and will die there. I walked up the overgrown path, brushing branches aside and wincing as the movement hurt my head. A tattered brown paper blind moved in the window of the front room; I reached through the hole in the wire screen and knocked on the door. It opened and Cressy stood there in slippers, pyjama pants and a buttonless cardigan. Pendulous breasted, toothless and with long, wispy white hair, he looked like a witch. But the thing in his hand wasn't a broomstick, it was a shotgun. He poked it through the hole so that it almost touched my chest.

'Go 'way,' he said.

I backed off a step. 'Take it easy. I just want to talk to you. My name . . .'

'I know you. Go 'way or I shoot you.'

I looked at the gun; the barrel was acned with rust, it was green around the trigger guard and the stock was dusty; but that didn't mean it couldn't kill me.

'Why?'

'Don't talk.' He lifted the gun a fraction. 'Just go.'

I was in no condition for side-stepping, ducking or for grabbing shotguns through wire screens. I went.

I was swearing, and my head was hurting as I drove back towards Glebe; if I'd had a dog I would have kicked it. I was driving fast down Cummins Street towards the turn up to Victoria Road, and when I touched the brake there was nothing there. My stomach dropped out as I pumped uselessly and started to flail through the gears and grab the handbrake, which has never had much grip. I fought the steering and felt the wheels lift as I wrestled the Falcon left at the bottom of the hill. The road was clear, the tyres screamed and I got round. I ran the car into the gutter, closed my eyes and shook; the tin fence at the bottom of the hill had been rushing towards me and what you mostly meet on the right around the corner are trucks—heavy ones. I felt as if I was walking on stilts when I got out to examine the car: there was no brake fluid in the cylinder. It's not a good way to kill someone; what if the victim thumps the brake a few times in the first hundred yards? But it *is* a good way to scare a man, like pushing a wall over on him. The more I thought about it the angrier I got.

I flagged down a cab and went back to Vincent Street. There was a lane running down behind the Frenchman's place, and I went down that and climbed over his decaying fence. The yard was a tangle of pumpkin vines, weeds and many, many strata of animal, vegetable and mineral rubbish. I crept past a rusting shed and almost whistled when I saw the back of the house: there were about twenty broken window panes on the glassed-in verandah, some smashed completely, others starred and cracked around neat holes.

I got my gun out and sneaked up to the side of the verandah; the Frenchman was sitting in a patch of sun at a small table with a flagon of red wine and a racing guide on it. A breeze through the bullet holes was stirring the paper and he moved his glass to hold it down. I couldn't see the shotgun. I wrenched the door open and went in; the Frenchman barely moved before I had the .38 in his ear.

'Sit down, Frenchy,' I said. 'I think I'll have a glass with you. Where's the popgun?'

He jerked his head at the door leading into the house and I went through into the kitchen, if you call a stove and sink a kitchen. The shotgun was leaning against a wall and I broke it open and took out the shell. I rinsed a dirty glass in rusty water. Back on the verandah the Frenchman was marking the guide with a pencil stub. He ignored me. I poured out some of the red and took a drink; it was old, not good old, stale old. It tasted as if it had been filtered through used tea leaves. I poured my glass into his.

'Who did the shooting?' I said.

He shrugged and made a mark with the pencil.

'Don't come over all Gallic on me, Pierre. I've had a wall drop on me, a shotgun pointed at me and my brakes taken out, and it all has to do with you.'

He looked up; his eyes were gummy and hair from his nostrils had tangled up with a moustache as wild as his backyard. 'I don't know what you're talking about. The shotgun? I protect myself, that's all.' He put some of the red down his throat as if he liked it.

'Protection? From me?'

He shrugged again. 'He shoots my house all to hell and tells me don't talk to you. So I don't. Now you have the gun, so I must talk to you.'

I put the gun away and sat on a bench under the window, then I realised what a good target that made me and I moved across the room.

'Who told you not to talk to me?'

'On the telephone, how do I know? Bullets everywhere, then the phone. Don't talk to Hardy. Hardy is tall and skinny with bandages. So.' He opened his hands expressively, they shook and he put them back on the table.

He was scared but he drank some more wine and got less scared. I offered him fifty bucks and cab fare to Central Station and he accepted. He said he could go to Gosford for a few days, and I said that sounded like a good idea. After I'd given him the money he got out a bottle of wine with a respectable label on it and we drank that. He gave me names of people who'd profit if Pat's dogs lost. The names didn't mean anything to me. I asked him if these men would dope dogs, and he smiled and said something in French. It might have been 'Do bears live in the forest?' but French was never my strong point at Maroubra High.

I spent the early part of the afternoon getting my car towed to a garage and persuading a reluctant mechanic to give it priority. Then I went home and rested; the red wine buzzed in my head as a background to the throbbing pain, but after a sleep and a shower I felt better. I collected the car and drove to Rozelle to confer with Pat and pick up Terry, who was visiting there. Pat's street is narrow and jam-packed with houses, but the blocks are deep, and Pat keeps his dogs out the back. He once showed me the kennels and the mattresses they sunbathe on and the walking machine they use when it's too hot or wet for the roads; it was like a country club except that the members were thin and fit. I didn't like them much and they didn't like me; without their muzzles I liked them even less.

Terry was out the front chatting to the neighbours when I pulled up. They'd known her since she started knocking a ball against the factory wall opposite, and even though they saw her on television now their attitude to her hadn't changed nor hers to them—it was that sort of street. Terry and I went inside to talk to Pat, who was drinking tea in the kitchen.

Pat is a widower of five years' standing but his house-keeping is as good as the Frenchman's was bad. Terry made coffee in the well-ordered kitchen; Pat tried to talk about my injuries but I wouldn't let him.

'The Frenchy gave me these names,' I said. 'What d'you reckon?' I read him the names and he chewed them over one by one. He sipped tea and smoked a rolled cigarette: Pat is small, brown and nuggety; his wife was six inches taller than him and gave her build and looks to Terry. Pat must have contributed warmth and charm because he has plenty of both. He was loyal to the game he was in too; he ruled out all the men I named as non-starters in the doping stakes. Two he knew personally, one was decrepit he said, and another was too stupid.

'It's none of them, mate,' Pat said. 'Could be some new bloke the Frenchy doesn't know about.'

'Yeah, I'll have to check that angle. Takes time though; this'll be costing you, Pat.'

'Worth it.' He puffed smoke at me and I coughed. 'Sorry, forgot you were a clean-lunger, like Terry. Good on you.' He drew luxuriously on the cigarette.

Terry and I went to a pub down near the wharf in Balmain. You can eat outside there, and hear yourself talk above the acoustic bush band. They have a couple of very heavy people to deal with the drunks and the food is good. Terry seems to eat mainly lettuce, and drink hardly at all; I was manfully doing my share of both food and drink when she told me that two of Pat's owners had pulled their dogs out.

'Hear about the doping, did they?' I said.

'Yes.'

'I thought that was a close-kept secret.'

'So did I, so did Dad. What does it mean, d'you think?'

I ate and drank and thought for a while. 'Sounds as if the doper spread the word.'

'That wouldn't make sense.' She took a tiny sip of wine, as if even half a glass would ruin her backhand.

'It might, if the idea is just to put Pat out of business, not to actually fix races. Does that open up a line of thought?'

'No.'

'Well, try this; it could be revenge.'

She almost choked. 'On Dad? Come on.' Then she saw that I was serious. 'Revenge,' she said slowly. 'We go in a bit for that on the circuit, but it's not common in real life, is it?'

That's another thing I like about Terry, although she's serious about her tennis she doesn't think it's 'real life'; she won't go on the gin when it's over. 'No, it's not common,' I said. 'In fact it's rare. "Maintain your rage" and all that, people can't do it mostly. But it does happen; we'd better ask Pat about his enemies.'

'I'm sure he hasn't any.'

'Everyone has.' She didn't like that too much; she doesn't like my suspicious nature or the work I do, really. It's a problem, and we spent the rest of the dinner talking about other things and getting over the bad spot.

Back in Rozelle Pat was still up, working on his books. We went through the tea and coffee ritual again and I asked Pat if he'd made any enemies in the game.

'Few,' he said. I glanced up at Terry.

'Any that'd want to put you out of business?'

He blew smoke and deliberated. 'Only one I reckon. Bloke was a vet and I gave evidence against him for doping. He didn't like it, and said he'd get me.'

'Why didn't you tell me about him?'

'Couldn't be him, mate. He's in gaol; he went to Queensland, got mixed up in something, and I heard he got ten years.'

'When was this?'

'Oh, four, five years ago.'

'He could be out, Pat,' I said.

Terry and I went back to her flat at Rushcutters Bay, near the White City courts, and she acknowledged that I could be on to something. We left it there and went to bed; it hurt a bit, what with the bruises and all, but it didn't hurt enough to stop us. The ex-vet's name was Leslie Victor Mahony, and it took me two phone calls and half an hour to find out that he'd been released from gaol in Brisbane three months back having served four and a half years of a ten-year sentence for embezzlement and fraud. I spent the next two days confirming that Mahony had come to Sydney and failing to locate him. There was a definite feeling that Doc Mahony was in town, but no one knew where, or they weren't saying.

At the end of the second day I was dispirited. Terry was playing an exhibition match but I didn't feel like going, and I didn't feel like reporting my lack of progress to her afterwards. The case was turning into a fair bitch and, weakling that I am, I got drunk. I started on beer when I got home, went on to wine with my meal and on to whisky after that. I woke up with a mouth like a kangaroo pouch. I stood under the shower for fifteen minutes, telling myself how not smoking reduced hangovers. All that did was make me wish I had a cigarette.

I was drinking coffee, and thinking speculatively about eggs, when the phone rang.

The voice said: 'I hear you're looking for Doc Mahony.'

I said: 'That's right, who's this?'

The voice said: 'Nobody. How well do you know Heathcote?'

'I know it.'

'You get there, and pick up a road that runs along the railway, going south. Where the bitumen stops you go right on an unmade road for two miles. You take a left fork, go down a dip and there's a shack on your right. Mahony's there.'

'You a friend of his?'

'I wouldn't piss on him. If you want him, he's there.'

He hung up and I tried to remember whether I'd heard the voice before. I thought I had but I've heard a hell of a lot of voices. I didn't like it at all; it looked to me as if a .22 had been used on the Frenchman's windows and a .22 bullet can kill you. An anonymous phone call, a shack in the bush—it sounded like a trap. It sounds crazy and probably had something to do with the brain cells I'd burnt out the night before, but I just couldn't get too frightened about a vet. I checked over the .38 carefully, took some extra ammunition and went to Heathcote.

I've heard people talk fondly about Heathcote as an unspoiled place of their childhood; it's hard to imagine it like that now. The sprawl on the western side of the highway is the standard, sterile, red brick horror-land where the garage dominates the outside of the house and the TV set the inside. Over the highway and the railway line though, the area has retained some dusty charm—if you like faded weatherboard houses with old wooden fences and roofs rusting quietly away. Up to a point I followed the directions I'd been given, but I'm not that green; I had a map of the tracks leading into the national park behind and beyond and I marked where the shack would be and circled up around behind it. I stopped at a point which I calculated would be about half a mile from the shack; it was a still, quiet day with the birds subdued in the sun. I closed the car door softly and started down the rough track towards a patch of forest behind the track. Things jumped and wriggled in the grass beside the track and I resolved to be very, very careful so that they wouldn't be jumping and wriggling over me.

The shack, as I looked at it through the trees, was exactly that—an ancient, weatherboard affair that had lost its pretensions to paint long ago. Grass grew in the guttering and sprouted out through the lower boards. I squatted behind a tree for ten minutes soaking up the atmosphere—no sign of a car, no wisps of smoke in the air, no coughing. I did a complete circle of the place at about seventy-five yards' distance, the way they'd taught me in Malaya. Still nothing. There are two theories about approaching a possibly defended place like this: one says you should keep circling and come in closer each time; the other has it that this causes too much movement and you should come in straight. The first way was out because there was a clear patch about fifty yards deep in front of the shack and I'm a straight-line man myself, anyway.

I made it down to the back door without any trouble. The building was a tiny one-pitch, three rooms at most. The noise I could hear inside was snoring. I gave it a few minutes, but it was real snoring, complete with irregular rhythm and grunts. I eased the door open and went in; floorboards creaked and the door grated, but Doc Mahony wasn't worried—he was lying on a bed in his underwear with a big, dreamy smile on his face—maybe he was dreaming of when he was young and slim and sober, which he wasn't any more. There was an empty bottle of Bundaberg rum on the floor and one half full on a chair beside the bed.

It was a dump comparable to the Frenchman's and the rural setting didn't help it any; you could hardly see through the dusty windows and the kikuyu poked up through the floor. I couldn't find the .22, which worried me, and I was also worried by the empty tins and the food and water bowls in the back room—I hadn't seen any sign of a dog. I filled the empty rum bottle with water and went back to the bedchamber. The Doc tried to ignore the first few drops but then I got some good ones down his nose and into his mouth and he spluttered and coughed and woke up.

His face was pale, grimy with dirt and whiskers, and lumpy like his body. He had a few thin strands of hair plastered to his head with sweat, and a few teeth, but much of the beauty of the human face and form was lacking. He opened his eyes and his voice was surprisingly pleasant-sounding.

'Who the hell are you?'

'I'm a friend of Pat Kenneally, Doc. You remember Pat?'

He remembered all right, alarm leapt into his pale, bleary eyes and he made a movement with his hand. He changed the movement into a grab for the rum but I wasn't fooled. I pushed the bottle out of reach and felt under the bed, and came up with a shoebox. I took my gun out and pointed it at Doc's meaty nose.

'Lie back. Get some rest.'

Inside the box was a notebook with Pat's address and phone number written on the first page. The next few pages were taken up with the names and descriptions of greyhounds. Some dog owners were listed with telephone numbers and addresses. Also in the box was an array of pills and powders, a couple of hypodermics and some bottles of fluid with rubber membrane tops.

'Nasty,' I said. 'Poor little doggies.'

He didn't say anything, but reached for the bottle again. There were still a couple of inches of water in the bottle and I poured enough rum into it to darken it up a bit. I handed it to him.

'You'll ruin your health taking it straight. Now, let's hear about the bricks and the car and the bullets through the Frenchman's house.'

He took a long swig of the diluted rum, swilled it around in his mouth and spat it against the wall. He followed this display of his manners with a racking cough and a long, gurgling swallow from the bottle.

'I don't know what you're talking about,' he gasped, and then took another swallow.

I tapped the notebook. 'What's this—research for a book?'

'I wanted to get Kenneally,' he said in the voice that was all he had left of his profession and self-respect, 'but I don't know anything about that other stuff—bricks and bullets.'

'It's God's own truth, Hardy.' The voice came from behind me; it was the voice on the phone and now I didn't even need to turn around to know who it was. I felt something hard jab the nape of my neck. 'Put the gun on the bed, Hardy. Do it slow.'

I did it very slowly, and then I turned. Johnny Dragovic had scarcely changed at all in the past six years since I'd seen him in court when my evidence had helped to get him eight years for armed robbery. Johnny was a tough kid from Melbourne who'd decided to take Sydney on; he knocked over a couple of bottle shops, and moved up to TAB agencies, with some success. The Board hired me and some other private men and I got lucky, heard some whispers, and we were waiting for Johnny at the right time and place. Blows were struck, and Johnny turned out to be not quite as tough as he thought. But he was tough enough, and the automatic pistol in his hand made him even tougher. I said, 'Dragovic,' stupidly.

'That's right,' he said. 'Glad you remember.'

My guts were turning over and I concentrated on getting my balance right and watching him carefully, in case he gave me a chance. I didn't think he would.

'What's it all about then?' I said.

'It's about eight years, five at Grafton.' The way he said it spoke volumes: he wasn't there to thank me for rehabilitating him.

'Put it behind you,' I said. 'You're not old.'

The gun didn't move. 'You bastard. I've kept going by thinking what I could do to you.'

'Thinking like that'll get you back there.'

'Shut up! I was nineteen when I got to Grafton, what do you reckon that was like?'

'Scary,' I said. I thought that if I kept him talking something might happen, he might even talk himself out of whatever he had in mind.

'That's right, scary. That's why I got you with the bricks and fixed your bloody car—to scare you.'

'You win. You did it, you scared me. I'm scared now.'

'You should be. I'm going to kill you.'

'That's crazy,' I said desperately. 'And not fair—I didn't kill you.'

He laughed. 'Sometimes, in that bloody hole, I wished you had.'

'What about him?' I gestured down at Doc who was listening and clutching the bottle like a crucifix.

'He goes out too,' Dragovic said. 'You kill him and he kills you. All in the line of duty.'

'It stinks, Johnny, it won't work.'

'It fuckin' will! I've planned this for a while, been watching you until the right deal came up. It'll look like you caught up with the bloke who shot up the Frenchy's house and you shot him and he shot you. You'll take a while to die, though.' He smiled and I could see how much he was enjoying it all, and how unlikely it was that he'd change his mind.

Mahony raised himself slowly on the bed and swung his legs over the side. 'This is madness,' he said. 'I don't want any part of it. I'm going.' He got off the bed and took a couple of shuffling steps towards the door before Dragovic reacted.

'Get back here!' he yelled. 'Get back.'

But Mahony opened the door and had half his body outside when Dragovic shot him. He crumpled, and I moved to the left and swung a punch that took Dragovic on the nose. Blood spurted and he blundered back, but kept hold of his gun. I made a grab for mine, missed and lunged out the door, nearly tripping over Mahony. I staggered, recovered my balance, and started to run for the trees about fifty yards away. I was halfway there when something stung my calf like ten sandfly bites; the leg lost all power and I went down, hard. Johnny Dragovic stepped clear of the doorway, carrying a rifle, and started to walk towards me. I lay there in the dust watching him and watching the rifle and when he was about twenty feet away I closed my eyes. Then I heard a shot and didn't feel anything, so I opened my eyes: the rifle was on the ground close to me and Dragovic was yelling and rolling around and a greyhound was tearing at his neck. There was blood on Dragovic's face from my punch, and a lot more blood on his chest from the dog's attack. He screamed, and the dog's head came up and went down twice. I sat up and grabbed the rifle; the dog turned away from the bloody mess on the ground and sprang straight at me. I shot it in the chest and it collapsed and I shot it again in the head.

I hobbled across and bent down, but one look told me that tough Johnny Dragovic was dead. The dog had a length of chain attached to a collar trailing away in the dirt. It looked as if Dragovic had secured the dog, but not well enough. More hobbling got me over to the shack where there was more death. Mahony's eyes stared sightlessly up at the blue sky; his mouth was open and some flies were already gathering around the dark blood that had spilled out of it.

After that it was a matter of rum and true grit. I took an enormous swig of the rum and started on the trek back to my car. When I made it I was weeping with the pain and there was a saw-mill operating at full blast inside my head. I got the car started and into gear somehow and kangaroo-hopped it back along the track until I reached a house. Then I leant on the horn until a woman came out, and I spoke to her and told her what to do.

Terry came to see me in hospital and Pat came and Sergeant Moles—it was like old times. The bullet had touched the bone but hadn't messed the leg up too much. No one wept over Doc Mahony and Johnny Dragovic, although Pat said that the Doc wasn't such a bad bloke, just greedy. Terry went off to play a tournament in Hong Kong, and one solitary night I went to the dog track and won fifty dollars on a hound named Topspin.

SILVERMAN

From *Heroin Annie* (1984)

If I hadn't been so busy worrying about money and my carburettor—the sorts of problems that beset your average private detective in the spring—I would have taken note of them out in the street. The car I did notice—a silver Mercedes, factory fresh. But then, that's not an impossible sight in St Peter's Lane. We get the odd bookie dropping by, a psychoanalyst or two, the occasional tax-avoidance consultant. I also saw a man and a woman in the car, nothing discordant about that really, as I went into the building and up to my office to move the bills and accounts rendered around.

I was at my desk wanting a cigarette (but fighting against it), with a light breeze from the open window disturbing the dust, when the door buzzer sounded. I got up and let them in. The woman walked over to the solidest chair and plonked herself down in it; she needed everything the springing could give her—she must have been close to six feet and wouldn't have made the light heavyweight limit. Her hair was jet black and her make-up was vivid. Of women's clothes I'm no judge; hers looked as if they'd been made for her out of good material. She got cigarettes in a gold case out of a shiny bag, lit up, and waited for the man to do whatever he was going to do.

He was a plump, red-faced little number with lots of chins and thin hair. His dark blue suit had been artistically cut, but the unfashionable lines of his body had easily won out. He looked like a funny little fat man, but I had a feeling that his looks were deceptive.

'I'm Horace Silverman, Mr Hardy,' he said. 'This is my wife, Beatrice. I'm in real estate.'

I nodded; I hadn't thought he was a postman.

'We are concerned about our son,' Silverman went on. 'His name is Kenneth.' I opened my mouth, but he lifted a hand to silence me. 'Kenneth left home a year ago to live with other students. He was attending the university.'

'Was?' I said alertly.

'Yes. He suspended his studies; I believe that's the term. He also changed his address several times. Now we don't know where he is, and we want you to find him.'

'Missing Persons,' I said.

'No! We have reason to believe that Kenneth is in bad company. There may be . . . legal problems.'

'How bad?'

'The problems? Oh, not bad. A summons for speeding, a parking violation. Others may be pending.'

'It doesn't sound serious. You'd be better off using the police, scores of men, computers . . .'

The red deepened in his face and his big, moist mouth went thin and hard; any affability he'd brought in with him had dropped away.

'I said no!' He slammed his palm down on my desk. 'I'm involved in some very delicate business negotiations; very delicate, with a great deal of money involved. The slightest complication of my affairs, the slightest hint of police hanging about, and they could fall through.' He got the words out with difficulty through the rising tide of his anger. He seemed intolerant of opposition. Maybe Kenneth knew what he was doing. The woman blew smoke and looked concerned but said nothing.

'Okay, okay,' I said. 'I'm glad of the work. I charge seventy-five dollars a day plus expenses. You get an itemised account. I take a retainer of two hundred dollars.'

He dipped into the bulging pocket of his suit coat and fished out a cheque book. He scribbled, ripped and handed the cheque over—five hundred dollars.

'Do you want them shot, or tortured to death slowly?' I said.

'Who?'

The woman snorted, 'Horace,' crushed out her cigarette in the stand and levered herself up from the chair. I gathered that they were going.

'Not so fast. I need names, addresses, descriptions, photographs . . .'

He cut me off by hauling a large manila envelope out of his other pocket and dumping it on the desk. I hoped his tailor never saw him out on the street.

'I'm busy,' he said shortly. 'All you'll need is there. Just find him, Mr Hardy, and report to me.' He'd calmed down; he was happiest telling people what to do.

'It could be unpleasant,' I said. 'He might be smoking cigarettes, taking the odd drink . . .'

'A full report, no punches pulled.'

'You'll get it.' I opened the door and he bustled out. She cruised after him, still looking concerned. He seemed to have brought her along just to prove that the boy had a mother.

I sat down at the desk again, propped the cheque up in front of me and opened the envelope. There were three photographs, photocopies of a parking ticket and a speeding fine and of a letter, dated two months back, from the Registrar of the

University of Sydney. It was directed to Kenneth at an address in Wahroonga. There was also a sheet of Horace Silverman's business paper half-covered in type.

The typed sheet gave me the low-down on Ken. Born in Sydney twenty-one years ago, six feet tall when last measured and slim of build, fair of hair with no marks or scars. The last meeting with his parents was given and dated—a dinner eight weeks back. Two addresses in the inner suburbs were listed, and it was suggested that the Registrar's letter had been sent to Ken's home address by mistake. His interests were given—tennis, bushwalking and politics. His major subject at university was psychology, and a Dr Katharine Garson was listed as his student counsellor.

The photos were black and white, good quality, good size. They showed a young man in his late teens or around twenty, all three shots roughly contemporaneous. Kenneth Silverman had it all—thick, wavy hair, even features, broad shoulders. I'd have taken bets that his teeth were good. One of the pictures showed him in tennis gear, and he looked right; in another he was leaning against a sports car and he looked right in that too. I couldn't see any resemblance to Horace, maybe a little to Beatrice. There were none of those signs—weak chin, close-set eyes—that are supposed to indicate, but don't, character deficiencies. Kenneth Silverman looked healthy and happy.

Sydney University was just down the road and Silverman's last known address was in Glebe, my stamping ground. I went down to the street and along to the backyard of the tattooist's shop where I keep my car. In an ideal world, I'd find the boy in Glebe before three o'clock, deposit my cheque, draw some out and be home in time to invite someone out to dinner.

The Fisher Library of the University of Sydney is a public place, like the whole campus. This statutory fact has been found useful by a few Vice-Chancellors who've felt the need to call the cops in. I got there a little after midday and looked up Dr Garson in the handbook—a string of degrees, senior lecturer in psychology. The Psychology Department was in one of those new concrete buildings that academics have allowed themselves to be herded into. They have as much personality as a bar of soap and, in my experience, they have a corresponding effect on the people who work in them. Not Dr Garson though; she'd done her concrete cell out with pictures that actually looked like people and places, and she had a flagon of sherry sitting on the window ledge.

'A sherry?' she said when she'd installed me in a chair.

'Please; then I can show you what good manners I've got, how well I can sip and murmur appreciatively.'

'Don't bother,' she said, pouring, 'piss is piss.' She set the glass on the desk near me and took a belt herself. 'So you're a private detective? Some of my colleagues wouldn't allow you on the campus, let alone in their rooms.'

'It's a public place.'

She raised one plucked eyebrow. 'So it is.' She finished her sherry and poured another. She had fine bones in her wrists and even finer ones in her face.

'I want some information about a student you counselled.'

She laughed. 'Unlikely.'

'I want to help him—find him, that is.'

She sipped. 'Perhaps he wants to stay lost.'

'He still can if he wants to.' I drank some of the sherry, dry. 'I find him, report to his father and that's that.'

'You don't look like a thug, Mr Hardy, but you're in a thuggish trade. Why should I help you?'

'One, you've got an independent mind, two, Silverman might be in trouble.'

She didn't jump out of her skirt at the name but she didn't treat it like a glass of flat beer either.

'Kenneth Silverman,' she said slowly.

'That's right, rich Kenneth who dropped out and disappeared. His mum and dad would like to know why. You wouldn't be able to put their minds at rest by any chance?'

'No.'

'Can't or won't?'

'Can't. I was surprised when he dropped out, he was doing well.'

'What did you do about it?'

She finished her sherry with an exasperated flick. 'What could I do? I counsel twenty students and teach another sixty. I wrote to him asking him to contact me for a talk. He didn't.'

'Had you counselled him much?'

'No, he didn't seem to need it.'

'It looks now as if he did.'

'Not really. He became radical at the beginning of the year. It happens to most of the bright ones, although a bit late in his case. The process sends some of them haywire but Ken seemed to be able to handle it. His first term's work was excellent, he trailed off a bit in early second term, nothing serious, then he just suspended for no reason.'

'Are you curious about that?'

'Yes, very.'

'Then help me.'

She took her time thinking about it. The process involved pouring some more sherry and tossing back the thick mane of chestnut hair.

'All right.' She held up her glass and sunlight sifted through the pale, amber fluid. 'You'd better talk to his girlfriend, Kathy Martin.'

'How can I contact her?'

'She'll be at my lecture at a quarter past two. She's a blonde with a suntan, you can't miss her.'

'You won't introduce us?'

'No.'

'Why not?'

She smiled. 'My reputation,' she said.

I finished my sherry, found out where the lecture was held, thanked her and left.

The lecture theatre sloped steeply and had front and back entrances. I killed some time with a sandwich and coffee and was back at a quarter past two watching the acolytes roll up for knowledge. I stood up the back, and tried not to be depressed by their impossible youth. One of the last students in was a blonde with her hair tied back; she had on a simple, sleeveless dress and sandals; her arms and legs and face were very brown. She sat down and got out a clipboard and looked like business as Dr Garson started in on R.D. Laing. I snuck out for coffee I didn't want and when I got back the students were dribbling out. I approached the blonde girl as she loped out into the quadrangle.

'Kathy Martin?'

'Yes.' Up close, she was the original outdoors girl with a demoralising sheen of good health.

'My name is Hardy, I've been hired by Mr Horace Silverman to look for his son. I understand you were a friend.'

'Yes.' I got the impression she wasn't a big talker.

'Well, can we have a chat?'

She looked at her watch. 'I have a tutorial in an hour and I haven't done all the reading.'

'It won't take long.' I herded her across to a bench. She sat down after looking at her watch again.

'When did you last see Kenneth?'

'Nearly two months ago.'

'Where?'

'At his place.'

'Where's that?'

'He had a squat in Glebe, Sweatman Street.' She gave me the number and I wrote it down.

'Why was he squatting? He had plenty of money, didn't he?'

'Kenny stopped taking his family's money. He went left, extreme left.'

'Did you?'

'Not so extreme.'

'Did you quarrel?'

She frowned. 'A bit, but we didn't split up, if that's what you mean.'

'You didn't?'

'No, he was around. I saw him, we did what we usually did. You wouldn't understand.'

'One day he was there and the next day he wasn't?'

'It wasn't a day-to-day thing.' She tapped her battered briefcase. 'Look, I really have to read this stuff.'

'Won't keep you a minute. What did you do about it—Kenneth's disappearance?'

'Nothing. I said you wouldn't follow. It wasn't a disappearance. The people he was in with, they do it all the time—go north, take jobs for money, you know?'

'So you weren't worried.'

'What could I do?' she snapped. 'I couldn't go to the police or anything, they were really *out*, in Kenny's terms. I didn't know his family. I just hoped he'd turn up; I still do.'

'What about the people at the squat?'

'They were raided. The house was taken over.'

'This was after Kenneth went missing?'

She paused. 'Kenneth sounds weird. Yes, I think so, soon after.'

I tried to digest the information and lost her while I did it. She got up and said goodbye in a voice that meant it. I thanked her and watched her walk away with that long, bouncy step and the thought came to me that Kenny had at least one good reason to stick around.

Sweatman Street has seen worse days; the big, two-storeyed, bay-windowed houses had been broken up into flats and rooms until recently, when small, affluent families had taken them over. More European cars and 4WDs than beaten-up Holdens with a rust problem. The street is down near the water and getting leafier and smarter daily and the pockets of poverty in it are not old-style—port and pension—but new-style: dope and dole poverty.

The address Kathy had given me was the last house in a terrace of twenty. It featured weeds and broken glass and peeling paint. The windows at the side and back were set too high up to see in. Around the back, I was surprised to find that all the fences dividing the yards had been removed. This left an immense space which was taken up with trees, rubbish and children's play gear in about equal proportions.

The broken windows at the back of the house were boarded up and the door was nailed shut. I gave it an experimental tug, and a shout came from behind me.

'Hey! What're you doing?'

He was big, with a lot of hair on his head and face. His jeans, sneakers and T-shirt were old and dirty. I stepped down from the door and tried to look innocent.

'Just looking,' I said.

He was close enough for me to see the aggression pent up in him and something else—there was a nervousness in his movements and a frozen look in his eyes that I'd seen before in speed-freaks and pill-poppers. I opened my hands in a placating gesture which he misunderstood, perhaps deliberately. He crowded up close and bumped me back against the crumbling brick wall. I wasn't ready for it, and lost a bit of breath.

'Take it easy,' I said. I put out a hand to hold him back and he swept it aside. His punch was a clumsy looping effort, and I couldn't resist it; I stepped inside and hit him short, just above the belt buckle. He sagged and I grabbed him under the arms to hold him up.

'Let him go.' Another man came from behind the trees; he was slighter and clean-shaven, and he dropped into a martial-arts pose about ten feet away from me. I let the bearded man slide down the wall.

'Don't be silly,' I said. 'All this is silly; I just want to ask a few questions. I'm looking for someone.'

'Do him, Chris,' my winded opponent said, and Chris didn't need any encouragement. He jumped up and let go a flying kick at my shoulder. It was a good, high jump, but the trick with this stuff is not to watch the acrobatics. I ducked under it and kicked the leg he landed on out from under him. He went down in a heap and the stiff-armed chop he came up with might have looked good on the mat but was way too slow in the field. I swayed away from it and hit him just where I'd hit his mate; and that was a mistake because he had washboard muscles there, but I had the combination ready and the next punch landed on his nose where there aren't any muscles, just nerves to cause pain and blood vessels to break. He yelped and threw his hands up over his face.

So I had one on the ground and one with a bloody face and no information. Then I heard a slow, ironic handclap; she was standing on the steps of the next house, dark and fat in a shapeless dress and with a cigarette between her lips.

'I didn't start it,' I said inanely.

'Who cares?' She seemed to find it all funny; flesh on her face shook as she laughed and she puffed at the cigarette without touching it.

I fished out my licence card and waved it in front of Chris and his mate.

'I'm a private detective. I'm looking for Kenneth Silverman; now who's going to talk to me? There's money in it.'

The woman took the cigarette out of her face and tried a fat, pursed-up smile.

'Now you're talking,' she said. 'Come along here.'

'Don't talk to him, Fay,' the bearded one said.

'Shut your head, Lenny. Come on whatever your name is, I'll talk your arse off.'

I went past my opponents and followed her to a back door in the middle of the row. We went into a kitchen that was neither dirty nor clean. I smelled something vaguely familiar, and sniffed at it.

'Candles,' she said. 'No power in here. I can make you a coffee, though.' She gestured at a small stove hooked up to a gas cylinder.

'Don't bother, thanks. Do you know Silverman?'

'Straight to it, eh? What about the money?'

I got out ten dollars and put it on the cracked linoleum-topped table.

'And another if I'm satisfied,' I said.

'Fair enough.' She bobbed her head and the fat bounced on her and ash fell down on to her lumpy chest. 'Yeah, I knew Kenny, he lived down the end there.' She waved back towards the scene of my triumph. 'He left when they cleared us out; no, a bit before that.'

'Who's "they"?'

'The developers—Forbes Realty. They own this terrace and a few others. Cunts!'

'What happened?'

'Came around one morning, about six o'clock, two big blokes with a guy in a suit. He told them what to do—they dumped all our stuff out; everything, every fucking thing, just out in the bloody street. Then they boarded the place up.' She laughed.

'What's funny?'

'I was thinking, Chris lost a fight that morning too—it's bullshit, that karate crap.'

I grunted. 'You said Silverman had gone by this time?'

She squinted at the ten dollars, remembering, or pretending to. 'Yeah, he wasn't in the house that morning. No sign of him. I think some of his stuff got dumped, but I'm not sure. It was a pretty wild scene.'

'Why are those two so jumpy?'

She spat the cigarette stub out onto the floor, put her thonged foot on it and fished a packet of Winfield out of her pocket.

'We've only been back a couple of weeks; it's been quiet, but you never know with that mob.'

I nodded, she lit up and puffed an enormous cloud of smoke at the window. I looked around at the artefacts of the squat—packing case shelves, a hose running in through the window to the sink, the small carton of milk on the table. She read my mind.

'You're wondering what a silvertail like Kenny was doing living in a dump like this?'

I pushed the money across to her. 'Yes.'

She picked it up and put it away with the cigarettes.

'Kenny and the others were taking on Forbes,' she spoke around the cigarette. 'Kenny was living here as a political act, that's what he said.'

'Who else was in the group?'

'Chris and Lenny, couple more. I think I've said enough, I don't know a bloody thing about you. Do I get the other ten?'

'You're not political yourself?'

'Shit no, I squat 'cos it's easy.'

'Did they have trouble with the developers before?'

'Oh yeah, plenty—slashed tyres, windows busted—usual things.'

'Anything since you moved back?'

'Not yet.'

'What sort of action did Kenneth and the others take?'

'Letters to the papers, attending council meetings, street meetings about the plan. They're going to build right down to the water, you know? We won't even be able to see the bit we see now.'

I gave her another ten dollars and went across to the dusty, cobwebbed window. Blackwattle Bay was an ugly, oily gleam under the dull grey sky and its Glebe shore was a blasted landscape of car bodies, timber and scratchy grass. The view was a long way short of cheerful but there was water in it, it promised better things; it was Sydney. I thanked Fay and tramped through the backyards; Lenny and Chris weren't in sight and I pulled myself up to one of the windows of the house Silverman had occupied. It was in bad shape; there were black-rimmed holes in the floorboards, and plumbing had been ripped out and hung limp and useless on the kitchen wall.

I drove to the post office and looked up Forbes Realty. The address in Norton Street, Leichhardt, niggled at me as I wrote it down. Back in the car I found out why—Kenneth Silverman's parking ticket had been incurred in Norton Street.

It seemed like time for some telephone research; I went home, made a drink and called a few people including Cy Sackville, my lawyer, and Grant Evans, a senior cop and friend. The results were interesting. Forbes Realty was a semi-solid firm and the word in financial circles was that it was over-extended. Its two leading shareholders were Horace Silverman and Clive Patrick. Silverman's interests were extensive and Forbes was a small part of his action. From Evans I learned that Forbes Realty had been burglarised eight weeks back and that enquiries were proceeding, also that a Constable Ian Williamson had stopped MG sports model JLM 113 registered to Kenneth Silverman and booked the driver for speeding. Evans arranged for me to talk to Williamson and that made one favour I owed him.

I reckoned I'd put in a day. It was time to tease out a few loose ends and do some thinking. I needed to know more about Forbes Realty and Kenneth's tactics; also, I was stalling: I didn't like the look of things and I might have to play a very careful hand. I bought some Lebanese food on the way home and washed it down with a few drinks. Then I took a long walk around Glebe; they were selling food and drink and fun in the main road and God knows what in the back streets and lanes. I nodded to the shop and street people I knew, and avoided the dog shit and cracks in the pavement by long habit. The water was shining under a clear sky and a light breeze brought a salty tang to the nostrils. You wouldn't have washed your socks in the water and every tree in the place was struggling against the pollution, but it was home and I liked it. Its minute foreshore didn't need blocking out with flats.

I went home and phoned a contact in motor registry. He got back to me an hour later with the information that Silverman's car hadn't been sold, traded, stolen or smashed in the last two months. It had disappeared. I went to sleep wondering about how Kenneth reconciled the car with his radicalism; I wondered whether Horace Silverman's delicate business negotiations involved Forbes Realty, and I wondered whether Dr Garson would accept if I asked her out to dinner.

At ten in the morning I phoned Horace Silverman and asked him about his role in Forbes Realty. He went silent and I had to prompt him.

'I can see you've been doing your job, Mr Hardy.'

'I hope so.' I was thinking fast, trying to guess at his meaning and keep the upper hand. 'Would you care to tell me all about it?'

There was another pause and then he spoke very deliberately. 'I don't know how you found out, but it's true—Kenneth and I had a falling out over Forbes Realty.'

I breathed out gently. 'How bad?'

'Quite serious. He was very critical of the firm, I suppose you know why.'

'Yeah. You didn't tell me he'd stopped taking your money.'

'That's true too. I'm sorry I wasn't frank, Mr Hardy. It's painful to discuss.'

I could imagine his cocky little face expressing the pain, and part of it would be due to having to apologise and explain. It seemed like the right time to suggest that we weren't looking at a happy ending.

'I suppose you hoped I'd find the boy quick and easy, and none of this'd matter?'

'Yes,' he said, 'something like that. I take it it's not going to be easy?'

'Right. Now, tell me about Forbes Realty; do those business negotiations you mention concern it?'

He snorted. 'No, not at all. That's a *very* big deal, Mr Hardy, and I don't want to discuss it on the phone.'

'Forbes is small beer to you?'

'More or less. It's a useful investment.'

'Are you actively involved with the company?'

'No, not really. I paid it some attention after Kenneth made his . . . allegations.'

'Were you satisfied?'

'I'm afraid I didn't enquire too deeply, other things took precedence.'

I'd heard that before—from parents who wept while children with scarred arms died in hospital, and from husbands who'd come home to empty houses and notes. Silverman broke in on these thoughts: 'Can you tell me what progress you've made, Hardy?' The Mr had gone, he was asserting himself again, and I wasn't in the mood for it.

'No,' I said. 'I'll call again when I can.'

It was close to six o'clock when I got to Erskineville; petrol fumes and dust hung in the air and Williamson, a beefy, blonde man, was sitting in his singlet on the front step of a terrace house breathing the mixture and drinking beer. We shook hands and I accepted a can.

'Evans told me to cooperate,' he said, popping another can. 'What d'you want to know?'

I got out the photocopy of the speeding summons and handed it to him. 'Remember this?' I drank some beer, it was very cold.

'Yeah, pretty well. That should have come up by now. What's going on?'

'He's dropped out of sight and I'm looking for him. Can you describe him?'

Williamson took a long suck on the can. 'He didn't get out of the car, so I can't be sure of his height and build—I'd guess tall and slim, maybe a bit taller and thinner than you. He was dark, narrow face . . .' He held up his hands helplessly.

'Hair?'

'Not much of it, dark and well back at the sides, peak in front, sort of.'

'Age?'

'Forties.'

'Clothes?'

'Suit—no shirt and tie, the jacket was on the front seat.'

'Where did he get the licence from, pocket or glove box?'

'Can't remember, sorry.'

'He was alone?'

'Right.'

'Did you see anything in the back of the car—clothes, suitcase?'

'Can't be sure, the interior light was only on for a second.'

'How was that?'

'Well, when I went up he opened the door as if he was going to get out but then he shut it again, you know those sports cars, they're short on leg room. Maybe there was something in the back, a bag, a parcel, I don't know. Why?'

'Just wanted to know if he was on a trip. You stopped him in Gymea, going south?'

'Right. He was doing 115, like it says.' He tapped the document and I reached over and took it back.

'Drunk?'

'No, he was driving okay and he looked and smelled okay.'

'Where did he say he was going?'

'Didn't ask.'

'What was his voice like?'

'Well, Silverman, I don't know. He wasn't Australian, some kind of foreigner.'

I finished the beer and set the can down on the wrought-iron rail. 'Thanks for the help and the drink.'

He waved it aside. 'What'll you tell Evans?'

'I'll tell him you cooperated.'

'Fair enough.'

•

The morning was grey and cool; I showered and shaved and dressed. The Smith & Wesson went into a holster under my jacket and I put a couple of fake business cards in my wallet. The wallet didn't look healthy so I banked Silverman's cheque and drew out some money in a thick stack of small notes. As I was packing it away I took another look at the speeding and parking tickets. The parking ticket was dated eight weeks back and timed at 7.30 a.m., the speeding ticket was thirteen hours later on the same day.

Norton Street was fairly busy when I arrived but I managed to park exactly where the parking attendant had booked Kenneth's sports car. The spot gave me a clear view of the Forbes office, which was a converted two-storey terrace house behind a high wooden fence. I could see the windows of the upper level and down a lane which ran beside the building. The parking place was legitimate now, but ceased to be so at 7 a.m. when a clearway came into operation.

I had only the vaguest idea of what I was going to do and I tried to think which of the business cards I had was the least incredible. I decided that I knew something about books and that I might be able to gauge the probity of the firm with the right approach. The small front courtyard behind the fence was covered in bark, and there were flowers in pots on either side of the solid door. I rang the bell and the door was opened by a girl who looked too young to be working; she had big eyes swamped in make-up, a lot of straight blonde hair, five-inch heels—and she still looked fifteen. I looked over her shoulder and saw a cigarette burning a hole in a piece of typing paper on her desk.

'Hey, your desk's on fire.'

She spun around, shrieked and snatched at the paper, which knocked the butt on to the floor, where it started burning the carpet; she also knocked over a vase of flowers and spread water across the desk. She started to cry, and I went in and picked up the cigarette. I eased the big blotter out of its holder and used it to soak up the water. She stood watching me while I dried the desk and dropped the cigarette and sodden blotter into a tin wastepaper bin. I also read the letter—it advised a shopkeeper in Newtown with an unpronounceable middle-European name that his lease would not be renewed. The door had opened into what would have been the hall in the original house, but the wall had been taken out and it was now a fair- sized office with two desks and several filing cabinets. The girl was fumbling on the desk for another cigarette. She got it going and sat down.

'Thanks,' she said. 'What can I do for youse?'

I handed her the burnt letter. 'You'll have to do this again.'

She looked at it. 'Shit,' she said.

I gave her the card that said I was a second-hand bookseller and asked to see Mr Patrick.

'You need an appointment.' She puffed smoke awkwardly and tried to look eighteen.

'I just prevented your office from burning down.'

She giggled. 'What do you want to see him about?'

I pointed at the card. 'I want to open a bookshop; I need premises.'

'Oh, you don't need Clive . . . Mr Patrick for that; Mr Skelton will do.' She swung around to the empty desk. 'He's not here.'

I leaned forward and dropped my voice. 'Well, you know, I might have to deal with Clive. You see, this is not just an ordinary bookshop, if you get what I mean.' I did everything but wink, and she got the message. Just then a short, well-stuffed guy in a pale blue suit bustled into the room. He had a high complexion, and pink showed through the thin fair hair that was carefully arranged across his skull. He shouldn't have been that heavy and thin on top, he wasn't much over thirty. The girl batted her eyes at him.

'Mr Patrick, Mr Henderson here wants to see you about business premises . . .'

'Give him an appointment,' he barked. 'Have you got the letter for that wog yet?'

She made her hands look busy on the desk. 'It's almost done.'

'Snap it up, Debbie.' He turned without looking at me once and went out of the room. The girl looked helplessly at me.

'He's nice really,' she said. 'Now when are you free?'

The front door swung open and a man came through. He was tall, dressed in a narrow-cut dark suit: narrow was the word for him, he had a long, thin, swarthy face with a sharp nose, his dark eyebrows grew in a V over his yellowish, slanted eyes. He had close-cropped black hair that receded on both sides and grew in a pronounced widow's peak in the front. His wolfish eyes swept over me as if he was measuring me for a coffin, then he dismissed me.

'Is Clive in, Debbie?' His voice was light and, although it sounds corny, musical. It also carried a distinct foreign accent. Debbie looked scared, and nodded mutely. He brushed past me and went down the corridor.

'Not Mr Skelton,' I said.

She pulled on the cigarette. 'No, Mr Szabo.'

'What does he do around here?'

She shrugged and pulled the desk calendar towards her.

'Don't bother,' I said. 'I think I'll look for a friendlier firm.' She looked hurt behind her cigarette so I was careful not to slam the door. I scouted the building and established that it had only two exits—the front door and a gate that led out to the lane at the side. I dodged the traffic across to the other side of the road, bought a sandwich and two cans of beer and settled down to watch.

A short, plump man with ginger hair arrived after ten minutes. If he was Mr Skelton he didn't look any more appealing than the rest of the gang. A bit after that Clive Patrick came out and drove off in a white Volvo, probably to a lunch he didn't need. Then Debbie emerged and tottered down the street; she came back with a paper bag, a can of Coke and a fresh packet of cigarettes.

I'd finished the sandwich and the beer and was feeling drowsy when Szabo stepped out into the lane. I whipped the camera up and started shooting. The shots in the lane wouldn't be much good, the one when he reached the street would be better. He sniffed the air like a hunting dog and looked directly across the street at me; I snapped again and could see him registering the car, my face and the camera and then he was moving. I dropped the camera and turned the key; a bus roared away from a stop and held Szabo up. I was clear and fifty yards away when he made it round the bus; I glanced back at him, wolfish visage and widow's peak—he didn't look happy.

I'm about as interested in photography as I am in flower arrangement but, like a true professional, I knew the man to go to. Colin Jones was an army photographer in Malaya; if you could see it, he could photograph it. He worked for *The News* now and we met occasionally over a beer for me to tell him how much I envied his security and for him to say how much he wished his work was exciting like mine. I stopped in Glebe, phoned Colin at the paper and arranged to meet him outside *The News* building.

When I arrived Colin was standing there, smoking a cigarette and looking like a poet. The printers were on strike and there were picket lines in front of the building. The picketers were harassing the drivers, who were loading the papers being produced by scab labour. Colin got me past the union men on the door and took me up to his smelly den.

'Contacts do?' he asked as I handed over the film.

I said they would, and wandered around the room looking at the pictures pinned on the walls; about fifty per cent of them were obscene. I used Colin's fixings to make a cup of instant coffee while I waited; the milk was slightly on the turn and the coffee ended up with little white flakes in it. I fought down the craving for sugar and a cigarette, and did some thinking instead. There wasn't much to do: Kenneth Silverman had been hanging around the Forbes Realty office one night and he hadn't been able to take his car away the next morning. That night, a Mr Szabo of that honourable enterprise had been booked for speeding while driving south in Ken's car, which may have had a bundle in the back. It was looking worse for Kenny every minute.

Colin sauntered in and handed me the prints. The light had been bad and my hands not all that steady, but the long, vulpine mug was there clear enough—identifiable.

'Brilliant work, Cliff,' Colin said ironically.

I pointed at his cigarette. 'Smoking kills.'

Colin tapped the prints. 'I'd say this joker could kill, too. When are you going to grow up, Cliff?'

'And do what?'

He shrugged. I put the prints away and we shook hands. On the drive home I thought about what Colin had said; I was near forty and felt it; I had a house about half paid for, a car not worth a tank of petrol, two guns and some books. I had a lot of scars and some bridge work; on the other hand, no one told me what to do, I had no office politics to contend with and most of the bills got paid, eventually.

Musing like this is dangerous, it means defences are down and self-pity is up. I was still musing when I walked along the path to my house and only stopped when I felt something hard jab into my left kidney.

'Let's go inside, Mr Hardy,' a lilting voice said. 'You've taken liberties with me, I think I'll return the compliment.'

I half turned but the something dug deeper, painfully, and I winced and stumbled forward.

'Take the keys out, slowly, and pretend you're coming home with the shopping.'

I did it just as he said; the envelope with the prints inside was in my breast pocket and felt as big as a bible. He told me to open the door and I did that too, trying to avoid any jerky movements and cursing myself for not observing some elementary security precautions. A car is the easiest thing in the world to trace and this was just the boy to be getting my registration down as I was driving away in Norton Street. While I'd been exchanging wisdom with Colin Jones he'd been doing his job.

There was no point standing around in the hall. He prodded me with his hand, not a gun. I went, I had no booby traps, no buttons to push to release incapacitating gas; from the way he walked and held the gun I could tell that a side step and a sweeping movement aimed simultaneously at his ankle and wrist would get my brains all over my wall. He turned on lights as we went and that put a couple of hundred watts burning in the kitchen. He backed away and I turned around to look at him. His face was like a V—he had a narrow head with a pointed chin; his dark eyebrows were drawn together and down under the hair that receded sharply on both sides.

He moved around a little getting the dimensions of the room straight and then he advanced on me keeping the muzzle of his gun pointed at my right eye. He was good and he'd done all this before. When he was close enough, he kicked me in the knee, and as I bent over he nudged me and I sprawled on the floor. I looked up at him thinking how nice it would be to get a thumb into one of those yellow eyes.

He smiled down at me. 'Don't even think about it. Now I see you have a gun under your arm and something interesting-looking in the inside pocket. Let's have the gun—easy now.'

I got the gun out and slid it across the floor towards him. He lifted the pistol a fraction and I took out the envelope and pushed it across too. I started to pull myself up.

'Stay there, in fact you can lie on your face.'

I could hear him fiddling with the paper and then I heard a snort.

'You're a rotten photographer, Hardy, I'm twice as handsome as this.'

I didn't say anything; he was either vain or had a sense of humour; either way I couldn't see what difference it could make to me.

'Where's the phone?' I pointed and he motioned me to get up and go. The knee hurt like hell but it held my weight. The living room has some bookshelves, a TV set and some old furniture, also a telephone. He waved me into a chair and I sat there opposite him while he dialled. The hand holding the gun was steady but he glanced uneasily at the photographs a couple of times. He still wasn't happy.

'Clive? It's Soldier, I've got Hardy; he's got a collection of pictures of me taken in Norton Street.'

The phone crackled and Soldier's knuckles whitened around the receiver.

'Listen, Clive,' he rasped, 'you're in this. If I have to knock off this guy you're going to be part of it, not like the other one.'

He listened again and when he spoke his voice had lost its musical quality; it was full of contempt. 'Of course I can't. We don't know where he's been or who he's talked to. There could be copies of the pictures. It's a two-man job, Clive.'

Clive evidently said he'd drop by, because Soldier put the phone down and wiped his hand over his face edgily. I didn't fancy what was coming up. It sounded like a pressure session, and Soldier looked like the boy who knew how to apply it. I felt sick and scared at the thought of what I had to do, but there was no cavalry coming. He told me to get up, and when we were both on our feet I made a slow, awkward lunge at him, giving him plenty of time to lay the flat of his gun along the side of my head. The sound inside my skull was like a rocket being launched and the colour behind my shut eyes was a blinding white, but I'd dipped with the blow a bit, and as I went down I thought *I can do it*.

I lay very still and let the blood drip into my ear. There was a lot of blood, luckily, and I was so afraid that my pulse must have slowed to ten beats a minute. He bent down to look at me, swore, and went out of the room.

Getting to the bookshelf was one of the hardest things I've ever done. It seemed to take forever, but my eyes were open and I was seeing okay when I clawed out the three volumes of Russell's autobiography and got my hands on the old illegal Colt I keep behind there. I pulled it out of the oilskin wrapping, cocked it and wriggled back to where I'd been. He came back into the room with a wet dishcloth in one hand and his gun in the other; his chest was thin, and covered in elegant beige silk. I shot for his leg but I was in no condition for shooting; the Colt jerked in my shaky hand and the bullet went into the embroidered pocket of the shirt. His yellow eyes flashed as the last messages his brain would ever send went through; and then blood welled and spurted and he went down backwards, awkward and dead.

I picked up his gun and put it in my pocket and then I got the dishcloth and dragged myself to the bathroom. My face was covered in his blood and I suddenly vomited into the basin. After a bit more of that I cleaned myself up as best I could and went back to the phone. Horace was at home, and I told him to drive to Glebe and call me from a public box in about half an hour. He tried to order me about, but I suppose something gets into your voice after you've just killed a man, and he didn't try it for long.

My head was aching badly now, but I examined it carefully and looked into my eyes and concluded that I had a mild concussion at worst. My treatment for that was time-tested—pain-killers and whisky. I took both upstairs and sat on the balcony to wait for Clive.

He arrived in the Volvo and he was all alone. I went down and let him in. He'd sweated a bit into the neck of the pastel shirt, but he was still the image of the over-fed businessman with nothing but money on his mind. I put my gun an inch or two into his flab and moved him down the passage to the living room. I still had a lot of blood on me and was feeling pretty wild from the codeine and the whisky and he did what I said without a murmur. He was scared. He almost tripped over the corpse.

'Soldier isn't quite with us,' I said.

He looked down at the bloody mess on the floor and all the golf and Courvoisier colour in his face washed away.

'You've been keeping bad company, Clive,' I said. 'Want a drink?' He nodded and I poured him a splash of Scotch. The phone rang, and Silverman told me where he was. Clive was still looking at Soldier and I had to jerk his hand with the glass in it up to his mouth.

'We've got a visitor,' I said. 'I'm going to let him in. You sit there. If you've moved an inch when I get back I'm going to break your nose.'

I got a miniature tape recorder out of a cupboard in the kitchen, and went through to answer the soft knock on the door.

Silverman started to say the things you say when you meet people with guns and beaten-up faces, but I told him to be quiet.

In the living room I sat him down with a Scotch and started the tape. I put Soldier's gun on the coffee table for added effect.

'What's Clive doing here?' Silverman said.

'Oh, he belongs. He murdered your son.'

That stunned Silverman into silence, and set Patrick talking as I'd hoped it would. There was nothing much to it. Patrick was in deep financial trouble, and hoped for the Forbes Realty deal on the Glebe land to pull him out. But he was running short of time and he got the wind up when Silverman Junior made a few enquiries about the firm. The squatters really got up his nose; he hired Soldier Szabo and some other muscle to help him there and Soldier was still around when Kenneth was caught snooping in Leichhardt.

'So you killed him,' Silverman said quietly.

'It was an accident, Horace,' Patrick muttered. 'Soldier hit him too hard. It was an accident.'

'Maybe,' I said. 'And maybe you killed him when you found out who he was. What else could you do?'

'It wasn't like that,' Patrick said quickly.

'The body might tell us something. Of course you had to get rid of the body—you should have thought about the parking ticket.'

'There was no ticket when we . . .'

'No ticket? Well, tough shit, they blow away sometimes. Did Szabo tell you about the speeding ticket?'

Patrick put his face in his hands. 'No.'

'What did you do with my boy?' Silverman said. All the imperiousness and arrogance had melted away. He was just a little fat man, sad, with quivering jowls and a bad colour. 'Where's my boy?'

I gave Patrick a light touch on the cheek with the gun.

'Answer him!'

'I don't know.' He looked at Szabo; the front of the stylish shirt was dark, almost black. 'He didn't tell me.'

'Clive,' Silverman said desperately, 'I must know, we'll get you off lightly. Hardy . . .'

I didn't say anything. Something like hope flared in Patrick's face for a second but it died. He was telling the truth and he had nothing to sell.

'He didn't tell me,' he said again.

After that we had the cops and an ambulance, and a doctor who looked at me and put some stitches in my head. I made a statement and Silverman made a statement, and Patrick phoned his lawyer. Eventually they all went away, and I drank a lot of Scotch and went to sleep.

They knocked down the houses anyway and built the home units, which look like an interlinked series of funeral parlours. I hear the residents have trouble getting their cars in and out. Clive Patrick went to gaol for a long time, and I got paid, but nobody has ever found any trace of Kenneth Silverman.

THE ARMS OF THE LAW

From *The Big Drop* (1985)

The voice on the phone was hoarse and not much more than a whisper. 'Hardy? This is Harvey Salmon.'

'Oh yeah,' I said, 'and who else?'

'Huh?'

'The way I hear it, Harvey, you haven't had a private phone conversation in years.'

'Don't joke, Hardy. This is serious.'

'Must be. When did you get out?'

'Today. I need your help.'

'Mr Salmon, I'd reckon you need prayers and airline tickets in about that order.'

'Stop pissing around. I want to meet you to talk business. D'you know the Sportsman Club, in Alexandria?'

I did know it although I didn't particularly want to; it was a dive that went back to six o'clock closing days and beyond as a sly grog joint and SP hangout. In those days the sport most of its associates were familiar with was two-up. I'd heard that it had gained some sort of affiliation with a soccer club, but it had still worn the same dingy, guilty look when I last drove past.

'It's one of my favourite places,' I said. 'Are you a member there?'

'Yeah, about the only place I still am a member.' His voice was bitter. 'Meet me there in an hour and we'll talk work and money.'

'I don't know . . .'

'A thousand bucks, Hardy, for two days' work.'

'Okay.' The phone clicked as soon as I had the second syllable out. I sat there with the instrument in my hand thinking that I was about to associate with a known criminal. But then, as a private investigator, I did that a lot of the time and it was what my mother had predicted I'd end up doing anyway. Besides, we're associating with criminals all the time—motor mechanics, doctors, real-estate agents—it was only the 'known' part that made this any different.

I needed the thousand bucks, not because business was especially slow. It wasn't; I had a few party-mindings and money-escortings to do in the days ahead, and I was on a retainer from a group of wealthy Ultimo squatters who were trying to keep leverage on the smelly company that owned their row of terraces. But things kept getting more expensive, like food and Scotch and sneakers, and it would take a lot of fear to turn me away from a thousand dollars.

The name Harvey Salmon generated a certain amount of fear, mind you. He'd been a key man in a syndicate the press had dubbed 'the rainforest ring' because the marijuana grown in Australia, or some of it, had been cultivated in rainforests. But the ring had operated on a broad field, importing from South-East Asia and exporting to the United States, and there had been the usual number of couriers killed and businessmen who'd found it expedient to go off into the bush with just their Mercedes and a shotgun.

The ring had collapsed under two simultaneous blows—the death, from a heart attack at the age of forty-three while jogging, of Peter 'Pilot' Wrench who'd been the chief organiser. Some said that Wrench had got his nickname from his early days of flying drugs into Australia through the open northern door, others said it was really 'Pilate' because he always washed his hands of a bad deal and a bad dealer. The death of Wrench threw the lieutenants into confusion and doubt, leading to the second blow. One of them gave interviews to certain law enforcement officers, which resolved the doubts of some of the others, who got long sentences to repent in. The interviewee was Harvey Salmon, who'd backed up his allegations with scores of hours of taped telephone calls. I'd heard a lot of that on the QT from Harry Tickener and other journalists; for public consumption, Salmon had got fifteen years a mere eighteen months ago.

It was 3 p.m. on a Wednesday afternoon, traffic in Alexandria was light and that made it a halcyon time of day. Alexandria seems to live on hope; the city- and airport-bound traffic moves through its broad and narrow streets like a cancer, but the area has been promised a park, a big project park. Acres of industrial land, including a bricking quarry and factory, have been slated for a development to rival Centennial. People were hanging on to their slum terraces and the real-estate operators were waiting the way a kidney patient waits for a donor. Meanwhile, the place is home to a few different ethnic groups and some restaurants to match—most of the restaurants will survive, most of the people won't.

I parked only three blocks away from the Sportsman Club, almost back into Erskineville, but that's nearby parking in Alexandria. At 3.30 the club already had a quota of drinkers—some of them afternoon specialists, some for whom the morning session had dragged on a bit, some for whom the evening had started early. I had to wait by a flyblown receptionist booth while my name was sent 'upstairs'. After I'd spent ten minutes comparing the fly spots on the glass of the booth to the blackheads on the nose of the young woman inside it, Harvey Salmon came down the stairs to escort me into the precinct.

Salmon was tall and heavy with thinning brown hair and an expression that suggested things were bad and getting worse. I'd never met him but his picture had been in the papers at the time of 'Pilot' Wrench's departure; in the flesh he looked heavier, thinner on top and even less sanguine. But gaol changes a man. He stopped a couple of steps from the bottom and studied me carefully. He wore a pale grey suit, white shirt and dark tie, suede shoes; I had on sneakers and jeans, an open-neck shirt and a leather jacket. I wondered which of us was dressed right. Salmon hopped down the last couple of steps with fair agility, gave me a nod and put two dollars between the sliding glass panels of the booth.

'Thanks, Teresa.'

Teresa didn't even glance up from *TV Week*. 'Kay,' she said.

I went up the short flight of stairs with Salmon, through a smaller drinking room with fewer poker machines than the one below, and into an office that was dark and musty. The only light was struggling in through some venetian blinds and the only places to sit were on the desk or on a rickety chair behind it. I sat on the desk and Salmon moved towards the chair. He also cleared his throat to speak but I got in first.

'How about a drink?'

'What? Oh yeah, sure, sorry.' He moved back and opened the door; for a minute I thought he was going to yell his order across to the bar but he didn't. He went out and I had about a minute and a half to study the room before he came back with two schooners. A minute and a half was plenty and I hadn't drunk schooners of Old for years. It wasn't such a good start.

When he was settled behind the desk and his glass, Salmon cracked his knuckles—I hoped he wasn't going to do that too often.

'I need someone around for two days,' he said.

'Try downstairs. If you're good company you shouldn't have any trouble.'

'I need someone who can handle a little trouble, if it comes up. Not that it will.'

'You never can tell,' I said. 'Especially in your game.'

He ignored me as if he had a set speech to deliver and was going to do it, no matter what. 'I was all set to fly out today, that was the deal.' He paused, maybe to see if I was shocked. I wasn't. 'But there's been some screw-up over the passport. I've got two days to wait, and I've got enemies.'

'Book into the Hilton, watch TV and wait.'

He ruffled the thin hair, making it look even thinner. 'I don't want to do that. Am I going to do that for the rest of my life? The cops say they're keeping an eye on me and also on certain people. But I don't know. Who can you trust?'

I drank some beer and looked at him; he wasn't sweating and he didn't look afraid, but maybe he just lacked imagination the way he, apparently, lacked a sense of irony.

'Where are you going?' I asked.

'R . . . South America. Same thing, see? The cops say they've squared it over there but I want to get a feel of what it's like. I'll have to get someone over there, but I want to do a few things while I've got these couple of days. Jesus, I've lived here fifty years, I don't want to spend the last two days in a hotel room.'

An appeal based on the pleasure of Sydney will get me every time. Salmon could see he had me and he took a confident gulp of his schooner before giving me the details. He had the use of a flat in Erskineville for the next three nights and expected to catch his plane on Saturday morning. He had a few places to visit, a woman to see. He wanted to have a few beers here and there; he wanted to go to the trots and the beach. He wanted me to stay in the flat and tag along with him. He'd give me five hundred now and five hundred on Saturday. I said I'd do it. Truth was, I was getting rather bored with party-minding and money-escorting.

We finished our beers and stood up together—the Sportsman wasn't the kind of place you wanted to stick around.

'Got a gun?' Salmon asked.

'Yeah. Got the money?'

'In the flat. Let's go.'

We left the glasses on the desk and went out of the office and through the bar. A couple of the drinkers looked at us but not with any particular interest that I could detect. Still, it's never too early to start doing a job well. Teresa had got to Wednesday in the *TV Week*; we went past her and out to the street. Salmon looked up and down it nervously.

'Where's your car?'

'Here's where you start living like a free man. It's about half a mile away.'

We walked down Margaret Street, which was fairly busy with shoppers and strollers, and turned into a quiet side street. Salmon didn't seem furtive but he wasn't introducing himself to people either. I noticed that he had a reasonable tan and not a gaol pallor and asked him about it.

'I did some gardening,' he said.

'I'm surprised they'd let you grow anything.'

He slowed down and gave me what passed for an amused look; the downward drooping lines of his face squared up a little. 'You'd be surprised what grows inside.' He patted down his wavy hair with a brown hand.

When we got to the car he hesitated.

'What's wrong?'

'What year is it?' he said.

'What does it matter? It goes.'

He got in. 'It goes with the flat anyway,' he muttered.

He directed me through the streets to one of the less grimy parts of Erskineville and we pulled up outside an ugly block of red-brick flats. I remembered that Harvey Salmon's address used to be given as 'of Point Piper' but he approached the building unconcernedly.

'It's not much,' he said. 'Cops reckon it's all they can afford. They reckon they've got a couple of the flats in the block so it's safe. What d'you reckon?'

We went down a narrow concrete path to thc back of the block and a narrow set of concrete steps that was flanked by a rickety wrought-iron handrail. Salmon got a bright shining key out of his pocket and unlocked the door. The flat was one of three with doors giving on to a skimpy walkway: no balconies here, no window boxes even.

Inside, the decor was nondescript, new but not very new, and bought from a catalogue rather than according to anyone's taste. I told Salmon to stay by the door while I checked the rooms: the small kitchen and smaller bathroom were empty, so was the bedroom. There was no one in the toilet. Salmon motioned me into the kitchen with a head movement. Out there he opened the fridge and got out a bottle of Reschs. I shook my head; he opened the bottle, poured a glass and drank it straight off. He poured another.

'The place could be bugged,' he whispered. 'What d'you reckon?'

That was twice he'd asked me; it was time I reckoned something.

'Let's not talk,' I said. 'I'll look around for bugs. Does the TV work?'

'Think so.'

'I'll watch the tennis. When're you going out?'

'Tonight. Sevenish. Think I'll have a kip.'

I cleared my throat and held out my hand.

'Oh, sure.' He reached into the breast pocket of his jacket and pulled out a wallet. He took out five hundred-dollar notes that looked as if they had plenty of company and handed them to me. I put the money in my jeans, peeled off my jacket and draped it over a chair and turned on the television. John Fitzgerald was serving to John Lloyd, 15–40. Salmon didn't even look at the screen. He scratched under his arm and went into the bedroom. I heard the springs groan as he flopped on the bed. Lloyd was at the net but he hadn't put enough snap into his volley and Fitzgerald lobbed over him: 30–40. I made a couple of cups of instant coffee in the kitchen and slept through a doubles match for an hour. Salmon came out and showered and we were set to go at 6.30. Before we went out the door he handed me twenty dollars.

'Expenses,' he said. 'Petrol, drinks and that.'

'Thanks.' I'd been on the job for about three hours and I hadn't done much that was very different from what I did when I wasn't working—except collect five hundred and twenty dollars.

The first stop was a pub in the Cross, where Salmon claimed to know a lot of people but they didn't seem to be around that night. We had a couple of drinks and he scratched up a word or two with a few blokes who didn't seem especially keen to talk to him.

'Just killing time,' he said as we hit the street again. 'This is the real business of the night: Lulu.'

I nodded politely; we were walking along Darlinghurst Road and there was a car cruising a few yards back and I was sure I'd seen one of the window-shoppers earlier in the night.

'You've got your tail,' I said. Salmon shrugged. A street girl wearing an open-weave top through which her nipples protruded and a mini-skirt that showed her meaty thighs, ambled out across the pavement and gave us the word. Salmon shook his head; I examined her closely but I was pretty sure she was the real thing and not policewoman-somebody.

'Tarts,' Salmon said. 'Wait'll you see Lulu.'

We went into a strip club opposite the fifty-flavours-of-ice-cream shop. Salmon showed a card and twenty dollars to the man inside the door and he took us through the smoke to a table down near the stage. I looked around to check for danger spots but I hardly needed to because the place was exactly like a dozen others I'd been in. Maybe I had been in there, it's hard to tell. There was a bar along one wall, maybe twenty or thirty tables, with just enough room for the drink waiters to squeeze between, grouped in front of a wide stage. The stage was covered by a black curtain that had trapped smoke and dust and dreams for too many years. Salmon ordered a double Scotch and beer chaser for himself and I settled for a single Scotch. It was cash on the barrelhead, of course, and he paid from that big roll that made me more nervous than anything else I'd seen.

After a while the show started and there's nothing to say about it except that it was slow and third- or possibly fourth-rate. The girls had dead eyes and their bodies seemed to come to life only spasmodically. Lulu was marginally more interesting than the rest if only because her enormous breasts looked real and when she glimpsed the wildly enthusiastic Salmon across the footlights she smiled with genuine invitation.

'Wasn't she great?' Salmon said. He waved for another drink; a few more and all he could hope to use those great tits for was a pillow.

'Yeah,' I said. 'She seemed to like you, too.'

'That's a hell of a woman, Hardy.' His voice had got slow and grave. Oh God, I thought, a slow, grave drunk. They're possibly worse than the fighting ones. At least you can tap the fighters on the nose, mop up the blood and put them to bed. He leaned forward across the table and whispered through the smoke haze and din of people talking loudly and drunkenly. 'Rang 'er up this morning. She's got a place behind here. I'm goin' back there in an hour, want you to keep an eye out.'

'Okay, but you'd better lay off the booze or you'll be wasting your money.'

'No money!' His voice went up suddenly. 'No money!'

'Okay, okay. Take it easy.' Slow and grave *and* fighting—the very worst kind.

At the appointed time a waiter beckoned to us and we got up and went through a small door at the end of the room beside the stage. The passageway was dark and there were a couple of rooms off it, one of which was framed in bright light. Salmon gave the waiter some money and he went away. Salmon steadied himself against the wall.

'Been a long time,' he said.

'Mmm?' I was trying to see the end of the passage in the dark. 'Need any help?'

'Funny. You just squat down there somewhere and wait for me.' He waved at the blackness ahead and knocked on the door. It opened and Lulu put her sequined breasts out into the passage, where they would have prevented overtaking. Up close her skin looked coarse and heavily powdered but she still had the genuine smile.

'Come in, Harvey,' she said. Salmon went in and I felt my way to the end of the passage. It did a right-angle bend, went down some steps and ended in a door that led on to a lane. I had a wide choice: the passage, the street or the stairs. Anyone who stands around in the street in the Cross after dark is asking for trouble; the passage was dark and smelled of cheap perfume and sweat. I chose the stairs.

I sat there in the gloom feeling sorry for myself and thinking that this job hadn't turned out to be much more exciting than party-minding. Some very recognisable sounds came from the room a few metres away; at least Harvey was having a good time. I sat there remembering good times and feeling the five hundred and five dollars in my pocket—I'd rather have had five dollars and someone to have a good time with. Then I got to thinking about whether you could have a good time with five dollars. It was boring on the stairs.

Whatever Harvey and Lulu did took about an hour and left Harvey looking as if he'd been dragged from the surf. He came lurching out with his shirt undone and his fly open. He smelled like an overused sauna.

'Never had annathin' like it,' he said. 'In-credible.'

'I got the impression you were regulars.'

'Huh? Oh, sort of. Coast clear? Less go, I need a drink.'

We went out into the lane and that's where they were waiting. Two big men, which made four big men, except that one of the big men was drunk and he was my responsibility. One of them stepped forward, looked closely at Salmon and ignored me.

'Salmon, we're going for a trip.'

'He's not going anywhere,' I said.

'Shut up, you. You can go back inside and look at the tits. We don't want you.'

I guessed that the bloke who hadn't spoken was the real muscle so I moved a little closer to him, taking me back towards the door. I gave him a short, hard right well below the belt and brought my knee up as his crotch came down. He groaned and gripped himself there; the other one was reaching inside his coat for something but I had a gun in my waist holster at the back and it came out smoothly as I turned around. I jabbed it hard into the talker's neck and then pulled it back and held it a few centimetres from his nose.

'Get back against the wall, Salmon,' I said. 'What's the other one doing?' I was staring into my man's eyes, trying to convince him that I'd pull the trigger if I had to. I seemed to succeed; he dropped his hand from his coat and stood very still.

'He's holding his balls,' Salmon said.

'You sober enough to kick them if he looks frisky?'

'Yeah,' he muttered. 'Where's those fuckin' cops?'

'We could find some,' I said. 'What d'you reckon?'

'No, what's the point?'

'Okay.' I moved the .38 a little closer to the nose. 'You see how things are. Mr Salmon's not vindictive. You and your mate can walk down there and turn the corner and go home or I can shoot you somewhere. What's it to be?'

'We'll walk,' he said.

I heard a shuffling step and then the dull sound of a hard kick being delivered and then another. A man groaned and whimpered. I held the gun steady.

'What?' I said.

'Nothin',' Salmon said. 'This one can crawl. Let's go.'

I moved back to the wall and we watched the guy who'd been kicked lift himself up off the ground and steady himself. Neither of them looked at us. They walked and hobbled down the lane and around the corner. Salmon and I went the other way out to the neon-lit street.

'You were good, Hardy.'

I grunted. 'Why'd you kick him?'

'I was feelin' good. He spoiled my night.'

The next day Salmon spent the morning in bed. He made a few phone calls in the afternoon, watched some TV. I went out and got some Chinese food and a paperback of *Dutch Shea Jnr* by John Gregory Dunne. We ate, I read; Salmon watched commercial television and went to bed early. I slept on the couch but not well; I spent most of the night reading and drinking instant coffee so that I'd finished the book by morning. Good book.

On Friday morning I told Salmon I needed some fresh clothes and wanted to go to the bank, so I had to get back to Glebe. That was all right with him because he wanted to go to Harold Park that night anyway. We had our discreet police escort over to Glebe, and I did my business with Salmon hanging around looking bored. Putting a couple of hundred in the bank to cover a mortgage payment probably wasn't a very big deal to him.

In the afternoon I watched some more of the tennis while Salmon yawned over some back-issue magazines he found in the living room.

'You miss these inside.' He flipped over the pages of a mid-year *National Times*.

'How did you find it? Prison, I mean.'

'Hot and hard. You ever been in, Hardy?'

'Not really, short remand at the Bay.'

He snorted derisively and seemed to be about to say something. Then he yawned and turned another page. John Alexander was giving ten years away to Peter Doohan and the games were going with service.

About half an hour earlier than I'd have thought necessary, Salmon announced it was time to go.

'It's too early,' I said. 'It's just down the road.'

'I want to get a good park.'

'I thought we'd walk. Do you good.'

'No. We drive.'

He was paying. We drove. I like Harold Park; somehow, even though they put in new bars and generally ponced the place up a few years ago, they managed not to kill the atmosphere. With the lights and the insects swarming in the beams and the

Gormenghast houses up above the Crescent, the track feels like a special place—just right for what happens there. The race call and announcements over the PA system boom and bounce around in the hollow so that everybody knows what's going on. You get a cheerful type of person at Harold Park—it's almost a pleasure to lose money there.

Some sort of change had come over Salmon. He was decisive about where he wanted us to park—out on the Crescent, well down from the Lew Hoad Reserve—and for the first time he showed a real interest in our police escort.

'Give 'em plenty of time to pick us up,' he said as I locked the car.

'If they're any good, they won't need help.'

'Just do as I say.'

We walked around to the main entrance in Wigram Road and I looked across to the pub.

'That's it,' I said.

'What?'

'The Harold Park—the pub over there. Didn't you say it was one of the places you wanted to visit before you took your trip?'

Salmon glanced at the pub, which was doing its usual brisk race-night business.

'Skip it,' he said nervously. 'The rozzers with us?'

They were, two guys in casual clothes looking like family men on a matey night out. They went through the turnstiles a few bodies behind us. I could feel the tension in Salmon as we stepped out of the light into an area of shadow in front of the stand.

'Okay,' he said. 'Now we lose 'em. Right now. We make for the exit over near the car.' He moved quickly, pushing through clutches of people heading for the bars and the tote; the mob swirled around us with no pattern yet, no fixed positions taken, and the gaps closed up behind us. I sneaked a look back after a while and caught a glimpse of the cops anxiously inspecting a toilet entrance.

Salmon moved fast on the way back to the car. He hugged the wall and people got out of his way.

'They likely to leave someone watching the car?'

I considered it. We hadn't been evasive at any time, rather the reverse; anyone who knew my habits would wonder why I'd drive such a short distance, but not too many cops knew my habits.

'Doubt it, but there's no time for a recce. That pair'll be on our hammer pretty soon.'

'Right. Let's go.'

'Where?'

'North.'

I took Victoria Road to the Gladesville Bridge and ran up through the back of Pymble to pick up the turn-off to Frenchs Forest. RBT seemed to have quietened Friday night down: the traffic moved smoothly and after Salmon got finished checking behind us for pursuit, he settled down and enjoyed the drive.

'Nice night,' he said.

'Yeah, where're we going?'

'Whale Beach.'

'Jesus, why?'

He gave a short laugh, one of the very few I'd heard from him. 'Not for a swim.'

The traffic stayed light on Barrenjoey, all the way past Newport to the Whale Beach turnoff. The Falcon handled the drive well, but Salmon only grunted when I commented on it.

'Fords are junk,' he said.

It was true that Fords weren't in abundance in the drives and on the road in front of the big houses. I saw Mercs and Jags, Celicas and the like, all looking good in the moonlight like the houses themselves. Salmon was concentrating on the terrain and when we reached a sign that said 'Public Pathway to Beach', he told me to stop.

'What's here?'

'Me cabin. Not too many know about it.'

We started down a steep and long flight of steps. I could see the water gleaming out ahead and heard the big surf crashing on the beach. About half of the houses were in darkness and the whole area was quiet and still apart from the sound of the sea and a few night birds calling. Halfway down the steps Salmon stepped over the rail and took a look into the blackness.

'Shoulda brought a torch,' he muttered.

'Don't you know the way?'

He glanced at me sharply. 'Sure, but it's been a while.'

We pushed through the bushes following a rabbit track until a squat shape loomed up in front of us. Salmon had taken his jacket off because the path ran slightly uphill and it was sweaty work on a mild night. He fumbled in a pocket and pulled out a bunch of keys. He handed me the jacket.

'Wait here, Hardy.'

I stood in the shadows holding the jacket and feeling like a five-hundred-dollar flunky; then I remembered that it was a thousand-dollar flunky and felt better. Salmon went up some wooden steps and took a long time selecting a key and getting it into the lock. Then he opened the door and took a long time turning on a light. The jacket felt heavy because there was a .45 automatic in one of its pockets. It was a long time since my army days when we practised stripping guns in the dark but I found I could still do it. I kept an eye on the light in the cabin while I ejected the bullet from the chamber, turned the top bullet in the spring-loaded magazine around and effectively jammed the thing as tight as a seized piston.

When Salmon came out of the cabin he was carrying a small canvas bag and wearing a look of satisfaction. I handed him the jacket.

'Want me to carry the bag?'

'Sure.' He gave me the bag and we pushed our way back to the path. The bag felt full of something but light; maybe it was toilet tissue for his trip.

Back at the car, Salmon shrugged his jacket on and took the bag from me. I looked up at the starry sky out to sea.

'Nice place,' I said.

'Yeah.' He was waiting impatiently for me to open the car.

'Changed a bit in the last year or so though.'

'Yeah.'

We drove back to Erskineville in virtual silence; it was an easy drive, giving me plenty of time to think. As far as I knew, nothing had changed much in Whale Beach for years—the affluent and trendy locals wouldn't permit it.

Salmon stowed the bag away in the bedroom and we had a Scotch before going to our respective beds.

'What time's your flight?' I was contemplating another Scotch, mindful of the hardness of the sofa.

'Eleven in the morning.'

'All fixed up?'

'Yeah. Goodnight, Hardy, and thanks.'

I couldn't sleep. I lay awake thinking about it and trying to figure what was going on. I felt sure things weren't what they seemed but that didn't take me far. I dozed and jerked awake with the same doubts and confusions crowding my mind. I didn't care about Harvey Salmon one way or another; as far as I knew he hadn't ever killed anybody, and in the world of organised crime his speciality was more in the organisation than the criminality. Still, I didn't like being so much in the dark. Around 7 a.m.

I called Harry Tickener, who writes on crime and politics for *The News*. He was grumpy about being woken up so early and I had to keep my voice low, which made him even grumpier.

'What can you tell me about Harvey Salmon, Harry?'

'At 7 a.m. nothing.'

'Come on, I need something. I know what he looks like, six-foot-two, fourteen stone; what about habits and so on?'

'Shit, Cliff, I don't know. Wait'll I get a cigarette. Okay . . . Well, fourteen stone's a bit heavy. I can't think of much, except that he's a tennis nut.'

'What?'

'Tennis, played it all the time, had his own court and that.'

'Thanks, Harry.'

'Any other time, Cliff. Not 7 a.m.'

He rang off and I put the phone down carefully. I was trying to digest the information when my flatmate came through the door wearing striped pyjamas and pointing the .45 at me.

'Heard you on the extension,' he said. 'Careless.'

'You're not Harvey Salmon.'

'No, but I've got this and you're still going to do what I say.'

He didn't tell me his name but he told me about the deal over the next few hours as he packed his bags and we waited to go to Mascot. As he understood it, an elaborate arrangement had been arrived at between Salmon and the State and Federal police. Salmon wanted two things—a new identity and a new life in South America (that was one) and a chance to pick up a bag of money from Whale Beach. The Federal police wanted information; the State cops wanted convictions. Harvey Salmon was released on licence in return for certain information; he didn't trust the police and he knew about a look-alike who was doing time in Grafton jail for fraud. The deal was that the look-alike would move around Sydney for a few days under police protection so that the real Salmon could get an idea of how effective that might be.

'What about the bag of money?'

'Salmon was dead keen to get hold of that. The State cops okayed it; the Federals don't know about it.'

'Why would the cops make a deal like that? Salmon'd sung already.'

'Not the whole song,' Harvey Salmon said. 'He keeps the last few notes until he gets his tickets and the bag at the airport.'

'What d'you get?'

'Some money and my freedom.' He grinned. 'And Lulu. Christ!'

'You can go back for more.'

He shook his head. 'Deal is, I leave Sydney for good.'

'Tough.'

'Yeah, now give me that gun you flashed outside the club.'

I gave him the gun, he took the bullets out and put them in his pocket before returning it. That made two inoperative guns and quite a relaxed atmosphere as far as I was concerned.

'What do you know about the cops who were tailing us?' I said, just to pass the time.

He grinned again; he was getting more relaxed by the minute and if he kept on grinning he might turn from a sad spaniel to a happy kelpie. 'I'd guess they were State boys the other night,' he said. 'Didn't care too much if Salmon got roughed up. They would've been the Federals last night; they're not supposed to know about the money, but they couldn't follow Neville Wran down Macquarie Street, anyway.'

'Probably right. Whose idea was it to bring me in?'

'Mine. I heard about you from Clive Patrick.'

'Is he in Grafton?'

'Yeah, copping it sweet. Be out pretty soon.'

I nodded and thought it over. I could take over now; the .45 was a liability and I was sure I had more moves than whatever-his-name-was. But I thought I might as well see it through.

'What about the other five hundred dollars?' I said.

'At the airport—after the swap.'

I drove to the airport. He checked a suitcase through to Rio, having collected his ticket and an envelope at the desk. He had a smaller bag as cabin luggage, about the same size as the bag he'd collected at Whale Beach.

Pan Am flight 304 to Rio de Janeiro was on time and would be boarding in an hour. He got his seat allocated and was heading for the baggage security check when things started to happen. First, a tall man stepped in front of us. He had a long, droopy sort of face, baggy eyes and was built on leaner lines than my companion.

'I'm Salmon,' he said. 'Let's have the bag and the ticket.'

The false Harvey Salmon was looking nervous; he fumbled in his jacket for the ticket and seemed to be playing for time. Two men detached themselves from a knot of people looking at a flight monitor and strode over to us. They were big, wore expensive suits and had short haircuts. One of them gripped the real Salmon by the arm. 'Would you come with us, sir?'

Salmon gave the man a tired smile. 'It's okay. I've got it here.' He tapped his breast pocket.

'Just come along, sir, and you too, please.' He looked sternly at the impostor and me and fell in behind us like a sheep dog. I thought he'd be a pretty good heel-snapper from the smooth confidence of his movements.

'Along here.' The man holding on to Salmon steered us across the floor and behind some shrubbery to a room marked 'Security'.

'What is this?' Salmon said. He got shoved firmly inside for an answer.

The room contained a desk with a chair drawn up to it and a row of chairs over by a big bright window. The sun was shining in and throwing long shadows from the divisions in the window across the pale carpet.

'We're police,' the arm-holder said. 'If you and Mr Salmon would just go over there and sit down, please.' He struggled to frame the polite words and to keep his diction smooth. Under the barbering and suiting there was a very rough customer. Salmon looked alarmed and angry; he moved his hand towards his pocket again.

'I've got it here.'

'I'm sure you have,' the cop said. 'Sit down.'

We sat, not side by side but a few seats apart. Salmon had broken out in sweat. The second cop put the bag on the desk and opened it. He nodded and turned to the impostor.

'Good. Got your ticket?'

The look-alike nodded and the cop carefully extracted a bundle of notes from the bag and passed them to him. 'Harvey Salmon' counted them, separated some and walked over to me. He held out the money; I sat still and he dropped the notes in my lap.

'Thanks, Hardy. I've got a plane to catch.' He didn't look at Salmon; he turned and walked out of the room. Salmon stood up and rushed across to where the policeman was zipping up the bag.

'That's mine,' he yelped. 'We had a deal. I get the money and you get the names.'

The policeman shook his head slowly and his smile was as cold and cheerless as a Baptist chaplain. The second cop moved in behind Salmon to do some shepherding.

'You've got it wrong, Harvey,' the bagman said. 'We wanted the money and no one wanted the names. No one wants you either.'

The other cop nudged Salmon. 'Come on.'

'No!' Salmon spun around desperately and looked across the room at me. 'Help me!'

The cop swung the bag in his hand and smiled again. 'He's done all he can. Harvey Salmon's flown to Rio. Come on.'

Salmon sagged and one of them grabbed him and held on hard. I sat there with an empty gun in my pocket and five hundred dollars in my crotch and watched them leave the room.

Three days later I sat in the home of my friend, Detective Sergeant Frank Parker, and told him about it. The telling took a bottle of wine and set up a strong craving for one of Frank's cigarillos. I fought the craving; no sense losing all the battles. Frank listened and nodded several times while he smoked and poured the wine.

'It's pretty neat,' he said when I finished. 'Must've been a lot of money in that bag?'

'Where would that have come from d'you reckon?'

Frank leaned back and blew smoke up over my head. 'Let's see, I'd say it would have been grateful contributions from people Salmon had kept quiet about. Mind you,' he gave me the sort of smile you give when you read a politician's obituary, 'that's not to say that some of their names wouldn't have been on the final list he was going to hand over.'

'Jesus. I still don't feel good about watching him being carted away to be cancelled.'

'Nothing you could do. Describe the man in charge, Cliff.'

'Big,' I said. 'Six-one or two; heavy but with a lot of muscle; smart suit; fresh everything—shave, haircut, the lot. Looked like he'd still be good at breaking heads and that he learned not to say "youse" and "seen" for "saw" not so long ago.'

Frank nodded and drew in smoke. 'He's an Armed Robbery D. Henry "Targets" Skinner. His turn'll come.'

TEARAWAY

From *The Big Drop* (1985)

'He's a tearaway, Cathy,' I said. 'You know it, I know it, everybody knows it. The best thing you could do would be to forget him. Get out of Sydney; go to Queensland. Kevin's caused you enough misery for a lifetime, it's all he's good at.'

'He never hurt anybody,' she said stubbornly. 'Never. Not anyone!'

'Just luck. He carried a gun—he pointed it, he never fired it but that's just a matter of chance. One split second can change all that and make him a murderer. That's still on the cards.'

I thought I had to be hard on her, but it turned out I was too hard. She'd come to me for help; she tramped up the dirty stairs and down the gloomy corridor and knocked on my battered door and all I'd done was cause her to drop her head onto my desk and cry buckets. I never did have much tact—a private detective doesn't use it much—but this wouldn't do. I came around the desk and gave her a tissue and made her sit up and swab down. Her boyfriend, Kevin Kearney, had broken out of a police van two days before. Kev and his three mates were on their way to their trial for armed robbery. One of them was shot dead twenty feet from the van; Kevin and the other two had got away.

He hadn't contacted Cathy, which was probably the first good turn he'd done her.

When she'd stemmed the flow and got a cigarette going, she filled me in on the shape and structure of her distress.

'He got word out to me that he was going to run. I got a car and some money and we were going . . .' She stopped and looked at me hesitantly.

'Call it Timbuktu, Cathy,' I said. 'What does it matter?'

'Well, I heard about the break-out on the news. Christ, I nearly died when they said one of them'd been shot. But . . .'

The cigarette wavered in her hand and she looked ready to cry again.

'It wasn't Kev,' I said gently. 'Go on.'

'That's all. He didn't come—no phone call, nothing.'

'I read about it. The cops say they've got no leads.'

She flicked ash; she was perking up a bit. 'Same here.' She opened her bag and took out a roll of notes and put them on the desk.

'Nine hundred bucks. It's the money we were going to shoot through on. Kev'd beat the shit out of me if he knew what I was doing, but I want you to find him.'

I looked at the money, thinking a lot but not saying anything. Cathy stubbed her cigarette out in an ashtray alongside the cash.

'Look, he's guilty, he'll get—what? Ten years? He'll serve—what? Six? That's not too bad. I can wait. On the run he's likely to get killed, and then I'd kill myself.' She grinned at me, finally showing some of the spark that made her one of the most popular whores in Glebe. 'You'd be saving two lives, Cliff.'

I grinned at her. 'When you put it like that, how can I refuse? But seriously, Cathy, it's bloody dangerous. Harbouring's a serious charge. One of them's dead, the cops won't really mind if they take out another couple.'

'I know. Just do what you can. He might've decided it was safer to go another way, he could be clear. I just want to know something.'

'All right.' I took the money; I didn't have any qualms about the way it had been earned—hell, I'd worked for doctors and lawyers; all manner of professional people.

'Where do you start?' Cathy said.

'With whoever it was gave you the nod about Kevin's break.'

That pulled her up short—it touched on the code of Cathy's world: don't name names, don't describe faces, don't take cheques. I waited while she lit up again.

'No way around it, love. It's the only way in.'

'Kevin wouldn't like it.' She blew smoke in a thin, nervous stream. 'Well, it was Dave Follan.'

She told where and when Follan drank, which was better than getting his address. I told her I'd stay in touch with her and report everything I learned straight away. She came around the desk on her high heels, put her behind in its tight denim on the desk, leaned forward to give me the cleavage and kissed me on the cheek.

'That's like having fish fingers at Doyle's.'

'What?'

'Never mind. I'll do what I can, Cathy. But I tell you one thing, you contact me if Kevin gets in touch with you. I don't want him wandering around with the wrong ideas about me.'

'He's a sweet guy really.'

'Yeah.'

She left and I leaned back in my chair and thought about Cathy and Kevin. I'd known them both in Glebe since they were kids. Kevin wagged school, stole things and played reserve grade football where he learned to drink and fight. I saw him play for Balmain a few times; I saw him in a police line-up and then

I saw him in a car that belonged to someone else. I was working for the someone else at the time, so I had a talk to Kevin. His ideas about property were loose; he was apologetic but unfussed about the car. I took it away, and we parted with mutual respect.

Cathy's path to the game was the usual one—good looks, lazy parents, bored teachers, boring schools, no skills, good times. She was at it by fifteen, and nine years later the marks on her were plain. Cathy had seen and touched it all; raw life and death had pushed and shoved her. She'd pushed back with good humour and a generous heart and very little else. She once told me she'd never read a book, and had watched TV for seventy-two hours straight when she was stoned. Her pimp—who I didn't know was a pimp at the time—hired me to protect him from another pimp. It all got messy and I ended up protecting Cathy. Then she met Kevin and he took over all the work.

When you want information about crims, talk to the cops, and vice versa. They spend half their lives on the phone to each other. I called Frank Parker and asked him what he'd heard about the escapee Kevin Vincent Kearney.

'Not a thing.'

'His best girl's anxious.'

'So she should be. Is she willing to help us catch him before he does something silly?'

'Not exactly.'

'It was a sweet deal of a break, Cliff. In retrospect the van driver reckoned there could've been half a dozen cars on the roads blocking him and slowing him down. They had a nifty little jigger to cut the hole. That all takes money, and there's only one way to pay that sort of money back.'

'Yeah, I know.'

'Our ears're open, but there's nothing yet. What've you got?'

'Nothing.'

'Cliff, leave it alone. It's bound to be sticky. Do a few compo investigations, do a few arsons. Leave it alone.'

I grunted non-committally and hung up.

In prison, men talk about escaping all the time. They talk about escapes that succeeded and those that didn't. They pool the knowledge, share the wisdom—the result is that they all do the same things when they're on the run and they mostly get caught. They talk endlessly about cars, which is one of the mistakes. Did you ever hear of anyone being apprehended in a taxi or a train? They steal cars and drive them in the dumb way they do everything else and they might as well be carrying a sandwich board—ESCAPEE AT LARGE.

Kevin was hooked on Volvos; he claimed they were safe, but no car was safe with Kevin at the wheel. Time was when a Volvo in Glebe would have stood out like a camel on Bondi beach, but that's all changed. Even so, it didn't hurt to cruise a few of Kevin's haunts—the gym off Derwent Street, the card room under the Greek restaurant in St John's Road, the Forest Lodge video outlet where Kev and the girls sometimes made their own movies—just in case there was a Volvo around that didn't belong. There wasn't, but it filled in the time until I could go looking for Dave Follan at the Glebe Grenadier.

The Grenadier is the sort of pub the vicar warned you about—it smells of smoke and spilt beer and a good time. It used to serve counter lunches that would stop a wharfie but they cut them down when the weight-conscious professionals moved in. But there's a bus stop outside, a TAB next door, no stairs to the pisser—nothing will ever drive the old-timers from the Grenadier.

I ordered a beer and looked around for the pub's social secretary—the man or woman who would know everyone who came and went and the colour of their socks. He was leaning his belly against the bar and watching the pool players. People slapped him on the shoulder as they passed and he greeted them by name without even looking at them. He was the man. I eased up to him with money in my hand ready to order.

'Good pub,' I said.

'Useta be, too many bloody trendies now.'

The clientele looked pretty solidly working class to me, but I respected his judgement.

'Dave Follan's a regular here, isn't he? He's no trendy, Dave.'

'Need more of him.' He finished his schooner and I gave the barman the signal as soon as his glass hit the bar. I finished too and ordered a middy. He lit a cigarette in the small space between drinks.

'Ta,' he sipped. 'You a mate of Dave's?' He looked at me properly for the first time; his eyes were lost in the beer fat and his small mouth was overhung by a wispy ginger moustache. He wore no particular expression and it was impossible to guess at his thoughts.

'Sort of,' I said. 'Wouldn't happen to know if he's coming in tonight, would you?'

He reached over the bar and poured the rest of the schooner into the slops tray. When he turned back to me he was holding the empty glass like a weapon. 'I would happen to know. I'm Follan, and I don't know you from Adam, mate. What the fuck d'you want?'

After the Hardy foot, I thought, *try the Hardy charm*. I grinned at him. 'Let me buy you a beer, I got off on the wrong foot then.'

He wasn't having any. 'You certainly did. What's your game?'

'Cathy told me you gave her the nod about Kevin's break.'

'Cathy should keep her bloody trap shut, then.'

'She's worried about Kevin, just wants to know he's okay.'

Follan's piggy eyes drifted along the bar to the right and left of us; it looked as if he could measure earshot to within an inch.

He sucked froth from his empty glass and somehow I knew it was to oil a lie. 'I dunno any more than what I told Cathy. I got the word from a bloke who was just out. Kevin told him to look me up. I gave it to Cathy word for word and that's all I know.'

'I could be lying about Cathy, I could be a cop.'

He signalled for more beer. 'Who gives a shit? I dunno where Kevin is.'

'That's a good safe story you've got.'

'It's true, too. Piss off.'

I downed my drink and walked away; before I left the bar I turned and looked back. Follan was jiggling his change like a man about to make a phone call. I walked up the street and moved my car to a point where I could see the pub door, but was hidden behind three or four cars. I was hungry and the two quick middies felt like a gallon on my empty stomach. A taxi pulled up immediately outside the bar door and Follan took three steps across the pavement and got in. 'If you drink, don't drive'—an honest citizen observing the law? Not likely; I U-turned dangerously and followed the taxi.

After fifteen years in the business of doing for people what they can't do for themselves, I thought nothing a human being did could surprise me. Follan proved me wrong; I thought he'd head for some Ultimo or Chippendale boarding house, or another pub, but the taxi drove to the Bellevue Hotel. Follan got out and waddled into the foyer as if he belonged there. I couldn't park and I didn't fancy hanging around behind aspidistras in the lobby anyway. I drove home, had a sandwich and some wine and sat out behind the house looking at the big city glow and smelling the big city smells. They jangle some people; they soothe me.

Dave Follan looked at me sullenly. I'd followed him from the Grenadier the next day to his flat in Avon Street, Glebe. I'd bailed him up as soon as he turned the key, pushed him in, and tried to impress him with my seriousness as much as with the .38. But I wasn't sure it was working. He sat on an overstuffed, floral-covered chair and looked belligerent. The flat was fussily decorated and arranged but the arrangements were fraying and breaking down as if the woman who'd set them up was no longer around. Fat Dave Follan looked incongruous amid the floral prints and china, but he didn't seem to know it.

'You won't use that bloody thing,' he growled. 'I'm just sittin' here wondering where to hit you.'

'It could come to that,' I said evenly. 'After we spoke the other day you made a phone call and then you went to the Bellevue. I want to know why.'

'You know what you can do.'

I took off my jacket and put the gun in the pocket, dropped the jacket over a chair. 'You're fat and I've got ten years on you. You'll get hurt and we'll break things. You really want to do it this way?'

'Yes.' He came up out of the chair heavily but not too slow. He expected his bulk to help but it didn't. He swung at me, I moved aside and he nearly lost balance.

'You've had a few too many as well, Dave. Don't push it.'

He swore and drove a pretty good punch straight at me. I took it on the shoulder moving back. He was slow to recover and I put my bunched right hand in his face, fingers near the eyes and the heel on the nose and pushed hard. He grunted and went down.

'This is silly,' I said. 'But if that's the way you want it, okay. I'll fix you up here, go to the Bellevue, find out what room you went to, give it a call and throw your name in. Be interesting to see what pops up.'

That got to him. The beer courage and the bully drained out of him. He got up slowly and eased onto the couch; his flesh spread and settled as he let it take his weight. That left him with the weight on his mind.

'Don't do that. Jesus, don't do that.'

I picked my jacket off the chair and sat down. 'Well, you can see where we are, Dave. You have to tell me why you're so scared.'

'I'm a dead man if I bloody do,' he muttered.

'It's up to you. Maybe I can keep you out of it. I could try. D'you have any choice?'

He shook his head. 'Wish the missus was here; I could do with a cuppa.'

'Where is she?'

'Dead. Month back.'

'Get on with it, Dave.'

His cigarettes had fallen on the floor and he reached down for them; the effort brought the blood back to his face, and I watched him scramble and wheeze until he had one lit. 'Big job on, of course. Interstate money.'

'Where from?'

'North. Kevin and the others are gonna do it. Cost money to get 'em out.'

'Why them?'

'It's a fuckin' cowboy job, that's why. You'd have to be bloody desperate to try it. They'll have other guns on 'em while they're doin' it. I picked that up by accident, wasn't supposed to.'

'Where and what?'

He sucked on his cigarette and let the smoke out slowly. 'I don't know, that's the truth.'

He could have been lying, it was impossible to say; he was going to lie at some point, I was sure of that.

'Why the message to Cathy?'

'That was a blind; Kevin reckoned she'd get a car and get some dough together. The cops'd watch her and he could stay outta sight—keep clear of her.'

'Where?'

'Don't know.'

That was all I'd get from him, I knew. We were manoeuvring each other; he'd said enough to make it not worthwhile for me to blow him to his principals; but if the worst happened and he had to front them he could claim he hadn't sung the whole song. They might leave him a toe.

I pulled on my jacket and shoved the gun in under my arm. 'I've got you by the balls, Dave. I can drop you in it with the cops or the other side. You know that?'

He nodded. 'Why would you?'

'I wouldn't need a reason. Last thing—give me the number at the Bellevue. That's it, just three little words.'

'Five oh six.'

'I thank you. You're on your own now, Dave. You'd better play it by ear.'

If you've got the room number, fifty dollars will get you the name of any hotel resident in the city. Room 506 at the Bellevue was occupied by a Mr Carpenter of Southport. My informant, who arranged transport for the guests and did a stint on the desk, threw in for free a physical description and that Mr Carpenter would be leaving the hotel at 10 a.m. the following day. He was new at the job—he could have negotiated that into another twenty.

The example of Dave Follan turned me off drinking for the night. I went to a film that tried to make me cry; it didn't, but it could have. I walked up through Hyde Park to Darlinghurst to drink coffee worth walking that far for. The blocking of the streets has caused the girls to move to William Street where they seem to be crowding each other a little. In Darlinghurst you do it in a terrace bedroom rather than the back seat of a car, but it's the same thing. I thought about Cathy, who made calls and went out to dinner more these days, but that's the same too.

Ten o'clock found me illegally parked and alert outside the Bellevue Hotel. Carpenter was easy to spot—a beefy, florid guy wearing a beige safari suit that might have cost five hundred bucks but still looked like a rag. He put two sizeable suitcases into a new Falcon wagon and we were off. My ancient Falcon followed the new model like a discarded bull trying to keep up with the new leader of the herd.

The drive wasn't far and wasn't scenic. The Falcon pulled up outside a blighted-looking terrace house in Enmore on the Newtown side. It was as un-neighbourly a house as you'll see around there—on a corner, with an empty factory next door and the railway across the street. It was a grimy, crumbling hulk, but it had one big advantage—you could get away from it in at least four different directions, and one route, by the tunnel under the railway, would take care of a pursuing car.

One of the plusses for my car is that it can look abandoned. I sat in it, hunched down, about four houses and two rusty galvanised iron fences away and watched the house. Two kids who should have been at school wandered past and looked incuriously at me. A dog helped things along by pissing casually against the front wheel, rubbing himself briefly on the tyre and ambling off. After a while a car pulled up outside the house, two men alighted and went inside. Pretty soon they all came out: Carpenter, the two new arrivals and three other men, one of whom was Kevin Kearney.

Kevin had grown a beard, lost weight and dyed his hair three shades darker, but his cocky walk, compensating for the fact that he was only five-foot-six, and the aggressive set of his shoulders were unmistakable. The party split up between the wagon and the car with Kevin riding separately from Carpenter. I had a moment's worry, but it passed—they followed the same route.

We drove in convoy to Five Dock. They pulled up within sight of the Great Western Highway intersection at a place where the canal goes under the road and there is a wide dividing strip and big grassy stretches on either side of the road. Houses are few and back where the priorities of highway and park have pushed them. I drove on and took a turn after the canal so that I could come back on the other side of the water and watch the group safely from pretty close quarters. The two parties coalesced, then split again. Carpenter and Kearney went towards the highway; Carpenter looked to be talking fast. The others broke into two pairs and moved around on opposite sides of the road. The two men who'd arrived later in Enmore went up a grassy bank to a high point above the road. A concrete bridge crossed another loop of the canal up there and they stood by it, looking down at the road and Kevin's two mates who smoked, glanced up and down the road and looked anxious.

Carpenter and Kearney joined them and Kevin did some nodding. Where they stood was a collection of yellow and black striped council gear—uprights, reflector lamps, long wooden bars—just the stuff for traffic diversion and road blocking. Carpenter turned and looked at the two by the bridge and Kevin's eyes followed his.

The two hill climbers came back down, the smokers stamped out their butts and everyone climbed aboard again for the ride back to Enmore. Carpenter's car peeled off and headed towards the city but Kevin and his mates were delivered safely home just as the westbound 12.45 rattled past their front door.

I was pushing my luck by trailing the other pair once they'd deposited the fugitives, but I risked it. They drove to Annandale and disappeared into a trucking yard. The sign on the fence said that interstate and international freight was handled there.

The curious thing was that I had a sense of having picked up a tail myself on this run. I tested the feeling around an Annandale block or two, but I was either wrong or it dropped off. It was something else to think about on the way back to Glebe for a late lunch and a very late drink.

Some of it wasn't hard to understand. The job was a hijack with no honour among thieves. Kevin and the boys were going to be under surveillance; Carpenter was putting up the money. Three things were unknown: what the cargo was, why Follan had called it a 'cowboy' operation and why Kevin hadn't been in touch with Cathy. She wasn't green; she would probably have driven the prime mover for Kevin if he'd asked her. The biggest question of all was—what was I going to do about it?

The first move was to get in touch with Kevin, and I didn't fancy doing that by driving up to the door. I sent him a telegram—to the name Kevin Vincent at the address in Enmore. I asked him to phone me and to keep everything under his hat; Kevin'd like that—there was an old-fashioned streak in him. His call came at a bit after five.

'Haven't seen you for a bit, Cliff. Have you still got all your hair, boyo?'

'Yes, Kevin. And your phoney brogue's as bad as ever. But I'll play along—why do you ask?'

'Because you've got a lot to keep under your own bloody hat and I wondered if there'd be the room, like?'

'Knock it off, Kevin. You're about to do something very silly.'

'What would you know about it?'

I thought about telling him but decided against it; Kevin was inclined to be irrational when he was angry. 'It stands to reason. You've got a job lined up.'

'How'd you get on to me?'

'A whisper. Cathy asked me to look for you. She's worried and she's got good cause. She says she'll wait for you to serve the five or six.'

The laugh that came across the line wasn't the old feckless Kevin laugh. It was harsh and bitter, and had not a shred of amusement in it. A prison laugh, maybe.

'Wait? Cathy? Her idea of waitin's to only be taking on one at a time.'

I didn't say anything; I was more interested in listening.

'Well, Cliff,' he said. 'You can tell her I'm in the pink . . . shut up!' I heard a short laugh and a scuffling sound, then Kevin went on in a steady voice. 'And I'll be in touch soon. She's not to worry.'

'Oh yeah, great! She'll eat that up, Kevin. That'll fix everything.'

'Soon means soon.'

'How soon?'

'Tomorrow.'

Jesus, I thought, *it's tonight*.

'Now, Cliff, you just get yourself a bottle of something good and settle down for a quiet night with your books. You hear me, Cliff? Get nosey and you're history. Got it?'

'Yeah.' He rang off, and I sat there holding the phone and thinking it had been one of the least productive conversations of my life. The three unknowns were still unknown and I still didn't know what I was going to do. I phoned Cathy, couldn't get her and chased her unsuccessfully through four telephone numbers, leaving urgent messages for her to call me.

The temptation to do as Kevin suggested, hit the bottle, was immense but I fought it. I had one big Scotch and left it at that. I spoiled some eggs trying to make an omelette of them, ate the mess and felt bad. Towards the back of my brain a voice was telling me to call Frank Parker, but I kept getting a picture of Kevin with his beard and dyed hair and I couldn't do it.

When the call came I nearly hurdled a chair to snatch up the phone. It was Cathy; she told me to wait until she came over, which would be in about an hour. She sounded steady and she didn't want to hear anything I had to say.

It was after ten when she arrived—in a black velvet jacket and white silk pants. Her face was unnaturally pale and her eyes were over-dilated and bright. She had a bottle of Black Label Scotch with her and she invited me to pour her a big one before she draped herself on the couch in my living room. She lit a cigarette and stubbed it out straight away, as if she didn't want to obliterate the odour of sex that clung to her. She drank some Scotch and arched up her shoulders and wriggled.

'I've been screwing my brains out,' she said.

'Is that right? It made you hard to find—I spoke to Kevin today.'

She drank some more, then she put the glass down and assumed a mock demure pose; she half-closed and dimmed her eyes and pressed her knees together. It disconcerted me; I wondered if she was drunk, but her coordination seemed perfect and she appeared to be under tight control.

'Tell me everything about it.'

'Well, he's in Sydney . . . and, ah . . . he hasn't been in touch for a good reason. He thought the cops'd be watching you and . . .'

'I'm a sort of decoy, is that right?' She said it brightly but with an edge of hate.

'I knew you wouldn't like it.'

'It's not so bad.' She picked up her drink and took a hefty belt. 'I always liked you, Cliff. Why don't I just slip into your shower and then nip into your bed? You know, I can make it seem like I never did it before.' She laughed. 'Or only once or twice. What d'you say?'

Any other time I'd have been tempted. I can be a sucker for fantasy and I hadn't been to bed with a woman that month or the month before. But the ulterior motive was just a bit too obvious.

'Cut it out, Cathy. This is a serious situation.'

Her mood changed instantly. She knocked off the rest of the Scotch and stood up abruptly. 'I'm going to have a shower anyway, to wash off the last of you bastards.'

Water ran; she had an instinct for where bathrooms were. I put some more Black Label in my glass and waited for her to come back clean and explain to me. I seemed to do a fair bit of that—waiting to be explained to—and it sometimes made me feel like a foreigner with an imperfect grasp of the language.

The make-up was gone when she came back; her hair was damp and she'd pulled the exotic clothes on as if they were a sweater and jeans. She looked, without the gloss, tough in a different way. She made herself another drink and got a cigarette going.

'I know all about it,' she said.

I stared at her.

'I mean, I know about the job. Five Dock?'

I nodded. 'How?'

She drank and her smile reminded me of Kevin's laugh over the phone—no fun in it. 'I knew you were good, that you'd find something, but I wasn't sure you'd be straight with me. So I had someone not as good as you trailing you around. He reported in to me this afternoon—all the details. It wasn't hard to work out what the job was. D'you know what they're lifting?'

I shook my head.

She gave that smile again and held up both hands. 'This, and this—booze and smokes. It's a hot load, going to get hotter. So you don't have to worry about honest citizens getting hurt.'

'How do you know all this?'

'Wasn't hard once I knew it was trucks and who the Queensland money was.' She looked at her watch. 'It's a pretty dumb game though—bloody well-guarded that shipment'll be. You did some good snooping, Cliff. The other bloke was impressed—you didn't spot him?'

'Maybe. Just at the end. Couldn't be sure. Cathy . . . did you try to talk Kevin out of this?'

She shook her head and drew on her cigarette.

'Why not? I did.'

'What did he say?'

'Not interested. Seemed very sure of himself.'

She consulted her watch again.

'Why d'you keep doing that?'

She got up. 'You won't go to bed, least you can do is take a girl for a drive.'

We were rolling past the Leichhardt Town Hall when she told me. 'You won't be able to get too close,' she said. 'It'll all be staked out. I told the cops.'

'God, Cathy! Why?'

She didn't answer; she just sucked on her cigarette and stared ahead through my dirty windscreen.

It was near midnight and a mist was rising off the canals and grass. Wednesday night, quiet, a good night for crime. The question of getting close never arose because it all happened as we skirted the park. The highway turn-off was in full view and I saw the high shape of a semi-trailer heading down the road. Then lights pointed crazily to the sky and there were flashes and flares out of the darkness. There was a sputtering of bright orange from up the hill where I'd seen the two heavies reconnoitring. The truck seemed to meander slowly down the grade, then pick up speed abruptly. Too abruptly: it skidded, lurched and rolled. There were dark shapes moving fast from the park and pairs of headlights suddenly cut through the dark mists. I stopped and braked without knowing it; the whole thing seemed to take an age with each separate part occupying its own bit of time, but in fact it must have been all over within a couple of minutes.

Cathy sat still and stared, and then she jumped and swore as her cigarette burned down to her fingers. She jerked open the door.

'What're you doing?' I reached across for the handle.

'I want to see. I was the fizgig, I've got the right!'

'Don't be a fool! You don't know what's going to happen. Who's dead, who's alive. You know what'll happen to you if they find out you put them in.'

She broke my grip on the handle and opened the door. 'Who cares?' she said.

I got out and followed her down the road and across a broad strip of grass. We were challenged a hundred yards from the scene by a shape that rose up from behind a bush. Cathy walked unblinkingly towards the gun.

'I want to see Matthiesson,' she said.

The cop fell in behind us and we went the rest of the way to the overturned truck and the cars each with flashing warning lights and one blue eye blinking tracers of light over still and moving figures.

Matthiesson was a bulky man in a flak jacket and bullet-proof gear. He held an automatic rifle and let its muzzle point to the ground when he saw Cathy.

'You shouldn't be here,' he said. 'And who's this?'

'A friend,' Cathy said dully. 'Where's Kevin?'

'He was hit. I'm sorry. I told you I couldn't make any promises.'

'Yes, you did. I want to see him.'

Matthiesson guided us across behind the truck. One of its wheels was turning slowly and bits of gravel were still falling from it. The overturned truck smelt strongly of liquor, and there were rivulets running from it and soaking into the small, dark, twisted shape on the ground. Kevin was on his back; his face was blotched with blood and one eye socket was a brimming pool. He looked like the death photo of Bugsy Spiegel. Cathy looked down at him and the tears started and fell down her face and onto the body. She just stood there, slightly bent over, and looked and wept. I moved over, put my arm around her and gently eased her away; she went, on feet that moved in a slow, hobbled shuffle.

Sirens started howling and the ambulances arrived and a team came to right the truck. There was a lot of swearing and one scream of pain as someone with bullets in him was moved. I got Cathy back to my car, gave her a cigarette and drove back to Glebe. She resisted nothing, accepted everything. Her shoes had blood on them and I made her kick them off at the door. I sat her down and wiped her face and made us both a drink. She drank it in a gulp and held out the glass for more.

'You asked why?'

I nodded.

'I went there to see him this afternoon. To Enmore. Just as I got there this girl came out. Great tall thing, all in pink. Kevin always liked them tall, pink's his favourite colour. Kevin came out with her. His hair was different and he had a beard. He shaved it off, did y'see?'

I nodded again.

'He came out with her and I watched.'

'Cathy, you couldn't be sure. She might have been with one of the other blokes. Anything . . .'

'She copped his special big feel just before she got into her car. I should know. I know what it meant.'

I didn't say anything.

'That's it,' she said. 'That's why.'

THE DESERTER

From *Man in the Shadows* (1988)

'I want you to find my son, Mr Hardy,' Ambrose Guyatt said to me. 'He's a soldier.'

An image from *Rambo* flashed before my eyes—gaunt men in rags screaming inside a bamboo cage. I'd watched the movie on a flight from Honolulu to Sydney because I'd finished my book and couldn't sleep. I'm over forty and carry a few unhealed physical and emotional wounds, which make me unfit for that kind of action.

'I don't understand,' I said.

'I should say he *was* a soldier. He went absent without leave.'

'For how long?'

'It's not clear. Some weeks.'

'Then he's a deserter.'

Guyatt shifted his well-padded behind on the unpadded chair I have for clients in my office. What's the point in making them too comfortable? They might decide that everything's all right and go away. Guyatt didn't. 'Technically, perhaps. You were in the army yourself, I believe. Malaya. You don't look old enough.'

'It went on longer than people think. If your son's a deserter, Mr Guyatt, the military and the police'll be looking for him. I can't see . . .'

'Julian didn't desert, or if he did he had a good reason. He's not some little guttersnipe; he's educated, he's got background.'

I held the smile in; I've seen backgrounds fade into the far distance and guttersnipes come up with the goods. I got out a fresh notepad and clicked my ballpoint. 'You'd better tell me all about it, Mr Guyatt.'

Like most people feeling their way into a subject, he found it easiest to start with himself. Ambrose Guyatt ran a very profitable business that had blossomed from paper and stationery into printing and copying. He told me that some years before he had worked twenty hours a day keeping abreast of things and making the right moves. 'That was when Julian was growing up,' he said. 'Naturally I didn't see much of him.'

I nodded and got ready to make my first note. 'How old is he now?'

'Twenty. He joined the army nearly two years ago. He was a champion athlete but he . . . didn't finish school.'

Guyatt was a short, stocky man with a balding head and a high colour. I'll swear he almost blushed when he admitted his offspring was a dropout.

I nodded again. 'Didn't finish the army stint either. Is that his problem, Mr Guyatt? That he can't finish anything?'

'I really don't know. It's a terrible thing to say but I can't claim to know him very well. We hardly spoke in the last years he was at home. Well, he wasn't really at home. He came in for clean shirts and money, which his mother gave him.'

'Would you have given them to him?'

'He avoided me. Never came when I was going to be around.'

I sighed. Young Guyatt avoided old Guyatt; old Guyatt avoided questions; I wondered what Mrs Guyatt avoided. 'Was he on good terms with his mother?'

Guyatt nodded.

'What does she have to say about it?'

'She's distraught. She says Julian loved the army and would never desert.'

I got a photograph of Julian, the licence number of his blue Laser, a few details on his pre-army life and the last date he had performed his duty at Waterloo Barracks. I also got the telephone number of one Captain Barry Renshaw.

'Step by step, how did it happen?'

'Julian didn't do anything about his mother's birthday. That had never happened before. She rang Waterloo Barracks and was told that he was on leave. That was a lie.'

'How do you know?'

'Julian had told his mother he was going to New Caledonia the next time he got leave, even if it was only for a week. He couldn't have gone. His passport's at home.'

'What then?'

'I rang and was told that my son had been posted as a deserter.'

I looked at my notes. 'You spoke to this Captain Renshaw?'

'No, someone else. I didn't get his name. Renshaw's been handling it since, but we've really heard nothing. Something has to be done.'

'I charge a hundred and fifty dollars a day and expenses,' I said. 'If I work on this for a month you'll be up for over four thousand dollars.'

'Do it. Please.'

I accepted his cheque. After he left, I stared at the photograph until I would have recognised the owner of the strong features, low-growing dark hair and steady eyes anywhere there was enough light to see by. Lately I'd done more debugging and money-minding than I cared for. It was good to have something to do some legwork on. Julian Guyatt hadn't been in the army quite long enough to throw off civilian contacts. I checked at his last two jobs, hung around the pub he'd frequented and spoke to a girl he'd taken out for a few months. The response was the same everywhere: 'Like we told the man from the army, we don't know anything.'

That left Captain Renshaw. I telephoned him and stated my business.

'I don't think I can help you.'

'Don't you want to find him?'

'Of course.' The captain clipped his words off as if they might straggle and sound untidy.

'I've found a lot of people. I might get lucky.'

'We've tried, so have the police.'

'You and the police have procedures, Captain. You treat all cases the same, cover the same ground. I can treat it as unique. I can feel around and try to find the handle. D'you follow me?'

'One silly young man. I hardly think . . .'

'That's what I mean. To his father he's more important than all your Leopard tanks put together. Give me some of your time, anywhere you like, please.'

'I don't know.'

I felt I was losing him. I spoke quickly. 'You tried to find Guyatt by looking into his civilian life, right?'

'Yes.'

'There you go. You need a fresh approach. You're an institutional man and you trust the institution.'

'What do you mean?'

I drew a breath, the next bit was risky. 'I'd check on his army life. Discreetly. I was a soldier myself.'

'Were you? Vietnam?'

'No, Malaya. Don't laugh, I'm not Methuselah. Captain, I'm going to look into this one way or another. I don't leak things to newspapers and I don't write books. Apart from the bare outlines, my files are in my head. You see what I'm getting at?'

'I do. Two o'clock, here at Waterloo Barracks. Suit you?'

I agreed and thanked him. Then I rang Guyatt and made my meagre report. It didn't sound like a thousand dollars' worth to me but Guyatt didn't complain. I asked him about the Laser and he told me that Julian had put a deposit on it and was paying it off from his army pay.

'What finance company?'

'Western, I believe. Madness! I lease, myself.'

I gave my name at a glassed-in, wired-for-sound guardbox. A silent sergeant escorted me down concrete paths, through sturdy metal gates and between some squat, undistinguished red brick boxes to a stylish aluminium and glass block. The sergeant led me down a corridor past some busy offices and knocked on a door marked Military Police.

'Mr Hardy.' A tall, thin man with sparse sandy hair got up from behind a desk and extended his hand. His face was about fifty years old; his uniform looked brand new.

'Captain Renshaw.' We shook hands and I sat in a straight-backed chair by the desk. The room was big enough to hold two other desks, three filing cabinets, a bar fridge and a large bookcase crammed with official-looking publications.

Renshaw pushed a pencil around on the desk in front of him. 'Probably won't surprise you to hear I looked up your record.'

'No,' I said.

'Decent enough. See you don't draw a pension or any benefits. Why's that?'

I shrugged. 'Stubborn. Let's talk about Julian Guyatt. What sort of a soldier is he?'

Renshaw took a file from the top drawer, opened it and ran his eye down the first sheet. 'Pretty good. No apparent weaknesses.'

'Specialist?'

He shook his head. 'No.'

'Have you got a psychological profile there? Any progress reports? Anything that suggests a reason for desertion?'

Renshaw kept his eyes on my face. 'Like . . .?'

'Gambling, drink or drugs, sex?'

'No.'

'Why was Guyatt's mother told he was on leave?'

'A mistake. An apology was made.'

I grinned. 'You're not being a lot of help, Captain. How about a drink?'

He looked puzzled. 'What?'

'There's a fridge behind you. I thought there might be a beer in it.'

He turned his upper body slowly and looked at the fridge as if he was seeing it for the first time. He reached forward and opened it. The seat of the swivel chair moved slightly. The fridge was empty. 'Sorry.'

'Don't worry. I'd like to talk to a couple of his mates.'

Renshaw consulted the file again. 'He doesn't seem to have had any close friends in the service.' He snapped the file shut. 'That's why we looked outside and why I think you're wasting your time. Unless you have any information which could be of help to us.'

I stared at him . . . The temperature in the room seemed to have dropped. Renshaw stood; I heard the sergeant's boots scrape the floor behind me. 'Goodbye, Mr Hardy.'

As an investigative interview it wasn't much to boast about, but I *had* got something. Captain Renshaw didn't know where the fridge was or that his chair swivelled—he hadn't spent more than ten minutes in that office before I arrived. If he was a military policeman, I was Frank Sinatra.

I wouldn't say I was encouraged, but at least I had something to bite on. When I checked with the finance company and found that Guyatt's payments had been made for three months ahead, I had a bit more. I did some more phoning—to the police to check on stolen and recovered cars and to a contact who can tell you useful things about credit cards. Result: several Lasers lost and found but not Julian Guyatt's, and he hadn't used his credit cards in the past month.

I slept on it and woke up feeling that I had enough to ring my client and make an appointment to talk to his wife.

The Guyatts lived in Greenwich, which isn't a part of Sydney I know well. I drove there in fine weather in the mid-morning and missed the street because a tree from a front garden was drooping over the sign. The place seemed to have more trees per square metre than anywhere else east of the Blue Mountains. I found the street and parked outside the long, low, timber house. Some distance off a car backfired and birds flew up from the trees. The noise they made was deafening.

Mrs Guyatt was a large, heavy-featured woman who had given her looks to her son. She seemed commanding and firm of purpose but she was just the opposite. As soon as I mentioned Julian's name her eyes moistened.

'I'll show you his room,' she said.

'I don't think that's necessary.'

She didn't listen. She led me down a passage towards the rear of the house and showed me into a large bedroom that had too much built-in furniture, too much carpet and too much window. It was an ugly room that someone had tried too hard to make comfortable. I stood uncomfortably while Mrs Guyatt showed me Julian's sports trophies—NSW Under-17 100-metres champion, 1984—tennis racquets and skis. There were no books. A poster on the back of the door showed a helicopter gunship in attack, a scene from *Apocalypse Now*.

Down in the over-elaborate sitting room we drank coffee while Mrs Guyatt told me what a good boy her son was.

'Did he have any friends?' I asked.

'Certainly. Chris Petersen, Phil Cash, I'm sure there were others.'

'These are army friends?'

'Yes.'

'Did you try to contact them?'

She looked distressed. 'No. I didn't know how . . .'

'Do you know where they come from, Petersen and Cash, or anyone else he was friendly with?'

'I don't think . . . I believe Phil Cash was from Gundagai. I think Julian said that. Otherwise, no. What has happened?'

'I'm trying to find out. You say you have your son's passport?'

'Yes. Julian left it here after his last trip to New Caledonia. Would you like to see it?'

I said I would. She left the room and came hurrying back, more flustered and distressed than ever. 'It's gone!'

'You're sure? You didn't misplace it?'

'No! I've never misplaced anything of Julian's. How could I? Someone has been in here and taken it.'

I tried to calm her down but didn't do a very good job. In the end I had to phone Guyatt at his office. He said he'd come home but he wasn't pleased at being taken away from his work.

I became aware of the car following me when I was a few miles from the Guyatts'. A grey Corolla. The driver wasn't bad at it but it's almost impossible to follow someone who spots you and doesn't want you there. I lost him in Hunters Hill between the Lane Cove and Gladesville bridges. I turned off Waterloo Road towards the city and outlaid some of Guyatt's money in a parking station as close as I could get to the GPO.

The country phone directories were a brand-new set. In a few weeks they'd have pages missing and entries obliterated, but for now they were the private detective's friend. There were only three numbers listed for Cash in Gundagai. The woman who answered at the first number had only been in the town a few weeks and gave a squawk of laughter when I asked her if she had a son. 'I'm a lesbian feminist separatist,' she said. 'If I had a son it wouldn't live twenty-four hours.'

The second number was the right one. Mrs Enid Cash confirmed that her son Phillip was in the regular army. 'There hasn't been an accident?' she said anxiously.

'No, nothing like that. I'm Captain Renshaw, Army Statistics. I'm afraid our records haven't been as well kept as they might have been. I'm trying to confirm the rural backgrounds of personnel. They're going to be in line for special benefits.'

'Quite right too. Well, our Phillip grew up on the farm here. He's a country boy.'

'Excellent. Let me see, he's stationed at . . .'

'Waterloo Barracks.'

'Right. He comes home on leave of course?'

'Always.'

'Thank you, Mrs Cash. You don't happen to know anything about a Sergeant Petersen, do you?'

'Chris Petersen, do you mean? How exciting! He must've been promoted. Phil will be pleased.'

'Yes. Is he a Gundagai man too?'

'Goodness me, no. He's a Victorian, from Benalla. Phil was always ribbing him about it. But he's from the country too so he'll be eligible, won't he?'

It took me four calls to locate the right Petersen in Benalla, but the story was much the same. Chris was a soldier who always came home on leave. One more call laid it out for me—the duty officer at Waterloo Barracks confirmed that Cash and Petersen were on leave. That would be surprising news to the old folks back home on the farm.

I puzzled about it as I walked through Martin Place back to the car park. I could understand three young men doing something else with their leave than what their mums expected, but the posting of Julian Guyatt as a deserter and Renshaw's manner needed explanation.

I'd parked five or six levels up, close to the fire stairs. I had my key in the door lock when the stair door opened and two men came out. I unlocked the door expecting them to go to their car but they suddenly swerved and jumped at me. They were big and quick; one hit me hard and low while the other grabbed my throat with his big, hard hand. He squeezed and I felt the darkness wrapping around me. He eased up and I fought for breath. He squeezed again; the puncher pulled me down so that we were squatting by the car. My knee hit the concrete. The darkness came and went again.

'Let it go, Hardy,' the squeezer said. 'Do yourself a favour and let it go. Understand?'

I shook my head. He put his palm on my forehead and slammed the back of my head against the car door. I felt the metal give.

'Forget about Guyatt or everyone'll forget about you.' He squeezed again and this time the darkness was thick and heavy and it didn't lift.

•

'The oldest trick in the book,' I said.

'What's that?' A man was brushing me down and helping me to struggle to my feet. I recognised my car; I didn't recognise him.

'You were really out to it,' he said. 'What are you, a diabetic or an epileptic or something? My aunt . . .'

I pulled myself up. 'No. I'm all right. Thanks a lot. I just had a sort of turn. Not enough sleep lately. Working too hard.'

'Better take it easy.' He moved away, happy to have helped, happy not to have to help any more.

'Thanks again.' I leaned against the car, massaged my bruised stomach and felt my stiff, aching neck. It must have been the two-car trick; let the subject see one car following him, drop that one off and keep him in sight from another. It's not something I've had much practice at, seeing that I work alone and can't drive two cars at once. But I should have thought of it.

I sat in the car for a while until I was sure my head and vision were clear. My attackers had cost Ambrose Guyatt some money by delaying me in the car park.

I reviewed the attack—very fast, very professional. If the fist that had hit my belly had held a knife and the hand that gripped my neck had gripped harder and longer, it would have been a classical jungle-fighting kill.

I drove home to Glebe watching for tails and not spotting any. The cat was outside the house, which wasn't unusual. But when I opened the door it didn't march straight in ahead of me. That was unusual. I waited in the passage and listened to the erratic hum of my refrigerator, the dripping tap in the bathroom upstairs, the creaking from the loose piece of roofing iron. All normal. I went in and looked around. The place had been quickly but systematically searched.

I made myself a drink and sat down to assemble what I had. It was a fair bet that my office had been searched too and if they hadn't found the file that carried Guyatt's name, his cheque and two or three other entries, they should go back to searching school. I was in a unique bind: I needed more information on Renshaw, Guyatt, Cash and Petersen. With civilians you can always find a source—a neighbour, a relative, a lover—but these men inhabited a closed world.

The only lead I had into Julian Guyatt's private life was his fondness for New Caledonia. There I had some room to manoeuvre. Ailsa Sleeman, an old friend, has sizeable business interests in New Caledonia and contacts to match. I called her, chatted about old times, and asked her to put out some feelers about Guyatt.

'I'll find out what I can,' she said, 'and you'll have to have a drink with us, Cliff.'

'Us?'

'I'm nearly married again.'

'Don't do it.'

She laughed. 'Maybe I won't.'

I had other things to do for the next few days and I did them. I didn't get in to the office for a couple of days and when I did I found the search had been rougher and more destructive than the one in Glebe. Papers were torn, things were broken and I got angry; my stomach was still sporting a dark bruise. I sat at my desk and brooded. Then I phoned Renshaw.

'Here's what I've got,' I said. 'A deposition from Mrs Guyatt that she was told her son was on leave. A taped conversation with the duty officer to the effect that Cash and Petersen are on leave plus taped conversations from their homes to say they're not. I've got a witness to my being assaulted in the car park and the licence number of a grey Corolla. I've got a videotape of your people searching my office. What d'you say, Captain? Are you going to tell me what's going on?'

Renshaw's short, barking laugh sounded far too confident for my liking. 'You amuse me, Hardy. I'll tell you what you've got—nothing! You called Gundagai and Benalla from a public telephone. Neither of your phones, office or home, has a recording device so you've got no record of any call to the duty officer here. I've never seen you, of course.'

'I've still got a client.'

'Listen, Hardy, I'll talk freely since I know you can't record anything I say. I'll admit that clumsy mistakes have been made. That's all I'll admit.'

'I don't think that'll satisfy Guyatt.'

Renshaw was calm, almost courtly. 'I think it will. I think his good lady's satisfied too. Why don't you ask them? Goodbye, Hardy.'

I've heard that tone of voice before; it's the tone of the fixer, the smoother-out of things who feels that he's done a good job. I drove to Guyatt's place of business in North Sydney. It was a busy operation—warehouse, printery and machine division topped by an office space that seemed to be in the process of expanding. I fronted up to a reception desk and told the young woman in charge that I wanted to see Ambrose Guyatt.

'Yes, he's . . . oh, have you got an appointment?'

Something about her manner and the bustle of the place suggested newness, innovation. 'I've never needed an appointment to see Ambrose before,' I said. 'What's up?'

She leaned forward confidentially. 'You haven't heard?'

'No,' I whispered.

The phone rang and she fumbled uncertainly with the buttons on the new-looking system. When she got the call properly placed she smiled at me. 'New contract. Big one.'

I felt a lurch in my stomach, just below the bruise. 'Oh, the army thing?'

'Yes, isn't it wonderful? Hey!'

I walked past the desk and pushed open the door she'd been guarding. Ambrose Guyatt sat with a phone at his ear in front of a paper-strewn desk. He was smiling as he spoke into the instrument. The smile faded as he saw me come into the room. He spoke quickly and hung up.

'Hardy.'

'Mr Guyatt.'

He reached into a drawer of his desk and took out an envelope.

'What's that?' I said.

He beckoned me closer. 'Cash instead of the cheque,' he said softly.

I was standing beside the desk now, looking down at him. His thin, dark hair was freshly cut and he was wearing a new suit. I took the envelope. 'Congratulations on the army contract.'

He nodded.

'Want to tell me where Julian is?'

'I can't.'

'Secret mission? Something like that?'

'I can't say a word.'

'I understand his mother's a proud and happy woman?'

His eyes widened as a faint doubt crept in. 'I think you'd better go.'

'I will. I'm sorry for you, Mr Guyatt. You're going to be a very unhappy man.'

'What . . . what d'you mean?'

I leaned close to him. I could smell his expensive aftershave and the aroma of cigar smoke. 'They don't make these arrangements for things that go right, Mr Guyatt. They do it for things that go wrong.'

He gaped at me as I walked out of the office.

•

I was right. Ailsa reported to me several days later. The information was fragmentary, hardly to be relied upon unless you had something to support it as I had. Julian Guyatt was part of a small task force that had been infiltrated into New Caledonia to operate against the Kanaks. It had been wiped out in the first exchange. Piecing it all together, the one-time Under-17 100-metres champion had been dead for twenty-four hours when his father first stepped into my office.

THE BIG LIE

From *Burn, and Other Stories* (1993)

Robert Adamo was a slender, medium-sized man with a slow, disconnected way of speaking. 'Mr Hardy, I hope you can help me,' he drawled. 'I've never hired a private detective before.'

'There's a first time for everything, Mr Adamo,' I said. 'I don't ask as many questions as an accountant or cost as much as a plumber. What's the problem?'

He glanced around my office for a moment, which is all the time it takes to register the minimal furniture and non-existent decoration. 'I want to find someone. That is, I saw her yesterday, but . . .'

'Hold on. Who're we talking about?' I'd already written Adamo's name and address on a foolscap pad, along with the fact that he ran a picture-framing and art restoration business in Paddington. Then I'd written MP, for missing person, and drawn the male and female symbols and a question mark.

'Valerie Hammond. She's my fiancée. We were going to be married in two months.'

I scratched out the male symbol. It took a bit of hacking and slashing through Adamo's reticence and shyness, but I eventually got something I could put down in point form on the pad. Adamo and Valerie Hammond had met when she'd come to collect a painting she'd had framed. They got engaged after six months. The date was set; then Valerie Hammond disappeared. She moved out of Adamo's house, where she'd been living for three months, quit her executive job with Air France and dropped out of sight.

'So you had an argument,' I said. 'What about?'

'No argument. Nothing. I asked her to marry me. She said yes. Then she was gone.'

'What did you do?' I said.

His long, bony hands were in his lap now, twisting and flexing. They were strong-looking hands, and Adamo himself was a strong-looking-man—straight dark hair, firm chin, high cheekbones. 'I . . . I looked for her, but I didn't know what to do. She took her clothes and she got a reference from Air France. She's very good at languages.'

It was a better start than some. Adamo was a very well-organised guy: he had a recent photograph of his girl, who was blonde, with a high forehead, big eyes and a sexy mouth—165 centimetres, fifty-five kilos. I did the conversions to the old system on my pad. Valerie was twenty-five to Adamo's twenty-nine; she'd learned French, German and Italian from her Swiss mother, and she and Robert had had a lot of fun in Leichhardt restaurants. His people were Italians who'd come out in the sixties when Roberto was a small boy. He was Robert now, and his Italian was rusty. I got the rest of the dope on Valerie—parents both dead, no siblings, only friends known to Adamo were Air France people he'd already talked to with no result. Valerie Hammond seemed to lead a quiet, very constrained life.

'Sorry to have to ask,' I said, 'but does she have any . . . peculiarities? I mean does she smoke a lot, or drink or gamble?' I gave a little laugh to help the medicine go down.

Adamo shook his head. 'Nothing like that. She is very quiet, a very private person. That's why I'm dealing with you rather than the police.'

'What does she spend her money on? She'd be on a good salary with the airline.'

'Don't know. We never talked about money. I'm very careful about money. Running a small business isn't easy.' His eyes flicked around the office again and I could sense him weighing up incomings and outgoings the way I did myself, periodically. 'All I can tell you is that she's careful about it, too.'

I made a note on the pad. 'She must've saved a bit then. You don't know what bank she used?'

He shook his head. 'She didn't have any money.'

'Excuse me, Mr Adamo, but you don't seem to have known a lot about the woman you were going to marry.'

'*Am* going to marry,' he said fiercely, 'when you find her.'

I nodded. His firmness deflected me from that approach. 'Tell me about seeing her yesterday.'

'In Terrey Hills. Mona Vale Road.' He checked his watch. 'At half-past three. She got in a Redline taxi and drove away. I was in my van. I'd been delivering a picture I'd restored.'

It turned out that he'd tried to follow the taxi but couldn't do it. I'd have been surprised if he could; following taxis is a lot harder than it sounds. He also didn't get the taxi's number, which was disappointing but not fatal. I took the photograph and got addresses and phone numbers and three hundred dollars from him—two days' pay—and told him I'd phone him within forty-eight hours.

'I love her,' he said. 'No matter what.'

'There could be problems you haven't anticipated, Mr Adamo,' I said. 'Emotional things . . .'

He shook his head. 'I deal with artists every day. I know about such things. They're a part of life. I want Valerie for better or for worse.'

He was serious and I was impressed. He lived in Lilyfield, only a hop, step and jump from Glebe, where I live. I could always drop in on him and take a look at the coop Valerie had flown. Unlikely to be necessary; people can be hard to find, but it's a matter of categories. Clean-living, good-looking quadrilingual blondes who get references from their employers aren't as hard to find as some.

It's not often in a missing persons case that you have the luxury of two clear, fresh trails to follow. As I get older, luxury appeals to me more. I rang Redline Cabs and spoke to a guy I know there who helps me because I once helped him. He undertook to find out from the service dockets which driver had picked up a fare in Mona Vale Road, Terrey Hills, approximately twenty-four hours ago, and to put me in touch with him or her.

Then I rang an employment agency that had once provided me with a typist when I needed one to make up a long and largely fictitious report. Amy Post was the typist; we'd had a brief, non-title, sexual bout and had remained friends. Amy was an executive in the company now.

'Amy? It's Cliff Hardy.'

'God, so it is. Let me guess—you need a physiotherapist who can do bookkeeping and house repairs.'

'I don't need anyone. I . . .'

Amy's voice went smoky. 'We all need someone, Cliff.'

'Sometimes,' I said. 'Right now, I've got a profile of a person who's left a job and is looking for another. I'll give you the details, and you tell me where she goes looking. Okay?'

'Okay. She, eh? Hmm.'

'It's business. A man's paying me to find her.'

Amy's voice went professional. 'Shoot.'

I gave her the details, such as I had, of Valerie Hammond's age, appearance, qualifications and experience. Amy said, 'Fluent in all of 'em?'

'So I understand.'

'Half her luck. She wouldn't need to be out of work a minute. And with a good reference? Shit, she could walk in anywhere and ask for top dollar. Got your pencil sharpened? No joke intended.'

Amy gave me a list of eleven likely employers—airlines, travel agents, convention organisers, consultants. I noted down the addresses and numbers and the names of her contacts at each place. Efficiency was Amy's god, and that was one of the things that had kept our affair light—she'd sensed that my ramshackle operation ran the way I liked it, and in a manner she couldn't bear. I drew a line under the last entry and thanked her.

'Glad to help. Are you sure this chick's a job of work for you?'

'Yes. Why?'

'Nothing. Just that she sounds interesting, and she'd be earning a hell of a lot of money. Bye, Cliff.'

I hung up and thought about what she'd said before dialling the first number. I'd made a dollar sign on the pad when I'd been getting information from Adamo. I underlined it and put another question mark beside it, and the word 'bank'.

The next hour was a minefield of answering machines, indifferent secretaries, hostile underlings and the occasional cooperative person. My spiel was that I was representing a legal client who needed to contact Ms Hammond, and Amy Post's name was my calling card. I positively eliminated eight of the organisations and was left with just three—Air Europe, a new charter-flight operation that could get you anywhere as long as you could pay the freight; a package-holiday outfit which specialised in booking clients into off-the-beaten-track hotels; and a consultancy that arranged computer linkups and interpreters in certain European locations. I could expect calls from these three when Amy's contacts were available and their commitments permitted. I made a separate note of the addresses—my time is important too.

Then I felt a little stir-crazy and went out for a drink and the paper. It was a cool, early November day, and the city seemed oddly quiet. There was nothing of interest in the paper, and I had to get out of the pub fast after one drink—it was the sort of afternoon you could easily spend in a bar, hanging around until the afternoon became evening and the evening night, and all you'd get out of it would be a headache. It wasn't so far to the Redline depot in Surry Hills and I decided to walk it and tell myself I was working.

'You missed him,' Bernie, my satisfied ex-client, said. 'Name's Wesley.' He waved at the phone on his desk. 'Be home now. Call him if you like.'

I sighed and called the number he gave me. Wesley had a deep, tuneful voice and sounded very tired. He remembered the fare.

'Where did you drop her?' I asked.

'Lindfield, I think. Yeah, Lindfield.'

'At a house, block of flats, what?'

Wesley's deep yawn came down the line. 'In the street, brother, just across from the railway station.'

I swore, apologised to Wesley and got his address in case I needed to talk to him about his impressions of the woman. Another question now and I was sure I'd hear him start to snore.

'No go, Cliff?'

I put down the phone. 'Tougher than I thought it'd be.'

Bernie clucked sympathetically and went back to his work.

That's the way it goes; one minute you think you can solve the whole thing between lunch and afternoon tea, and the next it's all questions and no answers. I went back to the office and looked at the three illuminated zeroes on the answering machine. No calls. I sat down and wrote up my notes on the Hammond case so far, the way the *Commercial Agents and Private Enquiry Agents Act* of 1963 requires you to do. I also completed the notes on a couple of other cases which had either been resolved or had petered out. Full of virtue, I drove home to an evening of TV news, spaghetti, red wine and Len Deighton. I worried on Len's behalf about the effects on his fiction of the Berlin Wall coming down. But not too much. Len could probably have more fun without a wall.

The calls came in the next morning, two of them with a little urging. At Conferences International, the outfit that set up the computer links and interpreters, I hit the bull's-eye. Yes, Ms Hammond was an employee and yes, certainly, the message to call me would be passed on to her. I sat at my desk and thought about cigarettes and mid-morning drinking, two habits I'd reluctantly abandoned, while I waited for the call. As a result, I was edgy when the phone rang.

'Mr Hardy?' A crisp, businesslike female voice. A voice used to cutting through the shit and getting things done. 'This is Valerie Hammond. I'm returning your call.'

'I'll be honest with you, Ms Hammond. I'm a private investigator. It's not a legal matter. I'm working for Mr Robert Adamo. He hired me to locate you.'

'I see. And you've succeeded.'

'He needs to talk to you, very badly.'

The voice started off flat, dull almost, and rose in pitch and intensity, losing control. 'No. Positively not. Tell him I don't want to see him or talk to him. I don't want to marry him . . . or . . . or have children or have anything to do with him. Do you understand?'

'No,' I said.

'That's all. Leave me alone!' The line buzzed and then went dead; she must have fumbled cutting the connection. Very upset. Very intriguing. Very unsatisfactory. How do you tell a client you scored a bull's-eye but the arrow fell out of the target? You don't. I hung up and ran down the stairs and along the street to where my car was parked. I drove straight to the Conferences International office in Bent Street and parked almost outside. Totally illegal, but I didn't expect to be there long. I got out of the car and circled the tall building on foot—smoked-glass windows, imposing entrance but no car park. I lounged in the street enjoying luxury again—I'd recognise her and she wouldn't know me from Harry M. Miller.

She came out fast, taller and blonder than I expected, but still Valerie H. as per the picture in my pocket. Her business clothes were smart and looked medium-expensive. No car. She stepped into a taxi, which had drawn up seconds before. The parking Nazi was just rounding the corner as I got back into my car and pulled away from the no parking zone. I jockeyed the Falcon into the traffic, a couple of cars behind the cab. I had my sunglasses on against the glare and a full tank of petrol; I had to hope that the driver was a sober type who signalled early and stopped for lights.

He was. The drive to Lindfield was almost sedate. I had no trouble keeping the cab in sight and staying unobtrusive myself. It was a little after eleven, with a fine, clear day shaping up. I squinted hard, trying to read something from the woman's demeanour. She sat in the back the way most women passengers do. Nothing in that. She seemed to be sitting very rigidly, but it might have been my imagination. The cab turned off the main road just past the railway station and pulled up outside a small block of red-brick flats. For the area, very low-rent stuff. There was no mistaking her distress now; she rushed from the cab, leaving the door open, and almost fell as she plunged up the steps towards the small entrance.

Shaking his head, the cabbie got out, closed the door and drove away. I parked opposite the flats; the sun was shining directly through the windscreen and my shirt was sticking to my back. It was suddenly very hot and still. The highway was noisy, and I heard a train rattle past. This little patch of Lindfield seemed to have missed out on the trees and the quiet and the money. I sat in the car and looked at the flats. It didn't figure. Amy said she must be earning a bundle. Adamo said she had no vices. So why was she living here? Like other people in my racket, I've been known to trace someone, phone the client with the address and bank the cheque. Not this time. I had to know more.

It wasn't nearly as hot out of the car. I flapped my arms to unglue my shirt, and put on my jacket. A sticker over the letterbox told me that Hammond lived in Flat 3. That was one flight up, a narrow door at the top of a narrow set of stairs. Ratty carpet, cheap plastic screw-on numbers, flimsy handrail, no peephole, no buzzer. I knocked and held my licence folder at the ready. The door opened more quickly than I expected. A big man stood there. He was moon-faced, with thinning fair hair. He wore a white T-shirt and jeans that sagged under his bulging belly. He was well over 180 centimetres tall and must have weighed over ninety kilos, much of it fat.

'My name's Hardy,' I said. 'I'd like to see Ms Hammond.'

Valerie Hammond shrieked, 'No' from behind the fat man and he reacted by brushing the folder away, putting a big, meaty hand on my chest and pushing.

Fat can be a problem if it comes at you fast. This guy was serious, but he wasn't fast. I stepped back, surprised but balanced, and he swung a punch. I'd almost have had time to put my licence back in my pocket before it got anywhere near me. As it was, I moved to one side and let the punch drift away into thin air. That upset and angered him. He lowered his head and bullocked forward, trying to crush me against the brick wall a few feet back. Couldn't have that; I jolted the side of his head with a short elbow jab and pushed at him with my shoulder as he blundered past. He hit the wall awkwardly with his knee and head, groaned and went down.

I looked through the open door. Valerie Hammond was standing there with a shocked, dazed expression on her face. Her eyes were full of terror, and her hands were fluttering like lost birds. I couldn't think of a thing to say to her. I took out a card, bent and put it on the frayed carpet just inside the door. Behind me, the fat man was struggling gamely to his feet.

I pointed to the card. 'I don't mean you any harm. Robert Adamo is concerned about you. Call me when you feel calmer. I don't know what your trouble is, but maybe I can help. I didn't want to hurt this guy.'

Her hands stopped at her face, almost covering her eyes. I stepped clear of the man trying to make a grab at me and went down the stairs. I realised that I was breathing hard but not from the mild exertion. Valerie Hammond's fear had shaken me more than anything that Fatty could have done. I peeled off my jacket and sat sweating in the car, wondering what to do next. It was one of those times when the distress you run into seems to outweigh the distress of the person who hired you. It happens and it's confusing. The only way to cope is to get more information. I started the engine and drove away, grateful for the breeze created by the movement and feeling an overwhelming need for a drink.

I had the drink in a North Sydney pub and reviewed my options. All very well to want more information, but where to get it? I couldn't give a work-in-progress report to Adamo as things stood, and I didn't see Conferences International as a promising source. The only other person who'd dealt with the lady was Wesley, the taxi driver with the tuneful voice. *What the hell?*

I thought. *He sounded bright, and she might have said something useful.* I had another glass of wine and a sandwich and rang Bernie at Redline, who told me that Wesley would be signing off at the depot about three o'clock. He'd tell Wesley I'd be there for a quick talk, but he warned me not to be late because Wesley would be buggered after his shift and wouldn't wait around.

Wesley was a Tongan, short and wide with a bushy black beard. He rubbed at the small of his back and flexed his shoulders as he spoke. 'Remember the lady well. Very upset, she was.'

'How d'you mean?'

'Crying. That's not so unusual there, you understand.'

'What? Where?'

'Where I picked her up—there in Mona Vale Road. Outside the place.'

'What place?'

'Some kind of institution for, you know, people with something wrong—mental cases, spastics and like that. Very sad place. But they treat them real good there. Looks very pricey—nice grounds, nurses in uniform, all that. But the visitors don't come away laughing. That all, brother? I'm bushed.'

I thanked him and Bernie and drove away with more questions in my mind but also some of the answers, maybe. I stopped at the post office in Glebe and located the Terrey Hills Nursing Clinic in Mona Vale Road in the phone book. Then I called in at the surgery of Ian Sangster, who is a doctor and a friend, and a lover of intrigue. I waited while Ian disposed of two patients and then went into his light, airy consulting room. Ian is a jokester: he poured two measures of single malt whisky into medicine glasses and lifted his in a toast. 'Good health.'

We drank and I told him what I wanted.

'It's a top-class joint. Very good, very expensive. But it's for serious cases, Cliff. I doubt you're ready for it yet.'

'You'll beat me to it if you keep knocking this stuff back the way you do,' I said. 'When will you know anything?'

'Tomorrow, late morning. I'll call you.'

That left me with another evening to kill. I went to a fitness centre in Balmain and hung around until someone turned up willing to play table-tennis with me. The deal is, you hire one of the squash courts, a table, net and balls for an hour at an exorbitant price, and play as hard as you can to get your money's worth. I played against a police sergeant from the Balmain station and let him win, four matches to three. In my business, you never know when a friendly police sergeant might come in handy.

I went into the office in the morning, paid a few bills, requested payment for the third time from a faithless client and generally waited for Ian's call. I plugged in a recording device and activated it when I heard Ian's voice on the line.

'Cliff,' he said. 'I've got good news and bad news. There's a patient named Carl Hammond who fits your bill. Aged twenty-three; the contact is his sister, Valerie Ursula . . .'

'That's it,' I said.

'Poor chap's in a very bad way.'

'What is it?'

'It's called kernicterus. This is the most severe case to come the way of the people there, and the worst I've ever heard of. Put simply, it's brain damage caused by jaundice at birth. The baby's red blood cells are broken down to such a degree that the liver can't cope with the by-products and this stuff called biliruben is released into the bloodstream. It's bile, essentially, a sort of stain that causes brain damage. Are you making notes or something?'

'I'm recording it, Ian. Go on.'

Sangster cleared his throat. 'Well, as I say, in a severe case a part of the brain is damaged and you get deafness, palsy, loss of coordination. Usually, in a case this bad, the baby is born prematurely and dies. That's called hydrops fetalis, for your information. Carl Hammond should have died. Some freak of nature kept him alive. A cruel freak, I'd call it. Not everyone would agree.'

'Can he . . .?'

'To almost any question you can put, the answer is no.'

'*Jesus.*'

'Not around when he was needed. I'm sorry, mate. This is grim stuff. He's there until he dies which could be tomorrow or ten years away. He requires complete care. The fees must be astronomical. Is that all you need?'

'Yes. No. What causes it?'

'The Rhesus factor.'

'What's that?'

'God, you laymen are so ignorant. No wonder we get so much money. It's an incompatibility between the mother's blood group and that of the foetus. The mother's metabolism sort of creates antibodies against the foetus, which pass through the placenta and fuck everything up. Get on to it early and you can do a transfusion and avoid the whole mess. Not in this case.'

'Why not?'

'Sorry. I don't know. It's a chance in a thousand sort of thing. Harder to detect twenty-odd years ago than now.'

I thanked him and rang off. I wound back the tape and played the conversation through again. Then I got out a dictionary and looked up some of the words while I made notes. I had an answer to one question now, at least—what Valerie Hammond did with her money. And, remembering her outcry on the phone, I had inklings of other questions and other answers. I resisted the impulse to go out for a drink before attempting to call Valerie Hammond. The only number I had was at work. Maybe she hadn't gone in today. I was almost hoping she hadn't when I heard her voice, crisp and confidence-inspiring, on the line.

'Valerie Hammond.'

She'd pulled herself together and sounded in better emotional shape than me. But what do you say? How do you tell someone you know their secrets and their nightmares? I tried to keep my voice level and calm, and I spoke very quickly. 'Ms Hammond, I don't want to distress you, but I know about your brother and your problem. I'm working for Mr Adamo, but I want to help you. Please talk to me. Please don't hang up.'

I heard the sharp intake of breath, could sense the struggle for control. 'I have to tell you I'm taking Valium which is the only reason I'm able to talk to you like this. What do you want, Mr Hardy?'

'To talk to you for a few minutes, face to face. If what I have to say doesn't make any sense to you I'll back off, report to Mr Adamo that I couldn't find you.'

'Very well. If it'll get rid of you. I don't mean to be rude, but you're a violent man.'

'I'll meet you outside your office building. We can talk as we walk. Play it by ear.'

'Did you follow me from work yesterday?'

Uncomfortable question, but it felt like time to play everything straight with her. 'Yes. I hope I didn't hurt your friend.'

'He's all right. He . . . he's just sharing the rent with me. It's an arrangement. I'm not . . . oh, what does it matter?'

This response was my first glimmer of hope; the first indication that she had some awareness of things outside the prison of her problems. 'In an hour, Ms Hammond?'

'Yes. I'll see you in an hour, Mr Hardy.'

She was on time and so was I. I walked up to her and we shook hands. It seemed like the right thing to do. She was wearing the same clothes she had on yesterday. So was I, as it happened. We walked along Bent Street past the government buildings, in the direction of the Stock Exchange. There were very few people about. We walked slowly. She said that she hoped this interview would be brief.

'Were you fond of Robert Adamo?' I asked.

'Very,' she said. 'Very, very fond. That was the trouble. I hadn't ever allowed myself to feel as much for anyone before. It was a mistake.'

'Why?'

'Robert wanted to marry me and for us to have children. I can't possibly do that, and you know why.' She quickened her pace slightly and spoke more quickly, as if she wanted to get the talk over. 'Oh, I know he loved me and he might have agreed not to have children. But that wouldn't have been fair on him. Or I might have weakened, or . . . or there might have been an accident. Anyway, my first duty is to Carl. I should never have got involved with Robert. He's too intense, too . . . good. His hiring you proves how serious he was. It was an awful, cruel thing for me to do.'

'I know this is painful for you, Ms Hammond, but I'd be glad if you could just answer a few questions. Why do you say you can't have children?'

Her high heels tapped faster. 'Because there is severe mental and physical disability in my genes.'

'Who told you that?'

'I didn't have to be told. Take a look at my brother, Mr Hardy.'

'Who told you?'

'My mother.'

'Did you ever enquire yourself about his condition, ask a doctor . . .?'

'No. I love Carl, strange as it may seem. I just want to make sure he's as happy as he can be. That's all. That's my life.'

'When did your mother die?'

'Six years ago. She left Carl in my charge.'

We'd reached a row of benches outside a new steel and glass tower. I steered her towards one that was shaded by a tree growing in a large wooden box. 'Sit down, Ms Hammond.'

She sat. The tension in her body was visible in every line; also the slight buffer zone created by the Valium between her and the world. On close inspection, she was a little too heavy-featured to be really good-looking, but she was impressive and there was energy and intelligence behind her sadness. 'I can't imagine what you have to say to me,' she said.

'Your mother lied to you,' I said. 'I suppose she was afraid that if you led a full, normal life you'd neglect your brother. She told you a very cruel lie. Perhaps she was ashamed.'

'That's impossible! My mother was never ashamed of anything. She was . . . was immensely strong.'

'I imagine so. Nevertheless, the disability your brother suffers has nothing to do with genetics, at least as far as you're concerned.'

'What do you mean?'

I had to resort to my notes, but I pride myself that I gave it to her clearly and accurately. I explained the medical terms and stressed that the whole Rhesus tragedy could be easily averted by today's technology. She sat perfectly still and absorbed it all. Tears were running down her face by the time I'd finished. She pulled a tissue from her leather shoulder bag and blotted the tears. Through all the distress her mind was razor sharp. 'If what you say is true, how is it that I was born normal and Carl had this terrible thing?'

'I'm not very sure of my ground here,' I said. 'It could be a matter of chance, but if not, I think you know the answer.'

'Different fathers?'

I nodded. 'And the reason for your mother's behaviour. Guilty people can be strong and vice versa. When did your father die?'

'A few years after Carl was born. They were very unhappy, my mother and father. They fought terribly. I was very young and didn't understand much. I thought it was because of Carl, or the money. But perhaps . . .'

She was sobbing now. I put my arm around her shoulders, and she rested her head against me. 'You've got a lot to think about,' I said. 'Most of it's very painful, but not all. You don't have to think of yourself as cursed or tainted. I don't want to push things, but Adamo's a good man. I don't see many, but I recognise one when I do. I think you'd find him understanding and sympathetic . . .'

She lifted her head and sniffed. 'He's very smart, too, isn't he?'

I remembered Adamo's firmness of purpose, his confidence that he could set things right if he just got a little help. 'Smart enough to run a small business profitably,' I said. 'I'm here to tell you that's tough. And smart enough to be in love with you and to hire me. Yes, I'd say he's pretty bright.'

THE HOUSE OF RUBY

From *Burn, and Other Stories* (1993)

'Good afternoon, sir,' the woman behind the table said. 'My name is Marcia. Do you want someone in particular, or a special service?'

'In a way,' I said. 'I'd like to see Ruby.'

Marcia was a nice-looking woman, thirtyish, with short curly hair and a humorous expression. The fact that her ruffled blouse was open almost to the waist and her make-up would have looked garish out of the dim orange light was to be expected. This was the House of Ruby, massage parlour and relaxation centre in Darlinghurst Road, Kings Cross, and the woman behind the table wasn't selling raffle tickets. She pressed a red button on the desk. The blue button, I knew, summoned two or three women in various states of undress. The red one, appropriately, summoned Ruby.

'Cliff, my love, you came.'

'Once or twice, Ruby,' I said. 'It's good to see you looking so well.'

Ruby is about fifty, and carries a lot of flesh on a large frame, but she carries it with style. Her hair is red and luxuriant, like her lipstick. She was wearing a purple silk dress that outlined her charms rather than displayed them. The dress was short, however; Ruby has great legs and those she displays. She reached for me with her ruby-ringed fingers and red-painted nails. 'Just you come in here, love, and I'll give you a drink and tell you a story that'll make you weep.'

'Private eyes don't weep,' I said.

Ruby burst into laughter, and I heard the woman behind the desk snigger a little too. Definitely the place to go to be appreciated for your wit, Ruby's. She took me through a door and down a short passage to her private suite, which is fitted out like an erotic dream—silk and velvet hangings, black and red decor, pornographic paintings and photographs. Ruby poured generous measures of Scotch into tall glasses and added ice. 'Put you in the mood, Cliff?'

'Sure,' I said. 'But it's just a bit overdone. I kind of get out of the mood from having been put in the mood, if you follow.'

She nodded. 'Me too, but it's what the punters like.'

I lifted my glass and drank down some good, nicely iced Scotch. 'How's Kathy?'

'Fine. Two kids.'

Kathy was Ruby's daughter, who I'd found one time after she'd run off on learning that her mother was a whore and a madam. Kathy was a convent-educated teenager at the time, and I'd taken her back to my place, where my tenant, Hilde Stoner, and I had talked to her for several days about life and the world. I'd shown her a bit of it, in the Cross and around Darlinghurst, and she got a different perspective on things. She'd been her mother's greatest supporter ever since, and Ruby was a friend of mine for life. I could've fucked my brains out for free forever if I'd been that way inclined. As it was, I'd availed myself of Ruby's services but twice, in moments of distress.

'So, what's the problem, Ruby?' I said. 'The girl out front looks nice—you seem to be keeping up your usual standards. Are you still catering to the taste for older women?'

Ruby drank deeply, which was a worrying sign; she usually sipped for a while and then forgot she had a drink. 'Of course. Best decision I ever made. You get a better class of client and a more mature employee—less trouble all round. And Marcia out there? She's the best. Professional woman, in the true sense of the word. She's a doctor, would you believe? Runs a small practice part-time and does an elegant job here as well.'

'So what is it? AIDS? Fred Nile picketing you?'

She waved her hand dismissively; the red stones in her rings glittered. 'AIDS. Nonsense. As safe here as in Turramurra. Safer. Not that it hasn't hurt business. All the publicity, I mean. But no, nothing like that. Sammy Weiss's trying to put the squeeze on me.'

'Sammy? Never.'

'Can you believe it? He owns the building, or most of it. I know that, and he knows that I know. So I pay him rent, on a lease. Fine.'

'He's putting up the rent?'

'No. He wants a percentage of my earnings, and he wants it to appear on the books as rent. He's negatively geared all over the bloody place. It's no skin off his arse, but I simply can't afford it. Not a hike of two hundred per cent.'

I'd been sinking down in my velvet chair a little, lulled by the Scotch and thinking the story wouldn't have much bite. Now I sat up. 'You mean double?'

'No, I do not mean double.' Ruby finished her drink in a swallow. 'I don't know what I mean. All I know is he wants the rent to go up this month by as much again as it is now and by that much again next month. What's that? He calls it two hundred per cent.'

'I'd call it treble,' I said.

'I call it ruin. Will you talk to him, Cliff? I pay that and I've got to run this place like a cattle yard—use kids, junkies, all that shit. I'd rather close up, and that'd put some decent women out of work. And I'm helping Kathy's husband get started as a nurseryman. I've got commitments. You know Sammy. I can't think what's got into him. He used to be a reasonable guy. Will you talk to him, Cliff? Please? I'm asking as a friend, and I'm paying. This is a business expense.'

I didn't like to see Ruby knocking back the Scotch as if she needed it, or the desperation in her eyes, so I said I'd talk to Sammy. That night I had nothing much else to do after I'd finished escorting a big gambler from the club in Edgecliff to the night safe in Woollahra, so I went looking for Sammy. Night is the only time to see him; that's when he eats dinner at the Jack Daniels Bar 'n' Grill and pays visits to several strip-joint nightclubs in which he has an interest. What he does in the daytime I don't know—sleeps or counts money, maybe both.

I found him in the Skin Cellar, a sleazoid hole in the wall around the corner from one of his classier joints in the Cross. The place was crowded, and the clientele was drunk and rowdy and giving the pre-owned blonde on the pocket-handkerchief stage a bad time.

'Get 'em off!'

'If I can't touch 'em, I don't believe 'em.'

'Shake it, gran'ma!'

The music howled deafeningly, a clatter of drums and electric machines. Through the smoke I spotted Sammy sitting at a table with two other men. This was normal. Sammy has a wife named Karen, pronounced Kah-ren, who keeps him on a tight, monogamous leash. What wasn't normal was the reaction of one of Sammy's companions as I pushed my way through the smoke and the drunken lurching that passed for dancing. He pushed back his chair and stood—thin and dark like me, but

188 centimetres, giving him that uncomfortable two and a half centimetre advantage and with an acne-eaten face to back it up.

'This guy's carrying, Sammy,' he grated.

Observant. I had my licensed Smith & Wesson .38 under my arm, the way the nervous winning gambler liked it. I nodded at Sammy, hoping to bypass the heavy, but he wasn't buying it. I saw the fist just before it hit me and ducked. I hadn't had a drink since mid-afternoon at Ruby's, or I might have been too slow. As it was, I had the adrenalin edge: I let the punch go past and hacked at the guy's shins with my right shoe. I connected and he yelped. He was reaching inside his jacket for something serious when I clipped him on the chin with a half-serious left hook. He was moving the wrong way, into the punch, and it snapped his neck back. That kind of pain makes you think about giving up, and he did. He slumped to the floor and I reached inside his coat, expecting to find a gun. Instead, my fingers closed over the handle of a chunky flick-knife held in a spring-loaded holster. I pulled it out, sprung the blade and dropped the knife on the floor. I brought my heel down hard on it.

'Sammy,' I said, 'what the hell d'you think you're playing at?'

'Don't move a muscle, shithead,' a heavily accented voice said close to my ear. I smelled sweat and aftershave. The other man at the table had slid away and come up behind me while acne-scars had been doing his thing. I stood very still because I could feel something digging into my right kidney and I knew it wasn't a broom handle. He dug the gun in some more and then moved it away. Professional. You know it's there, but you don't know precisely where. And it was no good thinking, *He won't kill me, not in a public place*. Above that racket a shot from a small calibre pistol wouldn't be heard, and a bullet in the leg is not a laughing matter.

'Sammy,' I said, 'this isn't your style.'

But Sammy Weiss seemed to be enjoying himself. His smooth, pasty face, normally fairly good-natured as long as things were going his way, was set in a scowl that he seemed to have grown used to. Sammy had put on weight since I'd last seen him, and lost some hair. But he was more snappily dressed and more carefully groomed—silk tie, shirt with a discreet stripe, lightweight double-breasted suit.

He snapped his fingers and his buffed nails gleamed briefly. 'Toss him out, Turk. Don't do no damage but, he's got a nasty nature.'

'Sammy . . .'

The pistol dug back in again, and the man I'd dropped was starting to get to his feet. Turk had all the moves; he jerked my elbow around, and you have to give when that happens. He prodded again and I found myself pushing through the crowd towards the door. I was confused by Sammy's behaviour, but not completely thrown. Before we got to the door I side stepped and watched Turk move automatically in the same direction. I dug my knee into his balls and reached for the gun, but he'd put it away and my move threw me a little off-balance. He recovered fast and stepped back—a medium-sized, dark guy, strongly built with a bald head and a thick, compensatory moustache. Stand-off. People were starting to notice us now.

'See you again, Turk,' I said.

He spat at my feet and backed away into the crowd.

I was still mulling it over the next morning—the change in Sammy Weiss from lair businessman who liked to flirt with the rough element to crime boss with minders—when Sammy's brother, Benjamin, knocked and walked into my office.

'I heard what happened last night, Cliff.'

'I hope you heard it right, Benjamin,' I said. No one ever called him Benny. He was an accountant, very straight.

'I heard there was a gun and a knife. Sammy's lost his mind.' He put his hat on my desk, lowered his small, neat body into a chair and ran a tired hand across his worried face. Benjamin is older, smaller and quieter; the brothers look alike only around the eyes, where intelligence is suggested.

'That's how it looked to me. What's going on?'

'First, would you mind telling me what you wanted to see him about?'

That's Benjamin, always getting the figures in the columns first. I told him about Ruby and Sammy.

'That's a good, steady business. The property's being well cared for, and it's appreciating. Things being the way they are, Ruby could probably handle a modest rent hike, but nothing like this.'

'I agree. What's got into your brother?'

'He's a changed man. Dresses differently, struts around with those two hoods. He's drinking and gambling more, acting the big shot. But all this is so heavy-handed, dealing with you and Ruby like that. If he tries it on the wrong people . . .' Benjamin shook his head and looked even more worried.

I knew what he meant. There were people in Sydney who'd take Sammy and Turk and the other guy apart just for fun. 'There must be a reason,' I said. 'A woman?'

'Come on. You know what sort of chain Karen keeps him on. No, I guess he's just bored. That plus the piece that appeared in *Sydney Scene* about him.'

'You've got me.'

'It's an insignificant little shoestring mag, run by a couple of queers. They did an article on Sydney's crime czars and somehow Sammy got a mention and a quote. Now he thinks he's Mr Big.'

'Jesus. That's dangerous.'

Benjamin leaned forward in his chair. 'I love Sammy, Cliff. He's a good man basically, always been very generous with me.

He's a good husband and father. I don't want to see him get into trouble. Could you . . .'

'Hold on. We're talking conflict of interest here.'

'I don't see why.' His small hands came up and he started ticking points off on his fingers. 'One, Ruby wants Sammy off her back; two, I want Sammy to wake up to himself; three, you'd like to get your own back on Turk.'

'Who says so?'

Benjamin smiled. 'I know you, Cliff.'

I thought about it, but not for long. I had to admit it was an interesting problem. Tough, but not too tough. And I had an affection for Sammy dating back to the days of the Victoria Street green bans, when he was on the side of the angels. Good business, as it turned out: he made money on his houses in the street. Still. 'What're Sammy's weaknesses?' I asked.

Benjamin didn't need his fingers. 'First, he's afraid of Karen; second, he's a hypochondriac.'

'That's interesting. Who's his doctor?'

'He never goes near them. He doses himself for his imagined illnesses. He tells me about them all the time, but I'm sure he's as healthy as a horse. So far.'

'Leave it with me, Benjamin, along with a couple of hundred bucks. I'll see if I can work something out.'

Benjamin wrote me a cheque. I gave him a receipt. He put on his hat and went, leaving me to do some thinking, of which two hundred dollars buys a fair bit.

Marcia was behind the table when I dropped in at Ruby's that afternoon. She had on another plunging blouse, and I had the feeling that the parts of her body I couldn't see weren't warmly clothed either.

'Ruby?' she said.

'No. I'd like to talk to you, doctor.'

She smiled, and I could see humorous lines under the make-up. 'Ruby's been chattering. I have to say she cheered up a bit after she saw you yesterday. She's been very down.'

'Do you know why?'

She shook her head and the jaunty, short hair bounced 'No. This is an excellent establishment, and business seems to be good. You're not a policeman, are you?'

'Private enquiries. My name's Cliff Hardy.'

It surprised us both that we shook hands.

'What do you want to talk to me about?'

For the second time that day I told the story of Ruby's troubles. This time there was a second strand—the metamorphosis of Sammy Weiss. Marcia listened intently, asking one or two questions. We had to break once while she dealt with a customer—for Henrietta and the special—but when I finished I felt as if I'd clarified a few things for myself as well as shared the problem with a good thinker.

'I like Ruby very much,' Marcia said. 'And I want to help. How can I? You haven't told me this for nothing.'

'You practise somewhere? You've got a surgery?'

'Hardly that. The front room of a terrace in Stanley Street.'

'That'll do. Is there something we could slip Sammy to give him the symptoms of a venereal disease—fever, discharge and so on?'

She took a deep, very distracting breath. I tried to sneak a look at her legs under the table. Well, it was that kind of a situation. 'Yes, there is,' she said. 'Cantharides'd do it.'

'What's that?'

'Spanish fly. Take enough, and you feel you're pissing razor blades.'

'What about . . . discharge?'

She shook her head. 'Harder. Massive vitamin C'd produce stains.'

'But no serious damage.'

She shook her head. 'Not in the short term.'

'How does it come, this stuff?'

'Granules. They're rather bitter.'

'Sammy has a couple of long blacks with his brother every morning and after work.'

'Three days,' Marcia said. 'Four at the most.'

I spoke to Benjamin in his office, which was a flat in a pre-war building in Riley Street, another of Sammy's holdings.

'A doctor and she's a whore? What's the world coming to?'

'Tell yourself it's getting more interesting,' I said. 'It works for me. All you have to do is slip this stuff into Sammy's espresso. Couple of days later you tell him he's looking terrible and offer to help. Make sure he takes a lot of vitamin C. Be subtle. If that doesn't work, be direct.'

Benjamin agreed to do it. Three days later he was on the phone to me. 'Sammy's desperate,' he said. 'I can't bear to see it. What's next?'

I gave him the telephone number and the address in Stanley Street.

'How am I supposed to know these symptoms?'

I'd done some checking on Benjamin in the quiet hours. It's always wise to check on a co-conspirator. There was more to him than met the eye. He had a personal interest in some of Sammy's assets, and he was not unknown at the House of Ruby. 'Benjamin,' I said, 'if your wife is the only woman you've ever shtupped, I'm a Dutchman.'

He disposed of that with a quiet cough. I repeated the address and told him not to worry. He called me at home that night.

'Tomorrow at 2 p.m., as planned,' he said.

'Good. Will he be alone?'

'Of course. You think he wants anyone to know about this? What's the matter, Cliff? Are you afraid of Turk?' It was the first time I'd heard an edge on Benjamin's voice since this business began. I was glad of it; it meant that he wanted Sammy straightened out as much as my other client did.

'Turk'll come later,' I said. 'Let's get this done first.'

Sammy turned up in a taxi at Marcia's terrace five minutes early. He was as nervous as a schoolboy buying condoms; he glanced up and down the street and then stared at the house. That must have been a comfort: Marcia's place had a neat, tiled frontage, just the right amount of greenery and a confidence-inspiring brass knocker. I was watching from the balcony. Sammy knocked. I scurried down the stairs and took up my position with the camera behind the screen in the front room. Marcia, wearing a short skirt, very high heels and a starched white lab coat, jotted down Sammy's details on a card. She arched a plucked eyebrow once, presumably at some blatant lie of Sammy's. I was alarmed; although her make-up was much toned down for the event, I was afraid she might overdo things. She didn't. Her instruction to Sammy to take off his pants was clinical. Sammy was so embarrassed he shut his eyes when she examined him. This allowed Marcia to open the lab coat. I had the silent camera whirring the whole time: Sammy's flaccid dick in Marcia's hands, the lacquered nails showing clearly; Marcia, her breasts dropping forward out of a lacy black bra under the starched white fabric and her hand clasped around Sammy's balls; Sammy, bent over, his underpants around his ankles, and Marcia behind him with the coat shrugged back on her shoulders, muscular thighs showing under the mini-skirt and her rubber-gloved finger probing Sammy's arsehole.

'Get dressed, Mr Jones,' Marcia said.

Sammy did, with relief. Marcia stripped off the gloves, washed her hands in a bowl and dried them on a white towel. Sammy sat on a plastic chair. I could see the sweat standing out around his receding hairline. Marcia picked up Sammy's card and made a few notes. She'd buttoned up the lab coat and assumed a prim, professional expression.

'Well, doctor?' Sammy said.

'You have nothing to worry about, Mr Jones. Your condition is the result of a dietary irregularity—lack of calcium, principally. Do you drink much milk?'

The gratitude and pleasure on Sammy's face was childlike. 'Never touch the stuff.'

'You've built up an imbalance in your body chemistry. I recommend milk and goat's cheese, also green vegetables. As much as you can get down.' Marcia scribbled on a prescription pad.

'Sure thing. And . . .?' Sammy said.

Marcia tore off the sheet. 'These pills. Twice a day before meals.'

'You mean three times a day.'

'No. Skip lunch. You should eat only a light breakfast and a high calcium dinner. No meat.'

'Pasta?'

'Light on the oil.'

Sammy jumped to his feet and thrust his manicured hand at Marcia's middle. 'Thank you, doctor. Thank you.'

'Here's your prescription. Have you got your Medicare card?'

'Let's make it cash,' Sammy said.

Benjamin and I had agreed that there was no point in lying, no working through go-betweens. We didn't want Sammy worried out of his mind. I arrived at Benjamin's office by arrangement late the following day to find the two brothers drinking coffee. Sammy said it was the first decent coffee he'd had in days. Benjamin didn't say anything. Sammy was expansive and ready to apologise for our misunderstanding of a few nights back.

I cut him off and spread the photographs out on the desk beside his coffee cup. I'm no artist of the lens, but the pictures were eloquent enough. Marcia looked delicious in her unfastened coat, Sammy's closed eyes could be taken for transports of ecstasy, and so on. Sammy looked at the photos and slowly reddened from his soft chin to his retreating hairline. He looked across the desk at Benjamin and his eyes were moist.

'You set me up. Your own brother.'

'It was for your own good, Samuel. Believe me, your own good, and mine and everybody's.'

'Your own brother.'

'I'm not your brother, Sammy,' I said, 'but I am your friend, or I can be if you play ball.'

'What's the rules?' Sammy said softly.

Benjamin got up and took the coffee pot off the warmer. He poured some more into Sammy's cup and filled a cup for me.

'First, you lay off Ruby. Leave her rent alone, don't hassle her in any way. Meet any reasonable requests she has as a good tenant.'

'And?'

'You stop pissing around with hoods like Turk. Stop acting the big shot.'

'Attend to business,' Benjamin said.

I sipped some of the terrific coffee. 'Exactly.'

'Or?' Sammy said.

'I take the pictures to Karen along with the doctor's report on you—that you presented for a suspected venereal disease and so on.'

Sammy snarled, 'Doctor!'

I said, 'She *is* a doctor, Sammy, and she gave you the straight goods. There's nothing wrong with you. You took a few doses of Spanish fly, which caused you a few temporary problems. That's all.'

The cloud that had been gathering on Sammy's brow lifted. 'You mean it? That woman really is a doctor?'

'Sure,' I said. 'I just got your urine tests back. You're clean.'

Sammy drank his coffee in one gulp. The flush in his face receded and he grinned. Then he exploded into laughter. 'You guys,' he said. 'You fuckin' guys. You finally get me to go to a doctor. Me, scared shitless of doctors. And I'm okay?'

I nodded. 'Sound as a bell. Sammy, while you're laughing, I can't quite see why you were worried. I mean, you haven't stepped out of line, have you?'

Sammy looked at his brother. 'You knew, didn't you?'

Benjamin nodded. 'I knew the scheme'd work, Cliff. Sammy worries about toilet seats, mosquitoes, knives and forks in restaurants . . .'

'You can catch things,' Sammy chuckled as he spoke.

It was time to cut through the hilarity. 'Okay, Sammy,' I said. 'I'm glad you're happy. We did you a favour, fine. But the terms still apply. Get ahold of yourself, or Karen makes your life a living hell. I don't need to spell it out, do I?'

Sammy shook his head; suddenly glumness enveloped him. 'It's not that easy.'

'How so?' Benjamin said.

Sammy waved his hand and it was almost as if he was saying goodbye to buffed nails and shaped cuticles. 'It's Turk,' he said. 'He's kinda . . . pressuring me. You know?'

'Don't worry about Turk,' I said.

A little checking turned up something odd and interesting about Turk. He didn't have a permanent place of residence; instead, he moved around a circuit of city hotels, staying two or three weeks at a time in one place after another. Not five-star hotels, but not fleapits either. The sorts of places I like to stay in myself, and where I stick out-of-town clients. Spending some money on the street and using the phone, I located his current hostelry, the Sullivan in Elizabeth Street, where I happened to know the security man.

Bert Loomis is an ex-cop, ex-bank security man, ex- quite a few things. He's fifty-five and looks every minute of it, especially around the eyes, which have seen most of the dirty things there are to see. I judged that fifty dollars would be about right, and it was.

'Fifteen minutes, Hardy,' Loomis said. I noticed that he didn't touch the knob, just slipped the card in the slot and edged the door open with his knee.

'Right,' I said. 'Where'll you be?'

'Nowhere.'

He jerked his head; I went into the suite and heard the door close behind me. I had to work fast, and Turk made it easy. He lived light—basic toilet articles in the bathroom, clothes in the closet and drawers. Condoms, a vibrator and pornographic material in a bedside cabinet. Beer and wine in the bar fridge, hard liquor on top. Two suitcases, empty. Dirty clothes in a heap in the corner of the little balcony room that overlooked the park. The drawer in the solid writing desk was locked and the Sullivan didn't run to a security safe for guests. I picked the lock and emptied the drawer out on the bed. Personal papers, money matters—bank books, cheque books, statements, bills from a firm of accountants, three passports.

I checked my watch. Twelve minutes. Time was up. I turned on the radio and dumped a drawer full of underwear onto the floor, where it could be seen from the doorway. Then I moved across to the door, opened it and left it propped open with the toe of one of Turk's high-heeled boots. According to the passports, Konstanides/Lycos/Mahoud measured 183 centimetres—he'd looked taller in the Skin Cellar and the boots explained why. I stood inside the bathroom, two metres from the doorway, with my .38 Smith & Wesson at the ready. I was there because I knew Bert Loomis couldn't resist a doublecross or a dollar.

Turk was quiet, but I could sense and smell him. He edged through the door, and I could imagine him standing in the short hallway, hearing the radio, looking at the mess on the floor. I could feel his tension. I stepped out with the .38 levelled at 150 centimetres. Turk was fast: he saw me, ducked, pulled out his own gun and came on. But the round hole staring at him had held his attention for just long enough, and I had the advantages of height and readiness; I moved aside, reached forward and clubbed his bald head with my metal-loaded fist. The barrel and trigger guard tore his skin, and the blow almost stunned him. His knees gave and I chopped at his right wrist, bringing my left hand down hard and bunched. He dropped his gun. I hit him between the eyes with my left and felt the knuckles protest. He fell forward and I kneed him in the chest as he came down.

After that, there was no fight in him. I pulled him into the bedroom and bound his ankles and wrists with four striped silk neckties from his closet. Bert Loomis put his head through the door, and I pointed my gun at him and he went away. Then I called the Immigration Department's investigations branch and told them I had an illegal immigrant in custody—an individual with multiple passports, multiple bank accounts, several driver's licences and a concealed weapon.

I had a beer from Turk's fridge while I waited for the Immigration boys. Turk and I didn't speak. I showed them the documents and

Turk's gun, and there wasn't a whole lot more to say. Turk's eyes blazed at me as they read him his rights and put the cuffs on.

'You shouldn't have spat at me, Turk,' I said as they packed up his belongings. 'I really didn't like it at all.'

Sammy Weiss was as relieved to get Turk off his back as he was to learn that he didn't have the pox or anything else. All he had to worry about was the photos, and I set his mind at rest about them.

'All you have to do, Sammy,' I said, 'is leave Ruby alone and behave yourself. Listen to Benjamin, do what he says. In six months, if you toe the line, I'll give you the pictures.'

We were in the Bar Calabria, drinking coffee. Sammy was wearing a quiet suit and tie and looking hurt. 'You don't trust me.'

'How do you spell it?' I said. 'Deal?'

'Deal. Really a doctor, huh?'

Benjamin was pleased and insisted on paying me over and above the two hundred retainer. He offered to do any accounting I needed free of charge. Ruby paid me as well—a couple of days' work, and expenses, such as my payment to Marcia, and for film and developing. It was a nice piece of business. After I'd collected the cheque and a drink and an enthusiastic kiss from Ruby, I stopped at the table by the door. Marcia was painting her nails and reading the *Independent Monthly*.

'You were great,' I said. 'Thanks.'

She looked up and blew on a wet nail. 'My pleasure. Anything else I can do for you?'

MEETING AT MASCOT

From *Forget Me If You Can* (1997)

I got drunk at Glen Withers' wedding and I got drunk pretty often after that without needing any excuse. I was late coming into the office more days than not, couldn't quite manage to return calls and cope with a hangover at the same time, and business began to suffer. I botched a summons-serving or two and that avenue of funds started to dry up. I was irritable, couldn't be bothered eating properly and lost weight. The cat left and didn't come back. There were days when I neglected to shower and shave, neglected to eat and the only thing I didn't neglect to do was find something to drink by mid-morning.

It was getting towards eleven o'clock and I was congratulating myself on not yet having had a drink, wondering if I could last until noon and doubting it, when a man walked into my office. I disliked him on sight, which is a sign of the way I was feeling. He was middle-height with a bulging beer gut, a high colour and not much sandy hair brushed across a pink scalp. His flabby face was scraped clean and he'd put on an aftershave that smelled like overripe pineapples. He wore a light blue summer suit with a white shirt, no tie, and he'd let the lapels of his shirt creep out a bit as if he really wished he was back in the seventies when shirts were opened wide over jacket lapels. He had the gold necklace to fit that style.

He took off his sunglasses and stared at me with pale, piggy eyes. 'Hardy,' he said. 'The private detective?'

I remembered that the filing card I use for a nameplate on the door had fallen off and I hadn't done anything about it. I thought about denying it, saying that Hardy had moved out and that I was the new tenant, but I couldn't summon the energy. 'Right,' I said and left it at that.

His eyes darted around the room. It was Tuesday and I hadn't been in since Thursday. A layer of dust covered the filing cabinets, battered desk and client's chair. When spruced up the decor can have a kind of rough charm; today it looked like stuff left over from a garage sale. He slapped the chair with a newspaper he was carrying and sat down. 'I'm Rex Hindle. I've got a job for you.'

Emotions warred in me. As I say, I disliked the look of him. I also disliked the look of myself. I had two days' growth sprouting, not a pretty sight with all the grey among the black, and I hadn't been near soap or a comb in a while. Anyone who'd want to hire me in that condition wasn't likely to be anyone I'd want to work for. On the other hand, among the junk on my desk were several pressing bills and an over-the-limit credit-card statement. I couldn't afford to be choosy, not right off the bat, anyway. Suddenly I wanted the drink badly and I briefly considered telling him to piss off and tapping the cask. Practicality, tinged with caution, won.

'There are certain kinds of things I don't do, Mr Hindle. Despite appearances.'

'Have to admit I'm fuckin' surprised. I was told you were pretty sharp.'

Now pride took over. I sat up straighter and gave him a keen-eyed look. 'I've been undercover for a while.' I scratched my chin. 'This is all a front.'

He nodded. 'So, you're busy?'

I shook my head and wished I hadn't. I *needed* the drink and three or four Panadols. 'It's finished. I'll be cleaning myself up later. This place too. How can I help you?'

'You do bodyguarding?'

'Sometimes. It depends.'

'I have to go to the airport and meet a couple of guys coming over from the fuckin' Philippines. They don't like me and I don't like them, but we have to talk. I've got some businesses there and things need sorting out. We'll go to the bar, talk and that's it. But I need to show them I'm not some sucker they can push around.'

It sounded manageable but I wasn't some sucker either. 'What sort of businesses?'

'What?'

'What sort of business are you in, in the Philippines?'

'Ferries. I own a couple of ferries. Real fuckin' money-spinners when everything's right.'

'What's wrong?'

He shook his head. 'I'm looking to hire you for a couple of hours, Hardy, not tell you the story of my life. Yes or no?'

'When is this?'

'Tomorrow morning. Plane gets in at ten.'

'What sort of business are you in here?'

'Jesus. I think I've come to the wrong place.'

I shrugged, almost happy to be out of it. 'Suit yourself.'

He half-rose from the chair, then settled back. 'Fuck it, they tell me you're good. Taxis. I own a couple of taxis. I even drive myself if one of the lazy bastards doesn't show up.'

By now my dislike of Mr Hindle was screwed up about as high as dislike could go. I had only one more card to play. 'Let's say three hours,' I said. 'Four hundred dollars an hour. Half up front, half when we say goodbye.'

He put his sunglasses back on and patted his thin, slicked-over hair. 'Deal,' he said.

I wouldn't say I turned over a new leaf, but I did stir the old one around a bit. I held off until six o'clock for the first drink and didn't lose count after that. I bought a barbecued chicken and some roast potatoes and salad in Glebe Point Road, took it home, put it on a plate and ate it with a knife and fork. The house was a mess and I left it that way but I made the bed before I got into it and after six and a half hours' sleep I got up pretty refreshed. I showered and shaved and put on a clean shirt. I'd got out of the habit of breakfast, but I brewed some coffee and drank it with milk and sugar.

Hindle lived in Hunters Hill so it wasn't much out of his way to pick me up. He drove a pale blue BMW that matched his suit of yesterday. Today he had on a cream number appropriate to the steamy weather. Only trouble was, his shirt was the same colour and there were dark sweat stains under his armpits. He was a lousy driver—too fast, poor reactions, no manners.

'Smartened yourself up a bit?' he said.

I nodded, watching the road the way he wasn't. 'When in Rome.'

'What?'

'Never mind.'

He took the route out through Redfern and I could see his eyes swivelling around as he paid more attention to the people on the pavements than the cars on the road. He blew out a breath as we waited at a light. 'Hot weather sure brings out the toey little virgins, doesn't it?'

A young black woman was crossing front of us. She was skinny with a very short skirt, a skimpy singlet top and very high heels. Hindle watched her avidly. The light changed and he roared away, burning off another car but misjudging the lanes so that he got wedged in and didn't make up any ground. When the going was clear he glanced across at me. 'What's the matter with you? Those Abo sheilas root like rabbits. Not fuckin' gay, are you?'

'That one could've been my granddaughter,' I said.

He laughed. 'Oh, I get it. No offence meant. No one told me you had a touch of the tar brush. Should've seen it, but.'

'Forget it,' I said. I'm an Anglo-Celt mix with a bit of gypsy and French thrown in somewhere, but I was in no mood to explain that to Hindle. Given the way he was driving, my main concern was to get to the airport alive.

We got there about forty-five minutes before the flight was due and Hindle pulled the BMW into a wide spot in the parking station but still almost managed to tickle a car in the next bay. We walked through the terminal. Hindle glanced at a monitor and then at his watch. 'They reckon it's on time but it'd be a fuckin' miracle. What about a quick one?'

I shrugged. I've always liked drinking in airport bars. It gives you the feeling that it could be you who's flying off to some exotic location or coming back with memories and experiences to feed off. Besides, he'd be paying. We went up to the bar, which hadn't been open long and still smelled fresh from the cleaning. There were little bowls of nuts and the air-conditioning was exactly right. In the appropriate company it would be a good place to spend a couple of hours getting quietly mellow. With Hindle, twenty minutes would be ample.

'What'll you have, Hardy?'

'Crown Lager.'

'Piss.' To the barman he said, 'I'll have a double Jack D with ice.'

The drinks came and Hindle paid with a fifty-dollar note; the barman struggled to make the change. I saw that Hindle had smaller bills in his wallet but the gesture didn't surprise me. I was glad I'd asked for four hundred an hour, sorry I hadn't made it five hundred. We drank and Hindle ate two serves of nuts. He tried to make conversation but I didn't respond. Eventually, like someone who finds comfort in screens, he spun around and gazed at a monitor displaying arrival times.

'What did I tell ya?' he crowed. 'Flight QF 870 from Manila delayed twenty-five fuckin' minutes. Wonder it's not an hour.' He snapped his fingers at the barman. 'Let's go again, buddy. And you might lay out a few more nuts. Drinkin' makes me hungry and eatin' makes me thirsty. Ha-ha.'

The barman did as he was bid, keeping his eyes down. Drinking full-strength beer at ten-thirty in the morning was sliding back towards the habits of the past few weeks, but Hindle was one of those people to make you put up barriers. I was reaching for some nuts when a woman walked into the bar. She wore a white dress and a short black jacket, white high-heeled shoes. She was Asian—long, straight dark hair, high cheekbones, ivory skin. Everything about her appearance was modest and restrained, but behind that was a kind of sexual invitation beyond words, beyond description. My jaw dropped before I collected myself, but the effect on Hindle was alarming. As if on autopilot, he sucked in his gut and firmed his chins, a low roaring sound seemed to come from his chest and little beads of sweat collected on his forehead. He wiped them away with one of the napkins that sat beside the silver trays of nuts.

'Jesus,' Hindle croaked, 'look at that.'

'Drink up. Plane's due in soon.'

He didn't even hear me. He was off in some warm, soft place where dreams came true. The woman sat at a table and the barman sprang into action with nuts and coasters at the ready. The woman smiled up at him, ordered and reached into her leather shoulder bag. The barman returned to his workstation and the woman took out a mobile phone. She seemed to have trouble with it and Hindle slid from his seat.

'Little lady needs an expert's touch,' he said.

It was hard to believe that he'd get anywhere with her, but I knew that confidence in a male was a powerful two-way aphrodisiac, and Hindle was almost secreting it. I watched as he walked across to the woman's table, gut in, glass held casually. She looked nervously up at him, technologically challenged, hitching a ride on the communications highway. I heard her tinkling laugh and his throaty buzz. I had to look away. He put his glass down on her table, sat and took the mobile phone from her. She drained her glass and Hindle signalled to the barman. I drank too, feeling slightly sick, a little dirty. I wondered why I was here, instead of in my car, driving off somewhere to serve a summons, or keeping an eye on a warehouse with faulty wiring and a big insurance cover with Glen likely to call soon and propose dinner or a movie or both . . .

Suddenly, Hindle was up and moving towards the door with the woman. I cursed myself for my inattention and stood up to find the barman almost hovering over me.

'Will you be settling the bill, sir?'

Hit the slowest mover, the daydreamer. Fair enough. 'Yeah,' I said. I pulled a ten-dollar note from my pocket and dropped it on the table. Hindle and the woman had moved to the door and I had the odd illusion that they were dancing.

'Fourteen dollars eighty-five, sir?'

'What?'

'The bill is fourteen dollars eighty-five.'

I threw down a five and headed towards the door, glancing at the monitor as I went—still a couple of minutes to go. Hindle and his companion were twenty metres away, moving towards a telephone. I relaxed and hung back. I had twelve hundred dollars at stake and didn't want to jeopardise it. This beauty was at least an adult and if she wanted to take on a beast it had nothing to do with me. I checked my watch again and that's when I saw two men block my view of Hindle and his companion. I took a quick step forward, then I felt a sharp sting beside my spine and a voice spoke softly, very close to my ear.

'You will move as I direct you. Slowly and calmly, or you are a dead man.'

I believed him. An expert with the right instrument can paralyse or kill you in a split second with scarcely a drop of blood. I don't know much about anatomy, but whatever was sticking into me felt to be in a vital place. I moved as requested, very slowly. The man was slightly behind me so that I couldn't see his face without turning, and turning was something I wasn't going to do. Smaller than me, smelling of tobacco, a soft stepper.

'What's happening?' I said.

'Don't speak please!'

Up ahead I could see that Hindle had two escorts, steering him in much the same way I was being steered. The woman was nowhere in sight. *Idiot,* I thought. *A decoy. Hindle went for it one hundred per cent and you didn't do much better.* We went out of the terminal and the procession continued across the road and into the car park. I felt the sweat run down my neck and I was so sensitised to the tiny pinpoint of pain in my back that I was sure it was still there, even though it probably wasn't. My gliding escort couldn't have a hand that steady. But by the time I'd worked this out we were in the car park with no one paying us any attention. Child's play for this guy to cut me down and roll me under a car. I kept walking, following Hindle and the others towards his BMW.

I was thinking fast but not coming up with anything useful. The two men with Hindle were small, compact types, neatly dressed in suits and wearing dark glasses. Hindle handed over his keys and was bundled into the back of the BMW, one of the men sliding in beside him. The other beckoned me forward. I moved towards the car. The beckoning became an impatient wave and I stooped more than was needed to get into the car. I knew I'd put some distance between myself and the man with the blade and I had room to manoeuvre with the other guy. I was set to spin and start hitting when the car park roof fell in on me.

Things were very blurry after that. I was aware of movement and voices but of only one visual image—a shot of Hindle's terrified face, drained of colour, running with sweat and with the jowls flapping as he shook his head.

The next thing I knew I was stationary and stretched out on my back behind a bush. I felt a leaf fall on my face and twitched away from it. My ears were ringing and when I opened my eyes the light made me shut them straight off. It felt as if I'd run into a wall.

After a while I pulled myself together and managed to sit up. The motivation was water—my throat was lined with bark and coughing detached bits of it and sent them scraping down my gullet. I stared, blinked and stared again. I was under a tree that grew beside a hole filled with sand. Beyond the hole I could see something smooth and green with a stick in the middle of it. I've woken up in some strange places, but behind bushes at the fifteenth green at Kogarah Golf Course has to be one of the strangest.

There were no players in sight. I got to my feet and steadied myself against the tree. A water bubbler was only a few metres away but it took time to get the confidence to make a try for it. I got there, rubbery-legged and sweating. The water was good for every part of me. I gulped it down, swilled it and spat, splashed it on my face, rubbed it into my hair and washed my hands. When I felt mostly human I checked myself over. It was three o'clock—I'd lost almost five hours. Everything else was there—home and office keys, driver's licence, NRMA, Medicare and credit cards, PEA licence. My .38 Smith & Wesson was still in its holster under my arm. I took off my jacket and unstrapped the holster, which was uncomfortable over my sweat-soaked shirt. The movement made me aware of a stiffness and soreness in my left arm. I pushed up my sleeve and saw the puncture mark inside my elbow.

I gave up carrying a wallet years ago, too easy to lose or have lifted. I distribute what money I have around various pockets and I touched them now automatically, not expecting to have been robbed. The right trouser pocket felt fuller than it should have been. I emptied the pocket; in addition to the couple of tens and a five I'd had left after paying for the drinks in the airport bar, I had twelve crisp, new hundred-dollar notes. That's when I knew for certain that Rex Hindle was dead.

I flagged a cab and went to the office, where I cleaned myself up and had a couple of medicinal Scotches. Probably not a good idea on top of whatever dope they'd shot into me, but I was in no mood to care. I sat behind my desk for a minute or two to see if there were any ill effects. All I could feel was the whisky doing me good. I ran through my story in my head and couldn't see any reason not to tell the truth.

The cops at the Kings Cross station don't like me particularly but they tolerate me. I put my story on tape over lousy coffee with Detective Senior Sergeant Kev Ingham, who heard me out, disapproval written all over his craggy face. I even mentioned the twelve hundred dollars.

'Shit, Hardy,' he said as he pressed the OFF button. 'That's one of the vaguest fuckin' statements I've ever heard. The only person you've been able to describe is the woman.'

'They doped me. Want to see the needle mark?'

'No, thanks. But it's a point. You'd better get down to St Vinnie's and get a blood test. I'll give you a chit. That might protect your arse a bit.'

'What d'you mean?'

'You're supposed to make a contract with your clients, right? Remember the fucking law? I didn't hear you mention a contract.'

I downed the dregs of the coffee and wished I hadn't. 'I haven't been at my best.'

'So we've seen, and heard. Your licence is shaky, mate. Get to the hospital and go home. You'll be hearing from us, or someone.'

I got up, feeling capable of making it to the door, just. 'Meaning?'

'I ran your Mr Hindle through the computer before you started burbling. He's known to the authorities, as they say.'

No trace was ever found of Rex Hindle or his BMW, or of the men and the woman who'd dealt with us at the airport. I was found to have a high level of some barbiturate in my blood and to have suffered a minor concussion. A committee that sat periodically to review complaints against PEAs censured me for failing to observe contractual procedures but, in view of my relatively clean record, my licence wasn't withdrawn. I cleaned up my act, knuckled down to some routine jobs and saw them through. I cut down on the grog and got back into playing tennis at the courts in John Street where Lew Hoad had blossomed.

A month later I got a visit from a Commonwealth policeman named Wilensky. I told him everything all over again and he did a lot of nodding and a little tapping on a notebook computer. He seemed quietly pleased and I asked him why.

'Rex Hindle was the ugly Australian personified,' he said. 'His ferries were floating brothels. He trafficked in young women, young men and drugs. He was slime, Mr Hardy. Your failure to protect him has left the world a better place.'

Which didn't make me feel better about myself. I also felt bad about losing Glen Withers and the cat, but I felt okay about the twelve hundred dollars.

BLACK ANDY

From *Taking Care of Business* (2004)

'I'm a literary agent but I'm not ringing to talk to you about your memoirs,' Melanie Fanshawe said quickly. 'A couple of people in the business have told me about your . . .'

'Rudeness?'

'Not at all.' Emphatic refusal. 'This is something quite different. Professional. I can't talk about it on the phone and I'm afraid I can't get to you today. Could you possibly come to me? I'm sorry, that sounds . . . I'm sure you're busy, too.'

She gave me the address in Paddington and suggested five o'clock. Suited me. I knew the area. There was a good pub on a nearby corner where I could have a drink when we finished, whichever way it went.

I was at her door a couple of minutes early. A tiny two-storey terrace described by the real estate sharks as a 'worker's cottage'. The door, with a small plaque identifying the business carried on inside, was right on the street. No gate. One step up. I rang the bell and a no-nonsense buzzer sounded inside.

Heels clattered briefly on a wooden floor and the door opened. Melanie Fanshawe was solidly built, medium-tall, fortyish. She wore a white silk blouse, a narrow bone-coloured mid-calf skirt and low heels. Her hair was dark, wiry and abundant, floating around her head.

'Mr Hardy?'

'Right.'

'Come in. Come through and I'll make some coffee and tell you what this is all about.'

I followed her down a short passage, past an alcove under the stairs where a phone/fax was tucked in. The kitchen was small with a slate floor, eating nook, microwave, half-sink and bar fridge. She pointed to the short bench and seats. 'You should be able to squeeze in there.'

I could, just. 'Small place you've got here.'

She laughed. 'I inherited it from my grandma. She was five-foot-nothing, but I've learned to turn sideways and duck my head.'

'I've got the opposite problem,' I said. 'I've got a terrace in Glebe that's too big for me.'

She boiled a kettle, dumped in the coffee, poured the water and set the plunger. 'How d'you take it?'

'White with two.'

She lifted an eyebrow. 'Really?'

'I'm trying not to be a stereotype.'

She laughed again. 'You're succeeding. They didn't tell me you were funny.'

I made a gesture of modest acceptance as she pushed the plunger down.

'Okay,' she said. 'This is it. I've got a client who's written a book. No, he's writing a book. I've got an outline and the chapter headings and it looks like amazing stuff.'

'Good for him. And good for you.'

She smiled that slightly crooked smile that made you want to like her. 'Yeah, sure. If he lives to finish it.'

I drank some of the excellent coffee. 'Here comes the crunch.'

'You're right. This book tells all there is to know about corruption in Sydney over the past twenty years—up to yesterday. Names, place-names and dates. Everything. It's going to be a bombshell.'

'But it hasn't been written yet.'

'As I said, the outline's there and the early stuff is ready. He's got the material for the rest—tapes, documents, videos. The thing is, as soon as it becomes known that this book's on the way, the author's life is in serious danger.'

'From?'

'Crims, police, politicians.'

I finished the coffee and reached for the pot to pour some more. 'You've only got an outline. Some of these things fizzle. Neddy Smith—'

'Not this one. This is for real. You know who the author is, and he specifically asked for you.'

'I don't follow.'

'As protection.'

'Who are we talking about?'

She drank and poured the little that was left in the pot into her mug. 'Andrew Piper.'

'Black Andy Piper?'

'The same.'

Ex-Chief Inspector Andrew Piper, known as Black Andy, was one of the most corrupt cops ever to serve in New South Wales. He'd risen rapidly through the ranks, a star recruit with a silver medal in the modern pentathlon at the Tokyo Olympics. He was big and good-looking and he had all the credentials—a policeman as a father; the Masonic connection; marriage to the daughter of a middle-ranking state politician; two children: a boy and a girl. Black Andy had played a few games for South Sydney and boxed exhibitions with Tony Mundine. He'd headed up teams of detectives in various Sydney divisions and the number of crimes they'd solved were only matched by the ones they'd taken the profits from. His name came up adversely at a succession of enquiries and he eventually retired on full benefits because to pursue him hard would have brought down more of the higher echelon of the force than anyone could handle.

Melanie Fanshawe looked amused at my reaction to the name. 'I gather you know each other.'

'I've met him twice. The first time he had me beaten up, the second time it was to arrange to pay him blackmail.'

She nodded. 'Doesn't surprise me. Well, he's telling all in this memoir—names, places, dates, amounts of money.'

'Why?'

'Did you know his wife died last year?'

I shook my head.

'She did. Then he was diagnosed with cancer. He says he's found God.'

'I don't believe it.'

'Which of the three?'

'The last. Black Andy is a corrupt bastard, through and through. If Jesus tapped him on the shoulder, Andy'd have one of his boys deal with him out in the alley.'

'He says he's put all that behind him. Cleared himself of all those connections. He wants to tell the truth so he can die in peace.'

My scepticism was absolute. 'Why not just write the book, confess to a priest, die absolved or whatever it is, and turn the royalties over to the church?'

She ticked points off on her fingers. 'One, he's not a Catholic. Some sort of way-out sect. Two, he needs the money—the advance for the book—to pay for the treatments he's having to give him time to finish it.'

'I paid him a hundred grand last year.'

'As I said, he claims to have broken all those connections. No income. Some recent in-house enquiry, well after his retirement, stripped him of his pension. At the time, he didn't care. But it's different now. From what he's told me, he had incredible overheads when the money was coming in—protection, bribes . . .'

'Booze, gambling, women.'

'All that. He makes no bones about it. It promises to be a unique inside account, Mr Hardy. A mega-bestseller. He needs it and, frankly, so do I.'

'How long does he think it'll take?'

'Six weeks, he says.'

'That's a lot of my time and someone's money. Yours?'

She gave me that disarming, crooked smile again. 'No, the publisher's, if I can work it right. The thing is, publishing houses leak to the media like politicians. I'm sure I can get the contract we need for this book, one with all the money bits and pieces built in, but as soon as I get it the news'll flash round the business and hit the media. I've told Andrew that and he says they'll come gunning for him from all directions. That's why he suggested, no, requested, you. Will you do it?'

It was too interesting to resist and I liked her. I agreed to meet Black Andy and talk to him before I made a decision.

'But you're more pro than con?'

'Yeah,' I said. 'I'm intrigued. But we get back to it—six weeks solid is big bucks.'

'I've got a publisher in mind who'll be up for it.'

'What about libel?'

'He'll cope with that as well. He's a goer.'

'Can I see what you've got from Andy already?'

She looked doubtful. 'He asked me not to show it to anyone until I was ready to make the deal, but I suppose you're an exception. I can't let you take it away, though. You'll have to read it here.'

She handed me a manila folder. It held four sheets of paper—the outline of *Coming Clean: The inside story of corruption in Australia.* I read quickly. No names, but indications that the people who would be named included well-known figures in politics, police, the law, media and business, as well as criminal identities. The fourth sheet was a list of chapter headings, with 'Who killed Graeme Bartlett?' as an example. Bartlett had been a police whistle-blower whose murder a few years ago hadn't been solved.

'This is it?'

'I've seen more. He showed it to me on our second meeting but he wouldn't let me keep it. He said it needed more work and he will only hand those chapters over to you. No you, no deal.'

Flattering, but very suspicious. There were harder men than me around in Sydney, plenty of them, but maybe hardness wasn't his priority. If he was genuine about his problem, Black Andy would have known that anyone he hired to protect him was liable to get a better offer. Some of the possible candidates would switch sides at the right price. My dealings with him hadn't been pleasant, but at least we'd understood each other. And perhaps my police contacts were something he thought he could make use of.

We came to terms. We'd only get to the serious contract point if I accepted the assignment. Short of that, for a bit of sniffing around and the initial meeting with Piper, I'd charge her a daily rate as a security consultant to her business.

I rang Piper that night and arranged to meet him at 11 a.m. in two days. I wanted the time to do some research on him and his new-found faith. He wanted to hand over more material to keep Melanie happy and convince me. He gave an address in

Marrickville and I scribbled it down. We were talking about Sunday. Okay by me, I wouldn't be doing anything else just then. Piper's voice hadn't changed, a Bob-Hawkish growl, but I fancied his manner was softer. Maybe my imagination.

I talked to Frank Parker, an old friend and a former Deputy Police Commissioner, and to a couple of serving officers with whom I was on reasonable terms. I found out nothing startling, but got confirmation that Black Andy's pension had been rescinded, that he was widowed and rumoured to be unwell. It's easy enough to put a rumour about. His main henchman, a former cop named Loomis, was in jail on an assault conviction. It wasn't quite what Melanie had said—Piper turning his back on his thug mates—but Loomis would have been his first linc of defence in the old days, and his absence added some credibility to the story.

I heard the hymn-singing inside when I located the address Piper had given me—the sect's meeting hall—and took my seat out of earshot on the other side of the road. Best vantage point, but it was hot and the bus shelter didn't give much shade. I hoped the word of God would end on time.

They filed out, more than a hundred of them, men, women and children, all neatly dressed. A few walked off, most headed for their cars. Among the last out was Black Andy Piper. Dark suit, white shirt, dark tie, despite the heat of the day. He spotted me immediately and beckoned me over. Same old Andy—do as I tell you. I gave it a minute, pretending to wait for the traffic, just to be bolshie.

By the time I'd crossed the road, Piper was standing on his own outside the hall. Maybe Melanie Fanshawe wasn't a good judge of weight, because he'd definitely trimmed down a bit. A hundred kilos, tops. He'd also grown a grey beard.

He looked thinner and older. His black eyes bored into me as I approached, then they drifted away and he seemed almost to smile. Almost.

'Hardy.'

'Piper.'

We didn't shake hands.

'Come in,' he said. 'I want you to meet Pastor Jacobsen.'

We went inside. A man sitting on a plastic chair in the front row of a crowded space turned around as we entered, stood and came towards us.

'Pastor, this is Cliff Hardy. The man I told you about.'

Jacobsen was a bit below average height, and thin. He wore a clerical collar, beige suit and black shoes. Not a good look. His hair was scanty and arranged in an unconvincing comb-over. Big ears, pale face and eyes, long nose, weak chin. His mouth was pink and damp-looking.

'Mr Hardy,' he said in a strong southern US accent. 'I'm honoured to meet you, sir. Well met in Christ.' He held out his hand and I took it. He closed his other hand over our grip and I immediately wanted to break free.

'Mr Jacobsen,' I said.

He released my hand slowly. 'I know Brother Piper puts his trust in you so I'll leave you to your business. Call me any time, Brother Piper.'

'Thank you, Pastor. I'll be at the bible class later this week. Mr Hardy will be my . . . shepherd, I trust.'

'Excellent.' Jacobsen picked up a bible from the lectern and walked away.

'C'mon, Andy,' I said when Jacobsen was out of earshot. 'This is bullshit.'

Piper sank down into a chair. 'Hardy, have you ever heard the saying, "There are no atheists in a slit trench under fire"?'

I sat in the row behind him. 'No, and that'd be bullshit too, because I've been there.'

He sighed and looked weary. 'What place does God have in your miserable life?'

I leaned over him. 'As Michael Caine says in *Alfie*, "A little bit of God goes a very long way with me".'

I'll swear he wanted to tell me to pray, but he held it back. He picked up a manila envelope from the chair next to him and handed it over. 'I have to clear up a bit in here and lock up. I'll see you later, Hardy.'

I drove to Paddington and went into the pub near Melanie Fanshawe's place. Quiet at that time on a Sunday. I bought a beer and used my Swiss army knife to cut away the tape. Chapter One was called 'The Bully' followed by 'The Rookie' and 'The Bag Boy', just as in the chapter list I'd seen. I read quickly. Piper explained how he'd been a bully as far back as he could remember and how a cop at the Police Boys Club had told him he was perfect police material. He named the cop and told how he and several of his colleagues, also named, had recruited Piper and some other boys to form a gang of burglars and car thieves.

He went on to explain how endemic corruption had been in the service despite the enquiries and attempts to clean it up. With his silver medal, rugby and boxing credentials, young Piper came to the attention of two detectives who controlled the flow of money between brothel owners, the police and politicians. Piper became the chief bagman while still a constable. The chapter had detailed information on meetings, amounts of money, bank accounts and, again, names.

'You opened it,' Melanie said as I handed the envelope over.

'Sure, wouldn't you in my position? This isn't a time for good manners. Just be glad I didn't copy it.'

We were on her little balcony, drinking coffee and looking out towards Victoria Barracks. 'You're very serious all of a sudden, Cliff. Is it that hot?'

'It is, if he can back it up. If he can't, it's defamation city.'

'Not our problem right now. What did you think of him?'

'What I've always thought—corrupt, devious.'

'And the minister?'

'I wanted to wipe my hand after we shook.'

She nodded. 'Me too. But he makes a good character in the book. How about the cancer?'

I shook my head. 'Don't know enough about it. He's lost some weight and the beard ages him. I'd like a couple of medical opinions, but we're not going to get them.'

She leaned back in her chair and drew in a breath. She was barefooted, wearing a halter top and loose pants, and her shoulders were tanned and shapely. Her nipples showed through the fabric of her top, and her toenails were painted red. There had been some chemistry between us I'd thought on our first meeting and it was fizzing now.

'Do you sleep with your clients?' she said.

I reached over and twisted her cane chair towards me. I lifted her feet from the floor and let her legs stretch out in my direction. I gripped the arms of her chair and slid it closer.

'No. But my client's more the publisher than you, right?'

The floor was pushing up at my back through the thin futon. I rolled over onto my side, propped, and looked down at her. She was one of those women who look younger and prettier after making love. Her hair fanned out on the pillow and she smiled up at me with her eyes, her mouth and everything else. The manuscript lay on the floor beside her. Great security, although neither of us had given it a thought for a while.

'Nice,' she said. 'I like older men.'

'Thanks a lot. Why?'

'They usually don't look as pleased with themselves as younger blokes. More grateful.'

'I am.'

She pulled me down and kissed me. 'You're welcome.'

We showered together in a stall that could barely hold us. We dressed and went for a walk. When we turned back into her street, she said, 'What're you thinking?'

'Why can't the publisher keep it all under wraps?'

'Doesn't work that way. People in-house have to see the manuscript: the lawyers, the possible editor. It has to get accepted by a board with a few members. Input from what they call the media liaison arm these days. Word will get out.'

We went into the house and she opened a bottle of wine. Something was niggling me about the whole business and I tried to sort it out as I drank the good dry white. Melanie did some work in her study and I wandered around looking at her books. Some were obviously by her clients, judging from the multiple copies, others were more familiar. I took down a bestselling sports autobiography and what I'd been searching for hit me. I fumbled and almost dropped the book.

Melanie looked up from her desk. 'What?'

'Who's the ghost writer?' I said.

She stared at me. 'I assumed . . . Shit.'

'Andy Piper couldn't write stuff like that to save his life. It's hard to tell from the outline and the chapter headings, but you have a look at the stuff he handed over today. I'm no judge of literature, but this reads like at least pretty fair journalism to me.'

She grabbed the envelope from her bag, slid the pages out and began reading. I put the sport bio back on the shelf and drank some wine.

'You're right, Cliff. It's rough and it'll need editing, but this is from an experienced writer.'

'Piper hasn't mentioned anyone?'

She shook her head. 'He wouldn't have to, necessarily. If he made a private arrangement with someone for a flat fee, it wouldn't have to involve me or the publisher.'

'Wouldn't come cheap, a ghost writer?'

She put the manuscript back together neatly. From the way she handled it, it had taken on a new meaning for her. She drank some wine.

'Depends on who it was and his or her circumstances. Writers don't make much money, even the good ones. Especially the good ones. I've steered through a few as-told-to jobs. Ten thousand and a share of the royalties and Public Lending Right'll do it mostly.'

'Andy says he doesn't have any money. Gave it to the sect.'

'Right.'

'So he's either got someone doing it for free or he's lying about being skint.'

'You're getting me worried, Cliff.'

I went over and stroked her frizzy hair. 'Didn't mean to. It's more my problem than yours. Either way, what it means is that he's got someone he trusts, apart from you and me.'

She took my hand and brought it down to close over her left breast. 'And what do you think about that, you detective you?'

'Interesting,' I said.

Over the next few days I dealt with routine matters. Melanie and I talked on the phone a few times and exchanged some emails. She'd keyed in Piper's manuscript.

'That's a lot of typing,' I said.

'I'm a gun typist.'

On Friday she rang to tell me that the contract with Bradley Booth, the publisher, was being signed as we spoke, and the advance would be electronically deposited in her account.

'Have you cleared the extra expenses with the publisher?'

'Yes. Bradley's excited about the book.'

'That's good because those costs cut in big time now. I'll send you my contract with Piper by fax, Mel, and leave you to sort it out with the publisher. Probably won't be able to see you till this is over. Better security for you.'

'Put a rocket up the writer, whoever he or she is.'

I rang Piper. He gave me the address of a flat in Edgecliff. The block was middle-range expensive. The upkeep of the building was good—clean stairs and landings, smoke detectors, fire extinguishers. I rang the bell at Piper's door and could feel him looking at me through the peephole. He opened the door. He was in his shirt sleeves and had a pistol tucked into the tight waistband of his pants.

'G'day, Hardy. Come in. What did you think of my book?'

'What makes you think I read it?'

'A snooper like you? No risk.'

I let that pass and allowed him to shepherd me down the short passage into the flat. The room we entered was big and light. At a guess there were three bedrooms, two bathrooms and a kitchen. Not bad for a man who'd given his all to Jesus. The big balcony, accessible through full-length sliding glass doors, worried me. I was about to say something about it when a man came in from one of the other rooms. He was a replica of Piper, thirty years younger—not as fat, dark hair, no beard.

'This is my son, Mark,' Piper said. 'He's helping me write the book. Mark, this is Cliff Hardy.'

Mark Piper looked as if he could've done a fair enough job of protecting his father himself. He wore a loose T-shirt, jeans and sneakers. His forearms were tattooed and there was nothing effeminate about the ring in his left ear. His manner was wary and his look close to hostile as we shook.

'Nice place,' I said to Andy.

'Mark's. He's by way of being a bit of a journalist.'

'I don't like the look of the balcony.'

Piper smiled. 'Out of bounds for me.'

They had it pretty well set up. Mark Piper had an iMac in one of the rooms and was taping Andy's recollections. The father slept in one room and the son in with his computer. The other bedroom was for me and for Reg Lewis, an ex-army guy I'd hired to spell me. Food was on tap from a local restaurant. No alcohol and no smoking. No women. Monkish.

Over the next few days we settled into a routine. Piper spent some time taping, not that much, and Mark tapped his keyboard. I stayed awake while they slept and slept when Rex Lewis was on duty. Andy insisted on going out to bible study in Lewisham on Friday night and hymn singing in Marrickville on Sunday. I had to sit in on these sessions. I wasn't converted. Andy and Mark weren't good company. They watched a lot of cable and commercial TV.

The news broke in a gossip column in one of the tabloids on Tuesday: 'A spokesperson for publishing giant Samson House confirmed that disgraced former New South Wales senior policeman Andrew "Black Andy" Piper is preparing his "tell-all" memoirs for publication. Piper is reported to be suffering from terminal cancer and to have found God. Sceptics remain sceptical; the guilty men and women aren't sleeping well.'

Sunday rolled around and I got behind the wheel of Piper's Mercedes ready to drive him to wherever the Reverend Dr Eli Jacobsen was selling his snake-oil. The car, not new, not old, was a pleasure to drive.

'Where to?' I asked.

'I fancy a drink.'

I almost lost control of the car. 'A what?'

'You heard me.'

He'd been swallowing variously-coloured pills several times a day, every day. 'Are you allowed to drink with all that medication?'

He didn't answer for a few minutes, as if he was chewing the matter over. He wasn't. 'Nobody tells Black Andy what to do,' he said.

'So, where?'

He heaved a sigh. He looked heavier and seemed more tired than in recent days. 'Clovelly Cove Hotel,' he said. 'I'd like to look at the water. Won a surf race there once.'

'I know you rowed, didn't know you swam.'

'You don't know a lot of things, Hardy.'

We parked close to the pub and walked to it with Piper in the lead, moving purposefully. I was hot in drill trousers, light shirt and cotton jacket to cover the pistol, and he must have been sweltering in his buttoned-up double-breasted suit. If he was, he didn't show it. He plonked himself down where he had a good view through the plate glass out to sea. Pretty safe. From that angle only someone on a boat could take a pot-shot at him.

'Get us a schooner of Old, Hardy.'

Maybe it was a test to see if I'd get pissed on the job. Maybe he'd just had all the piety and healthy living he could take. Or maybe he'd ring the Reverend Eli to come and save him from sin at the last second. I bought the drinks—a middy of soda and bitters for me—and took them to the table.

He didn't hesitate, took a long swig and pointed at my glass. 'What's that piss?'

'Don't worry about it.'

'I won't.' He drank deeply and leaned back in his chair. It creaked under his weight. I hadn't noticed him eating more lately but then, he was a messy eater and it wasn't something to watch voluntarily. He looked fatter though. Schooners of Old would help that along nicely.

It happened very quickly at first, then seemed to slow down to half speed. The man walked into the bar, headed towards the taps, then swivelled quickly and took two long steps in our direction. He was only a few metres away when his hand came up with a gun and he fired three times. The shots were shatteringly loud. Piper grunted and toppled back. My gun was in my hand and I shot twice as I saw his gun swing towards me. I hit him both times, and his arms flew out and he went down and back as if he'd caught a knockout punch.

The bar erupted into shouts and swearing and breaking glass as some of the patrons stayed rooted to the spot and others headed quickly for the door. I put my pistol on the table in front of me and drew in a deep breath. My eyes were closed and the cordite smell invaded me and made me cough convulsively. When I recovered, I found Black Andy Piper standing beside me, finishing the last of his drink. His suit coat was open, his shirt was unbuttoned and the Kevlar vest under it was an obscene grey-green colour.

'Knew I could rely on you, Hardy,' he said. 'Give the cops a call on your mobile, eh? It'd look better from you.'

It was a total set-up, of course. Charles 'Chalky' Whitehead was a former friend and associate and later bitter enemy of Piper. He knew that a no-holds-barred account of Black Andy's life would point the finger at him for a number of crimes, including murder. Piper, without his henchmen and gone soft on religion, was too tempting a target for Whitehead to resist. He wasn't the brightest and when he'd tracked us to the hotel he didn't ask any questions, just came in blasting. He'd have lined up a rock-solid alibi beforehand.

Black Andy needed to get rid of Whitehead, who was competing hard with him for control of some lucrative rackets. He had someone planted in Chalky's camp who got the word to him where he'd be and when. I did the job for him, legitimately. Whitehead died before the ambulance arrived.

The police made noises about suspending my licence, but the facts were clear, with plenty of witnesses. The cops weren't serious; no one was unhappy about Whitehead being out of circulation.

Piper had no intention of publishing a book. He paid the advance back to the publisher, including Melanie's commission. He tried to pay me for my services but I told him where to put it. He reclaimed the partial manuscript from the publisher and from Melanie, threatening to sue them unless they complied. They did. What happened between him and the Community of Christ I never found out and didn't want to know.

My affair with Melanie petered out and died when she asked me if I wanted to write my memoirs.

DEATH THREATS

From *Taking Care of Business* (2004)

The young man sitting across from me was the colour of teak and looked about as tough. There was no fat on him and he'd slid snake-hipped onto the chair as if he was flexible enough to sit there and bend his legs up around his head if he'd wanted to. He was wearing jeans and a polo shirt and his forearms were sinewy. His handshake was that of a heavyweight although he had the build of a welter, light-middle at most.

'Billy Sunday advised me to get in touch with you, Mr Hardy,' he said.

I nodded. 'And how is Billy? Haven't seen him in a while.'

His lean face fell into sad lines. 'Not the best. You know how it is with us blackfellas; fifty's old. And Billy hasn't exactly taken care of himself. Crook kidneys.'

'Sorry to hear it. He could handle six blokes at a time in his day. Joel Grinter, did you say your name was? How can I help you?'

'D'you follow golf?'

'No. I've heard of Greg Norman and Tiger Woods. That's about it.'

He smiled and his face came to life. Very young life—he couldn't have been much over twenty, but he conducted himself as though he was older. 'That's a start. I'm a professional golfer. Rookie year. I've won once already and had three top tens.'

'You'd be making a quid then?'

'Yeah. Doing all right. Plus Lynx are making noises to sign me up. That's where the real money is.'

'Good for you. It's a better business to be in than boxing. You can keep all your marbles.'

'Right, if I can stay alive. I've been getting death threats.'

He told me that he was from Canungra in Queensland, had won a scholarship to the Sports Institute in Canberra and had been a top amateur. Now he was staying in Sydney with his coach, one Brett Walker, who lived in Lane Cove. He was due to play in a tournament at Concord, starting tomorrow. After he won his first event in Queensland some months back, he got a new car.

'Nothing flash. A Commodore. Some mongrel wrote "Golf is a white man's game" with a spray can down one side. Bloody hard to clean up. That's pretty funny seeing that a black man is the best in the world and another black man is in the top ten.'

'Who's that?'

'Vijay Singh. Fijian Indian. He's won two majors. Anyway, I figured it was Queensland, you know—rednecks, ratbags . . .'

'But?'

'But the other day I got this.' He lifted his hip, took a newspaper cutting from his pocket, and passed it across to me. The article was from the *Telegraph* and was about him. It was fairly standard sports stuff, with a photograph of him hitting a shot and sketching his background and career and touting him as the future of Australian golf. But not according to the person who'd drawn a gun on the cutting in red with a bullet travelling towards Joel Grinter's head.

'I'll admit it scared me,' Grinter said. 'Put me off my game. I played lousy in the pro-am.'

I looked blank.

'It's a game you play a day or so before the tournament. There's a little bit of money up and businessmen and such pay to play with the pros. It's supposed to be a fun day, but I was looking over my shoulder every second shot. I was in the trees and the sand more than I was on the fairway.'

'I get the idea,' I said. 'I don't blame you. But don't you blokes have a management arrangement with some mob or other? Don't they lay on the security?'

He looked troubled. 'Yeah, that's right. And there's a couple of management companies after me to sign with them. I haven't decided who to go with but they might shy away if they hear about this. Lynx, the one I like, might not be as keen about me. It's not like with Elvis—you can't sell golf gear using a dead man.'

'I guess not. So what d'you want me to do?'

'Find out who's behind this and stop them.'

'Big ask. I thought you were just going to hire me as a bodyguard.'

'That, too.'

I smoothed out the news cutting on the desk as I thought about it. The death threat probably wasn't serious, just some nutter, and bodyguarding usually isn't a long-term commitment. I thought about Billy Sunday and his crook kidneys and how he'd saved me from having the shit beaten out of me some years back. 'You're on,' I said. 'We have to sign a contract and you have to pay me some money. I'll knock the rate down on account of Billy.'

He pulled out a cheque book and shook his head. 'No way. I'll pay my whack.'

I had no idea what his golf earnings were but a new Commodore doesn't come cheap so he could probably afford me with room to spare. We did the paperwork and he took on that look people do when they've hired a detective. Nothing's been done or achieved, but they feel better. I took out a notebook and poised a pen. 'Okay, Mr Grinter . . .'

'Joel.'

'Joel. What does your coach think about all this?'

'Brett? I haven't told him.'

'Why not?'

'Ah, I don't want to worry him. He's got enough on his plate.'

I got the names of his contact at Lynx Sports and at the two other management companies who were bidding for him—Golf Management Services and Sports Management International.

'Which one do you favour?'

He shrugged. 'Dunno. Depends whether I go to Europe or America, or play the Australasian and Asian tours for a season. SMI's the shot if I go overseas. Brett reckons I should. I'm still thinking about it.'

'What does your family think?'

'Mum and Dad are dead. Died real young. No brothers or sisters. There's people close to me, like Billy and them, but they don't know anything about the business.'

'Where're you going now?'

'The gym for an hour or so and then back to Brett's. Early tea and early to bed. I've got a six-thirty tee-off tomorrow.'

That wasn't welcome news because I thought I'd better stick with him over the course of the tournament to see if I could spot anyone taking an undue interest or displaying signs of hostility. I knew a little about the geography of Concord and had the impression that some houses had backyards that bordered the golf course. Not ideal. He said he'd arrange for me to get a pass that'd let me in for free and give me access to certain places that were off-limits to the public.

I pointed to the cutting. 'Can I keep this?'

'Sure. Happy to see the last of it.'

I said I'd be there in the morning but that he shouldn't notice me. We shook hands and he left.

This time I read the cutting carefully. Both of Joel's parents had been stolen children. Light-skinned. His father's work in an asbestos mine had killed him in his late thirties; his mother died soon after with belatedly diagnosed diabetes a contributing factor. Joel spelled all this out in an interview he gave after his win and he also made the point that all four major golf championships that year had been won by black men. Up-front stuff.

I hauled out the phone book, located the numbers for GMS and SMI and spoke to their media liaison officers, posing as a journalist for Harry Tickener's paper. Harry would always cover for me. I put the hypothetical to them that a sportsman or sportswoman they were thinking of taking on was getting death threats. What would their reaction be?

'We'd snap him or her up,' the SMI man said. 'Great publicity, plus we've got guys to cope with that sort of thing.'

'What effect could it have on a career?'

'On sales of products, zero. On appearance fees a plus, a big plus. People like danger.'

'If it's not directed at them.'

'Hey, you don't get it. How many people d'you think tried to get close to Salman Rushdie to feel the vibe?'

The GMS man was more circumspect. 'Handled right it could play. As long as it didn't go on too long and the man or the woman didn't make inflammatory statements.'

'But you wouldn't shy away?'

A pause. 'No, but we'd surveille it to see if it was bona fide. People have been known to devise such things to lift the interest quotient.'

I thanked him and rang off, thinking that if I heard any more language like that I'd have to have my ears syringed. But it gave me things to think about. I had a feeling that Joel hadn't been completely frank with me but I couldn't put my finger on where the feeling sprang from. Fake the death threat to up the price? I didn't think so. I rang Lynx and laid it on a bit thicker. I got a similar reaction to the publicity possibilities as long as the threat didn't actually eventuate. That made a difference.

'Dead sports stars are forgotten as soon as the funeral's over. And death threats give sports a bad name—puts the parents off. On balance I'd say a definite no-no.'

I trailed around after Joel on the first day of the tournament and I found it a bloody long walk in the sun. At least I could get under shade for some of the time and have a few beers. Also I wasn't swinging a club and bending down to place and pick up a ball. Golfers might not always look fit but they must be. I heard nothing in the crowd to suggest that there was anything but goodwill towards Joel. I'd advised him to try to keep trees and other people between him and the spots where back fences bordered the course and, as far as I could tell, he did it and I saw nothing suspicious. Knowing stuff-all about the game, it seemed to me that he played well, but he wasn't happy.

'Three over,' he said.

'Better than the blokes you were playing with.'

'But maybe not good enough. The cut's likely to be two over or even one. Means I have to be one or two under tomorrow.'

'Can you do it?'

'Sure I can do it. I've shot a sixty-five around here. I can do it if I can just clear my bloody head.'

'Look, I've seen and heard nothing alarming. It could all be just bullshit.'

He didn't seem interested and went off to practise his putting. I hung around, kept an eye out, followed the Commodore back to the address he'd given me, Brett Walker's house in Lane Cove, and called it a day.

The next day I found out what a tough game professional golf is. The cut mark was set by the general standard of play in the field and on the second day it was better than the first. Because of the calmer conditions, the pundits said. While other players, including two of the three Joel was playing with, were starting to hit the ball longer and straighter, Joel struggled.

'He'd be stuffed if it wasn't for his short game,' a man in the gallery said. 'Christ, can he get it up and down.'

'Abo eyesight,' another bloke said, and his tone was admiring.

Towards the end of the round Joel started to pull himself together. He pounded the ball down the middle and got it on the green close to the cup on three holes in a row. Shouts went up as his putts dropped and I gathered he was in with a chance. The crowd following him built suddenly.

'I'm new at this, mate,' I said to the bloke who'd commented on Joel's eyesight. 'What's going on?'

'He needs to birdie the last to make the cut.'

'Which means?'

He looked at me as if I shouldn't be allowed out alone. 'It's a par five, means he has to get a four or better.'

'I get it. What if he doesn't make it?'

'Then he's out his travel and accommodation, and his entry fee and his caddie's fee. He goes home with bugger-all.'

Joel hit his drive into the trees on the left and the gallery groaned.

'Great out,' my informant said as Joel's ball came sailing out of the trees onto the fairway. 'He can do it.'

'Too far,' another spectator said. 'He can't get on from there. Christ, he's taking the driver.'

My informant told me what I needed to know without me having to ask. 'He's using his driver off the deck. It's really designed for hitting off a tee. Incredibly hard shot.'

Joel took a deep breath, set himself and swung. I feared for his spine from the way he wound himself up and let go, but he made contact and the ball took off low and climbed like a fighter jet until it was sailing high towards the green. A roar went up from the crowd gathered there and I felt a thump on my back.

'He made it,' my new friend said. 'He bloody made it.'

We moved as quickly as we could to the green. I was caught up in it now and shouldered my way forward to get a good look. There were two balls on the green, one a little short of it and another in the sand bunker on the right.

The man in the bunker took two shots to get out and the crowd groaned. The guy who was short of the green rolled his ball up close to the cup and the crowd clapped. Then it was Joel's turn because he was furthest away. The distance wasn't quite as long as a cricket pitch but near enough. There seemed to be several rises and falls in the surface between him and the hole. He walked around, surveying the putt from every angle, consulted with his caddie, then walked quickly up, took one look along the line and struck.

'Baddeley-style,' someone said.

The ball took the slopes, rolling first away from the hole and then towards it. It gathered speed, then lost it as it got nearer. If the birds were singing and the cicadas scraping I didn't hear them. The ball seemed to be drawn towards the hole. Then it stopped, half a roll short. A sigh went up from the crowd and Joel dropped his putter and buried his face in his hands in anguish.

I spoke to Joel briefly after the game but he seemed to have lost interest in everything. His coach, Brett Walker, a big, red-faced, freckled character, had a few words with him and then turned away to talk to a journalist.

'I'm a broken-down ex-Queensland copper,' I heard him say. 'But I can hit a six-iron two hundred yards.'

Joel drank a couple of quick cans and then headed for the car park. I followed him at a discreet distance. Disappointed and with drink inside him, he'd be vulnerable if his enemy was about, but nothing happened. He drove steadily enough and turned off into the park a couple of hundred metres from the Walker house. I kept him in view, staying out of sight. He left the car and joined a girl who was sitting on a bench under a tree. They went into a clinch that seemed to last for ten minutes, and when they broke it they stayed as close together as they could.

They talked intently and interspersed the talk with kissing and hugging. There was some headshaking and nodding and more kissing and then the girl turned away and headed back towards the road on foot, leaving Joel sitting on the bench. I followed her, feeling slightly ridiculous ducking behind trees. She turned and looked back and for a second I thought she'd spotted me, but she was waving to Joel. I was closer now and saw that she had tears on her face and was young, very young.

She walked up the road and turned into the driveway of the Walker house. A woman came down to meet her: same slim build, blonde hair and body language—clearly her mother. They argued heatedly.

I drove back to the course, where players were still finishing their rounds. My pass got me back in and I found Brett Walker sitting on his own at a table near the beer tent. There were four empty cans in front of him and he had another in his fist. Fourex. I sat down opposite him and he stared at me blearily.

'You did it, didn't you?'

'Did what?'

'Sent the threatening messages to Joel.'

He swigged from the can. 'Bugger off, whoever you are.'

'I'm the private detective Joel hired to find out who's been threatening him. And I have. You don't like his relationship with your daughter because he's Aboriginal.'

For a minute I thought he was going to throw the can at me and I almost hoped he would. It would have given me an excuse to hit him. But he drained it and crushed it in his big, freckled fist. 'I can't help it,' he muttered. 'It's the way I was brought up. I can't bloody stand the thought of it.'

'What did you hope to achieve?'

'Get him to sign with SMI and piss off to America.'

'Brilliant. He'd probably take her with him.'

'She's seventeen, just.'

'I've seen them together, mate. You've got Buckley's.'

'Jesus. I need another beer.'

He staggered off and I almost felt sorry for him. He returned with two cans and thrust one at me. I cracked it and took a swig. 'Thanks. I hope you're not planning to drive home.'

'Wife's coming to get me.'

'Is she with you on this?'

'Christ, she doesn't know.'

'She does. I've seen her and your daughter going at it hammer and tongs. Couldn't have been about anything else.'

'Bloody snooper.'

'That's right, and I've snooped on things like this for twenty years and learned a few things. You're out of your depth. The surest way to pair them up is for you to stick your nose in.'

'I didn't think he was smart enough to do something like hire a detective.'

'I'd say he's very smart. Smarter than you. You need to come down out of your tree into the twenty-first century.'

Maybe I was still hoping he'd cut up rough, but it didn't take him that way. He sighed and shook his head and seemed to lose interest in his beer. He lifted his head and glanced across to where players were hitting on the practice fairway. I followed his glance and saw Joel Grinter spill balls onto the ground and start hitting.

Walker watched Grinter's long fluid stroke. 'Missed the bloody cut, knows I'm pissed off with him about something. And he's out there practising. He's got a beautiful swing, hasn't he?'

'He has.'

'Shit, I think you might be right. I've been a mug. Well, that's the end of us.'

'Why?'

He looked at me. 'Well, you're going to tell him, aren't you?'

I drank some more beer. 'It's a good drop, Fourex. I don't have to tell him, not if you're fair dinkum and leave it alone. What's the expression? Play it as it lies?'

'What'll you tell him?'

'I'll think of something. Deal?'

It took a while for him to answer and that was encouraging. You don't change the habit of a lifetime in an instant if you're serious. Eventually he thumped himself on the side of the head as if to drive the idea home and nodded. 'You're not a bad bloke for someone who knows bugger-all about golf. Deal, and thanks.'

I phoned Joel a week later at Walker's and got him after Mrs Walker answered.

'Hardy here, Joel. How's things?'

'Okay. Brett was shitty with me about something, but everything's much better now. Real good in fact.'

'Fine. I see you're playing in Canberra next week.'

'I'll kill 'em. How'd you get on? I haven't had any more trouble.'

I told him I'd found out that a retired footballer with mental problems had been responsible for the spraying and the clipping. I said he'd gone off his medication and had harassed some other Aboriginal sports stars, but he was back under treatment.

'How'd you find all that out?'

'Professional secret.'

'Jeez, that's another load off my mind. Thank you.'

'I'll send you a bill. Keep swinging.'

LAST WILL AND TESTAMENT

From *The Big Score* (2007)

'I'm dying, Cliff,' Kevin Roseberry said.

'Says who?'

'The doctors and me.' He tapped his pyjama-clad chest. 'I can tell.'

'Doctors have been known to be wrong,' I said. 'Even you've been wrong once or twice, Kev.'

Kevin Roseberry was seventy-five but looked older. He'd been a lot of things in his time—wharfie, boxer, rodeo rider, boxing manager. When he won two million dollars in a lottery he hired me, who'd known him just as someone to drink with in Glebe, to get a blackmailer off his back. It wasn't hard, the guy was an amateur, easily persuaded of the error of his ways. Kevin and I became friendly after that. He bought a big terrace at the end of my street, held some great parties. Now he was in a private room in a private hospital and I was visiting.

'I've been wrong heaps of times, but not now. The big C's got me and they reckon I've got a month at the most. No kicks coming. After the life I've led I was thankful to make it to the new century, let alone two years in. I've got that doctor you recommended onside.'

'Ian Sangster?'

'He's a good bloke. He's put me onto another quack who knows the score. I'm going home next week and he's arranged for a nurse who'll know what to do.'

I nodded. That's exactly what I'd want for myself—not that it'll ever happen.

Kevin used to be big but he'd wasted badly. Even his craggy bald head looked smaller. His voice was still the hoarse bark it had always been and his eyes were bright under the boxer's scar tissue. He pointed to his bedside cabinet. 'Let's have a drink.'

I opened the cabinet, took out a bottle of Teachers and two glasses. I poured two generous measures and handed him his. We raised the glasses in a silent toast to nothing in particular.

'I've got a problem,' he said. 'Who to leave my bloody money to.'

'I could take some of it off your hands. Just say the word.'

'Funny. You can tell jokes at the wake. No, this is serious. You didn't know I had a kid, a daughter, did you?'

'Never saw you with a pram.'

'Yeah, well it was all a fair while ago. I didn't treat the woman well and I never had much to do with the kid, nothing in fact. Back then, it was work, fights, the rodeo circuit, grog and more grog. You know.'

'You've got the scars to prove it.'

'You bet I have. The thing is, I'd like to help the kid and her mother. It bloody worries me, Cliff. I'm on the way out and I've been a selfish bastard all my life. I don't believe in any of that religious crap, but I'd like to go with a sort of clean slate if I can. Does that sound nutty?'

'No, Kev. It sounds like a decent man trying to do a decent thing. Nothing wrong with that.'

'Good. Thanks. You helped me once and I want your help again. I want you to contact the girl and her mother and tell me how things stand with them.'

'Meaning?'

'Well, last I was in touch with Marie, and this is nearly ten years back, she wanted nothing to do with me. Warned me not to try to get in touch with the girl. This was just before I came into the money, but I had a bit and I wanted to know if Marie and Siobhan needed anything. Marie said she was doing fine, so I backed off and I thought, fuck her. But now things are different. The house is worth the best part of a million. I blew a fair bit on horses and having fun, but there's still a couple of hundred grand left. It's invested and brings in a decent amount. Now if Marie's doing well that's fine, but Siobhan's in her twenties and I don't see why her mother should still speak for her. Shit, she might have children, my grandchildren. The money could be useful for them if not for . . . you see what I'm getting at.'

'Why can't you get in touch yourself—ring up or write?'

Kevin shook his head and the loose skin on his neck was grey and mottled. 'I tried. I rang the last number I had but the people I spoke to had never heard of her. I didn't know what else to do and I'm too crook to go hunting them up. But that's your game, isn't it—finding people?'

'Part of it. I can give it a shot, Kev, but people can move a long way in ten years. Women marry and change their names. How old would Marie be?'

'Twenty years younger than me, mid-fifties. I met her when I was managing a middleweight who fought Jimmy O'Day. She was some kind of cousin or auntie or something of Jimmy's.

A good bit older, Jimmy started real young. She was at the fight and afterwards we got talking and that.'

'She's Aboriginal?'

'Just a bit, like Jimmy.'

'That bit can mean a lot these days. You'd better give me the names and the address and anything else that might be useful. Got a photo?'

He gestured at the cabinet. 'In my wallet. A couple of snaps from back when we were sort of together. Siobhan was just a baby.'

Snaps was right: they were polaroids and pretty faded. In one of the photos, Kevin, with more hair on his head and flesh on his bones, stood beside a tall woman who was carrying a baby. In the other, Kevin was holding the baby securely in his big, meaty hands, but the look on his face suggested he was afraid of dropping it. The woman was handsome rather than pretty, with strong features. Impossible to tell her colouring from the old pictures, but dark rather than fair, I thought. I put the photos back in the wallet. Kevin took it from me and extracted a wad of hundred-dollar notes.

'Eight hundred do you?'

'For starters, sure. You might have to hang on a bit longer, Kev. These things can take time.'

'I'll try, mate, but don't count on it.'

I got Marie's last known address, in Leichhardt, and left him there with the television on and the remote in his hand that was like a claw.

I remembered Jimmy O'Day. He was a fast-moving middleweight back when boxing was very much in the doldrums. He fought in the clubs, had a few bouts in New Zealand, and won the Commonwealth title, which meant practically nothing at all. I saw him once at Parramatta and thought he was pretty good without being sensational. He was a boxer rather than a puncher, and that didn't please the pig-ignorant club crowd all that much. He dropped out of sight after losing the title to a Māori fighter. I still had contacts in the boxing world and it might be possible to get a line on Marie O'Day through him if all else failed.

It took me a couple of days to clean up a few other matters before I got around to visiting Leichhardt. The young woman at the address Kevin had given me, a neat single-storey terrace not far back from Norton Street, remembered Kevin's call and could only say she knew nothing about former residents.

'I think it had been a rental property in the past,' she said. 'Tess and I had a lot of repairs to do when we bought it.'

I got the name of the agent she'd bought through, thinking they might have had the letting of the house beforehand, and thanked her.

'Does the house have a history?' she asked. 'Like a criminal past?'

'Why do you say that?'

'Oh, you look like a policeman or . . . something.'

I rewarded her with an enigmatic smile.

Ten-plus years ago, when Marie O'Day was there, Leichhardt was already gentrifying, with properties turning over quickly as people took their capital gains elsewhere and new residents moved in, renovating and restoring. None of the houses in the vicinity looked as if they were owned by old-timers who knew everything that went on in the street. I knocked on a few doors and got confirmation of that impression. As a last gasp I tried the corner store at the end of the street, one of the few survivors. The proprietor was an elderly Italian man with limited stock, just hanging on. I bought some things I didn't need and asked him how long he'd had the shop.

'Twenty years, mate.' His accent was pure Italo-Australian.

I showed him my PEA licence. 'I'm looking for a woman who used to live at number 76. Her name's Marie.'

He shook his head. 'They come and they go.'

'Good-looking woman, darkish maybe, with a child.'

He sparked up. 'Oh, *si*, Marie, with the kid. I couldn't never get the name right.'

'Siobhan.'

'Yes. I called her honey because of the colour of her hair. Beautiful hair.'

'She was in here a lot, Marie?'

'Most days. Nice woman. No trouble. She do something wrong?'

'No. I don't suppose you know where she went when she left here?'

He rubbed his hands together and looked around at his meagre stock. 'I'm trying to remember. Some people say, "Carlo, I'm off to Queensland", and I say, "Take me with you"—for a joke, you understand. But no, Marie, she just . . .'

'What?'

'*Si*, I remember. Her cousin paid her bill. I let her have a little bit of credit because she always paid when she got her pension. But I didn't see her to say goodbye, "*ciao*"—she used to try to speak Italian. But this man came in and paid. He said he was her cousin.'

'What did he look like?'

Carlo squared his shoulders and set his fists in front of him. '*Fallo così!*'

'A soldier?'

'No.' He drew his index fingers across above and through his eyebrows. 'With the scars. Like you. A boxer.'

Trueman's Gym in Erskineville retains the name although Sammy Trueman died years ago. It has undergone periods of prosperity and adversity, renovation and neglect. Now, with boxing in Sydney on the upswing, partly due to the charisma of Anthony Mundine, the gym has attracted a respectable number of wannabe fighters paying respectable fees for the facilities. Footballers use it and some actors, waiting for the follow-up to *Cinderella Man.*

For generations the gym has served as a poste restante address for fighters and trainers often too down on their luck to afford proper accommodation. A couple of sports journalists drop in regularly in search of colour for their columns. I go there once in a while just to stay in touch with the business I had thought of taking on professionally until a hard left hook from Clem Carter in an amateur six-rounder convinced me otherwise. I'd done some work for a couple of the trainers and managers over the years, scaring off touts and persuading promoters to pay what they owed.

Wally Tanner was one of those trainers and I knew he hung out at Trueman's, always on the hunt for a promising fighter. I didn't think he'd trained Jimmy O'Day, but O'Day had certainly put in time at Trueman's and there was a good chance Wally would know something about him.

In the old days a boxing gym smelled of tobacco smoke, sweat and liniment, now it's just the sweat and liniment. It was early in the afternoon, not the best time when most of the fighters have jobs and only get to the gym after they knock off, but Wally was there watching a couple of heavyweights plodding around the ring.

He nodded to me. 'G'day, Cliff. Look at these no-hopers. It's a disgrace to let 'em in a ring.'

'As they say—they're slow but they can't hit.'

'That's right. Haven't seen you for a while. What brings you around?'

'D'you remember Jimmy O'Day?'

Wally turned disgustedly away from the ring to watch a skipper and a kid working on the speed ball. They didn't please him either. 'Sure I do. He was a good boy—good, not great. Why?'

'I'm trying to locate a cousin of his named Marie. I'm told they were pretty close at one time.'

Wally was an old-school racist. 'Yeah,' he said, 'well they're like that, aren't they? Especially when one of 'em's got any cash. Jeez, they bled Dave Sands dry. Lionel too, I reckon.'

'Any idea where Jimmy is now?'

'Be in Redfern, wouldn't he?'

'Come on, Wally, keep up. There's Aborigines in parliament, in the law, in business.'

'Not ex-boxers. The money goes and they get on the grog.'

'Have it your way. I'll ask someone else.'

'Hang on, don't get shitty. I don't know anything about a cousin, but I did hear that Jimmy was doin' something. What was it? Oh, yeah—he's got a band. They play country music.'

'What's the name of the band?'

'Dunno. I just heard someone mention that Jimmy was the leader. I suppose he plays the guitar and sings. Don't they all play the guitar and sing, the leaders?'

'Mick Jagger didn't play guitar, though I gather he does a bit now.'

Wally would've spat into the sawdust in the old days, now he just sneered. 'That ponce. Big in the bedroom, but I'd like to see him inside the ropes.'

'The man's over sixty.'

'So am I, and I can still go a bit. Better than them two.' He turned away to watch the cumbersome sparrers and I left him to it.

It was a lead of a sort, and what you always dread in the early stages of an investigation is the absolute dead end. Avoid them for a while and you can start to make progress if you know your business.

I don't buy many CDs these days after replacing a lot of my seventies vinyls and cassettes. I don't really keep up much since Cold Chisel and Dire Straits, though I quite like The Whitlams. With country music I mostly preferred the women—Patsy Cline, Lucinda Williams. I'd bought Kasey Chambers' first album at Hot Music at the Cross and that's where I went next.

The place is distinguished from many others by having staff who know about the stuff they sell and how to get it if it's not in stock. The young woman I approached had a fair amount of silverware in her face, a lot of eye make-up and an indoor pallor.

'Excuse me,' I said, 'do you happen to know about a country music band with a leader named Jimmy O'Day?'

'Would that be James O'Day?'

'Could be.'

'Well, sure—they're called the Currawongs. Want to hear them? They've got two albums.'

She put a CD on and gave me the headphones. I'm no great judge of country, but the music sounded tight and professional. The lead singer had a sweet voice, something like Gram Parsons. I listened to a couple of tracks and nodded.

'I'll take it.'

I produced the plastic and as she was inspecting the CD and wrapping it, I asked if she knew where the band played.

'You like it that much, eh? Maybe you want the other album?'

'This'll do for a start.'

'Okay, worth a try. Their webpage is on the line notes. You can probably find out from that. I know they tour a lot, like all those groups. Have to make a living, dude.'

'Don't we all, isn't it a pity?'

I took the CD to my office and inspected it. The album was simply called *The Currawongs*. The photograph of the band was small and dark and I wasn't able to identify O'Day from that. Any one of the four—keyboard player, two guitarists and drummer—could have been him, but the notes said that James O'Day was the keyboard man, singer and lyricist. I looked at the photo again but couldn't match the man at the piano with the kid I'd seen in the boxing ring nearly twenty years back.

As you'd expect, the band's webpage was Currawongs.net. I got it up and learned more. One of the guitarists was Brian O'Day, James's brother, and the drummer, Larry Roberts, was their cousin. The other guitarist was Luke Harvey. The band had evolved from several earlier groups and taken their name a few years back. They'd toured the east coast extensively and played at the Byron Bay Blues and Roots Festival. Biographical information was sketchy; no ages were given, there was no mention of Aboriginality or boxing, but the title of one of the songs, 'Blues for Jimmy Sharman', struck the right note. Sharman Senior and Junior were the bosses of the most famous of the old-time touring boxing-tent shows. It was looking good.

As the cluey woman in the music shop had thought, the band's dates were listed on the website. In two days' time they were playing at the Bulli Hotel in the Illawarra. Easy drive, pleasant setting. I took the CD home and played it. It didn't make me want to rush out to buy the other one, but I liked it well enough. The songs had a freshness to them and varied between bluesy laments, standard country stuff and something verging on hard rock. There seemed to me to be a touch of the Stones in country mood, with a bit of Van Morrison, maybe some Paul Kelly, and that note in O'Day's voice that reminded me of Gram Parsons, especially on the downbeat tracks. I listened closely to 'Blues for Jimmy Sharman':

You went in much too often
And you got real beat down
When the country boys who took a glove
Weren't just the usual clowns
But you stayed at it longer
Than they ever thought you might
'Cos your woman and kids was hungry
And Dad you had to stand and fight.

Sounded as if he knew what he was singing about.

I phoned Clarrie Simpson, one of the journalists who frequented Trueman's and someone I occasionally had a drink with. We shot the shit for a while. Clarrie was semi-retired and glad to talk.

'Remember Jimmy O'Day?' I asked.

'Yeah—held the Commonwealth Mickey Mouse middleweight title, briefly.'

'Know anything about his background?'

'I should. I wrote a piece about him.'

'His father?'

'Tent fighter with Sharman Junior.'

Thank you, Clarrie. 'How old would Jimmy be now?'

Clarrie's of an age where everyone not as old as him seems to get younger. 'Not old,' he said. 'He started young and he quit right after that Kiwi beat him. Nasty, that was. He got cut badly above both eyes and they didn't stop it as soon as they should have. I'd say early forties. Anything in this for me?'

'Could be, not sure.'

'Typical.'

I rang the Bulli Hotel and found out you could book a table close to the stage for a meal and a ticket to the show for a price that wouldn't take too much of Kevin's retainer. Pay by credit card. Why not?

I booked into a Thirroul motel, thinking that I'd probably have a drink or two and wouldn't want to drive back. A short hop from there to Bulli. Great old pub on the highway, heritage-protected for sure. The structure had been preserved and the renovations hadn't destroyed the charm. A Hyundai people-mover and trailer were parked in the lane beside the pub. The room where the band was to play held about twenty tables and there was plenty of standing room with a bar at the back. I gave my name and was shown to a small table off to one side with a clear view of the stage. I ordered a bottle of Houghton's white burgundy and the barramundi with chips—what else do you eat on the coast within the sound and smell of the waves?

The wine was cold and the food was good. The room filled up quickly with all the tables being taken and the standing room packed. Evidently the Currawongs had a following. They came on about ten minutes late, which is pretty standard. The MC just spoke the band's name to raucous applause and went off. Before the lights went down I got a good look at the keyboard man. James was Jimmy all right—the same dark curly hair, olive skin and fluid movement. I couldn't see the boxing scars but, like me, he had the heavy brows that stretch the skin and lead to cuts. The band tuned up briefly and launched into one of their country rock numbers I hadn't heard. The crowd had and showed its approval.

They played for forty-five minutes, switching from fast to slower but never slow, and keeping the energy up. James, as I told myself to think of him, was active at the electronic keyboard, standing up when appropriate and giving it some body as well as fingers. All four seemed to be on top of their game with some good slide guitar at times and nice harmonies. They took a ten-minute break and came back with more of the same. James didn't do the corny stuff of introducing the band, but each member had a couple of solo moments that said more than words. I paced myself with the wine and still had a third of the bottle left when they did their last song and their encore. I was probably one of the oldest people there, but I was on my feet and cheering like the youngest.

'James will be signing CDs in the bar when he catches his breath and has a drink,' the MC announced.

A crowd clustered around as O'Day propped himself against the bar with a beer to hand and chatted to the people buying the record. As I got closer I could see the scar tissue, which gave him a slightly threatening look. Even if you didn't know he'd been a fighter, he'd strike you as someone not to mess with. I took the album I didn't have from the roadie who was supervising the business and paid cash for it. I hung back until I was the last in the line.

'Hi,' O'Day said, 'enjoy the show?'

I handed him the record. 'I did.'

'What name?'

'Cliff Hardy. I'm a private detective and I want to talk to you.'

He paused the pen over the record. 'Yeah, what about?'

'I saw you fight a couple of times when you were called Jimmy.'

He scrawled something illegible and stood. 'Good for you. I'm off now.'

'Hang on.'

I moved to stop him and suddenly the roadie and someone else were beside me, hemming me in against the bar as O'Day slipped away. The roadie threw a punch. I ducked it and gave him a hard one to the ribs that crumpled him. The other man attempted to kick me in the balls and I up-ended him. He came back quickly in a karate stance. By this time some of the hard-core drinkers had clustered around, ready to enjoy the second show of the night. I didn't oblige them. I pulled out my wallet and held up my PEA licence card.

'Federal police,' I said. 'Don't make things worse for yourself.'

He straightened his body and unflexed the stiffened fingers. 'Sorry, I was just . . .'

'Doing your job. It's okay.'

The drinkers lost interest. I looked about but the roadie had gone. I went out onto the tiled verandah and around to the side where the band's people-mover and trailer had been parked. Gone. When I went back into the pub the karateist had faded away as well. Great work, Cliff, I thought, you scared everyone off and learned bugger-all.

I went back into the room and recovered my bottle. My hair was in my face, my shirt was half pulled out from my pants and I was angry. A frightened-looking kid behind the bar handed me a cork and I gave him a nod that didn't make him any happier. A woman came bustling towards me; she was angry, too.

'I don't care who you are,' she said. 'I'm going to report you for causing a disturbance here.'

'Who're you?' I said.

'I'm the events manager.'

'In your place I'd do exactly the same thing, but think about it. Would a bit of a stoush after the band finished playing really do your venue a lot of harm? I don't think so.'

She was smart enough to take the point. She was pushing middle age but holding up well. She wore a white blouse, blue velvet jacket and black trousers with heels that made her tallish. Her hair was dark with red highlights.

'You're not a policeman,' she said.

'No. I told Jimmy O'Day that before things got wild.'

'Jimmy?'

'We go back a bit. You are . . .?'

'Rennie Ellis. Well, you've made life interesting tonight, but you'd better take your bottle and go.'

'Who was the guy with the karate moves?'

She shrugged, nicely. 'I don't know.'

'I think you do. I'm booked into the Thirroul Lodge, room six. I'll be there until 10 a.m. tomorrow. I'd like to talk to him and I could make it worth his while.'

'Goodnight,' she said.

At the motel I parked the wine in the mini-bar and opened one of the small Scotches for a nightcap. I'd barely tasted it when a knock came on the door. I opened it and Rennie Ellis stood there with a trench coat draped around her shoulders and a bottle in her hand.

'We got off on the wrong foot,' she said, and handed me the bottle. 'A peace offering.'

I took the bottle—champagne. 'Come in.'

She moved past me and looked at the room. 'A while since I've been here,' she said. 'Not bad. They're trying.'

'I was having a nightcap. Want a Scotch?'

She dropped the coat on a chair and sat down on the arm. 'I'll take the other half, sure.'

She was a good-looking woman with a full figure and the sort of confidence that comes with experience on top of adequate self-esteem. She sipped at the Scotch, bent easily and picked up the book I'd put down beside the chair intending to read it for a while before going to bed.

'*Dark Safari*,' she said. 'Paul Theroux. What's it like?'

'Good. Confirms my feeling that I don't want to go to Africa.'

'What do you want?'

'To know why you're here.'

'Knew you'd be direct. Anything else?'

'I asked you in, didn't I?'

She drank the rest of the Scotch. 'I saw you in action in the pub. I was impressed.'

'Didn't come across to me.'

'That was for the management. I'm here for me now.'

It was a semi-invitation I couldn't refuse. We finished the Scotch in the mini-bar and opened the champagne. She told me she was a swimming instructor not getting too many clients given the time of year. She said she was tired of young surfies and old hippies. At some point she moved to the bed and we were sitting together and things went on from there. She kissed as though she needed to, and so did I. She had a condom in her coat pocket and by the time I'd kissed her breasts and slid my fingers inside her I was ready. We pulled back the covers and made love vigorously enough to pull the sheets away from the mattress. After we finished we clawed at the sheets and blankets, suddenly aware that it was cold.

'Hey,' she said. 'My first private detective.'

'How d'you know that?'

'Someone heard you speak to James O'Day. That someone told me.'

'Is it the person I think it is?'

'Could be. Tell you in the morning. I've got another rubber—think you're up to it?'

'Not now.'

'In the morning?'

'Possibly, just possibly.'

Rennie was the sort of woman who knew what she wanted and what she was prepared to give. We were comfortable together in the morning—both feeling better about the world and ourselves.

'Where's the breakfast?' she asked. 'The soggy toast and the cold coffee?'

'I don't eat breakfast.'

'Oh Christ, an ascetic.'

I pointed to the miniature Scotches and the empty champagne bottle. 'Hardly.'

She had a quick shower and got dressed. 'Well, that was fun, Cliff, and I'm going to get Claude to call in on you. He might know why James O'Day took off like that and why they heavied you—tried to, at least. Are you trouble for him, the singer?'

'Not at all. Would you believe I just want some information about his auntie?'

She laughed. 'Big case.' She blew me a kiss and was gone.

I showered and dressed, tidied the room a bit, put the condoms and the bottles in the rubbish bin. The day had dawned fine but cool and I could smell the sea as I stood outside the room with a cup of instant coffee. A Holden ute, about the same vintage as my Falcon, pulled in to the slot beside it. The man who got out looked bigger and darker in the daylight than in the pub gloom. He wore jeans and a sleeveless T-shirt that revealed his muscles and tats. There were rings in both his ears—not a good idea if you're serious about fighting people who know how to fight.

'You'd be Claude,' I said. 'G'day, my name's Cliff.'

He didn't offer to shake hands, but he didn't try to kick me. 'Rennie says you're okay.'

I nodded.

'You freaked Jimmy out a bit last night.'

'Didn't mean to. Come inside. Want some coffee?'

He smiled. 'You're a private eye, on expenses, right? How about a beer from your mini-bar?'

We sat at the table in the room, me with my instant and him with a Crown Lager. He drank half of it in a gulp. 'Hits the spot. Rennie mentioned money, too, and she says you're not after James for nothing dodgy. How much money, bro?'

'Depends—on a scale from a hundred to two hundred depending on the information.'

'Not a lot.'

'Got a better offer right now, Claude? Look, I've got no grief for Jimmy. I saw him fight when that was his name.'

He drank some more beer and looked less hostile. 'Yeah? He was good, wasn't he? I was too young to see him.'

'Pretty good and he quit when he was ahead. He's in a better business now. Might hurt his ears, but it won't scramble his brains.'

'Right. That's why martial arts is better, I reckon, 'cept there's no money in it.'

'Which brings us back to where we were. Why did Jimmy sic you guys onto me and take off like that? What's he worried about? Tell me that and I'll pay you something, tell me how to get to talk to him and I'll up the ante.'

'Tell me what you're on about first. Then I'll think about it.'

I made myself another cup of coffee, got him another beer and told him, without mentioning names or sums of money. When I finished he rolled the bottle in his hands as an aid to thought and decision-making.

'That was a pretty neat move you made on me in the pub.'

I shrugged. 'I always think one foot off the ground leaves you vulnerable.'

'If the other guy's quick enough. I was a bit pissed, a bit slow.'

I nodded. It was probably true. He was circling; I played along. 'How d'you come to know Jimmy anyway? Are you related?'

He laughed. 'You think I'm an Abo? I'm Maltese, mate. I played in the band for a while, wasn't good enough when they got on to the bigger gigs and recording and that. No hard feelings. I do a bit of work for them now and then. I'm good at the electrics. Okay, well Jimmy had this manager who ripped him off every which way. The guy's a crook, but he's still trying to get a share now that they're getting bigger. I reckon when you said you were a private detective Jimmy thought you were on his case. That's why he gave Chicka and me the sign.'

I took two fifties from my wallet and handed them over. 'That again if you tell me how to reach him. But you contact him first and tell him I'm not any sort of threat.'

'If you've lied to me, I'll fuckin' . . .'

'I'm sure you would, but it's not like that and you know it.'

'He hangs out in Newtown, him, a couple of the guys, and Jimmy's wife.'

He gave me the address and I tossed across my mobile phone. 'Give him a ring.'

He shook his head. 'Too early, man, they wouldn't have got back till late and probably had a bit of a blast, you know. Good gig, sold some records.'

Claude gave me the phone number off the top of his head and said he'd ring at around midday. He advised me to call mid-afternoon when they'd be 'mellow'.

They say that terminally ill people can get a surge from good news. I rang the hospital and left a message for Kev that I was making progress.

I took my time on the drive back to Sydney and it was almost midday when I reached Newtown. I had a quick drink in the Marlborough and then threaded my way through the narrow streets to the address Claude had given me. It was a two-storey terrace on a corner, two blocks from King Street and a block away from the Memorial Park. Biggish place, room for quite a few people. There looked to be a small courtyard out the back with a vine of some sort growing wild. The narrow front porch was mostly taken up by the wheelie bin and the two recycling bins, but there was space for a couple of pot plants that looked as though they got a certain amount of tending. No broken-down sofas, Jack Daniels bottles, defunct TV sets. Rock groups had cleaned up their act.

I parked fifty metres away and used the mobile. I got an answering machine telling me the names of the residents and asking me to leave a message. My response was interrupted.

'This is James O'Day. Claude phoned me about you. Where are you?'

'Outside.'

'Stay there. I'll come out and we can go for a walk.'

I met him in the middle of the street. Newtown people walk on the street because the footpaths are narrow and often blocked by overhangs from front gardens and the trees planted in the gentrification era. He still looked like a middle-weight—medium tall, sloping shoulders, narrow waist. He wore jeans and a flannie, denim jacket with a sheepskin collar. He held out a hand, not to shake, a gesture of apology.

'Sorry,' he said.

'You should be. You cost my client two hundred bucks.'

He smiled as we walked down the street towards the park. 'That what you paid Claude? Good for him. You said you saw me fight. Was that just a line?'

We reached the park and began walking down a path beside a wall covered in graffiti, some of it not too talent-less. 'No, I saw you a couple of times when you won. I didn't see the one you lost.'

He took his hands from the pockets of his jacket and touched the scar tissue. 'I got cut. Best thing that ever happened to me.'

'How's that?'

'Made me quit before my brains got mushed. You've done a bit yourself, eh?'

'Amateur only, before headguards came in. I did enjoy the show and I did buy the record. Bought the first one, too, when I was trying to get a line on you.'

'Wow, that could put fifty cents or more in my pocket. Okay, now we're here let's get to it. Claude said you're looking for someone in my family. He was a bit vague, the way you were, I suppose.'

This was evidently a familiar walk to him and he was setting a cracking pace. He swerved off onto another path and I had to trot to catch him.

'Sorry,' he said. 'I've mapped out this kilometre track and I do five or six circuits when I've got the time.'

'Terrific. I do something the same around Jubilee Park in Glebe, but right now I'd rather talk than trot.'

'Fair enough.'

We cut across the grass where some kids were kicking a soccer ball around, past a group that looked to be in some kind of therapy session, to a bench in the sun. Just to appear professional, I took out my notebook and leafed through it.

'About ten years ago, you paid a corner store bill for a woman named Marie O'Day in Leichhardt. The shopkeeper said you looked like a fighter. I got onto an old-timer at Trueman's who knew you'd gone into what he called the music business. Tracking you down wasn't that hard after that but then . . .'

He smiled again, the smile he'd given to the photographers in his fighting days and on the stage in his new incarnation. 'We ran into a spot of bother. Okay, I'm impressed with your investigative skills. Did you find out that after boxing I went to TAFE to get an education and worked on my piano playing until I was game to perform in public?'

'No.'

'You just thought I segued from middleweight champ to rock star?'

I was getting sick of this. 'Look, Jimmy,' I said, 'I don't give a fuck about your brilliant career. I've got a client who needs to make contact with Marie O'Day and any kids she might have—to her and their advantage.'

He wasn't used to being talked to like that and his first reaction was antagonistic. He swivelled on the bench and his handsome face took on the sort of look boxers wear when they touch hands before the fight. I didn't react—not what he expected. He struggled for control.

'All right,' he said. 'I deal with too many arseholes.'

'And too many people who're scared of you.'

'I suppose. You've got it right. Marie's my cousin. She was leaving Leichhardt and she was short of money so I paid her bill. Wasn't much.'

'You ever heard of Kev Roseberry?'

'Might've, not sure.'

'He's the bloke Marie took up with and had the child by. He trained some bloke you fought and that's how they met.'

'I don't remember him. When I was fighting all I thought about was fighting. Full stop.'

'Marie didn't tell you who the father of the child was, and you didn't ask?'

He shook his head. He'd relaxed by now and was half turned away, watching the people in the park. His voice was full of irony, sarcasm, anger. 'You know what Abo women are like, fuck anyone.'

'That's a bloody stupid thing to say and you know it.'

He sagged against the backrest and all the aggression was gone. 'They call me an Uncle Tom, you know, some of the people, because I don't make a thing about being Aboriginal.'

'That's understandable, sounds as if you've got a problem with all that. I'm sure you're not alone, but I'm not your psychiatrist. Roseberry's dying of cancer. He's got some money to leave and he wants to know about Marie and about her kid, Siobhan, if there's any grandchildren and if they need help. No, make that if Marie'd accept it. She told Kev years back that she didn't want to know him.'

'How did he treat her?'

'With neglect.'

'Got a guilty conscience now, has he? Is he some kind of religious freak?'

I sighed. 'I'm getting tired of talking to you, Jimmy. Can you tell me anything about Marie and Siobhan or not? Yes or no. Yes, and I'll be grateful, no, and you can fuck off and I'll tackle it some other way.'

'You're a hard bastard, aren't you?'

'Sometimes not, sometimes I have to be.'

'What's in it for you?'

I got up and started to walk back towards the path. A soccer ball came skidding towards me and I kicked it back as hard as I could. The kid closest to me shouted when it went past him.

'Sorry,' I said.

I got to the path and kept walking. I heard footsteps behind me. O'Day tapped me on the shoulder.

'Come back to the house. I'll help you find Marie, but it's tricky.'

O'Day took me through the house to a back room he'd set up as an office-cum-recording studio. There were guitars lying around, a drum kit, a couple of keyboards and electronic equipment I couldn't identify. He rolled and lit a joint, which he offered me. I refused.

'Got a beer?'

'Juicehead.'

He fetched a can and we sat facing each other over a tangle of cables.

'Marie's had a lot of trouble in her life,' he said. 'Grog, blokes, illness. She went hyper-political and got into demonstrations, sit-ins, protests. She got bashed by the police and hurt pretty badly. She's on a disability pension and just getting by. I help her out from time to time, but she's proud and doesn't like it. I do it through a third party. Also, she reckons I've sold out to whitey.'

'What about Siobhan?'

From just puffing, he now drew deeply on the joint, sucked the smoke in and held it down. Then he did it again. He seemed to need the comfort of it, or perhaps something else. I took a sip of beer and waited.

'She's with Marie. She's got a kid. They're doing it tough.'

'Where are they?'

'She won't accept charity from—'

'Whitey, okay. This isn't charity, Jimmy—it's long overdue support money from a decent man trying to make amends.'

'Marie doesn't admit there's any decent white people.'

'And that's as stupid a thing as what you said before.'

'I know. Okay, I'll tell you where they are and you can try your luck.'

'You won't come with me?'

He sucked hard on the joint again and shook his head.

'Why not?'

He'd smoked the joint almost down to the end but he wasn't done. He drew on it again until it must have singed his fingertips. 'You wouldn't understand.'

'Try me.'

He let the roach fall to the floor, got up, went to one of the keyboards, hit some switches and began to play. Straight blues riffs. He was stoned. He kept playing, seemingly in a trance. I looked around the room and saw a desk with a computer and printer wired up to other equipment. I opened a drawer in the desk and found a contact book. There was an entry for 'Marie O' with an address in Marrickville but no telephone number. I copied down the address and left him to do whatever he thought he was doing, wherever he thought he was.

My mobile rang as soon as I started the car. It was a nurse at the hospital where Kev was being treated. She said that Mr Roseberry's condition had deteriorated and that he wanted to see me urgently. He'd asked the medical staff to hold off on palliative medication until my visit.

'It's that bad?' I said.

'I'm afraid so.'

I drove to the hospital and was ushered into Kev's room. A man I didn't know was there with Kev's doctor, who I had met, and a nurse. Kev was propped up in the bed and the life seemed to be leaking out of him. His voice was a croak.

'Sorry to rush you, mate. Is she alive, Marie?'

'Yes, Kev.'

'And the kid?'

'Yes.'

'That's all I needed. You'll do the right thing, I know. Okay, let's get this bloody thing signed. This is Ed Stewart, Cliff. He's a solicitor and pretty honest for a lawyer. That's a joke, Ed.'

Stewart smiled dutifully and produced a document that he, Kev and the nurse signed. The effort seemed to drain Kev to the dregs. He held out a hand and I shook it, gently. 'Ed'll explain it to you, mate. I knew I could count on you and . . .'

A spasm shook him and robbed him of the power of speech. He nodded at the doctor and closed his eyes. The nurse shepherded Stewart and me out of the room. We stood in silence outside the door for a second before walking away.

'I hope I'm up to making a joke as I go out,' Stewart said.

'Me, too.'

We went into a waiting room and Stewart showed me the paper. 'This is Kevin's last will and testament, revoking all others, while of sound mind, blah, blah. He had me draw it up this morning. It leaves his estate to be divided equally between Marie

O'Day and her daughter Siobhan. And there's provision for any issue Siobhan might have. You are named as the executor.'

'What if I hadn't been able to confirm that they were around?'

'He seemed to have every confidence that you would.'

Kevin Roseberry died that night. As executor I was responsible for his funeral arrangements. I made them and tossed up whether to contact Marie and invite her along. I decided not. Dealing with her was going to be tricky enough without it happening in an emotion-charged atmosphere. Kev was cremated; I said a few words, so did some of the denizens of the pubs he'd frequented. We had a bit of a wake at the Toxteth Hotel and that was that.

Stewart, the solicitor, said he'd put Kev's estate through the probate process and then it'd be up to me to arrange the distribution of the assets. No point in putting it off any longer. I drove to Marrickville, located the flat in a small block sitting in a sea of concrete, no balconies, and wearing an air of defeat. I knocked and the woman who answered was recognisable as Marie of the photograph, but only just. She was rail-thin and haggard; her dark, wiry hair had a wide white streak in it of a kind I'd seen before. Not a cosmetic touch—the effect of hair growing back on the site of a serious wound.

'Yeah?' she said, packing as much hostility as it was possible to get into the word.

'Ms O'Day, my name's Hardy. Your cousin James O'Day gave me your address because there's something very important I have to discuss with you.'

'What would that be?'

'Can I come in, please? It's to do with quite a lot of money and better discussed in private.'

'I don't want any money from Jimmy.'

'It's not from him.'

'I don't know anyone else with money.'

'You knew this man. Come on, it won't take long.'

For a minute I thought she was going to slam the door but she didn't. She stepped back and let me push through and follow her. I doubted that she'd ask me to sit down or do anything even mildly hospitable. The front door opened straight into the living room, which was shabby but tidy. There was a TV set and a cheap CD player, a well-stocked bookshelf and a milk crate filled with baby toys near one of the chairs.

She was wearing jeans, sneakers and a faded black cardigan. She crossed her thin arms over her thin chest and gripped her shoulders as if she was physically holding herself together.

'Well?' she said.

'Kevin Roseberry died a couple of days ago.'

'Well that's one less white prick.'

'He had quite a lot of money when he died.'

'Bullshit. What he didn't piss up against a wall he gave to the bookies and the TAB.'

'He won a lottery, Ms O'Day. He owned a house worth almost a million dollars and there's a couple of hundred thousand in investments. I'm a private detective. Kevin hired me to find you. He wanted you and your daughter to have the money. I understand there's a grandchild, too.'

Her hands flew from her shoulders to her face and she collapsed into a chair. She lost colour and her olive skin went a blotchy pink.

'What's wrong?' I said.

'Crook heart.' She fumbled in the pocket of her cardigan and got a pill jar in her shaking hand. 'Get me a glass of water, will you.'

I went through to the kitchen and filled a glass. When I got back she was struggling to get the top from the bottle. I helped and shook a pill out into her hand. She got it to her mouth and I helped her steady the glass as she drank.

'Thanks,' she said. The colour slowly returned and she pulled herself up from the slumped position. 'Sorry about that.'

'Jimmy told me you were ill.'

'Jimmy talks too bloody much. So he told you about Siobhan and the baby, eh? They're at the park just now. Lovely little kid. Prick of a father, but, just like . . . Did I hear you right—Kevin left over a million bucks?'

I nodded.

'To me and Siobhan?'

'And the grandchild. Kevin hoped there were some.'

She drank the rest of the water. 'Sit down, Mr . . . whatever your name is.'

I sat and she looked around the room. 'Crummy, isn't it? All we can afford on a couple of pensions. Look, who's got the say about this money?'

'When I told Kev I'd located you he made me the executor of his will, so the answer is—me.'

She said nothing for a minute, fixing me with a stare that seemed to strip me bare. 'Kevin wasn't a bad man. Just weak, like so many.'

'Black and white,' I said. 'And like some women.'

The first smile I'd seen from her appeared, making her look younger and stronger. 'You're not so bad. Okay, let's see how you handle this—I've never been certain that Siobhan was Kevin's child. Could've been one of a couple of others. I was a wild girl at the time. You've met one of the other possibles.'

'Jimmy.'

'Right. He's sure she's his although she's fairer than both of us. Buggered him up and he gave me a very hard time when I kept saying I wasn't sure, which was the truth. Oh, I know he gets a bit of money to us from time to time. Bet he doesn't know I know.'

'That's right.'

The smile came back. 'Men. All right, Mr Detective, what d'you make of all that? Kev's left his dough to a woman who fucked around, and a child and grandchild who might not be related to him at all.'

I didn't even have to think about it. The will was rock solid, there was no clause about verifying parenthood or anything like that.

'Kev was a gambler like you said, Marie. I reckon he'd have taken a punt.'

I put the Currawongs CDs on the shelf somewhere between the Beatles and Dire Straits and whenever I play them I raise a glass to Kev.

BREAK POINT

From *The Big Score* (2007)

'You play tennis, right, Cliff?' Sydney Featherstone said.

'After a fashion,' I said.

'Come on, your mate Frank Parker told me you played at White City. Schoolboy championships.'

'Yeah, got to the third round of the doubles. Newk and Roche had nothing to worry about.'

'But you know the difference between a topspin backhand and a lob?'

I nodded. We were in the bar of the Woollahra Golf Club. Featherstone was a senior partner in a sports management agency with top-level clients in a variety of sports. They had men and women on their books, Australians and internationals. Doing well, Frank had told me when he arranged the meeting. An old mate putting business my way.

'We're thinking of signing this kid, Cameron Beaumont. He's just turned eighteen.'

'I read about him,' I said. 'Reached hundredth in the world the other week.'

'That's him. Stands about one-eighty-five, ideal for tennis, weighs eighty kilos. Leftie, quick; held the New South Wales junior one hundred metres record. Bench-presses his weight plus quite a bit more. Looks like Tom Cruise with legs.'

'Sounds like money in the bank. What's the problem with the superstar-to-be?'

'He goes missing for days at a time. No one knows where or why.'

'A girlfriend.'

'Nothing wrong with girlfriends on the tennis scene. Within reason. If that's it, fine. But why the secrecy?'

'A boyfriend, then?'

'Those who know him say not.'

'When he comes back is he out of shape, distracted?'

'No. Plays just as well as ever or better. It's a mystery we need to solve.'

'Why? Let him have his privacy.'

'Are you kidding? There's no such thing in elite sports.'

'Is hundredth in the world elite?'

'At his age, potentially.'

'Lleyton Hewitt won an ATP event at sixteen, I seem to recall.'

'He had the background. This kid's a battler, up from nothing—local courts, no support. Both parents dead. He was fostered out as a kid. Pillar to post. You know how it is. He got on the satellite circuit at sixteen through a sports master at school and he's been going through the opposition like a dose of salts. It's a hand-to-mouth living but he's come on strong just recently.'

'Why hasn't he been picked up before this?'

'That's a funny thing. A couple of sponsors and management mobs have approached him but he's pissed them off. Must be waiting for a top-drawer offer.'

'Have you approached him?'

'Not yet. There's one thing I haven't told you. He takes off on these jaunts from time to time over the last year or so, but always after he wins a tournament or comes close. He's playing in an event next week that he's got a shot at winning. A few of the top players have pulled out injured and Beaumont's in really good form. Got in on a wild card. He's bound to take off—should give you a chance to see what's up.'

'Why is it important that I know something about tennis?'

'You're going to have to watch him play. Be bloody boring if you didn't like the game. Plus, Frank said you were a good judge of character. That comes out on a tennis court, win or lose, wouldn't you say?'

'Sometimes,' I said.

Beaumont was playing late in the afternoon of the first day and I arrived in time to watch him. Just as well. He was up against a veteran who'd beaten a lot of top players in his time. He had a good serve and a wide variety of shots plus experience. It didn't matter. Beaumont blew him away in under an hour with a mixture of power and guile.

Featherstone turned up at my shoulder as I was loading sun-dried tomato and cheese onto a biscuit. The second glass of white wine, out of a bottle with a label, had gone down well. 'Impressive, huh?'

'Definitely. I'd like to see him up against someone his own age, especially a runner.'

'Not next time up. He's got a qualifier who can scarcely believe he got through the first round. But if the other matches go according to the seeds and he keeps on like he started, he'll meet Rufus Fong in the semi. He can run.'

Cambo, as the papers had decided to call him, advanced to his semi-final with Fong. I went along, found a seat in the shade, and witnessed the most devastating destruction of a top-liner by a newcomer since the unseeded Boris Becker won Wimbledon. Fong hadn't won a Grand Slam event but he'd come close, and had more than a dozen other titles to his credit. He could run all right, but he couldn't hide. Other players made the mistake of giving him angles. Fong's speed allowed him to run the balls down and his strength permitted him to return the angles with spades. Beaumont hit straight at him with extraordinary power. Fong had to either get out of the way or play defensively, moving back and off-balance. No contest. Beaumont volleyed away Fong's weak returns with ease, dispatched his serves, and never went to deuce on his own serve.

Beaumont was demonstrative on court, lamenting his occasional misses—never on crucial points—and giving himself the odd triumphant fist. But he had charm. He applauded his opponent's few successes with sincerity and shrugged off the several bad line calls he got. At the net, having won, his handshake appeared genuine, and he chatted with Fong all the way to the umpire's chair. No chucking away of sweatbands, just a courteous wave to the crowd and the signing of a judicious number of autographs.

In the final, Beaumont played an American hardcourt specialist who gave him some trouble. The American dropped the first set but came back strongly to win the second in a tie-break. Beaumont served some double faults and appeared rattled. But he was his old self in the third. He broke serve early, held his own easily, broke again and held and the American wilted. Beaumont won the match 6–1 in the third set and that's when I started to go to work.

Beaumont must have checked out of his hotel in the morning because, after the victory ceremony was over and he'd had some obligatory interviews and some photos taken, he changed his clothes, loaded his tennis gear into the back of a beat-up 4WD, and took off. Thanks to my pass, I was close by in the privileged parking area and I dropped in behind him as he left the car park, picked up the motorway and headed west. Not the coast then, but there was nothing wrong with the mountains at that time of year.

Beaumont drove fast but well. His 4WD laboured a bit on the hills and I had no trouble keeping tabs on him in my recently serviced and tuned old Falcon. Daylight saving was a week or so away and the light started to fade quickly in the late afternoon. He stopped in Katoomba, went to an ATM for money and then spent up big on groceries. The carton of cigarettes surprised me, as did the bottle of brandy and the six-pack of beer he bought at the pub after showing his ID. I didn't have to show mine to buy a half-bottle of Bundy. I had a sleeping bag and a donkey coat, but if I was going to spend a night in the mountains I thought I might need some internal heating as well.

Beaumont drove as if he knew the back roads well. We were soon on dirt, winding through the bush. There was no traffic and I had to hang well back, keeping tabs by the flashes of his brake lights. Eventually, after a hill climb, a descent and another climb, he pulled up outside a cabin set back from the track and shielded by a long stand of she-oaks. By then I was on foot watching this from a sheltered place. I'd stopped a hundred metres away when I heard his noisy engine turn off.

We were at a decent elevation and it was cold. I wrapped the coat tight around me and watched as Beaumont came back to his car to unload the supplies. The cabin door opened and a tall man stood in the dim light—at a guess from a Tilley lamp—inside. Beaumont handed him a box and scooted back for another. The two went inside and the cabin door closed. The windows were curtained but I could see another light come on and silhouettes of the figures moving inside.

It was cold but quiet, and I managed several hours of fitful sleep with a few periods of wakefulness in between. The extra chill just before dawn woke me and I got out to piss, stamp around and get the stiffness out of my limbs. No mail, no neighbours for kilometres—a perfect hiding place. For what? For whom?

I had gym clothes in the car—sweat pants and top, T-shirt, sneakers. I changed into them and equipped myself with a couple of the tools of my trade—binoculars and a good camera with a zoom lens. I'd had nothing to eat since some canapes back at the tennis while Beaumont was accepting his horrible crystal trophy and his no doubt very welcome cheque. My stomach was growling as I took up my position and saw wisps of smoke from the cabin chimney drift up into the clear blue sky. I could smell the eucalypts and the scents of all the other trees and bushes whose names I didn't know. One of the names for us PEAs is snooper. I was one now and, in this setting, quite happy about it.

They came out around eight o'clock. I got a good long-range shot of the man. He was fortyish, shorter than Beaumont but more strongly built. Both men carried tennis racquets and Beaumont had a string bag full of balls. Keeping under cover I followed them to where there was a clearing about half the size of a tennis court. Beaumont's companion was smoking. He puffed away while Beaumont did some stretches and warm-up exercises. For the next thirty minutes Beaumont had balls belted at him, aimed high, low, left and right, at very close range. He missed only two, getting his racquet solidly onto them and knocking them clear of the other man—except one which caught the older man on the shoulder and spun him round. He dropped his racquet and a spasm of coughing erupted from him. Beaumont comforted him with an arm around his shoulder. When he recovered, the session began again. They must have had fifty balls in the bag and Beaumont darted around picking them up from the ground and in the thin scrub around the clearing when they'd all been used. Then they started over again.

After that Beaumont chopped wood at the back of the cabin for an hour. There was a pile of old railway sleepers in a lean-to shed. He carried them out, chopped through them, making half-metre lengths, and then split the lengths with a block-buster. I'd done something similar as a punishment fatigue in the army, and I knew how hard that old weathered wood could be. It made me tired just to watch him.

The day warmed up and the insects buzzed and birds sang. I snapped a few more photos in a better light and with a better background. As a city man born and bred, a few hours in the country goes a fair way with me and I was getting tired of holding my position behind a tree. Beaumont's host brought out two mugs of tea or coffee. They squatted companionably near the chopping block. The man smoked and spiked his mug with brandy. He also had another coughing fit.

Beaumont changed into shorts and a singlet and set off along a fire trail into the bush. He was away an hour and came back moving at the same speed as when he'd left. I was about ready to call it quits. The relationship appeared to be somewhere between fraternal and professional. Whatever it was, it certainly wasn't going to do the boy's tennis career any harm.

I ducked down suddenly when I saw the man moving towards where I was hiding. I was working mentally on a paparazzi story when he stopped a few metres away. He looked quickly back at the cabin, sucked in several deep breaths, bent over and vomited heavily into a pile of leaves. He recovered, used a stick to clean up, and went back to the cabin. I got a much better look at him then and he was somehow familiar. I'd seen him before, or his photograph, but I couldn't remember where or when.

I went straight to the office, hooked the camera up to the computer and printed out copies of the photographs. I picked out the best shot of the mystery man and made a couple of blown-up copies. I studied the face intently: square jaw, thin mouth, heavy brows, straight nose, thick grey hair worn long. No scars. I looked at it too long so that in the end the feeling of familiarity had gone.

The FBI or the CIA could no doubt have run it against the millions of other faces they have digitally recorded and search for a match. Not an available facility for a one-man operation in Newtown. My best bet was Harry Tickener, a journalist who has worked the streets, boardrooms, courts and parliament in Sydney longer than he likes to recall. Harry's up with the technology, but he receives so many emails a day you're lucky to hear back from him within a week. I took one of the photos and went to see him in his Surry Hills office, where he runs an online newsletter that prints stories others are afraid to touch.

Harry groaned when he saw me walk in the door carrying two styrofoam cups of coffee. 'Jesus Christ, there goes an hour's work,' he said.

'But here's the best coffee in Sydney.'

He grinned, took the top off his cup and flipped it towards the bin. Missed. 'Thanks, Cliff. Always good to see you. What's up?'

I put the photo on his desk, keeping it covered with my hand. 'Take a quick look at this. Just get an impression and see if a name springs to mind. I felt I knew the face but I've studied it too long.'

I uncovered the image. Harry looked at it, blinked and snapped his fingers. 'Jesus Christ,' he said. 'I'd swear that's Daniel Murphy twenty years down the track. You've found him. Where is he?'

I shook my head. The name triggered the recollection I'd been searching for. Daniel Murphy was an international hockey player who'd killed his wife's lover. The couple were separated at the time with a young child and Murphy had been told that the lover had a record of child abuse. He shot him, went on the run and wounded a policeman before he was captured. His counsel stressed the mitigating circumstances, but the wounding of the cop counted heavily against him and he was sentenced to eighteen years to serve twelve before being eligible for parole. Murphy had escaped from Goulburn gaol four years into his sentence, injuring an inmate and a guard, and had never been recaptured.

I said, 'It wasn't quite twenty years back, was it? What happened to the wife and child?'

'The wife committed suicide when Murphy was convicted. That's all I know.'

Usually, when Harry helps, I promise him the story if it can be told when everything sorts out, if it sorts out. The strike rate isn't that good, but there wasn't a chance of it happening this time. I thanked him and left him grumbling.

Using the name I had, I trawled through the *Sydney Morning Herald* database and came up with the information in detail. My recollection was confirmed, with additions: Murphy had emigrated from Ireland to Australia when he was barely more than a youth and had no relatives here. His wife's maiden name was Wexler. She'd been a street kid with emotional problems and when found dead in her flat from a drug overdose the infant was dehydrated and suffering from various illnesses to do with malnourishment and neglect. It was odds-on that the child had been put in care and fostered out to become, in time, Cameron Beaumont.

I emailed Sydney Featherstone that I was on the job, making progress and that the omens were good. I drove straight back to the mountains and pulled up outside the cabin early in the afternoon. I approached the building and a dog, tethered near the steps to the front porch, began barking loudly. I stood where I was and waited.

Cameron Beaumont opened the door and looked me over suspiciously. Despite my jeans and leather jacket I might still have been a cop. Can't tell these days.

'What do you want?' he said.

'To talk to you and Daniel Murphy.'

That rocked him. He looked over his shoulder and his body language directly contradicted what he said: 'There's no one here of that name.'

I held up the photograph. 'Was yesterday.'

Like all great tennis players, he had vision like a jet pilot and he didn't need to come any closer to see the picture. 'Who are you?'

'We can talk about that and a few other things.'

The dog kept barking. I heard hacking coughs coming from inside and then Murphy appeared in the doorway.

'He's sick,' Beaumont said.

I nodded. 'I know. I saw him chuck his guts up yesterday. You didn't.'

Beaumont turned his head. 'Dad?'

Murphy shrugged. 'Don't worry, this had to happen some day. You a reporter?'

'No, I'm a private detective and right now I'm thinking about all this staying private. That is, if you'll talk to me. You could start by calling the dog off.'

'Quiet, Max,' Murphy said. Raising his voice caused him to start coughing again. When he recovered his breath he invited me in. I went past the dog and Beaumont into the cabin. It was a mobile home that had been put up on stumps and ceased to be mobile. It was cramped but everything appeared well ordered and arranged. Several windows were open and there was a fresh eucalyptus scent mingling with the smell of cigarettes. Everything was spotlessly clean except for an ashtray brimming with butts.

'Make some coffee, Cam,' Murphy said, 'and we'll let the man tell us who he is, first off.'

Beaumont moved towards the back of the room and ran water. Murphy sat on one side of a built-in eating bench and indicated to me to sit opposite. I put the photo on the surface and showed him my PEA licence.

Murphy lit a cigarette. 'I met a few blokes in your game inside.'

'You would,' I said. 'Hazard of the job. I've been there myself.'

I told them my story and then Daniel Murphy told me his. After he escaped from gaol he'd made his way to Queensland, where he worked on fishing boats, and then to Wollongong and into a plastics factory.

'Little show,' he said. 'No one cared who you were or where you came from. I got a driver's licence in a false name, Medicare card—the works. One day there was a chemical spill—dioxin—and I got two lungs full, thank you very much. Like inhaling that Agent Orange shit. Fucked my lungs first and then it spread. I took a payment to keep quiet about it. Didn't like doing it, but I couldn't afford to make a fuss.'

By the time we'd finished the coffee Murphy had worked his way through a few more cigarettes. He asked Cameron to get him a drink and the young man set a couple of cans on the table.

'Doesn't drink himself,' Murphy said as he cracked a can. 'Smart.'

'How did you end up here?'

'I had some money. Went to Sydney and tracked Cameron down. I always meant to do it but I didn't have the chance till then. Wasn't easy, couldn't go through official channels, but I had a few names from people who'd written to me in the early days in gaol. I found him. Doesn't look much like me, but he's the spitting image of my dad as I remember him. Show him the photo, Cam.'

Cameron produced a faded, slightly creased photograph of a man in football togs with a 1950s look to them. Murphy was right—the resemblance was striking.

'That's all I've got of him. He was a champion Gaelic footballer. He was IRA and the Brits killed him.'

Cameron had hardly spoken a word. Now he handled the photograph like a precious relic, smoothing it in his big, strong hands.

'Anyway, when I found out that Cam was a tennis champ I was that proud. I'd had a pretty useless life up to that point and I decided I'd do something with the time I had left.'

'Dad's a natural sportsman,' Cameron said quietly.

'Was,' Murphy said. 'Any ball game, I could play it.'

'We met up about eighteen months ago when I was battling away in the satellites. His training and help got me to where I am now.'

'You'll be well inside the top one hundred after that win,' I said. 'I saw it.'

Murphy stubbed out another cigarette and looked at me. 'I wish I had. I'd give anything to see him play, but it's too big a risk. Too many people who'd pick me.'

'You could wear a disguise,' I said.

Cameron smiled. 'Yeah, we thought of that, but Dad hasn't got the breath to get up stairs and that. And he needs to smoke all the time, and . . .'

'Couldn't handle it, Hardy,' Murphy said, 'and the way the fucking world's going with the pricks in charge now, they'd come down on him like a shit shower for having a crim for an old man and harbouring him. Cam's been seen around here. They'd put it together.'

Murphy and I drained our cans. He fiddled with a cigarette and then put it down. 'I've had chemotherapy and it only made me worse. I haven't got long. I know how to take myself out peaceably and I'll do it when it gets too bad. We've talked about it—Cam and me. He'll help me to disappear.'

Cameron's eyes were wet. 'And every fucking thing I win'll be dedicated to him in my mind and in my heart.'

'The question is, Hardy,' Murphy said, picking up the cigarette and lighting it, 'what are you going to do?'

I reported to Featherstone that his intended client was merely doing some specialised training on his own in a bush location. No girls, no boys, no drink, no drugs. Featherstone was edgy about it, but when he heard that a pitch from another management group had fallen on deaf ears, he agreed to go along.

Daniel Murphy died six weeks after our first interview. I'd seen him a few times subsequently, did a bit of ball collecting. Cameron contacted me when his father died and I went up there and helped him with the burial. We put Daniel Murphy deep in the ground in the national park at a place where the birds sing and the insects buzz and the leaves fall softly.

AN ABC OF CRIME WRITING

This ABC of Crime Writing was not intended as a 'how to write crime' exercise, but perhaps that's what it is. Things don't always turn out the way a writer planned. I wanted to provide a kind of tour through the work of crime writers I'm familiar with, drawing attention to some of the key ideas, styles and devices they use to write their stories. I found myself occasionally offering advice, suggestions, a strategy, preferring one way of doing things to another, but that was still a very secondary motive.

Agreeing with Michael Wilding's injunction that 'crime fiction is not literature, it is entertainment', I wanted to be entertaining. So I made fun of certain writers and their characteristics, quoted amusing snatches of dialogue and tried never to be prescriptive or solemn. When I looked through an early draft I realised that I had in fact written my version of a 'how to write crime' manual.

I believe that the best and possibly the only way to learn to write crime stories is to read a great many of them. Read for relaxation, enjoyment, perhaps for information, perhaps merely to pass the time. Read, read often and read a lot of different stuff. Read everything you can find of authors you like and sample the work of others you like less. This is certainly what I did. From an early age I read a variety of crime novels, from the pulp of Carter Brown to the polish of Nicholas Blake, from the clue-puzzle cosiness of Agatha Christie to the grime and danger of Dashiell Hammett.

I read vast numbers of the enormous output of John Creasey, who has serial characters the Toff, the Baron and Inspector West. These are essentially polite books. Increasingly, though, I favoured the impolite authors—Peter Cheyney, James Hadley Chase, Dashiell Hammett, Raymond Chandler and Ross Macdonald. Over time I acquired all of Hammett and Chandler—novels and story collections—in green Penguin paperbacks, and all of Macdonald in various paperback editions.

As a break from study as an undergraduate and postgraduate research, which included overseas travel and fieldwork in places like New Guinea, the Solomon Islands and Fiji, I read and re-read these authors. I remember sharing a cramped space aboard a patrol boat in the Solomons with a touring District Officer and us both pulling out copies of Chandler's *The Big Sleep* for our kerosene-lamp-lit, mosquito-net-shrouded night-time reading.

American writer Robert B. Parker, the author of many crime novels, who wrote his doctoral thesis on Hammett, Chandler and Macdonald, said, 'When the time came to write I found I could write.' I suspect he experienced the same thing as me: soaked in the plots, the rhythms, the cadences of the hard-boiled writers, he discovered he could, without too much difficulty, produce his own version, giving it his personal stamp.

So this catalogue reflects my own journey through the rich and diverse field of crime fiction and may provide shortcuts for aspiring writers. It is necessarily selective; no one could cover all the crime fiction available, and well-informed readers will see gaps and prejudices. There is, for example, a subset of the genre with priests as investigators to which I am averse. Not to mention investigators in ancient Greece, Rome and Egypt, and cat and dog detectives. Readers will see that I have read and drawn on the work of more male writers than female. I find it easier and more satisfying to immerse myself in the male world with its emphasis on violence, graphic description, action and all the fragilities of men.

My preference for the hard-boiled over the runny-yolked is obvious. But there is interest and pleasure to be found every time the social fabric is torn by a homicide and the effort is made to restore it . . . temporarily.

—PC

Acknowledgements

Thanks to Jean Bedford, Linda Funnell, Michael Fitzjames (for the illustration that opens this part, 'M is for mean streets') and Michael Wilding

A *is for* **action**. This is a matter of balance. Some writers, like P.D. James, have very little; some, like Mickey Spillane, have too much. If the low-action model is adopted, the characterisation, dialogue and descriptions had better be good. They were in James's early novels but when she padded them out with descriptions of furniture and architecture ('mullioned windows' adorn many country houses), things slowed to a halt. Spillane's violence was overkill, literally.

A woman I was talking to at some book gathering asked me what kinds of books I wrote. I was writing crime, spy and historical stuff at the time and said I wrote action novels. 'Oh, I hate action,' she said. Her favourite author? Jane Austen.

A *is also for* **adultery**. This has lost its potency as a force in crime fiction. In the past, concealment of it could be a prime motive for a murder. Once the chief ground for divorce, 'irretrievable breakdown' has sidelined it. It may still play a part if a pre-nuptial agreement comes into the picture.

A *is also for* **age**. The age of the chief character in a long-running series of books can create a problem for the author. Agatha Christie virtually ignored the problem; Hercule Poirot, a middle-aged refugee from Belgium when introduced in *The Mysterious Affair at Styles* in 1917, would have topped a hundred by the time of his final activities in the 1970s. Christie aged him slowly without comment, though admittedly he was pretty old and infirm by the end.

Robert B. Parker chose not to age his chief character Spenser, a private eye, at all. Had he done so he would have been in trouble. Spenser fought Jersey Joe Walcott, former heavyweight champion, when he was, say, twenty and Walcott was in 'the twilight of his career.'[1] Given that, he would have been in his nineties by the time of his last case in *Sixkill* (published posthumously in 2011). Spenser is still appearing in a continuation of Parker's books by Ace Atkins.

John D. MacDonald, creator of Travis McGee, said that an author could credibly age a series character at one-third the natural rate. This is a good working formula.

A *is also for* **alcohol**. This is an essential ingredient. I advise giving protagonists a drinking problem, which they struggle, more or less successfully, to control. This provides narrative texture. Reformed alcoholics are also a possibility, especially if they fall off the wagon from time to time, but AA meetings aren't a lot of fun and the struggle to remain dry can become tedious. The Matthew Scudder novels of Lawrence Block (*The Sins of the Fathers*, 1976, and following) and the Dave Robicheaux novels of James Lee Burke (*The Neon Rain*, 1987, and following) provide examples.

An incidental alcoholic character is very useful, especially in private-eye novels. The investigator can exploit this weakness, feel slightly guilty about it but still get the job done.

The classic ambivalent comment about drinking is at the end of Chandler's *The Big Sleep* (1939): 'On the way downtown I stopped at a bar and had a couple of double Scotches. They didn't do me any good. All they did was make me think of Silver-Wig, and I never saw her again.' That's getting a lot of resonance out of a couple of drinks.

---

1 This is a rare example of sports fan Parker getting things wrong. Strictly speaking, Walcott did not have a twilight. He retired after his second loss to Rocky Marciano in 1951. The television series based on Parker's book took years and weight off Spenser by having him fight José Torres, a light heavyweight world champion in the 1960s.

B *is for* **backstory**. In most crime novels, especially private-eye books, something in the past, preferably murder, surfaces in the present and causes distress. Investigation therefore involves the past and the present, providing a rich texture and helping to fill up the pages to publishable length.

Sometimes the matter in the past is very distant and obscure. The plot of Dashiell Hammett's *The Maltese Falcon* (1930) is embellished by a myth about the gifting of a golden bird by the Spanish king to the Knights Hospitaller during the Crusades. The details don't matter. This was a brilliant exotic touch, providing a backdrop to an intricate, sordid contemporary story.

A misplaced trust, rooted in family history and tradition, with details provided, is a good backstory setting. Then, in the here and now, A assures his lifelong friend B that he had nothing to do with the death of C in the past. B defends A to detective E who doesn't believe him and comes to suspect B. Then A's unreliability becomes clear, probably through the intervention of love interest F and things move towards a resolution. Examples abound.

B *is also for* **blackmail**. This is not as popular a theme as it once was. Decriminalisation of homosexuality removed one avenue for this form of extortion and our expectation of ethical behaviour from politicians and business leaders is now so low their transgressions don't need to be hidden. It was a very useful crime for writers, because, unlike others, it forced the perpetrator to maintain some form of connection, however temporary, with the victim. This provided opportunities for the blackmailer to make mistakes and gave the investigator a sporting chance.

When blackmail featured in crime novels it was usually as a precursor to murder, as in *The Big Sleep*.

B *is also for* ***Bradshaw's***. For over a hundred years, *Bradshaw's* was the bible of railway travellers in Britain. It was consulted by investigators like Sherlock Holmes, Hercule Poirot, Sexton Blake, 'Bulldog' Drummond, and others who needed to move around the country.

Bradshaw's provided writers in the 'Golden Age' with plot points (see Agatha Christie's *Death in the Clouds*, 1935, using the continental Bradshaw's). The publication issued frequent amendments and updates. Woe betide the suspect whose alibi relied on the arrival of the 8.15 from Kings Cross to Ely at 9.10 who'd failed to recognise *Bradshaw's* notice of the cancellation of the 8.15 service on the day in question.

The chief exponent of the railway mystery, in which time-tabling figured along with other aspects of the railway system, was the former railway engineer Freeman Wills Crofts.

A contemporary writer, Edward Marston, has attempted to revive the railway mystery (see H for historical).

B *is also for* **butler**. Did the butler ever do it? I can't recall an example but I haven't read Agatha Christie, Ngaio Marsh, Georgette Heyer or Dorothy L. Sayers exhaustively. Given the convention that it's where suspicion should fall in the country-house story, if he had it in for the master or mistress of the house, other family members or a guest, it would be unwise for the butler to do it. Better to sublet the act to a footman or gardener.

In 1933 Georgette Heyer worked a twist in *Why Shoot a Butler?* The butler is the first victim.

C *is for* **car**. Given the tedious prevalence of car chases in crime stories on film and television, it is surprising to see that cars play a comparatively insignificant part in books. Police detectives just use the pool cars, except for Colin Dexter's Inspector Morse, who drives a venerable Jaguar. Ian Rankin's John Rebus drives a battered Saab when not using a pool car. Lee Child's Jack Reacher has no car at all. How could it be otherwise? He doesn't have a licence or a fixed abode. When he needs wheels, he borrows, usually from a woman.

C *is also for* **CCTV**. Closed circuit television now keeps watch on vast areas of modern cities. London, in particular, is said to be intensely covered but so are capital and provincial cities in many countries. CCTV footage figures prominently in many crime novels, especially the later ones of Barry Maitland (*Silvermeadow*, 2000, and others). The footage is notoriously grainy and flickering, which allows technicians to play walk-on parts.

In the early days of CCTV, video cassettes were often wiped and reused, to the frustration of investigators. Now, with high-capacity disks and hard drives, the images can be captured and held for all time. Contemporary criminals in fiction can use the footage to their own advantage, a good example being in Lee Child's *One Shot* (2005).

C *is also for* **clue puzzle**. Coined by the pioneers of mystery fiction, Wilkie Collins, Edgar Allan Poe and Arthur Conan Doyle, this was the dominant mode until the advent of the hard-boiled style (see H for hard-boiled). Agatha Christie was the queen of the clue puzzle but there were many contenders—Ngaio Marsh, Georgette Heyer, Margery Allingham, Dorothy L. Sayers (the latter two with upper-class protagonists) and others. Most of the writers in this mode were women, but some men contributed—John Dickson Carr, Freeman Wills Crofts and the Poet Laureate Cecil Day-Lewis, who wrote under the pseudonym Nicholas Blake.

One of the many variants of the clue-puzzle style was practised by Erle Stanley Gardner in his Perry Mason stories (*The Case of the Velvet Claws*, 1933, and following), where witnesses could be tripped up by apparently minor discrepancies (see C for courtroom drama).

C *is also for* **coincidence**. To be avoided at all times.

C *is also for* **complication**. Raymond Chandler's plots were complicated because he often cobbled together bits from short stories to form the narrative and because he didn't care. 'Scene is more important than plot,' he wrote, and I agree with him. Some critics suggest that a death in *The Big Sleep* is unattributable. Others disagree. I don't care.

In the Golden Age of crime writing, the time of Christie, Sayers, Marsh et al., complications were often resolved in the last chapter when characters were called together, often, interestingly, in the library. Unreality was entrenched.

As a yardstick, no plot should be so complicated that an experienced crime reader cannot explain it within twenty-four hours of finishing the book. After that, with the reader almost certainly deep in another book, explanation cannot be expected.

C *is also for* **courtroom drama**. Setting aside the formulaic contrivances of Erle Stanley Gardner, the courtroom drama as an acknowledged contemporary subset of the crime genre was kicked off by Scott Turow's *Presumed Innocent* (1987). Understandably, the style has flourished most in the United States where the legal system, with its elected judges and district attorneys, plea bargains, bail bondsmen and capital punishment making for corruption and high stakes, has provided a rich field.

John Grisham became a leading practitioner with a series of novels (*A Time to Kill*, 1989, and following) that became hit films—little Tom Cruise in *The Firm*, big John Cusack in *The Runaway Jury*, for example. Other contributors are Steve Martini, Michael Connelly and John Lescroart.

C *is also for* **criminal protagonist**. E.W. Hornung, brother-in-law of Arthur Conan Doyle, began publishing stories in the *Cornhill Magazine* about gentleman thief A.J. Raffles in the 1890s. These were collected and published as *The Amateur Cracksman* in 1899. This 'soft' approach to having a hero working outside the law was continued by Leslie Charteris in his Simon Templar ('the Saint') novels (*Meet the Tiger*, 1928, and following).

In *The Killer Inside Me* (1952), pulp writer Jim Thompson created one of the most psychotic of criminal protagonists. A sane and in that way tougher criminal protagonist was introduced by Donald E. Westlake, writing as Richard Stark, in his violent novels about Parker, who steals and kills. The first of these, *The Hunter* (1962), was filmed as *Point Blank* in 1967, with Lee Marvin perfectly cast as Parker (renamed Walker).

Australian Garry Disher's character Wyatt, who first appeared in *Kickback* (1991), is violent in a violent world but has a personal moral code in which his most violent actions are directed towards those who deserve it.

This style, as practised by Stark and Disher, is perhaps the epitome of hard-boiled, in that the protagonists' emotions, if any, are screwed down tight.

C *is also for* ***Crockford's Clerical Directory*****.** This listing of the Anglican clergy, which began publication in the mid-nineteenth century, was an essential tool for investigators when the bona fides or the career of a clergyman character needed to be checked in the clue-puzzle mysteries of the early twentieth century. Many a vicar was exposed as an imposter, and some were found to have either shady pasts or dubious connections. Vicars figure less frequently in crime fiction now but otherwise nothing has changed.

D *is for* **death**. The British Crime Writers Association stipulated on its formation that a book must include a murder to qualify for a Golden Dagger award, and I agree. An induced suicide might just do. Then the question arises of how soon the murder should occur. Some books, of course, have it on the first page. Unless the murder has occurred before the story begins, I would say it should be within the first quarter of the book.

D *is also for* **doctor**. Very useful characters, doctors. Absolutely essential in police procedurals where one is needed at a crime scene and a pathologist is needed to perform an autopsy, at which some investigators, like Chief Inspector Morse, feel queasy (see S for squeamishness). Others, as in Stuart McKenzie's books, for example, indulge in mordant humour. Doctors may be good guys, family friends, the possessors of knowledge like hidden abortions and secret children, or bad guys—Dr Feelgood drug providers, dodgy plastic surgeons and torturers.

D *is also for* **dream**. Dreams provide useful punctuation points for writers, allowing the action to slow down or be reprised in the consciousness of a character. It is permissible for an investigator to gain an insight through a dream. A dream is a handy way to invoke a memory, which can deepen characterisation, suggesting perhaps a vulnerability not before glimpsed, but the device should be used sparingly to protect the illusion of reality.

D *is also for* **drugs**. Drugs have figured in crime fiction from day one. Not surprisingly, given his own addiction, opium figures in Wilkie Collins's *The Moonstone* (1868), and think of Sherlock Holmes and his 'seven-per-cent solution'. Opium was inevitably part of the picture when Sax Rohmer's Dr Fu Manchu was around.

DEATH *TO* DRUGS

Drugs have figured more prominently in American than in British crime fiction. Raymond Chandler adopted the 'reefer madness' stance, in which a marijuana smoker was inherently unreliable.

Once Mafia novels came on stream (see M for mob), drugs moved to centre stage. Drugs figure interestingly in Mario Puzo's *The Godfather* (1969), where older mafiosi shy away from drug trafficking while the younger, 'made' guys see it as where the money is. The young guys win the battle and, in fiction and in life, the big city mob and drugs have always been closely associated.

In more recent times, writers' attention has shifted to the importation of drugs across the southern border of the United States. Don Winslow's *The Power of the Dog* (2005) is a powerful example with an enormous body count.

E *is for* **email**. A contemporary crime novel without email would be like Sherlock Holmes without telegrams.

E *is also for* **empathy**. With a couple of notable exceptions, most crime novels have at least one empathetic character—someone to like, if not love. This is built-in with partnership stories. If Holmes is too cold for your taste, Watson's bluff affability may appeal; if Morse is too acerbic, sensible long-suffering Lewis may excite your sympathy.

But there is no one to like in *The Maltese Falcon* (John Huston and Bogart humanised Sam Spade somewhat in the film) or in Hammett's Continental Op novels. It is a similar situation with James Ellroy. His cop hero Lloyd Hopkins (*Blood on the Moon*, 1984, and two others) is virtually a psychopath. This was deliberate. After he'd stopped writing about Hopkins, Ellroy was asked what had happened to him. He replied that he'd probably died of AIDS.

Also eschewing empathy as far as his protagonist was concerned was Andrew Vachss in his Burke series of novels beginning with *Flood* (1985). The theme was child abuse and Vachss said of Burke that he was writing about a vision of hell and didn't want a knight-errant as the guide.

E *is also for* **exercise**. There are no half-measures here. Detectives either do or don't. Robert B. Parker's Spenser does. He spars with Hawk in the gym and, as he says tersely, 'Lifts some'. Sue Grafton's Kinsey Millhone jogs to work off the effects of her disgusting fast food diet.

Spade and Chandler's Marlowe, operating well before Jim Fixx's *The Complete Book of Running* changed the world, stayed in their suits throughout. Ian Rankin's Rebus knows he should exercise but has another drink instead; Morse wouldn't dream of it. At the extreme end is Rex Stout's Nero Wolfe, who is so obese he can hardly move and has to use Archie Goodwin to do the legwork.

It's a matter of which demographic the writer is appealing to—jock or slob.

E *is also for* **expertise**. Early detectives like Holmes and Poe's Dupin were experts in things like ciphers, poisons and determining the brands of cigars from the ash. Later practitioners were more like Ross Macdonald's durable Lew Archer—handy with their fists perhaps and bright enough, but with no special skills. A change came with Jonathan Kellerman's psychologist Alex Delaware and Patricia Cornwell's pathologist Kay Scarpetta. Their skills were central to cracking their cases. Chief Inspector Morse was an expert at cryptic crosswords and classical music, which helped occasionally, but mainly gave him opportunities to be smart at Detective Sergeant Lewis's expense.

F *is for* **father**. The worst father in crime fiction (filmic) is Noah Cross in Robert Towne's superb screenplay of *Chinatown*. Cross fathered a child on his own daughter and has designs on the resultant daughter/granddaughter. Few others come close.

General Sternwood in Chandler's *The Big Sleep* combines a louche decadence with a likeable cynicism. He admits to having passed on his own vices to his daughters but believes they may have cultivated a few of their own.

Detectives as fathers can work well, as with Rebus and his accident-prone daughter and with Michael Connelly's half-brother characters, Harry Bosch and Mickey Haller, whose two daughters get together. The main function of a daughter in a crime novel is to make a father character vulnerable. Sentimentality can cause this to go badly wrong, as in James Lee Burke's Robicheaux novels, where it oozes over Robicheaux's daughter Alafair. The only acceptable attitude is tough love.

F *is also for the* **FBI**. Ever since Inspector Lestrade in the Sherlock Holmes stories, there have been incompetent policemen acting as foils to the brighter protagonist. In recent times this role has often been assumed by FBI agents. The G-men are seen as unwieldy and bureaucratic and sometimes corrupt. There is a reluctance to call the FBI in and scepticism about its methods.

A notable exception is Clarice Starling in *The Silence of the Lambs* (1988) who is well and truly up to the job, at least until the foolishness of the novel *Hannibal*. The heaviest verbal put-down of the Bureau comes in one of the Jack Reacher novels where it is characterised as the Federal Bureau of Incompetence.

F *is also for* **film adaptation**. Crime fiction vies with the Western as the genre to be most adapted for films. Some of the best adaptations in my opinion are *The Hound of the Baskervilles*

(1939), *The Maltese Falcon* (1941), *Get Carter* (1971), *Death on the Nile* (1978), *True Confessions* (1981), *The Silence of the Lambs* (1991) and *LA Confidential* (1997). Among the worst, for missing the style and essence of the original story, have been the 1978 remake of *The Big Sleep*, *V.I. Warshawski* (1991) and the 2000 remake of *Get Carter* (one of the worst films of all time).

Far and away the best original screenplay for a crime story is Robert Towne's *Chinatown* (1974).

F *is also for* **food**. Investigators, criminals and suspects have to eat and many writers make eating part of the texture of their books. As noted, Kinsey Millhone eats fast food but also dines frequently at a local Hungarian restaurant where she has friends and sometimes learns things. Ian Rankin laments the sugar- and salt-laden Scots diet, but eats it. A popular takeaway for his characters is vindaloo and chips but Inspector Rebus himself, a purist, favours rice with his curry. Menus in southern novels, like those of James Lee Burke, Carl Hiaasen and James W. Hall feature shrimp, po' boy sandwiches and dirty rice.

Harry Bosch eats on the run and buys take-out to indulge his daughter. He microwaves TV dinners and frozen pizzas. Robert B. Parker's Spenser is a gourmet cook and we get recipes and descriptions of culinary activity. He is also a beer snob but apparently knows or cares little about wine.

Lee Child's Jack Reacher is a big guy, six-foot-five and a hundred and twenty pounds. He eats a lot, mostly in diners, where he favours cheeseburgers for dinner and pancakes with maple syrup for breakfast. Happily, he walks so far hitch-hiking that he keeps his weight under control.

Meals feature prominently in clue-puzzle country-house mysteries, where an absence at breakfast or the wrong use of an implement at dinner can set hares running.

G *is for* **gambling**. In his 1971 survey of British mystery fiction, *Snobbery with Violence*, Colin Watson has a chapter entitled 'De rigueur at Monte'. This pointed to the frequency with which British writers in the Golden Age took their characters to Monte Carlo to gamble or to observe gambling. E. Phillips Oppenheimer's *Murder at Monte Carlo* (1933) is a prime example. Gambling has not figured much since then in crime fiction, though it crops up in Dick Francis's racing novels (see H for horses), and Peter Temple's character Jack Irish (*Bad Debts*, 1996, and following) is a punter and variously involved in the world of racing.

G *is also for* **ghost**. Quite rightly, ghosts are almost entirely absent from crime fiction. The only acceptable 'ghost' is one that turns out to have a perfectly rational explanation as in *The Hound of the Baskervilles* (1902).

In the novels of the mother-and-son team writing under the name Charles Todd (*A Test of Wills*, 1996, and others), a Scotland Yard detective, Ian Rutledge, a survivor of World War I, has on his conscience and in his consciousness a 'ghost' in the form of the voice of his dead Sergeant Hamish McLeod, who taunts and provokes Rutledge as he goes about his work. This is a device admired by some readers and deplored by others.

G *is also for* **guilt**. Guilt is no longer as popular as it once was in crime fiction. Once guilt could cause characters to confess to crimes, to name accomplices and to commit suicide. Guilt operated strongly when more people espoused versions of Christianity where guilt is in-built. Catholics could avoid guilt by confession but this could help a story along by inspiring guilt in priests who came into the possession of guilty knowledge.

Characters in contemporary novels in more secular times either don't feel guilt when psychopaths (see S for serial killer) are able to rationalise it away, being aware in a hard world that, like conscience, it is a luxury and a negative impulse. Approved characters feel guilty about infidelities, neglect of children, deception of colleagues, but few self-respecting murderers would feel guilty about having killed someone.

G *is also for* **gumshoe**. This is a colloquial term for a private detective, implying that such operatives require rubber-soled shoes for their clandestine work. Another term is 'shamus', whose origin is obscure. It surfaces in the hard-boiled stories of the late 1920s. One suggestion is that it's an amalgam of the Hebrew word 'shamesh', meaning servant, and the Irish name Seamus, a common name for police detectives. This seems unlikely and 'origin obscure' remains the best account while the jury is out. 'Peeper' is another name hailing from the time when private detectives were commonly engaged in divorce work—peeping through keyholes and under blinds and taking photographs of adulterous activity (see L for Latin tag).

G *is also for* **gun**. They're not essential; knives, clubs, poisons and garrottes will do, but guns are the most efficient killers. Usefully, they leave clues behind—bullets, bullet casings, powder burns—giving investigators something to work with. A ballistics expert in an obligatory white coat, unbuttoned, is a serviceable character. Fingerprints on firearms have become less interesting for investigators. For one thing, everyone now knows to wipe a gun and for another, given the millions of guns in America, most of those used in crimes end up in the drink. The hit man with a favourite gun is a complete anachronism.

A book with guns as the absolute movers and shakers of action is George V. Higgins's debut novel *The Friends of Eddie Coyle* (1970).

G could also be for gloves, in this context, as in shooters wearing them, and modifications of guns like the sawing off of stocks and barrels can leave tell-tale signs behind.

Guns can be overdone. There are too many in the novels of Don Winslow and T. Jefferson Parker. Here the classics differ. Raymond Chandler said, 'When in doubt have a man come through a door with a gun in his hand.' On the other hand, writers might take note of Philip Marlowe's observation, 'Such a lot of guns around town and so few brains.' I think it's in the book; it's certainly in the film, with Bogie's sibilance working full on.

G *is also for* **guts**. They may be spilled metaphorically or literally, or, again metaphorically, displayed by the protagonist. At some point in a crime novel a hero should come under threat and display not foolhardiness, but a judicious courage.

H *is for* **habits**. Series characters typically have habits—Sherlock Holmes plays the violin, Hercule Poirot drinks tisanes and fusses with his moustache, Philip Marlowe plays auto-chess, Inspector Morse does cryptic crosswords, Nero Wolfe grows orchids. The function of these habits is to humanise the character and to alert readers to the workings of their minds. When Holmes scrapes the strings we know he is thinking deeply; when Morse cracks a difficult cryptic clue we know he is at the top of his game, and so on.

Conversely, for a criminal, a habit is a weakness, allowing an investigator to anticipate an action or set a trap.

H *is also for* **hard-boiled**. This is the accepted term for the tough school of crime writing that evolved in the United States in the 1890s and found its expression in magazines like *Black Mask* and *True Detective*. The first hard-boiled writer is generally thought to be Carroll John Daly, whose stories were dark, violent and uninterested in redemption. The origin of the term is interestingly discussed on the website The Straight Dope.[2] It has a history dating back to the nineteenth century, had a vogue in post-World War I New York and was firmly attached to the seminal writing of Dashiell Hammett and Raymond Chandler.

The characteristic mode of hard-boiled stories is that they exhibit little of the emotional response of the characters to the events happening around them. Broadly speaking, the investigators are too busy surviving and fending off threats to describe their feelings or to admit to having them about the wider world. This characteristic, though modified, persists in contemporary crime writing (see P for pulp).

2 www.straightdope.com/columns/read/1475/

H *is also for* **historical**. The list of historical crime novels is so extensive you could not live long enough to read them all. The subgenre has been popular at least since the work of Edith Pargeter, who wrote under a number of pseudonyms, most notably Ellis Peters. Her first novel had the unpromising title of *Hortensius, Friend of Nero* (1936), but she achieved great popularity with the series of medieval novels featuring Brother Cadfael, set at a time when the English throne was in wild dispute. The books inspired a short-lived television series.

Peter Lovesey has been a prolific writer of historical crime novels. His series character Sergeant Cribb (a descendant of bare-knuckle, prize-fighting champion Tom Cribb—another example of the usefulness of boxing as texture in crime novels) first appeared in *Wobble to Death* (1970), about the odd Victorian interest in marathon pedestrianism. As so often with successful English novels, a television series resulted.

Anne Perry, who was involved as a teenager in a murder in New Zealand, has produced a great number of historical crime novels. Her first novel had the evocative title *The Cater Street Hangman* (1979).

Cherry-picking among the many practitioners, Edward Marston's Domesday novels are worthy of attention. The protagonist is in the service of William the Conqueror and surveys the kingdom's resources while solving crimes in different counties and cities he visits. *The Wolves of Savernake* (1993) was the first of these interesting and informative books. Less successful to my mind, after admittedly a small sample, has been his series about the British railway network beginning with *The Railway Detective* (2004), set in 1851.

Pre-eminent among contemporary English historical crime novelists is C.J. Sansom, whose series about hunchbacked lawyer Matthew Shardlake, set in Tudor times, rises well above the ruck.

Beginning with *Dissolution* in 2003, all subsequent books have been eagerly awaited by devoted readers. Interestingly, Sansom presents a much less sympathetic portrait of Thomas Cromwell than does Hilary Mantel in her Man Booker prize-winners *Wolf Hall* (2009) and *Bring Up the Bodies* (2012).

Historical crime writing is much less common in the United States than in Britain. When set in the nineteenth century, American crime stories tend to appear as Westerns, for example Ron Hansen's excellent *Desperadoes* (1979) and *The Assassination of Jesse James by the Coward Robert Ford* (1983).

Books about the Mafia are an exception to this. There was a historical dimension to *The Godfather*. Dennis Lehane provides another exception with his powerful book *The Given Day* (2008), set in Boston in the early years of the twentieth century. It focuses on crime and corruption, while his *Live by Night* (2012) is a convincing and compelling evocation of the Prohibition era.

A trio of crime novels set in Sydney in Victorian times by Martin Long—*The Garden House* (1989), *The Music Room* (1990) and *The Dark Gateway* (1991)—received much less attention than it deserved.

H *is also for* **hit man**. Contract killers, also known as button men or torpedos, figure in many crime stories. Their characteristic MO (see L for Latin tag) is a close-range shot to the head with a low-calibre pistol. Hit men tend to be off-stage characters, less the focus of investigators' interest than the person who put out the contract.

Richard Condon's 1982 novel *Prizzi's Honor* tells the story of a husband and wife, both contract killers, who are hired to murder each other.

H *is also for* **homicide** (see D for death), and also for humour. Humour is a matter of judgement. Too much, as in the novels of

Kinky Friedman, and the result is ludicrous; none at all and the effect is deadening. The one-liners stand out in Robert B. Parker's novels. 'Work for you?' Spenser says to someone objectionable wishing to hire him. 'I'd rather spend the rest of my life at a Barry Manilow concert.'

In the 1960s, Joyce Porter's novels about bumbling, venal Detective Chief Inspector Wilfred Dover (*Dover One*, 1964, and following) were charming and funny in an old-fashioned English manner. Janet Evanovich has achieved much the same effect with an utterly up-to-date American idiom in the Stephanie Plum series (*One for the Money*, 1994, and following). 'I'll touch it,' Steph's feisty grandmother exclaims when a flasher invites the women to feel his member. Great scene.

H *is also for* **Hong Kong**. Australian William Marshall wrote a series of crime novels, beginning with *Yellowthread Street* (1975), featuring detectives Harry Feiffer and Christopher O'Yee, set in Hong Kong. The books provided the basis for a British television series and sold well in the 1970s and 80s.

With its interesting geographical location, political history, affluence and gambling culture, Hong Kong has provided a vibrant setting for crime writers. Michael Connelly's twelfth Harry Bosch novel, *Nine Dragons* (2009), is one example.

H *is also for* **horses**, which didn't figure much in crime fiction after Arthur Conan Doyle's 'Silver Blaze' story until Dick Francis mounted up. In a succession of best-selling books, ex-jump-jockey Francis had various damaged (one-armed, deaf, traumatised) protagonists, always middle class or above, dealing with villains lurking around the stables and the racetracks. The early books had, if the expression can be excused, pace, good inside information and sufficient characterisation to make them enjoyable. But they became increasingly formulaic to the point of being repetitive and displayed ever more conservative attitudes—understandable perhaps in one who rode for the late Queen Mother.

It has emerged that the books were practically written by Francis's wife, Mary, who researched and developed them. When she died the job was taken over by his son Felix, who continued to write them after his father's race was run.

I *is for* **incest**. This taboo subject does not figure much in crime fiction. However, two American taboo-defiers, James M. Cain and Jim Thompson, were preoccupied with the subject. Cain is said to have begun, and abandoned, a literary novel dealing with incest. His book *The Butterfly* (1946) is about it. Thompson, probably a victim of child abuse and certainly a witness to it, writes about incest in *Heed the Thunder* (1946) and *The Alcoholics* (1953) and touches on it in other works.

I *is also for* **India**. A number of writers, Indian and non-Indian, have set stories on the subcontinent but India has not achieved the popularity of the Scandinavian setting (see N for Nordic). Perhaps the most successful series of novels set in India are those of H.R.F. 'Harry' Keating about Inspector G.V. Ghote of the Bombay police (*The Perfect Murder*, 1964, and following). Keating avoided two pitfalls of writing about Indian characters—parody and condescension.

I *is also for* **indigenous**. The first notable indigenous detective was Australian—Arthur Upfield's Napoleon Bonaparte. In a series of novels in the 1930s and 40s, Upfield had great success with part-Aboriginal (white father, black mother—the reverse would have been unthinkable at the time) Bonaparte. The books were distinguished by their accurate descriptions of the Australian bush. They were well-intentioned but racist, in that Upfield seemed unaware of the patronising condescension in the character's name (harking back to the deplorable days of the 'King Billy' brass nameplates given to Aboriginal elders) and making Bonaparte's intellectual abilities (he held an MA) attributable to his white ancestry while his instinctive talents came from the black side. The books are almost unreadable now on this account and for their sexism, stereotypical characters and stilted dialogue. However, Upfield's books sold well in England and America.

Thirty years ago, at a writing conference in Stockholm, American author Tony Hillerman told me he'd been influenced by Upfield's books, serialised in the *Saturday Evening Post*. If so, and he wasn't just being nice to an Australian a long way from home who only had two books to his credit, this was the best thing Upfield did. Hillerman's best-selling and award-winning novels about Navajo tribal policemen Joe Leaphorn and Jim Chee really put the indigenous detective on the map. Books like *The Blessing Way* (1970) and others combine a profound understanding of Native American culture with sound crime-writing technique.

Hillerman's books have been much imitated and there are now other indigenous investigators on the scene such as Inuits and, for all I know, Ainu and Veddas.

I *is also for* **insanity**. Insanity often plays a part in crime novels: sometimes as a motivation, sometimes as an excuse. Carmen Sternwood in *The Big Sleep* is insane, but compassionate Philip Marlowe believes she can be cured. Howard Hughes is insane in James Ellroy's *White Jazz* (1992) and *American Tabloid* (1995) and cannot be redeemed—but that's Ellroy. And Hughes.

Insane characters provided backdrop until Thomas Harris placed Hannibal Lecter centre-stage in *Red Dragon* (1981) and *The Silence of the Lambs* (1988). Mad, cannibalistic Lecter is like a force of nature—preternaturally intelligent and vicious, the energetic focus of the books' plots, although in captivity for much of the time. It's hard to imagine how he could be surpassed as a sociopath and psychopath. Unfortunately, in *Hannibal* and *Hannibal Rising*, Harris overplayed his hand.

I *is also for* **internet**. Like other technological advances (see E for email, M for mobile phone, P for photograph and T for texting), the internet has had a profound effect on the plotting and texture of crime fiction. Investigators and criminals now have vast amounts of data literally at their fingertips and much plodding work can be avoided. It cuts both ways, with brilliant law-enforcement computer technicians vying with crazed criminal geeks.

Typically, characters like Harry Bosch and Jack Reacher have only a nodding acquaintance with the technology. Their talents lie elsewhere.

I *is also for* **'in the wind'**. This is a term in American crime fiction for a character who has gone into hiding or whose whereabouts are unknown.

J *is for* **Jack the Ripper**. Probably no series of crimes has inspired so many books, fiction and non-fiction, as the Whitechapel murders of 1888 in which five prostitutes were killed and mutilated. The perpetrator was never found. The name 'Jack the Ripper' was signed to a note sent to the London police, purporting to be from the killer. It was almost certainly a hoax but the name stuck.

Serious study of the crimes is known as Ripperology and two notable examples of works that attempt to identify the Ripper are Stephen Knight's *Jack the Ripper: The final solution* (1976) and Patricia Cornwell's *Portrait of a Killer: Jack the Ripper, case closed* (2002). Candidates for the perpetrator have included Prince Albert (the grandson of Queen Victoria), artist Walter Sickert, royal physician Sir William Gull and professional cricketer Montague Druitt. Frederick Deeming, who killed women and children in England and Australia and was hanged in Victoria, has also been proposed as a possible culprit.

The list of novels dealing with the crimes is very long and has drawn in historical figures such as Oscar Wilde and fictional characters like Sherlock Holmes.

J *could also be for* **jail** but no one much spells it that way these days.

J *could be for* **jogging** (see E for exercise) or **joke** (see H for homicide) but it's also for **journalist**. Journalists stand very low in social esteem, down with used-car salesmen apparently, but they rate much more highly with crime writers. They are very useful characters as the holders and purveyors of information. Investigators can use their knowledge as a shortcut to gaining an understanding of people and circumstances and use their publishing power to further a cause, as in Stieg Larsson's *The Girl with the Dragon Tattoo* (2005, and following).

Journalists make very good partners for male detectives because of their contacts, but also conflicts of interest can arise between the journalist's need to publish and the investigator's need for security. This can make for dramatic clashes and resolutions as well as providing a desirable balance.

But times have changed and the internet has reduced the usefulness of journalists to investigators. Female journalists are also now more likely to be in the visual, rather than the print media, which has had the effect of making them better looking but dumber. A book making critical use of a TV journalist is Lee Child's *One Shot* (2005). Unhappily, this didn't make it a good book.

J *is also for* **juries.** These are crucially important in American crime novels, as the death penalty is still a possibility, less so in civilised countries where it has long been scrapped. John Grisham's *The Runaway Jury* (1996) focuses on the bizarre US system of jury selection and manipulation. Juries are also central to Michael Connelly's Mickey Haller series of novels, starting with *The Lincoln Lawyer* (2005, and following) (see C for courtroom drama).

J *is also for* **justice**. Justice is assumed to be blind or capricious in crime novels, otherwise there would be no need for ethical lawyers, honest cops and private investigators.

K *is for* **knife.** The knife is a 'wet work' murder weapon with a lot to recommend it—a silent operation if properly delivered, the possibility of fingerprints and DNA, blood typing (rendered less useful by the discovery of DNA), and distinctive shapes and cutting edges allowing different white-coated experts to parade their knowledge. As the title suggests, Jonathan Kellerman's *The Butcher's Theatre* (1988) makes good use of knives, and of course they come into play in any book based on the Whitechapel murders.

It's worth noting that knives are the only weapons that give Jack Reacher qualms, before he starts breaking wrists and arms and dislocating shoulders.

In cases of domestic fatalities, knives are usually found in kitchens.

K *is also for* **knight and squire.** This is a term coined by Barry Maitland for pairings such as Colin Dexter's Morse and Lewis, Reginald Hill's Dalziel and Pascoe, and Ruth Rendell's Wexford and Burden. It was to get away from this formula that Maitland chose to use the male and female team of Brock and Kolla in his police procedural series (*The Marx Sisters*, 1994, and following), although it should be noted that in romantic historical fiction squires sometimes turn out to be women, with obvious consequences.

L *is for* **laboratory** (see D for doctor and S for squeamishness). Since the advent of Patricia Cornwell's medical examiner Kay Scarpetta (*Postmortem*, 1990, and following), crime writers have increasingly felt obliged to introduce laboratory scenes into their stories—white coats, petri dishes, latex gloves. There is a variety of ways to handle these scenes—humorously, clinically, sceptically. Perhaps the best approach, a challenge yet to be met, would be to combine all three.

L *is also for* **Latin tag**. Some of the most common are habeas corpus, in situ, modus operandi, sub judice, in flagrante delicto. Most crime writers have little Latin and less Greek but they must know these terms.

L *is also for* **loan sharking**. This peculiarly American practice occurs in many crime novels where the debt incurred has to be paid one way or another. *The Vig* (1990) by John Lescroart has loan sharking as its central theme.

L *is also for* **locality**. Some writers are intensely identified with their chosen localities—Dashiell Hammett with San Francisco, Raymond Chandler with LA, Georges Simenon with Paris, Ian Rankin with Edinburgh. Some writers (see R for research) invent their localities—Ed McBain, Ross Macdonald and Sue Grafton for example. The only rule is that the localities be interesting in their own right and believable.

L *is also for* **locked room**. Introduced into what was then called 'sensational fiction' by Edgar Allan Poe in 'Murder in the Rue Morgue' (1841), the locked-room mystery was popular in the Golden Age—the 1920s to 1940s. The exemplar of the device was American-born John Dickson Carr, who mostly lived in and wrote about England. His 1935 novel *The Hollow Man* was voted the best locked-room mystery of all time in 1935 by a panel of seventeen crime writers. It is likely to retain the title because the style is out of fashion, although some contemporary writers employ it; examples are Peter Lovesey's *Bloodhounds* (1996) and Kerry Greenwood's *Murder in Montparnasse* (2002). Carr's protagonist, Dr Gideon Fell, lectures on the subject in the book and this is sometimes published as a stand-alone essay.

The device in the hands of Carr and others always strains credulity.

L *is also for* **love.** Love suffuses crime novels—except those of James Ellroy, where nobody loves anybody or anything. Characters kill for love and die for love. They love their jobs, their houses, their money. Investigators love their wives (often estranged) and their children—more often one child and usually a daughter. Some investigators love the natural world, as James W. Hall's Thorn loves the Florida Keys.

Morse loves classical music, Bosch loves jazz, R.D. Wingfield's Jack Frost loves sausage sandwiches. Dr Watson, of course, loves Sherlock Holmes but doesn't know it, while Robert B. Parker's Spenser loves Hawk but can't admit it, even though Susan Silverman might be tolerant.

M *is for* **mean streets**. 'Down these mean streets a man must go who is not himself mean, who is neither tarnished nor afraid.' Raymond Chandler's stylish famous formulation is odd, given his work. Philip Marlowe is initially seen in Chandler's first novel, *The Big Sleep*, not in a mean street but outside General Sternwood's mansion. Marlowe, in fact, spends more time in high-class gambling joints onshore and afloat, respectable apartment buildings, doctors' rooms and out-of-town resorts than on mean streets. But the formulation could hardly go, 'Down these mean streets a man must sometimes go . . .'

Streets are meaner in Hammett and much meaner in later writers like James Ellroy.

M *is also for* **Miranda**. The Miranda warning has been a part of police procedure in the United States since 1966. There is no precise text for arresting police to follow but they must advise suspects of the following: they have the right to remain silent; anything they say may be used in evidence against them; they have the right for an attorney to be present at any interrogation and, if they cannot afford a lawyer, a court-appointed attorney will be provided.

In crime fiction police observe or violate these rules as circumstances dictate.

M *is also for* **mob** or **mafia**. The quintessential mob book is Mario Puzo's *The Godfather* (1969), which laid down the ground rules, introducing us to consiglieri, 'made' guys and the code of silence. The mob is a very useful device, allowing organised crime to be a threatening and controlling presence without ever having to specify details. The mob can be thought to be behind a series of murders for two-thirds of a book before it becomes clear that the perp was a rogue cop or a CIA guy or a lawyer.

The mob can be located anywhere up and down the east coast of the United States, in California and Nevada but never in the mid-west except in Chicago or possibly Kansas. The best mob book in recent years is Don Winslow's *The Winter of Frankie Machine* (2006) in which a mafia hit man tries to retire. There was talk of a film with Robert de Niro, who has played mafiosi so often he must sometimes think he is one.

The Russian mafia has begun to figure in American and British crime novels. In its home-grown manifestation it is best seen in Martin Cruz Smith's books (*Gorky Park*, 1981, and following).

M *is also for* **mobile phone** (cell phone in the United States), which has changed the plotting and pace of crime novels. Where detectives used to have to locate pay phones or stay by a home, office or hotel-room phone, they can now move around freely. Mobiles are good for tracking people, which can work both ways—for good or evil. They are bad for the environment because characters throw them from high buildings or into the nearest lake or river to avoid being tracked.

There are dangers for writers here. Ian Rankin's *Standing in Another Man's Grave* (2012) makes a greater use of the mobile phone—calling, texting, messaging, photographing and sending photographs, voice recording—than I've seen before. It threatens to dehumanise, over-digitalise, the story.

The change wrought by the mobile was underlined in the British TV series *Life on Mars* where a character, thrown back to the 1970s, howls, 'I need my mobile.'

'Your mobile what?' is the only response he gets. The short-lived American adaptation was deprived of this joke. 'I need my cell' just wouldn't work.

M *is also for* **morality**. Investigators have an ill-defined, self-devised moral code, rarely spelled out. It can be very flexible, as in the case of Sam Spade, who is sexually amoral—he has seduced his partner's wife and rejects her when attracted to someone else. But when the partner he has cuckolded is killed he says, 'When a man's partner is killed he's supposed to do something about it.' Who supposes this? He does.

M *is also for* **morgue** (see D for doctor and S for squeamishness).

M *is also for* **motivation**, of which there must be one, or several. Along with means, motivation is one of the big three (see O for opportunity) and the chief one is money.

M *is also for* **multiple killings**. These are usually the work of individuals (see S for serial killer) but occasionally take the form of massacres. Massacres are on the cards whenever Mexican and South American drug cartels are on the scene. The best exchange at a massacre scene is in Cormac McCarthy's *No Country for Old Men* (2005) where the deputy says, 'It's a mess, ain't it, Sheriff?'

'If it ain't,' the sheriff replies, 'it'll do till a mess gets here.'

The lines were reproduced word for word in the Coen brothers' 2007 award-winning film of the book, something rarely achieved by novelists.

N *is for* **name**. For series characters, names are very important. Arthur Conan Doyle considered 'Sherrington' before settling on Sherlock, a wise choice. The names often encode the qualities of the characters. Raymond Chandler gave his detectives various names, including Malory, before settling on Marlowe. A theory that this was the name of one of the houses at the private school Chandler attended was exploded when it was discovered that the house name wasn't used in his time. (Such is the interest of writers in this matter.) It seems most likely that Marlowe is resonant of Malory and his *Morte d'Arthur*. The name of Robert B. Parker's Spenser is a deliberate and poetic evocation of the past. The same goes for Timothy Harris's character Thomas Kyd in *Kyd for Hire* (1977) and *Goodnight and Good-bye* (1979). Kyd was an Elizabethan playwright.

The name Morse suggests codes and clues appropriate to the character; Mike Hammer and Tiger Mann, Mickey Spillane's characters' names, need no explanation.

Garry Disher says that he wanted a name with a 'short whiplash quality' for his series character Wyatt and that he probably had Wyatt Earp in the back of his mind when he decided on the name.

Michael Connelly and John Lescroart chose unusual first names for their series characters—Hieronymus and Dismas; the first is a fourteenth-century Dutch painter, the second the name given by tradition to the repentant thief on the cross in the biblical legend of the crucifixion. The names permit some amusing exchanges in the books and privilege educated readers—nothing wrong with that.

N *is also for* **noir**. A French film critic of the 1940s defined certain Hollywood films as film noir, pointing to the use of dimly lit scenes, shadows, and dark actions and motives. Since then film historians have argued that the style was accidental—an attempt by studios to save money on lighting rather than to add atmosphere. Whatever the truth of this, the term was taken up by later critics and reviewers of both films and books to describe a certain kind of morally ambiguous and dramatically tense story (see H for hard-boiled). This led to ridiculous descriptions, from a literal perspective, of films like the brightly lit *Chinatown* and books set in the high bright sun such as the Elvis Cole novels of Robert Crais (*The Monkey's Raincoat*, 1987, and following) as noir. It remained a useful and more or less accurate term for books such as those by Philip Kerr in the gloomy Bernie Gunther series (*March Violets*, 1989, and following), which are aptly described as 'Berlin noir'.

'Tartan noir' is a term loosely applied but best used to describe crime writing set in Scotland where the characters and the setting share characteristics—bleakness, toughness and harshness. The protagonists are of the anti-hero type—cynical and without illusions—and the social scene is unforgiving.

An early example was the work of William McIlvanney (*Remedy is None*, 1966, and following). The novels of Ian Rankin, Stuart MacBride and Denise Mina (*The Field of Blood*, 2005, and following) fit the category better than some other Scots writers like Val McDermid.

N *is also for* **Nordic**. After the success of the de facto husband-and-wife writing team Maj Sjöwall and Per Wahlöö with their Swedish police procedurals featuring Martin Beck (*Roseanna*, 1965, and following), there was a falling away in translation of Scandinavian crime novels, although they continued to be written and to be popular locally.

That changed with the translations into English and popularity of writers like Peter Høeg, Henning Mankell, Anne Holt and others in the 1990s. Since that time there has been an avalanche of 'Nordics'—from Sweden, Norway, Denmark, Finland and Iceland. The extraordinary sales of Stieg Larsson's *The Girl* trilogy in the 2000s built on the success of earlier writers.

The best survey and appraisal of the Nordic crime-writing scene is Jean Bedford's 'The Nordic Phenomenon' in the *Newtown Review of Books*, 28 February 2012. There is, she argues, a hunger among progressively inclined readers for stories from a part of the world that, in theory and to a degree in practice, has fairness-to-all social settings.

The exotic climate and geography, too, seem to exercise a fascination for readers, which has provided encouragement and a degree of success to writers basing their stories in Canada and Alaska. It hasn't worked at the other end of the globe. As far as I'm aware there are no crime novels written and set in Tierra del Fuego.

N *is also for* **nostalgia**. Once a crime series is underway the protagonist inevitably expresses nostalgia for a time when he or she was younger and life was simpler. This can provide engaging punctuation points in the narrative and readers enjoy references to places they once enjoyed, music they once listened to, sports stars they once admired. It's a device that bonds writer and reader.

It isn't always appreciated that those writers who become tired of their characters, as Arthur Conan Doyle did of Holmes, Chandler did of Marlowe and Fleming did of Bond, generally yearned for the time when the enterprise was fresher. It shows.

O *is for* **OMCG**. This acronym for outlaw motorcycle gang is gaining currency in Australia, with governments becoming ever more enthusiastic about limiting the freedoms of the citizenry.

'Bikers' (the US term works much better than the Australian 'bikies') are usually associated with the manufacture and distribution of mind-altering drugs rather than crimes against persons or property. Increasingly, as with many criminal organisations, their violence tends to be directed principally towards themselves.

Hunter S. Thompson apart, not many writers have chosen to get close enough to motorcycle gangs to write about them. A common attitude is summed up by comedian Roseanne Barr: 'I hate bikers. They're dirty, they smell, they have tobacco juice in their beards, they shit by the side of the road—and that's just the women.'

O *is also for* **omniscience**. In effect third-person narrators are omniscient in that they are in possession of all the information and control everything. This contrasts with the first-person style (standard although not universal with private-eye stories) where the action is seen from the point of view of the character/narrator—who only knows so much and must find out more. Certain detectives in what might be called the old school—Holmes, Poirot and Rex Stout's Nero Wolfe, for example—are omniscient in their inherent superiority over the forces they have to contend with. It is significant that they are sexless—attachment to a woman or women would constitute an impermissible weakness.

O *is also for* **opportunity**. This is very much needed by a would-be murderer, but in most cases it needs to be contrived or set up. The danger here is in leaving behind evidence of the arrangement. With the opportunity taken and the murder committed, it becomes necessary to cover the tracks. One method is the alibi, but it can be tricky. Alibis can be broken down. Another method is to deflect suspicion onto someone else. This only works if the murderer is considerably smarter than the investigator, which may appear to be the case, but only temporarily.

In the clue-puzzle mystery the opportunity is crucial and must be uncovered. In the weakest examples it can be done by a coincidental meeting or a chance remark. This is shaky ground. In the hard-boiled school, the opportunity may be given, even admitted, by the perpetrator, and the challenge becomes, 'Prove it.' Then it turns into a battle of wills and other forces intrude (see V for violence).

O *is also for* **output**. Like many authors of Westerns, some crime writers have been notable for the extraordinary number of books they've published. Belgian Georges Simenon published over four hundred novels; Agatha Christie about sixty-six, and others, like Erle Stanley Gardner and Leslie Charteris, also have long bibliographies to their credit.

Edgar Wallace produced so many books, dictating them and once publishing eighteen in a single year, that an English newspaper printed a cartoon in which a bookseller offered a volume to a customer saying, 'Have you read the midday Wallace?'

The biggest producer was British writer John Creasey, who started late, did not live to a great age, and published more than six hundred books. Creasey, who also had an active political life, wrote under a variety of pseudonyms and had a number of serial characters. His books written under the name J.J. Marric are competent police procedurals, while others, like many of the Inspector Roger West books, are superficial and unconvincing. There is no detailed biography of Creasey, and how he was able to write so much remains a mystery.

By contrast, Arthur Conan Doyle, Dashiell Hammett and Raymond Chandler produced comparatively few books, but their place in the crime-writing pantheon is secure.

P *is for* **passion** (see L for love and S for sex).

P *is also for* **pastiche**. Pastiches of popular crime stories have often been written, with the most notable source being the work of Arthur Conan Doyle. A recent count listed close to a hundred Sherlock Holmes pastiches, parodies and imitations, of which one of the earliest and possibly the best was Nicholas Meyer's *The Seven-Per-Cent Solution* (1974).

Pastiches have been written of the work of Rex Stout, Agatha Christie and other leading lights. To mark the centenary of his birth, the estate of Raymond Chandler commissioned Robert B. Parker to write a continuation of 'The Poodle Springs Story', which Chandler had left unfinished at his death. This was published in 1989 as *Poodle Springs*. In 1991, also with the estate's approval, Parker published *Perchance to Dream*, a sequel to *The Big Sleep*.

P *is also for* **perpetrator**. Arch-villains like Arthur Conan Doyle's Professor Moriarty, Sax Rohmer's Dr Fu Manchu and Ed McBain's Deaf Man (see P for police procedural), are long out of fashion. The lone serial killer is probably the most favoured subject of all in contemporary crime fiction (see S for serial killer).

Perpetrators can be male or female, black, white or Asian or a mix of any of these. A skilful writer can enlist the reader's sympathy for a perpetrator, as when young Vito Corleone kills the Mafia street boss in *The Godfather*, but only up to a point. Perps can be rich or poor but, as Sophie Tucker famously observed of personal circumstances, 'rich is better', which holds true for crime writing.

P *is also for* **photograph**. Scene of crime officers (see S for SOCO) take photographs of crime scenes, some of which can be blown up to reveal detail, but that is about the extent of the usefulness of photography in modern crime fiction. The 'Brownie and bedsheets' era, where private detectives took photos of actually or spuriously cooperative adulterous couples (see G for gumshoe) is long past. Ever since suspicion was aroused about the photograph of alleged John F. Kennedy assassin Lee Harvey Oswald posed with a rifle (was the shadow in the right place?) the potential for doctoring photographs has limited their usefulness as either evidence or accusatory material. With digital photography, any misrepresentation of arms, legs, faces or sexual organs is possible.

P *is also for* **plot**. One of the greats of crime fiction, Raymond Chandler, made a pronouncement on this subject that aspiring crime writers should take into account: 'Scene is more important than plot.' This is sage advice; many tyros become frustrated and bogged down trying to devise and control complicated plots. Many, perhaps most, crime readers are interested in the elan of the story rather than the twists and turns.

P *is also for* **poison**. Once popular as a murder method—the more exotic the better—poison is now little used.

P *is also for* **police procedural**, a subset of the genre more or less invented by Ed McBain in his 87th Precinct series (*Cop Hater*, 1956, and following). These books reproduced facsimiles of documents—reports, mug shots, fingerprints, letters etc.—to represent the nitty-gritty of the materials the cops had to work with. McBain had an engaging set of characters, particularly Steve Carella with his deaf-mute wife, Teddy, and Cotton Hawes, prey to certain weaknesses (though the writing could get sentimental). There was also a potent recurring villain, the Deaf Man.

The term now applies to any book featuring teamed, organised police work as exemplified by Stuart MacBride, Ruth Rendell, Reginald Hill and Barry Maitland. R.D. Wingfield's novels about Detective Inspector Jack Frost (*Frost at Christmas*, 1984, and following) and Ian Rankin's Rebus novels are not strictly police procedurals because the protagonists typically do not follow procedure.

P *is also for* **politics**. Politics and crime intersect in life as well as in fiction, as any newspaper will affirm. Politicians rarely make heroes or favoured characters but they make excellent perpetrators and victims because so many people dislike them and there are so many possible motives for their crimes or victimhood.

Generally speaking, conservative politicians make the best villains because, as the saying goes, 'reality has a left-wing bias'.

P *is also for* **primal scene**. Psychiatrist Geraldine Pederson-Krag theorised that the addictive appeal of mystery fiction relates to the primal scene—the child's witnessing of or curiosity about sex between the parents. She argued that the child's observation of the clues—closed doors, nocturnal sounds, clothing disturbances etc., excite the child's curiosity, which contains strong oedipal elements.

Mystery fiction reactivates this interest, leading to the compulsive reading of crime stories. Whether sound or not, this is an extremely useful theory for crime writers, who are frequently asked to account for the popularity of the genre. The usual answers go to a vicarious thrill from reading about crime and violence and its all-pervading presence in the world. Ho hum. A writer could advance the psychiatric theory and either stop the questioner in his or her tracks or open up an interesting discussion, according to whether the questioner is worth talking to.

P *is also for* **probable cause.** A version of this rule exists in many jurisdictions, with varying effects. In general it provides that a law officer must have reasonable grounds to arrest a person, search a person or a person's property, or have a search or arrest warrant issued in respect of a crime committed or in prospect.

Non-observance of the rule and the difficulty of applying it figure prominently in American crime fiction (see C for courtroom drama).

P *is also for* **profiler.** Profilers are often to be found in police procedurals. As with identikit drawings, it is fairly unusual for the profiler's work to crack the case. Profilers are very passive, mostly to be found at their desks clicking keys. They have, it seems to me, a fairly interesting but very cushy job. Like weather forecasters they are never called to account when they get it wildly wrong.

The compelling exception to this is brilliant, sexually dysfunctional psychologist Dr Tony Hill in the novels of Val McDermid (*The Mermaids Singing*, 1995, and following).

P *is also for* **pseudonym.** Some crime writers adopt pseudonyms to cope with and conceal their enormous outputs, as in the cases of John Creasey, Edgar Wallace and others (see O for output). But sometimes it is done for a variety of other reasons. Alan Yates, for example, wrote as Carter Brown simply because he thought the name sounded better. Gore Vidal produced several crime novels under the name Edgar Box to mark a separation between his popular and literary work. Kenneth Millar wrote under a couple of closely related names before settling on Ross Macdonald. The reason was to avoid confusion with the work of his wife, who was published as Margaret Millar.

The multiplicity of the pseudonyms of Creasey and Wallace are long forgotten, and who now knows that Georgette Heyer also wrote as Stella Martin, or that Martin Cruz Smith also wrote under the name Simon Quinn? Pseudonyms are hard to maintain—crime readers now are well aware that Jack Harvey is Ian Rankin, Barbara Vine is Ruth Rendell and Robert Galbraith is J.K. Rowling.

The writer to most successfully achieve long-term anonymity through the use of a pseudonym was Rodney William Whitaker, an American academic who published best-selling novels like *The Eiger Sanction* (1972) and *The Loo Sanction* (1973) as Trevanion. Whitaker also published academic works under his own name and books in other genres under different pseudonyms.

P *is also for* **pulp**. The name derives from the poor quality of the paper on which mass-market magazines were printed. Those on better paper, like the *Saturday Evening Post* or the *New Yorker*, were known as 'slicks' and cost a lot more. The leading American crime writers James Ellroy (until he ran off the rails), Michael Connelly, Harlan Coben, Jeffery Deaver, Dennis Lehane and Elmore Leonard (before he became a parody of himself) owe much to the pulp writers of the 1930s and 40s.

I take Chandler's remark that 'Hammett gave murder back to the people who commit it' to mean that the pulp writers democratised crime writing. Henceforth murders would be committed and investigated by ordinary people using ordinary language, or people only marginally out of the ordinary experiencing the pressures of everyday life.

The same is true of the Britishers like Rankin, MacBride and others. Crime investigation as the province of the aristocracy and gentry lingers on, though, in the Adam Dalgleish books of P.D. James (*Cover Her Face*, 1992, and following), and the Inspector Thomas Lynley (who is the Earl of Asherton) books of Elizabeth George (*A Great Deliverance*, 1988, and following).

Q *is for* **question**. Questions are the warp and woof of crime novels. 'Where were you on the night of . . .?' The subject had better have an answer. Private-eye novels, in particular, amount to the detective making house calls and asking questions. The questioner may get truthful answers, untruthful ones or a beating but the questioning will persist. The list of questions is almost infinite—who, why, when, where, how, how much, how often . . .?

R *is for* **rape**. Rape is sometimes, but not always, an accompaniment to serial killings. Semen analysis is high on the list of pathologists' skills. The rape of a prostitute can sometimes be the subject of jokes by hard-bitten cops, but the rape of a child never. Homosexual rape occurs in prisons and the threat of it—'You know what happens to smooth-looking guys like you in the joint?'—is often used as a threat to suspects, who mostly cooperate. Who wouldn't?

R *is also for* **research**. Some crime writers carry out extensive research, some do very little. Elmore Leonard took to using professional researchers to take photographs of places and provide descriptions and impressions of them, their transport systems, weather, and so on.

Most writers, I suspect, as I do, research in the way a bird builds its nest—selecting precisely and only what is wanted. Best-selling authors need to produce quickly and regularly, and the last thing writers need is to get bogged down in research. Chandler kept a book about guns on a shelf above the typewriter and found what he wanted without needing to join a pistol-shooting club. Because crime is in the air, on the street and in the media, simply being alive and able to see and hear provides material.

Fiction writers have a great advantage over journalists and non-fiction writers. When an actual place that is otherwise just right for atmosphere and sociology is wrong in some crucial aspect, the solution is simple—use the real stuff, make up the rest and invent a name. This saves a lot of work looking for somewhere else. Ed McBain went further. His city was totally fictional though very detailed. It had the illusion of reality and left him free to model locations on real places and tweak them as he pleased.

R *is also for* **robbery.** This is a minor crime in the writer's lexicon but it often acts as a precursor to the central business, which is murder.

R *is also for* **rule.** Many crime writers have suggested rules for the craft, such as Chandler's celebrated 'When in doubt have a man come through a door with a gun in his hand' (see G for gun), which was surely tongue in cheek. Agatha Christie's tip for the clue-puzzle writer, though never explicitly stated, was her practice of writing the last chapter first.

Elmore Leonard's ten rules[3] are justly celebrated (see W for weather) but writers should also take note of one golfing guru's overriding tip—'Ignore all tips.'

3 'Tips from the Masters', Gotham Writers, www.writingclasses.com/toolbox/tips-masters/elmore-leonard-10-rules-for-good-writing.

S *is for* **security**. In the best crime fiction no important characters are secure.

S *is also for* **sentimentality**. Literary critics define sentimental writing as that in which the emotion generated is excessive for what is being described or dramatised. It is the besetting sin of American crime writers since the 1950s such as Ed McBain, Robert B. Parker, James Lee Burke and others. The problem seems to be that, having been let off the leash to use violence and obscenity as much as they please, some writers feel a sense of guilt about this freedom and balance it with sentimentality about parents, children, lovers and country. The British and Australian counterbalance of cynicism and disillusion is more appropriate.

S *is also for* **serial killer**. Writers outdo each other in devising motivations and methods for serial killers. Probably the most bizarre example occurs in Lee Child's novel *Running Blind*, in which several young women are found dead in their own bathtubs, which are filled with green paint. There is no apparent cause of death.

Jack Reacher is dragged in by the FBI to help the investigation. Only a spoilsport would give away the reasons for, and causes of, the deaths. It's sufficient to say that Child has to be credited with inventing a completely original and very unpleasant mode of exit.

Following the example of the Whitechapel Killer, a twisted hatred of women is a powerful trigger. Such killings give the writer scope to explore subjects like DNA, semen traces, mutilation patterns and to speculate about the enormous spectrum of human sexuality.

A spate of serial killings gives an opportunity for a differently motivated single-focus killer to insert a joker into the pack to deflect attention and investigation from the serial killer.

S *is also for* **series.** Whether or not to write a series is not always the writer's decision. After the success of a first book, publishers often desire a sequel and the writer refuses at his or her peril. Once launched, a series is hard to stop for a variety of reasons. When a potent character has been created, it's tempting to simply put him or her through the paces again and again. In a sense the books write themselves.

Publisher pressure can be relentless because it's easier to market a book in a series than a one-off—it takes less thought, which appeals mightily to publicists. The dangers to the writer come if he or she wishes to branch out, to write one-offs, start a new series or, even worse, write in another genre. Type-casting, stamping the writer as 'the creator of', may cripple the ambition.

John D. MacDonald, creator of the colour-coded Travis McGee series (*The Deep Blue Good-by*, 1964, to *The Lonely Silver Rain*, 1985, and many others in between) found a way around this. When his publishers gave him grief over a non-McGee novel, he said he'd written one called *A Black Border for McGee* and would kill the best-selling character off unless the publisher gave the non-McGee effort the full treatment. It was in his safe at home, he said.

MacDonald died and no such manuscript was found. He was bluffing. Travis would have approved.

S *is also for* **sex.** A distinction has to be made between sexual language and sexual action. James Ellroy's books, for example, are awash with four-letter words but even the usually mild sex scenes are few.

Spenser and Susan Silverman fuck a lot but the bedroom door is firmly closed. In fact very few crime writers do R-rated scenes. Most attempt a minimalist approach:

'Want to?' she said.

'Yes,' I said.

So we did.

That kind of thing.

S *is also for* **SOCO**. Scene of crime officers (SOCOs), or crime scene investigators (CSIs), are important minor, atmosphere-providing characters in crime novels. They wear white protective suits and booties, latex gloves and shower caps. They work within an area taped off by the first cops to arrive at the scene and spend a lot of time bent double looking for footprints and cigarette butts. They drop what they find into evidence bags, which, contrary to many writers' beliefs, are made of paper. Plastic has the capacity to pollute the evidence but it may be used when it is raining, which it usually is in crime scenes in Ireland, Scotland and the north of England.

S *is also for* **Southern Africa**. There are a large number of South African crime writers. The only one I'm familiar with is James McClure, whose series about detectives Kramer and Zondi (*The Steam Pig*, 1971, and following) enjoyed international success in the 1970s.

Rhodesian-born Scots writer Alexander McCall Smith has enjoyed enormous success with a series of novels set in Botswana beginning with *The No. 1 Ladies' Detective Agency* (1998, and following). My attempt to read the first book failed; I found it impossibly twee and paternalistic.

S *is also for* **sport**. Dick Francis's racing novels (see H for horses) are the most prominent example of the sports mystery—if horse racing can be considered a sport. Other sports are less suitable; there have been good and less good crime novels centred on golf and tennis, with perhaps the most notable being Martina

Navratilova's *Total Zone* (1994) and others. The books received a lukewarm reception.

By far the most appropriate sport to provide a context for a crime novel is boxing. Budd Schulberg's *The Harder They Fall* (1947) qualifies as a crime novel, with its plot involving deception, exploitation and death. Boxing features in several of Robert B. Parker's Spenser novels and is a dominant force in the dark and violent world of one of James Ellroy's best books, *The Black Dahlia* (1987).

Without actually featuring in the story, boxing is often used as a point of reference in crime fiction to suggest manly character, from Sherlock Holmes in 'The Sign of the Four', to Ross Macdonald, where Lew Archer claims to be the nephew of a man who went fifteen rounds to no decision with 'Gunboat' Smith, the 'Great White Hope' when African-American Jack Johnson held the world heavyweight title (*Find a Victim*, 1954).

S *is also for* **squeamishness**. As noted (see D for death) some investigators exhibit squeamishness at crime scenes and autopsies. Most writers do not, the exception being P.D. James who takes care not to have a witness to a murder be depicted as someone who cannot cope with the event—a child or a parent, for example. James is thus sparing herself, the characters and the reader. She is in this regard more the nurse than the queen of crime.

S *is also for* **story**. Crime fiction is mercifully free of the kind of writing that does without story in favour of . . . who knows what?

The very best of the pulp writers, Jim Thompson, provided a definition that embraces everything from his noir classic, *The Killer Inside Me* (1952), to *Romeo and Juliet*. 'There is only one story,' Thompson wrote: 'Things are not what they seem.'

S *is also for* **suicide**, which is still a common fate for suspects who turn out to be perpetrators.

S *is also for* **survival**. Of stylistic necessity, first-person series characters must survive. The way to handle this is to make the threats to them credible enough for the reader to, in a sense, suspend this knowledge and feel the weight of the threat. Third-person stories about series characters are not hampered in this way and a writer may kill the character off, as Nicolas Freeling did Piet Van der Valk in *A Long Silence* (1972) and Colin Dexter did Endeavour Morse in *The Remorseful Day* (1999).

A writer who has killed off or retired a series character might revive him in a retrospective story and get away with it once or twice. Nicholas Freeling, unsuccessfully, tried a version of this with two books about Van der Valk's wife (see N for nostalgia). Colin Dexter said he wouldn't do it.

Another method of sustaining a series after a character's retirement is to bring him back to work on cold cases, as Michael Connelly did with Harry Bosch in *The Narrows* (2004) and as Ian Rankin did with Rebus in *Standing in Another Man's Grave* (2012).

S *is also for* **suspect**. Some suspects are merely red herrings but they swim for quite some time before being caught and discarded. Too few suspects and the story can be too thin; too many and it gets cluttered. The red herring suspect is the chief legacy of the old clue-puzzle mystery and the trick is to develop the character or situation just sufficiently, and no more, so that the matter can remain open for a good part of the book.

Variations on the theme include the protagonist (even the first-person narrator) being an apparently credible suspect for a considerable time. Suspects may complicate matters by making confessions—sometimes to deflect attention from someone to be protected or through mental aberration. The disturbed false confessor is common in sexual cases, with offenders eager to proclaim their guilt. They are pretty easily spotted and become part of the sad backdrop in the tableau of modern urban life, as a serious critic might say.

T *is for* **terrorist**. Terrorists crop up in crime fiction from time to time—increasingly, these days—but never very usefully. Their inevitable failure and destruction limit their serviceability.

Black Sunday (1975), Thomas Harris's pre-Hannibal Lecter novel, presented a fresh approach to the terrorist story. A deranged Vietnam vet who flies a television blimp over US sporting events plans to explode a bomb containing a vast number of steel darts over a Super Bowl game. He doesn't.

After I read it I waited impatiently for his next, *Red Dragon*, and the rest is history. The film had Bruce Dern, as one critic said, 'at his unhinged best' as the nutter. Dern was every bit as good as Anthony Hopkins but, in the nature of things, there was no sequel.

T *is also for* **texting**. A modern crime novel without texting would be like Sherlock Holmes without twice-daily mail delivery.

T *is also for* **threat**. Without threats there is no story. In a serial killer book (see S for serial killer) the threat is that he or she will kill again. In a kidnap story the threat is that the victim will die. In the police procedural the threat may come from within the police department; superior officers may be stupid, corrupt or both. In the best PI stories the protagonist should be placed under threat of some kind but another threat lies within his or her own character—in the balance between weaknesses (drink, sex, misplaced loyalty) and strengths (courage, persistence, honour). Threats are everywhere in crime fiction, as in life.

T *is also for* **title**. Titles are crucially important. *The Maltese Pigeon* doesn't work nor does *The Long Sleep*, not because of the familiarity of the real titles but because the wrong words don't carry the right resonance. Crime writers choosing titles have a multitude of choices.

Some, like Garry Disher, go for the impact of a single word—most of Disher's novels in the Wyatt series have one-word titles.

The most common crime fiction title is one starting with the definite article. There are thousands of examples. A very long list of famous titles of this kind begins with Wilkie Collins's *The Woman in White* (1860). Michael Connelly uses the style throughout his Mickey Haller series from *The Lincoln Lawyer* (2005) to *The Gods of Guilt* (2013).

Five words seems the ideal length for a longer title—James M. Cain's *The Postman Always Rings Twice* (1934) or James Hadley Chase's *No Orchids for Miss Blandish* (1939), for example. Six words, as with *The Far Side of the Dollar* (1965) seems a touch too long. Ross Macdonald should have dropped the first definite article.

The violent vigilantism of Mickey Spillane's Mike Hammer is unambiguously announced in titles like *I, the Jury* (1947) and *My Gun is Quick* (1950), while the even more violent intent of Hannibal Lecter is totally masked, indeed deflected, by Thomas Harris's title *The Silence of the Lambs*.

As mentioned, John D. MacDonald colour-coded his Travis McGee novels. He said he did this to make it easier for buyers to remember what they'd read and recognise a title as new. Why Sue Grafton chose to alphabetise her titles—*A is for Alibi* (1982) through to *Y is for Yesterday* (2017)—and Janet Evanovich to adopt a number code—*One for the Money* (1994) to *Hardcore 24* (2017)—is not clear. If Grafton had wanted to continue the series beyond another book (she died before she could get to Z) she'd have had to think again about titles, but Evanovich won't.

T *is also for* **tobacco**. Holmes, famously, smoked a meerschaum pipe; Sam Spade rolled his own (presumably Bull Durham or something similar) and other Hammett characters smoked

Fatimas like their author; Marlowe (like Chandler) smoked a pipe and cigarettes. Poirot did not smoke but his offsider, Captain Arthur Hastings, was a pipe smoker, as was Simenon's Maigret. Simon Templar smoked because it was the sophisticated thing to do. Mike Hammer smoked Luckies, what else?

Smoking gave writers useful punctuation points in the scene—pauses, distractions, opportunities for reflection. It's been sorely missed as an aspect of sympathetic characters since the US Surgeon General's report of 1984. Smoking is now reserved for dubious characters more flawed than the protagonists—women in particular.

Some reformed smokers, like Michael Connelly's Harry Bosch or Lee Child's Jack Reacher, have stressful moments when they wish they still smoked but they don't. This is in contrast to recovering alcoholics like James Lee Burke's Dave Robicheaux, who have similar moments of temptation and succumb.

T *is also for* **torture**. Torture is more common in spy and historical novels than in crime fiction but in books involving ruthless organisations such as the Mafia and drug cartels, torture is used to gain information or expose traitors. Seldom, though, is torture there as a sadistic indulgence or a fit punishment.

For most serial killers, dismemberment and display are post-mortem. 'Buffalo Bill', the serial killer in *The Silence of the Lambs*, subjects his incarcerated victims to severe mental torture but this is not his object. He wishes to fatten them so that their flayed skins will help him in his transgendered delusion to create a 'girl suit'. Their physical pain simply does not figure in his calculation and is all the more horrifying for that.

Mutilation occurs, as when fingers or parts thereof are sent to solicit ransoms, but this is not torture per se. Torture takes time and crime fiction is, or should be, fast-paced.

The threat of torture is another matter. A powerful example occurs in Don Winslow's *The Winter of Frankie Machine* (2006) when Frankie takes a man out into the desert, strips him naked, and sits in front of him sharpening a knife to a flaying keenness. The guy talks.

T *is also for* **trench coat**. The trench coat, usually with the collar turned up and the belt loosely tied, has been de rigueur for private eyes in films, on television, in comics and in illustrations ever since Humphrey Bogart shrugged into one in the film of *The Big Sleep*. But I cannot think of a book in which a PI wears one.

T *is also for* **trial** (see C for courtroom drama).

T *is also for* **true crime**. The shelves in bookshops groan under the weight of books about crimes that have actually happened. I cite a selection with which I am familiar. Truman Capote's *In Cold Blood* (1966) and Norman Mailer's *The Executioner's Song* (1979) are sometimes designated 'non-fiction novels' or 'creative non-fiction' but I regard them as true crime books. Also in this category is Robert Lindsey's *The Falcon and the Snowman* (1979). True crime shading into memoir is Mikal Gilmore's account of the crimes and death of his brother Gary, *Shot in the Heart* (1994). More strictly true crime are Dominick Dunne's *The Two Mrs Grenvilles* (1985) and Gerold Frank's *The Boston Strangler* (1966).

Ten Rillington Place by Ludovic Kennedy (1961) details the murders committed by John Reginald Christie in the 1940s and 50s in London. *Fred and Rose* (1995) by Howard Sounes, deals with the multiple killings by Fred and Rose West, one of the victims being a cousin of English writer Martin Amis.

In Australia, Lindsay Simpson and Sandra Harvey wrote a number of widely read true crime books including *Brothers in*

Arms (1989) and *The Killer Next Door* (1994). John Dale's *Huckstepp: A dangerous life* (2000) about Sallie-Anne Huckstepp, prostitute, drug addict, associate of criminal Warren Lanfranchi and murder victim, is a compelling work.

True crime books often provide the basis for film and television treatments.

U *is for* **undercover**. Undercover cops occur frequently in crime fiction. They are usefully ambiguous characters treading a fine line between criminality and law enforcement. Quite often they fall over the line to the wrong side, at least for a time. Undercover cops are under intense pressure from both sides of the line and many do not make it to the denouement. If an undercover cop dies early, interesting questions arise—was the death caused by the good guys or the bad guys and does it matter which?

U *is also for* **underworld**. This term is now little used. It comes from a time when the criminal classes were thought to be located in ill-favoured parts of big cities such as the East End of London or the Bowery in New York. Now the crooks are to be credibly found everywhere, in Mayfair and on Park Avenue as like as not. Generalised terms like organised crime or the mob (see M for mob) now serve the purpose.

U *is also for* **university**. The university or campus mystery has had capable exponents from Dorothy L. Sayers' *Gaudy Night* (1935), set in a fictitious Oxford college and featuring her characters Lord Peter Wimsey and Harriet Vane, onward. Robert B. Parker's first Spenser novel, *The Godwulf Manuscript* (1973), was set in a university and reflected Parker's years as an academic.

Robert Barnard, another academic who became a successful crime writer, wrote *Death of an Old Goat* (1974), set in a thinly disguised University of New England, where he had held a teaching position. Don Aitkin, a distinguished academic political scientist, wrote a light mystery novel set in a university, *The Second Chair* (1977).

The campus mystery provides a ready-made set of characters—academics, administrators, students, and such elements as ambition, career and examination pressures, plagiarism, cheating and sexual misalliances that make a heady brew. Several of Colin Dexter's Inspector Morse novels involved doings in Oxford colleges where these forces come into play.

V *is for* **vicar** (see C for *Crockford's Clerical Directory*).

V *is also for* **victim**. Victims can be drawn from either sex or anything in between and from all walks of life. They are preferably young for sympathy's sake and, if old, are best depicted as either helpless or rich. Dead criminals are not necessarily victims. Their criminality may have deprived them of that status unless they have some redeeming features, such as a firm, long-standing friendship with an unblemished (or slightly blemished) protagonist.

Victims have to be identified, which allows pathologists, computer freaks and old-time cops (particularly in the case of dead prostitutes) into the act. Victims can be either hidden or ostentatiously displayed, according to the perpetrators' particular needs. Occasionally a victim may leave a clue to the killer—a bloodied word on a wall, a scrap of clothing clutched in a dead hand—but an efficient killer will clean up properly afterwards.

V *is also for* **violence**. In crime fiction, violence has escalated since the time of Sherlock Holmes and the sedate Golden Age. It took on a mindless, fascist character in the work of Mickey Spillane and a psychologically disturbing tone in the pulp novels of Jim Thompson, Cornell Woolrich (*The Bride Wore Black*, 1940, and others) and other pulp writers like Steve Fisher (*I Wake up Screaming*, 1941).

Violence is more nuanced in the hard-boiled school of Hammett and Chandler. In the work of the post-Chandlerians and the legions of crime writers now operating, it becomes a metaphor for the state of society, a pointer to personal and institutional corruption.

W *is for* **Washington, DC**. Washington is often described as the crime capital of the United States and not only because the government is based there. It is the setting for most of the novels of George Pelecanos (*A Firing Offense*, 1992, and following).

W *is also for* **water**. It's amazing how many fictional killers persist in drowning people in baths and dumping their bodies in the sea. Child's play to the pathologist. Such murderers also fail to realise that bodies thrown into the sea, rivers and lakes will rise to the surface unless properly trussed and weighted. They deserve to be caught.

Water is good for showering after a hard day's investigation and for having sex while doing so. It's also good for crossing in ferries, and allowing investigators, informants and even perpetrators to have safe conversations.

Some writers specialise in water-borne stories. Anne Perry has the Thames River Police while Travis McGee often takes to the water in his houseboat, *The Busted Flush*.

There is a good deal of water about in the novels of James Lee Burke, James W. Hall and Carl Hiaasen, in the forms of the Gulf, the bayous and the Florida Everglades. There is also shrimp at cook-outs and po' boy sandwiches.

W *is also for* **weariness**. Investigators are often described as 'world weary' and why not, given the number of jobs they've undertaken. Maigret is the world-record holder at 76 novels and 28 short stories; Spenser 40 novels; Lew Archer 18 novels and about the same number of short stories; Harry Bosch, 18 novels and counting.

The weariness, of course, is metaphorical for pragmatism and lack of illusion. Investigators are not physically weary when long stake-out hours are required or a man comes through a door with a gun.

W *is also for* **weather**. It would be interesting to do a survey, but I doubt if there has ever been a crime novel that does not mention the weather. Like the state of traffic on the roads, fluctuations in the stock market and current news events, the weather provides a useful punctuation point, slowing down the narrative and providing texture while plots thicken and develop.

Weather is even more useful as a signifier of the mood of characters, the physical surrounds to the action, the atmospherics of the story. However, Elmore Leonard's first rule of writing in his list of ten is: 'Never open a book with weather'.

W *is also for* **witness** (see C for courtroom drama).

X *is for* **xenophobia**. Xenophobia was a mainstay of early crime writers like Sax Rohmer (towards the Chinese). Interestingly, xenophobia is two-edged in Sax Rohmer—Fu Manchu plots the elimination of the 'white race' while a white character screams at him, 'You yellow devil.' We have Sapper's Bulldog Drummond castigating the Germans, while in the Sherlock Holmes stories lascars are never to be trusted. It's less common now and writers take care to vary their villains—in the United States if the villains are Vietnamese in one book, they'd better be Cubans in the next; in Britain West Indians/Russians; in Australia Italians/Lebanese, and so on.

Unapproved characters give xenophobia full rein but their aversions are more likely to be directed at other races than nationalities, although everyone despises the Swiss.

Y *is for* **Yeti**. So far, to my knowledge, no Yetis have appeared in crime fiction but the range of the genre suggests that it might happen. I seem to remember some books that featured a sasquatch or the fear of the creature, but I retain no other details.

Z *is for* **zeitgeist**. The zeitgeist of crime fiction is that a world of violence, hatred and greed can be countered by intelligence, humour and courage, but only partly and temporarily because there are more books to write.

Z *is also for* **Zen**. Buddhism figures very little in crime fiction because the word itself suggests peace and harmony, whereas the atmospherics of crime fiction stress violence, hatred and greed.

Australian Colin Talbot's 1995 mystery novel is entitled *The Zen Detective*, and of course there is Michael Dibdin's Italian detective Aurelio Zen (*Ratking*, 1988, and following).

CRIME AND CRIME WRITING, THE COLUMNS

When Linda Funnell and I began the online review journal the *Newtown Review of Books* (https://newtownreviewofbooks.com.au) seven years ago, we thought we would like a regular columnist to add interest to the site. We asked Peter if he would do it and from our first post in March 2012 he only ever missed a few weeks when he was hospitalised. He ended up writing over 300 columns for us, usually of about 500–600 words. Many of them were snippets from a writer's life; others were discussions of books he had read or was reading;

some were social or political commentary. Some were personal history. Some were reminiscences of people he had known who had somehow impressed him. We gave him carte blanche. The selection that follows centres mainly on writing or writing-related themes.

In the last few years of his life, when he could no longer write for extended periods, these columns were his only outlet. He hated missing deadlines and we usually had several columns up our sleeves. We still had one unpublished when he died.

—JB

ON BEING REVIEWED

18 November 2016

The worst review I ever got was back in my academic days. My MA thesis, 'Aborigines and Europeans in Western Victoria from First Contact to 1860', a typically cumbersome title, was published in 1967 by the Institute of Aboriginal Studies in Canberra as an occasional number in a series of monographs. An academic at, I think, La Trobe University wrote a devastating critique pointing out its factual errors, inadequate research and faulty theoretical underpinnings. Although the thesis had gained me the degree and a PhD scholarship, I was chagrined but not humiliated.

I excused myself with the thought that I'd done the best I could under the circumstances—time and the pressure of teaching. An easy out, perhaps, but I doubt that anyone ever writes anything under ideal conditions. Writing isn't like that; those who wait for ideal conditions probably don't ever write.

My subsequent academic books were respectfully reviewed without setting my career alight. When I embarked on a freelance writing journey, I had at first bad and then very good luck.

My history of prize fighting in Australia, *Lords of the Ring* (1980), probably took me longer than any other book to write. It involved a lot of research and recasting but my high hopes for it were dashed. It was published by Cassell, a publisher that was soon to be subsumed. It received almost no reviews and the one promotional event organised had me seated in a mocked-up boxing ring close to the cosmetics section in the David Jones Sydney store with a pile of books by my side. Not a single buyer! One woman, taking pity on me, chatted briefly about her son who had been a boxer.

The first Cliff Hardy novel, *The Dying Trade* (1980), was also made an orphan when the American publisher McGraw-Hill cancelled its Australian fiction list, of which my book was one of the two published. Happily, because of its novelty, the first home-grown, as it were, Australian crime novel in decades got positive reviews from all quarters and was picked up, along with the next two in the series, as a paperback by Pan and then, as I continued to produce rapidly, by Allen & Unwin, by then embarked on their enterprising and successful Australian venture.

Over the years, with many books in different genres, I've had no seriously damaging reviews. One reviewer of perhaps the tenth Hardy book suggested that the blows the detective received on the head would've been mentally damaging. I took notice and when it was sometimes necessary for the protagonist to be out of action, I found other ways. Stuart Coupe, a friend, wrote that reading *Aftershock* (1991), the Hardy novel about the Newcastle earthquake, 'was like watching paint dry'. It hurt at the time. I console myself with the fact that it is one of the most popular of my books borrowed from libraries and as an ebook.

Overall, I have only had two disappointments at the hands of reviewers. One has been that their treatment of my historical novels, which I consider to be my best writing, never generated public enthusiasm or good sales. The other is the paucity of reviews of the autobiography *Damned if I Do* (2013) (co-written with euthanasia campaigner Philip Nitschke). Newspapers, magazines and their editors are evidently as terrified as politicians of dealing with this issue, which has overwhelming support in the Australian population. Its time will come, and this brave and pungent book may one day be seen in its true light.

ON BOOZE

21 September 2012

Patrick White worried about his drinking. He told biographer David Marr there were times when he drank half a bottle of spirits a day and wine as well. He consulted doctors, almost hoping, Marr suggests, for a diagnosis of alcoholism, which would relieve him of responsibility. White gave up drinking for months at a time but always went back to it. This is a pattern familiar to drinkers who are not physically addicted to, but emotionally dependent on, alcohol.

Alcoholism and heavy dependence are common features in the lives of writers. At a rough count, more than ten per cent of the writers listed in John Sutherland's compendium *Lives of the Novelists* fall into this category. Some of the better-known are Samuel Johnson, F. Scott Fitzgerald, Ernest Hemingway, Dashiell Hammett, Raymond Chandler, Patricia Highsmith, John O'Hara, John Cheever and Kingsley Amis. For a better gender balance, one could add Dorothy Parker and Jean Rhys. There are poets like Robert Burns and playwrights like Eugene O'Neill.

It's easy to see why rock musicians, performing at high voltage night after night, need something to keep them going even if they are getting money for nothing and their chicks for free.

But why is it that alcohol looms larger in the lives of writers than, say, architects?

In his study of Faulkner, Fitzgerald, Hemingway and O'Neill, *The Thirsty Muse*, Tom Dardis argues that genetics is the critical factor predisposing these writers to alcoholism. The drug, he believes, may have stimulated their early work, but ultimately led to a decline into mediocrity or worse for all but O'Neill, who quit.

The argument holds up well for these four and would certainly apply to Chandler, whose father was an alcoholic. But whether it would apply across the board is doubtful.

While it's easy to establish that the writers mentioned (and many others) drank, it's harder to tell whether they drank *while* they were writing.

We know that Hemingway, after his back was injured in a plane accident, wrote standing up, with his typewriter on top of a refrigerator. Did he have a bloody Mary on top of the fridge as well? We don't know. Chandler claimed he could type accurately while he was drunk, which suggests he drank while writing.

When writing, I usually work for about an hour in the morning, from around eleven o'clock to noon, and in the late afternoon, from around 5 to 6 p.m. During both sessions I drink a sizeable glass of wine, sometimes two.

I believe that alcohol releases certain inhibitions and helps me project myself into my characters, to imagine actions and scenes I've never experienced or to transmute actual experiences into the material of fiction.

Over the years, for various reasons, I've given up drinking for quite long periods. I've written books in these dry spells and no one has deemed them better or worse than others. So I *can* write without booze if I have to, but it's not as much fun.

ON THE ORIGIN OF HIS IDEAS

31 March 2017

The question 'Where do you get your ideas from?' is often put to authors, especially crime writers. When I was busy at the trade I tended to fob questioners off with answers about my imagination and how I had picked up on things I'd overheard when I was a journalist or listened to on radio or seen on television.

There is, of course, much more to it than that, and now that I'm in retirement I've thought about a more considered response because people seem to be interested.

My first detective novel, *The Dying Trade* (1980), was simply an exercise in trying to write the kind of hard-boiled detective novel I admired from Chandler, Hammett and Ross Macdonald. I piled everything in—a missing person, corrupt cops, sex and violence. The next, *White Meat* (1981), derived from my knowledge of boxing and the research I'd done for my history of prize-fighting in Australia, *Lords of the Ring* (1980). I'd been to many fights and talked to boxers in gyms and pubs. I knew how it all worked. The third, *The Marvellous Boy* (1982), came about because I wanted to write a little about

Canberra, where I'd spent years as a postgraduate student and academic.

After that the books came thick and fast—including the novels and the short stories, I calculate that Cliff Hardy must have dealt with about a hundred cases—and I forget the genesis and the plots of most of them. But a few are clear in my memory.

The only short story I can remember the spark for is 'The luck of Clem Carter' in the collection *Heroin Annie* (1984). I'd been captivated by the opening line of Ernest Hemingway's *The Sun Also Rises* (1926): 'Robert Cohn was once middleweight boxing champion of Princeton. Do not think that I am very much impressed by that as a boxing title, but it meant a lot to Cohn.' I thought it would be interesting to imitate it and see if anyone noticed. From memory (I don't have a copy of the book to hand) my lines were: 'Clem Carter was the welterweight boxing champion of the Maroubra Police Citizens Boys Club. The title didn't mean much to most people, but it did to me because he beat me for it.' The story, one of my best I think, was about mateship. No one ever noticed my homage.

Wet Graves (1991) was inspired by a passage in Peter Spearritt's book *Sydney Since the Twenties* (1978), which gave an account of the people killed in the construction of the Harbour Bridge. Their bodies were recovered but it occurred to me that there might still be undiscovered corpses under the bridge and I built up a story to develop the thought.

The Greenwich Apartments (1986) had its beginning in my friend Bill Garner's account of renting a supposedly empty flat and finding a suitcase under a bed containing, I think, photographs. I changed the photos to video cassettes and that set the story in motion.

Torn Apart (2010) gestated for many years. When I was at university in Melbourne I got a letter from a friend in Sydney enclosing a clipping from a Sydney newspaper. It showed a student demonstration at the Melbourne University campus and the head and shoulders of one student was circled. My friend commented on my participation. But, although the photograph looked exactly like me—the height and build, the hair, the expression, even the clothes—I'd been nowhere near the demo. The idea of a doppelganger stayed with me for decades until I incorporated it into *Torn Apart*, providing Cliff Hardy with a look-alike.

Apart from Sydney locations, places where I've lived or visited were quite often the stimuli for stories—the south coast of New South Wales, the Central Coast, the Blue Mountains, New Caledonia, Norfolk Island. If I racked my brains I could probably come up with some other triggers but this is enough to make the point that it didn't take much to set me off.

ON LEE CHILD

1 March 2012

Patrick Gallagher, the publisher at Allen & Unwin Australia, asked me some time ago if I'd ever thought of writing a novel *à la* Lee Child. I had to admit I hadn't read Lee Child. I checked with Jean, who consumes eight novels a week, mostly crime. 'Oh,' she said, 'his character's a sort of superhero.' Not my kind of thing and I told Patrick so.

A bit later Jean bought Lee Child's fourteenth book, *61 Hours*. With nothing else on hand, I read it and was very impressed. Jack Reacher, ex-military MP, now a vagabond whose only luggage is a folding toothbrush, finds himself in a frozen, troubled North Dakota town. Trouble is Jack's business. The writing was crisp with no padding; the characters were well drawn and the plot held me. I realised I'd been missing something.

Always in the market for a good read, over the next year or so I borrowed from libraries or bought second-hand most of the Jack Reacher novels. Reacher, six-foot-five and 220 pounds, was puissant to the max but credible. He was an original creation, a free-as-the-air wanderer owing nothing to other literary heroes I could think of.

The books were patchy, with some much better than others. The couple written in the first person, such as *Persuader* (2003), were weaker than the third-person books. Reacher, and his manifold abilities as fighter, thinker and lover, was better observed from without than portrayed from within. Several of the books harked back to Reacher's career in the military, but most were set in the present, a present that Lee Child was able to render convincingly.

While the character is American, the writer is English, and this enables him to avoid the sentimentality that disfigures so many American heroic characters—Robert B. Parker's Spenser in the later books is a notable example. Child's books are full of fresh information about places, weaponry, and the civil and military authorities. Jack is good in the city but better in the country. In *Nothing to Lose* (2008), in his depiction of the two isolated Texas towns Hope and Despair, Child achieves a nightmarish, almost Dantesque, atmosphere. In this book, Child's best in my opinion, you can learn a great deal about the US military's inexcusable use of depleted uranium.

So I looked forward eagerly to the next Reacher novel. *Worth Dying For* (2010) was pretty well up to standard, with Jack setting things right in backwoods Nebraska. The next book, *The Affair* (2011), was a shocking disappointment.

The Affair was set in the past and focused in part on the circumstances surrounding Reacher leaving the army, something that had been alluded to in earlier books. But it had a tired feel and the matter apparently at issue—a murder in a Mississippi town close to a mysterious army base—lacked bite. Uncharacteristically, the plot relies on red herrings and the shadowy figures pulling the strings remain shadowy. Reacher's love interest is the local sheriff, a character virtually recycled from an earlier book, and the scene where they achieve simultaneous orgasms as the room rocks to the vibrations set off by an express train is simply ludicrous.

Every writer is allowed a flop, but the lack of energy in *The Affair* is worrying. Even the title suggests a lack of effort. Child's seventeenth Reacher novel, *A Wanted Man*, is due out this year. I'll approach it with caution—probably via a library rather than a bookshop.

ON HIS EDITORS

29 April 2016

In a writing career of more than forty years I've had dealings with dozens, perhaps scores, of publishers' editors. Some have been excellent, some good, some just all right and a few terrible.

I can't remember much about the editors of the handful of academic books I produced. My impression is that they were mainly concerned with the accuracy of footnotes and indexes rather than the quality of the writing.

I first encountered serious and helpful editing from Carl Harrison-Ford, who edited my history of boxing, published as *Lords of the Ring* in 1980. This was my first attempt at non-academic history and I struggled with the material. At one point I had the idea of changing to a fictional approach. I had only the slightest of credentials as a fiction writer at the time and Carl, wisely, talked me out of this. He also encouraged me to adopt a thematic rather than a chronological approach and this resolved many problems. I remain proud of the book, which continues to be cited, and grateful to Carl.

When it came to fiction I was lucky in having Jean as a first reader and copyeditor to civilise the raw product. The editor at McGraw-Hill for the first Cliff Hardy novel, *The Dying Trade*

(1980), smoothed away a Melburnian's ignorance of Sydney and I feel sure contributed to the book's success in that way. To my shame I've forgotten her name and did not credit her, an omission I've tried to rectify in subsequent books with other editors.

I struck trouble with an editor in one of my early historical novels. She clearly disliked the story, the characters and the style, and her editorial work was dismissive. We battled. The book didn't sell, so perhaps she was right, but she became a successful writer herself later and our meetings subsequently on panels and at gatherings were amicable.

Not so with another editor. I've forgotten the book involved but again, she was unsympathetic. I remember that she wrote in the margin beside a passage in which I described the abilities of a character, 'What an all-rounder!' I took exception to this and her whole editorial manner and insisted that another editor be assigned, the only time I've done this. I later heard her described as 'the rudest person I've ever known', a judgement I endorsed.

The Journal of Fletcher Christian (2005) was a tricky book to compose. It was a fictional account purporting to be Christian's work and was preceded by a narrative explaining how the supposed manuscript had come into my hands. Meredith Curnow and Roberta Ivers at Random House showed great, almost embarrassing, faith in the book and worked long and hard to conquer its difficulties. I made sure to acknowledge them for helping me to produce what I think was one of my best books.

No editor has done more to ensure that my Cliff Hardy books appear in as finished a form as possible than Jo Jarrah, working for Allen & Unwin. Jo has edited more of the series and caused me more annoyance and gratitude than anyone else. She has received the manuscript after I've dealt with Jean's copyedit and the publisher's reader's report and has never failed to find flaws—inconsistencies, mistakes of time and place, stylistic awkwardness.

More importantly, she has sometimes seemed to understand Hardy's character better than I have myself. She once pulled me up short with the comment that 'Cliff has lost his mojo'. That required a serious reappraisal and I've kept it firmly in mind ever since.

ON EL DORADO

27 January 2017

I got a phone call from my agent. This was unusual. Usually she emails me along these lines:

'Dear Peter (we like to observe the formalities), I've just processed a royalty from a set of your ebooks. I'm sorry it's so little but . . .'

I'll reply thanking her and telling her that it'll pay a bill or two. But a phone call . . .

'Peter,' she said, sounding excited. 'Your ship has come in.'

I didn't know I had a vessel at sea. 'What's her name, the *Marie Celeste*?'

'Very funny. I mean that I've had a contact from a film producer . . .'

'Hold on,' I said, 'is this one of those producers who wants an option for peanuts but swears he can get Mel Gibson on board if we can kick in for his expenses . . .?'

'Mel's too old for Cliff,' she said. 'No, this is Randy Frost, who produced three films in the *Blackout* franchise and *Blood in the Water*.'

'Never heard of them or him.'

'Where have you been? He called from Hollywood. He's got HBO and Google money. He's offering five million for the rights to Hardy and he's interested in a couple of the Browning books and one of the historical novels, and his nephew Clint, who's a documentary maker, wants to do a true crime thing for the History Channel about your book on Mad Dog Moxley and . . .'

This is a daydream of course, but it indicates a certain disappointment I sometimes feel about my writing career. Wouldn't it have been nice to get Cliff Hardy up on screen a few times? With Cate Blanchett in a cameo (all that could be afforded) as a femme fatale. To have made a rip-snorting Australian Western out of my novel *Wimmera Gold* (1994) with Anthony Mundine as a bare-knuckle prize-fighter and Hugo Weaving as a villain. To have captured the darkness of William Cyril Moxley and Depression-era Sydney on grainy black and white film?

It wasn't to be: the local market is too small, there is too little money around, foreign competition is too great and my books have failed to achieve international penetration.

I hasten to say that I'm not really complaining: to have made a living from writing for forty years, to have never, as I not entirely playfully put it, had to go out to work for all that time and to have enjoyed writing, has been a boon and a privilege. But still . . .

ON LITERARY VS POPULAR FICTION

4 August 2017

From time to time discussion still arises about the difference between literary and popular fiction, and their respective merits. Those of us interested in the topic are often divided.

Michael Wilding made his position clear when he wrote somewhere that, 'Crime fiction [and by extension other forms of genre fiction] is not literature; it's entertainment.' As a practitioner I am inclined to agree. While hoping to provide well-written stories with at least some serious matter to engage serious minds, my primary purpose has always been to entertain.

But the matter can't rest there. I recently heard Ian Rankin, surely one of the best crime writers, make a case for the genre. I don't have the actual quote, but he said something like this: if you plan to go to another country and wish to inform yourself beforehand of the society's hopes and fears, divisions and successes, read the local crime writers. They will give you a better understanding than voices from the commentariat.

That seems to lift the genre up a few notches and it's remarkable how very many countries have a flourishing output of crime fiction. Rankin's pronouncement could easily bc put to the test.

A while ago I watched Jennifer Byrne's program, *The Book Club*, on ABC television. Two of the panellists were Lee Child, author of the Jack Reacher novels, many of which I've read, and Matthew Riley, the author of techno-thrillers, none of which I've read, and one historical novel, which I gave up on, thinking it very bad. They both claimed that they could write literary fiction if they wanted to but had chosen not to for various reasons.

I find this a dubious claim. I feel there is a difference between the two kinds of writing and that one deserves more critical appraisal than the other. This feeling was reinforced when I listened recently to the audio version of Ian McEwan's *Nutshell* (2016). The conceit of this book is that an unborn foetus can hear everything through the uterine wall—voices, music, footsteps, the rustling of clothes, radio, television and podcasts. What's more, he (the foetus) has fumblingly discovered his gender and can interpret this information to construct a world he has yet to see. He can intuit or guess at appearances, motives, terrors.

The audacity of this idea is matched by the brilliance, breadth and depth of the language; the range of reference; the subtlety of ideas encompassing such matters as climate change, nuclear annihilation, sexual politics and much more. There are passages—such as the foetus's awareness of sensations when his mother's lover is fucking her; his concern for the effect on him on another occasion when she swallows sperm; and when he attempts suicide by strangulation by the umbilical cord—that shocked me in a way I didn't think genre writing could do.

This, inescapably, is the craft of writing and the power of the imagination working together at high intensity to create something challenging and new (to me, anyway—I could never get through more than a few pages of *Tristram Shandy*): literature.

Graham Greene clearly thought there was a difference between his two sorts of writing, designating some of his novels as 'entertainments'. I'd be happy to resort to one of my favourite authors, Somerset Maugham, to sum up. Maugham described himself as being at the very front of the second rank. It's all just writing when all's said and done, and perhaps the leading genre writers such as James Ellroy, Val McDermid, Bernard Cornwell, Rose Tremain, Adrian McKinty and Ursula Le Guin should be assigned an honourable place at the very front of the second rank.

ON RETROSPECTIVES

9 February 2018

A good number of authors who've employed series characters have written what are called in the business retrospectives—that is, stories that hark back to earlier events in their characters' careers. John le Carré did so with *Smiley's People* (1979), tracing previous strands in his main characters' professional and personal lives, and again in *A Legacy of Spies* (2017), which is essentially a memoir by Peter Guillam, one of Smiley's colleagues in the secret service.

Ian Rankin has done the same with John Rebus. I did it twice, with *Matrimonial Causes* (1993) and *That Empty Feeling* (2016).

The 2016 book, my second-last, gave me the welcome chance to write about my interest in boxing. I don't remember much about the earlier book except that Cliff Hardy's then girlfriend asked him to tell her about an early case, which he did. I was pleased with myself for coining the term 'box Brownie and bed sheets' in describing the activities of private detectives in that benighted time. I cannibalised a short story to produce the novel, a procedure for which Raymond Chandler was notorious. I have to admit that neither of the two retrospectives were as popular as the standard here-and-now books, perhaps partly because people didn't want to be reminded of the old divorce laws and partly because of the widespread hostility to boxing.

A recent book by Michael Connelly, *Two Kinds of Truth* (2017), provides an interesting further example. Connelly is a bold writer who takes risks. Not only has he brought in characters from other books—Mickey Haller from *The Lincoln Lawyer* (2005) has teamed with Connelly's main man Harry Bosch in several books (this has been done before, by Tony Hillerman with Jim Chee and Joe Leaphorn, and Ian Rankin with Rebus and Malcolm Fox)—but in a dangerous bit of postmodernism Connelly goes so far as to mention the film of *The Lincoln Lawyer*, and he runs his contemporary story parallel with his retrospective case, giving them more or less equal emotional and narrative weight. This is a first as far as I know.

One of the appeals of the standard here-and-now double-plot novel is the tension set up between the two strands. Will the two stories come together and if so, how? This adds to the reader's interest. Inevitably they do.

In the case of *Two Kinds of Truth*, the stories were so disparate—one a thirty-year-old case involving legal manoeuvres and the other an intensely contemporary matter concerning opium addiction and the Russian mafia—that it was difficult to see how they could fuse. This was constantly on my mind as I listened to the audio version. They did fuse in a highly dramatic fashion to my complete satisfaction.

I found a couple of the recent Bosch novels a bit below par but this one delivers the goods. Not that it smells of the lamp, but an immense amount of research must have gone into its substance and considerable craft into its construction. To my mind, although I don't know the entire field (who could?), Connelly is the prince of American crime writers.

ON HIS SWANSONG

30 June 2017

I was scheduled to appear at the Sydney Writers Festival on 27 May. I was keen to do this because it'd be my swansong, my final book having been published in January, and also because I'd be 'in conversation' with actor, journalist and author Graeme Blundell. I've known Graeme for many years, from our Melbourne days. He is an aficionado of crime fiction who has reviewed a number of my books favourably and we'd done a similar gig successfully once before.

But by the time of the session I was in hospital with a cast on my leg. Could I do it in a wheelchair? I decided I could—with more than a little help from my friends.

The day arrived and a first-class nurse from the hospital, a Nepalese man named AJ, helped me to dress and compose myself in the wheelchair and trundled me out to the wheelchair taxi. If you've never been in one of these vehicles, try to keep it that way. I imagine it's something like being locked in a Black Maria. (Are there still Black Marias?) The chair is bolted in, you are strapped in, and the windows are so small and high up that all you can see are roofs and the tops of trees.

At the Hickson Street wharf the driver alerted Allen & Unwin publicist Andy Palmer, and he appeared to detach me from the taxi and take me to the Green Room. I was early; I got a glass of wine, chatted to Andy about our long association, and Jean, Patrick Gallagher (the head honcho of Allen & Unwin), and Blundell turned up. Then it was off to the venue, the Loft.

I was concerned about the setting. Given the wheelchair, would we have to do it on a level with the audience? Not ideal. No problem—there was a device to lift the chair up to the level of the stage. I would've preferred this be done with the audience in place for the dramatic effect, but this was apparently not the way. Up I was put, and I was in the wheelchair, miked up, a glass of water and Blundell beside me, as the audience came in. Given my poor vision I couldn't tell how big the auditorium was but I was told it was mostly full.

Graeme opened by inviting me to explain my condition. I told them I had had a blackout in the kitchen and that the stove, the sink and the fridge had hit me as I fell. This got a good laugh *and* sympathy.

Jean had advised me not to play the whole session for laughs as I sometimes did, and I obliged. Under Graeme's astute questioning I spoke about how I tried to create realistic characters with realistic problems, plausible plots and a social and political texture to work with the necessary sex and violence—to execute the popular-fiction writer's craft, in other words.

I did make jokes, particularly about Shane Maloney, whom I accused of cutting deeply into my audience as well as being more widely translated than me. Blundell picked up on this and told how, when overseas somewhere, he'd mentioned that he was an Australian writer, and someone had asked, 'Oh, are you Shane Maloney?'

'Thanks for that story, Graeme,' I said. 'You've made my day.'

The session went well, with some good questions from the audience. One in particular I chewed over. I was asked if I missed Cliff Hardy as a sort of partner. I said I didn't, not really, but perhaps a bit. I certainly missed chances to use his voice, to comment on things I heard and saw now that I could no longer write.

I was winched back down and signed about thirty books—a gratifying result in these hard times. Then it was back into the hands of Andy Palmer, my minder, and once again into the Black Maria after saying goodbye to Jean and others.

I was met at the hospital by Doug, another top-notch nurse, who wheeled me back to my room, heated up the dinner waiting for me and completed some injecting and pill administration. And so to bed, after a good event only made possible by willing helpers. Cliff Hardy himself could hardly have asked for better.

ON THE NEDDIES

13 October 2017

I was recently honoured by the Australian Crime Writers Association with an award commending me for my long career as a writer in the genre. Michael Robotham, himself deservedly a past winner of Best Fiction awards,[4] spoke of my work in a way that touched me deeply. I've previously won several other awards from the Association and when I told a friend, a Scotsman, about the Ned Kelly award—nicknamed a Neddy—he was astonished that we should name our awards after a criminal.

'We don't regard him solely as a criminal,' I said. 'Given extenuating circumstances and statements he made, we regard him as at least partly a rebel.'

'He was a murderer,' he said.

I explained that, prior to the events at Stringybark Creek where three policemen were killed, Ned's only offences had been for assaulting police and for horse stealing.

He interrupted, 'That was a hanging offence.'

4 This year's winner, with a twopeat (as we say in footy), was Adrian McKinty for *Police at the Station and They Don't Look Friendly.*

'Not in Australia,' I said. 'He served three years in gaol for it. The second offence against the police, committed under extreme provocation, was more serious. It was then that the gang went into hiding and were posted as outlaws with rewards for their capture.'

'They murdered three coppers.'

I told him that, despite the gang not being posted as dead-or-alive fugitives at that stage, there is evidence that the police party that went after them were a semi-vigilante group who carried equipment designed to strap dead bodies to horses.

'So in one sense the gang acted in self-defence,' I said.

He remained sceptical but I'd outlined the circumstances that caused contemporaries and later generations to take a more favourable view of the Kellys. The authorities were provocative, heavy-handed and oppressive towards hard-scrabble settlers, many of whom, like the Kelly brothers, were descendants of convicts.

Nevertheless, it remains curious that we name our awards as we do. The United States has no Jessies (I'm thinking of Jesse James) and Britain no Ronnies (as in Great Train Robber Ronnie Biggs). Well, who cares? Let them have their Gold and Silver Daggers and their Edgars. We're different and I've never heard of anyone refusing a Neddy on the sort of grounds my friend raised. I'm proud of mine—all of which in some way represent Ned's armour, painted indelibly into our consciousness by Sidney Nolan. And besides, my maternal grandmother's maiden name was Kelly and it was my mother's middle name.

Footnote: Another past Neddy winner I'd like to name is Patrick Gallagher, the publisher at Allen & Unwin, who published most of my Cliff Hardy books as well as many by other local crime writers. The recipient of a Lifetime Achievement Award in 2002, Patrick has been in no small measure responsible for the popularity and marketability of the genre in Australia today.

ON WRITING HIS FINAL BOOK

13 January 2017

With *Win, Lose or Draw* from Allen & Unwin, published on 3 January this year, I have produced my last book. Early reviews and notices suggest that it is in no way inferior to the forty-one others in the Hardy series. So why stop?

Certainly not because I tired of writing about Cliff Hardy. I have immensely enjoyed the time I spent with each book—feeling out the characters, allowing the plot to develop (I never pre-planned a story) and having the freedom to comment through the fiction on life and death, sex and sport, the city I love and places I've been. I admit that the books have taken me longer to write recently, say two to three months, rather than a month and a half as in the past, but this was because I had less to do—my other novel series having come to an end. But it was also because I wanted to extend the pleasure of putting Cliff through his paces—having fun, getting things off my chest.

When I was in my thirties my eyesight was threatened as a result of long-term type 1 diabetes. The argon laser (introduced to this country by Fred Hollows, whose autobiography I was later to co-write) saved my sight. And I wrote many books over the following years.

A few years ago my eyesight deteriorated as a result of the scars from the lasering thickening and cutting down the area of retina I had to work with. My response to this, with nothing corrective to be done, was to write in a bigger font on the computer. Starting perhaps three or four books back I began to write in 18 point. This piece I am now writing in 36 point!

My eyesight deteriorated still further after I finished the manuscript of *Win, Lose or Draw* to the extent that it became difficult for me to manage on the computer—to use the spell checker, to access certain functions, even to locate the cursor. The effort it would take to write a novel under these conditions would be exhausting and the pleasure would be nil.

It has been suggested that I could dictate, as many writers have done, or use voice-recognition software, but these strategies wouldn't work for me. I loved sitting down with a glass of wine beside me, opening the file and clattering the keys with my two index fingers and one thumb. I loved seeing the words appear on the screen and to be immersed in the world I was creating out of my imagination and memory and physically with my hands. To do anything else wouldn't feel like writing.

So I had no idea this book would be my last when I wrote it and that's good. Knowing that could have imparted a tone—perhaps regret, perhaps self-pity—wholly inappropriate to Cliff. As it was, I gave it an ending intrinsic to the story, a very Cliff Hardy ending. And I'm happy with it.

LIST OF BOOKS

FICTION

Cliff Hardy series
The Dying Trade (1980)
White Meat (1981)
The Marvellous Boy (1982)
The Empty Beach (1983)
Heroin Annie (1984)
Make Me Rich (1985)
The Big Drop (1985)
Deal Me Out (1986)
The Greenwich Apartments (1986)
The January Zone (1987)
Man in the Shadows (1988)
O'Fear (1990)
Wet Graves (1991)
Aftershock (1991)
Beware of the Dog (1992)
Burn, and Other Stories (1993)
Matrimonial Causes (1993)

LIST OF BOOKS

Casino (1994)
The Washington Club (1997)
Forget Me If You Can (1997)
The Reward (1997)
The Black Prince (1998)
The Other Side of Sorrow (1999)
Lugarno (2001)
Salt and Blood (2002)
Master's Mates (2003)
The Coast Road (2004)
Taking Care of Business (2004)
Saving Billie (2005)
The Undertow (2006)
Appeal Denied (2007)
The Big Score (2007)
Open File (2008)
Deep Water (2009)
Torn Apart (2010)
Follow the Money (2011)
Comeback (2012)
The Dunbar Case (2013)
Silent Kill (2014)
Gun Control (2015)
That Empty Feeling (2016)
Win, Lose or Draw (2017)

Ray Crawley series (co-written with Bill Garner)
Pokerface (1985)
The Baltic Business (1988)
The Kimberley Killing (1989)
The Cargo Club (1990)

The Azanian Action (1991)
The Japanese Job (1992)
The Time Trap (1993)
The Vietnam Volunteer (2000)

Richard Browning series
'Box Office' Browning (1987)
'Beverly Hills' Browning (1987)
Browning Takes Off (1989)
Browning in Buckskin (1991)
Browning P.I. (1992)
Browning Battles On (1993)
Browning Sahib (1994)
Browning Without a Cause (1995)

Luke Dunlop series
Set Up (1992)
Cross Off (1993)
Get Even (1994)

Young Adult fiction
Blood Brothers (2007)

Historical fiction
The Gulliver Fortune (1989)
Naismith's Dominion (1990)
The Brothers Craft (1992)
Wimmera Gold (1994)
The Journal of Fletcher Christian (2005)
Wishart's Quest (2009)
The Colonial Queen (2011)

Other fiction

The Winning Side (1984)
A Round of Golf: Tales from around the greens (1998)
Standing in the Shadows: Three novellas (2013)

NON-FICTION

Biography

Fred Hollows: An autobiography (with Fred Hollows) (1991)
Fighting for Fraser Island: A man and an island (with John Sinclair) (1994)
Ray Barrett: An autobiography (with Ray Barrett) (1995)
Heart Matters: Personal stories about that heart-stopping moment (edited with Michael Wilding) (2010)
Damned if I Do (with Philip Nitschke) (2013)

Autobiography

Sweet & Sour: A diabetic life (2000)

True crime

Mad Dog: William Cyril Moxley and the Moorebank killings (2011)

Sport

Lords of the Ring: A history of prize-fighting in Australia (1980)
The Picador Book of Golf (edited with Jamie Grant) (1995)
Ringside: A knockout collection of fights and fighters (edited with Barry Parish) (1996)
Best on Ground: Great writers on the greatest game (edited with John Dale) (2010)

LIST OF BOOKS

Pacific history

Passage, Port and Plantation: A history of Solomon Islands labour migration, 1870–1914 (1973)

The South Sea Islanders and the Queensland Labour Trade by W.T. Wawn (edited by Peter Corris) (1973)

The Cruise of the Helena: A labour-recruiting voyage to the Solomon Islands by J.D. Melvin (edited by Peter Corris) (1977)

The Journal of John Sweatman: A nineteenth century surveying voyage in North Australia and Torres Strait (edited with Jim Allen) (1977)

Lightning Meets the West Wind: The Malaita massacre (with Roger Keesing) (1980)